"Castille takes the MC genre and lights it on fire! I want my very own Sinner's Tribe Motorcycle Club bad boy!"
—Julie Ann Walker, *New York Times* bestselling author

"A sexy and dangerous ride! If you like your bad boys bad and your heroines kicking butt, *Rough Justice* will rev your engine. A great start to a new series!"
—Roni Loren, *New York Times* bestselling author of *Nothing Between Us*

"Raw, rugged and romantic, *Rough Justice* is so gorgeously written you'll feel the vibration of the motorcycle engines in the pit of your stomach, smell the leather and fall in love with this story!"
—Eden Bradley, *New York Times* bestselling author of *Dangerously Bound*

Praise for
***USA Today* and *New York Times* bestselling author**
SARAH CASTILLE
and her sizzling-hot romances . . .

"Castille's debut is steamy."   —*Publishers Weekly*

"Hot, hot, hot."   —*Nocturne Romance Reads*

"Smart, sharp, sizzling and deliciously sexy . . . a knockout."
—Alison Kent, bestselling author of *Unbreakable*

★ CHAOS BOUND ★

Sinner's Tribe Motorcycle Club

SARAH CASTILLE

St. Martin's Paperbacks

This is a work of fiction. All of the characters, organizations, and events portrayed in this novel are either products of the author's imagination or are used fictitiously.

CHAOS BOUND

For information address St. Martin's Press, 175 Fifth Avenue, New York, NY 10010.

ISBN: 978-1-250-10409-0

Printed in the United States of America

Our books may be purchased in bulk for promotional, educational, or business use. Please contact your local bookseller or the Macmillan Corporate and Premium Sales Department at 1-800-221-7945, ext. 5442, or by e-mail at MacmillanSpecialMarkets@macmillan.com.

St. Martin's Paperbacks edition / July 2016

St. Martin's Paperbacks are published by St. Martin's Press, 175 Fifth Avenue, New York, NY 10010.

10 9 8 7 6 5 4 3 2 1

To my wild one

★ ACKNOWLEDGMENTS ★

Many thanks to my long suffering family, for encouraging me even though it meant no dinner.

Thanks to Danielle Gorman for keeping me organized and sane; and Mandy Lawler and Danielle Barclay for helping me share the Sinners' stories; and to Casey Britton for her awesome story comments.

To the hardworking people at St. Martin's Press for bringing this story to life; and much thanks to my editor, Monique Patterson, for her brilliant insights and whipping it into shape; and to my awesome agent, Laura Bradford, for believing in this series from the get-go.

Most thanks of all to my Harley man for his love and support, and always having his bike ready to ride.

★ ONE ★

Naiya Kelly knew he would come for her.

O God, by Your mercy, rest is given to the souls of the faithful, be pleased to bless this grave.

She just hadn't expected it so soon.

Appoint Your holy angels to guard it and set free from all the chains of sin and the soul of her whose body is buried here . . .

And certainly not at the cemetery in the middle of her mother's burial service.

So that with all Thy saints she may rejoice in Thee forever.

She repeated the words in her head, praying for the same deliverance the priest sought to give her mother, although they both knew Laurie Kelly was going to hell.

Which is exactly where Naiya would be going as soon as the priest finished the service, because the devil stood waiting for her on the other side of the wrought-iron gates.

She focused on the holy water the priest sprinkled over the coffin, each perfect drop beading on the rough-hewn wood. Anything but turn and meet the dark, steady gaze of her mother's killer—the man who had brutally stripped away Naiya's innocence seven years ago, and was back for more. No, not a man. A monster.

Viper. President of the Black Jacks Motorcycle Club (MC). Self-styled outlaw biker king of Montana.

Her fingers slid over the ring on her left hand—silver, with four crossed sabers on a black background. The Good Mark of the Phantom. It was the only clue she had to the identity of her father now that her mother was gone. As a child, she'd read every Phantom comic book she could get her hands on, imagining her father had left the ring for her as a form of protection because he couldn't be with her. The Phantom had no superpowers but relied on strength and intelligence to defeat his foes.

So how was she going to escape a cemetery with only one gate and six outlaw bikers waiting for her in a sea of chrome and leather?

Salvation from our enemies and from the hand of all who hate us . . .

Her hand curled around the bouquet of roses she had brought to lay on her mother's grave, her fingers white from the morning frost. Usually she loved Montana's autumns for the brilliant colors and cool evenings, but an early cold snap had sent the leaves tumbling from the trees, and Devil's Hills had gone from green to brown overnight, brutally ripping away the tail end of what had been a beautiful Indian summer.

Shine on those who sit in darkness and death's shadow . . .

She hadn't been back to Devil's Hills since she'd run away seven years ago, but the small, former mining town hadn't changed at all. With it's pretty main street adorned with brightly colored historic buildings, an abundance of American flags and eclectic shops, and nestled against a backdrop of snow-covered mountains, it was hard to believe the town was the seat of the largest Black Jacks MC chapter in Montana and not a tourist paradise.

Naiya plucked a petal from one of the white roses as the priest prayed. White for the purity her mother had lost the day she met Viper. White to wipe the slate clean. Grandma Kelly had been a devout Catholic and had done her best to save Naiya's mother's soul, but once Viper got his fangs into her, there was nothing Grandma Kelly could do. His poison had tainted not just Laurie's life, but Naiya's, too.

I am the resurrection and the life. The one who believes in me will live, even though they die; and whoever lives by believing in me will never die. Do you believe this?

No. Of course she didn't believe it. She would be dead the minute she left the cemetery, or at the very least wishing she was dead. She could feel Viper's eyes boring into her, staining her soul. He probably had a needle all ready to get Naiya addicted to the same drugs he'd given her mother to keep her willing and compliant.

Naiya's mother had been Viper's favorite sweet butt— one of many women who hung around the MC, doing chores and servicing the needs of the bikers in exchange for safety and a place to live—and second only in importance to his old lady, the biker equivalent of a wife. Naiya couldn't see the appeal of a forty-year-old meth addict to a man who could have any woman he wanted, especially when he'd demonstrated a taste for fifteen-year-old girls.

In the end, Naiya's mother had paid a high price for Viper's attention: death by overdose in Viper's bed. At least Grandma Kelly wasn't alive to see it.

Amen.

Naiya glanced over at the tombstone beside her mother's grave etched with her grandmother's details: *Marjorie Grace Kelly, wife of Peter Kelly (deceased), mother of*

Laurie, beloved grandmother of Naiya. She didn't remember much about Grandma Kelly's funeral, only that
she'd been afraid for the first time in the nine years since
she was born. Grandma Kelly had always taken care of
her, and after that day, she had no one. Well, almost no one.
Her drugged-out junkie sweet butt mother didn't count.

The priest sprinkled the casket with holy water. She
missed Father Doyle who had been a fixture in the church
as long as she could remember. He had led the service
when her grandfather died and had been very close to
Grandma Kelly. If not for Father Doyle, she might have
made an even bigger mistake than going to the Black Jack
clubhouse on her fifteenth birthday.

In a low, soothing voice, the priest asked again that her
mother's soul rest in peace, and then he made a prayer for
mercy.

Mercy.

A sob welled up in Naiya's throat as she contemplated
her last few moments of freedom. Not even Viper would
dare step foot onto holy ground, but even if he did, who
would stop him? The priest? The cemetery workers standing ready with their shovels? No one else had come for
the funeral. Junkies didn't have many friends.

And neither did she.

After her mother sold Grandma Kelly's house and blew
the money on drugs, they'd been forced to live above a sex
shop with a cruel, brutal Black Jack named Abe. Parents
didn't want their children associating with the daughter of
a drug addict and bike gang whore, and she'd been ostra-
cized at school. Naiya took refuge in books, her only saving grace her intelligence and her determination to succeed
at school so that she could leave the biker life behind.

Eternal rest grant unto her, O Lord.

Damn the Black Jacks. Damn Viper. Damn her own
stupidity for coming back to Devil's Hills. But there was

no running from Viper. She knew he'd kept tabs on her in college; she'd heard the Harleys, seen the occasional Black Jack cut. If she tried to run, he would hunt her down. The Black Jacks were one of the most powerful outlaw MCs in the country, and second only to the Sinner's Tribe MC in the state.

And what kind of daughter wouldn't bury her mother? Even if her mother had done nothing to save her when Viper decided to give Naiya a birthday present she would never forget.

Happy fifteenth birthday, love. Now lie still and shut the fuck up.

The gate creaked. Heavy footsteps thudded across the grass behind her. Trembles wracked Naiya's body. The priest intoned the last prayer, and Naiya placed the flowers on her mother's coffin.

"Good-bye," she whispered.

And let perpetual light shine upon her.

A hand clamped down on her shoulder, and Naiya fought back a whimper of fear.

May she rest in peace.

"Amen."

"No use praying, love," Viper murmured in her ear. "God's not gonna save you now."

Sometimes Holt "T-Rex" Savage found pleasure in the pain.

In the furthest recesses of his mind, he could tell good days from bad.

On the bad days, Viper didn't come to the dungeon. On those days, Holt suffered as his body tried to heal from countless months of torture. He felt every bruise, every cut, every lash, every bone that had broken and not reset. His lungs burned with every breath. His heart ached with every beat. His blood crusted beneath the manacles that held him to the wall.

But worse were the memories that assailed him when he stared at the Sinner's Tribe cut—the leather vest worn by all outlaw bikers—that Viper had pinned to the cinder block wall with the dagger Holt received when he patched into the Sinner's Tribe.

His cut. His club.

At least they had been until the Sinners betrayed him.

The Sinner's Tribe MC—the club he had loved, the bikers he had called brothers, the president he had respected above all men, the man he had called friend—were nothing to him now. He had sacrificed for them, offered himself to Viper to save the life of the Sinners' VP's girl, Evie, and in return they left him to suffer and die.

Funny how history repeated itself. Except this time his sacrifice hadn't landed him in juvenile detention, but in hell.

Yesterday should have been a good day. On the good days, Viper tortured him until his mind went blank, erasing memories, hopes, and dreams, wiping out the pain of betrayal and replacing it with fantasies of revenge.

Revenge had given him the will to live. Revenge against Viper and the Jacks. Revenge against Jagger and the Sinner's Tribe. Once he was free, his wrath would know no bounds. He would surrender himself to the beast within until it had drunk deep of betraying biker blood.

But yesterday was different. Viper was excited. His dark eyes glittered in the semi-darkness of the dungeon beneath the Black Jack clubhouse that had been Holt's home for countless months. Viper pulled out equipment he had never used before, tortured Holt without needing a break to rest his arms or to laugh or talk with the men who always accompanied him for what he called his "workout" sessions.

He was going to have a woman he had wanted for years, he'd said.

A girl he'd tasted once and never forgotten, he'd said.

The daughter of the sweet butt who had inconvenienced him by dying in his bed.

A replacement for the woman Holt had snatched away with his ridiculous sacrifice that had landed him in Viper's dungeon and opened his eyes to the fact the Sinners were not the loyal brothers Holt thought they were.

All of which meant Viper didn't need Holt any more. He would be working out his stress between the poor girl's soft thighs. His whip would taste her smooth, creamy skin. His chains would circle her slim wrists. Her blood would stain his sheets. And he would drink the nectar of her screams.

Today was a bad day. The worst of all days. There was no pain Holt didn't feel, no breath he didn't fight for, no beat he didn't have to squeeze from his heart. Today he wondered if there would be a tomorrow because even revenge was losing its battle to sustain him.

Holt stared at the cut on the wall. The Sinner's Tribe patch was barely visible in the thin light that shone through the outer door. He remembered the day Jagger had given him that cut. The bar filled with his brothers, chanting his road name, "T-Rex." The pride that swelled his chest when Jagger threw the cut over his shoulders. And later, the emotion that welled up in his throat when his best friend, Tank, gave him the dagger. It had been the best day of his life.

His chest seized, and he gritted his teeth. This is why he fought back the memories. Nothing hurt more than emotional pain.

Light flickered against the wall, and the door scraped open. Holt drew in a deep breath and blinked as his eyes adjusted to the light.

This was it. The last day had finally come. He felt no

fear, no longing, and no sadness. Nothing but regret that he hadn't had a chance to exact his revenge. If he'd been a praying man, he would have prayed that this would be the end of his suffering. But he wasn't. So he closed his eyes, and he made a wish.

His wish didn't come true.

"Fucking bitch." Viper shoved a woman into the dungeon so hard she fell to the floor. "You're mine now, and you'll damn well learn to behave. Blame your mother for dying with a shitload of debt. Your new place is in my fucking bed with your legs spread wide, your pussy wet, and your mouth open only to suck my cock. And if you ever try to pull that kind of crap on me again, you'll be joining your fucking mother in her grave." He slammed the door shut, plunging the room into darkness.

For a long moment, the woman didn't move, and Holt wondered if Viper had hurt her. He opened his mouth to speak, but, with his tongue dry and swollen, no sound came out.

An ear-splitting scream filled the dungeon. He heard the rasp of her breaths, fists on metal. Through the thin light streaming beneath the door, he could make out the barest outline of her body as she let loose a string of curses that would put even the most hardened biker to shame.

Holt wanted to go to her, tell her she was wasting her breath. No one would find her in Viper's dungeon. And even if someone heard her cries, no one would come to her aid. But with his wrists manacled and one ankle chained to the floor, he couldn't move. Weak from hunger, thirst, and loss of blood, he couldn't even rattle the chain to let her know she wasn't alone.

Sobbing, the woman bent down and slid her fingers under the door. She cursed again, filthy words interspersed with such rapid breaths he wondered if she would hyperventilate.

"It'sokayit'sokayit'sokayit'sokay." She curled up beside the door for a few minutes, muttering to herself. And then she sprang up, her hands sliding over the door and the wall beside it, searching, shouting so loud Holt's ears rang. "Help."

She still hadn't turned around, and he thought this was a dangerous thing. If she had any sense, she would protect her back. But this woman wasn't thinking about the dangers in the dungeon. Between sobs and shouts, she railed against Viper as if she couldn't contain the fire inside her no matter how hard she tried.

If he could have moved his lips, he would have smiled.

Finally, she found the light switch, and the naked bulb overhead flickered on. Holt squinted as his eyes adjusted the light. Viper kept him in darkness save for the days he came to visit, and on those days Holt didn't want to see what Viper had in store for him.

He must have made a sound because she whirled around to face him, hands raised, eyes wide. Her gaze flickered over the implements on the walls—whips, chains, iron bars, knives, axes, and all manner of torture devices Holt had never encountered before but with which he was now intimately familiar—the hooks in the ceiling, the toilet in the corner that was just far enough for his chains to reach, and the blood stains on the floor.

Not all his blood. There had been another man in the dungeon when he'd first been captured. A dark-haired Devil Dog who had made the mistake of sleeping with one of the Black Jacks' old ladies. After beating the poor bastard to death, Viper left his body on the dungeon floor and moved Holt to a different dungeon in a different location where Holt was subjected to everything he'd witnessed and more. When Viper returned Holt to his original cell, the Devil Dog was gone, and everything had been rebuilt as new. But the horror was old and endless.

Finally, the woman's gaze fell on him. She gasped and her hand flew to her mouth. Holt tried to make out her face, but with his eyes swollen and crusted with dried blood, and unused to the light, she was nothing more than a blur.

"Ohgodohgodohgodohgod." She took one step toward him, then another. When she crouched down in front of him, he managed to widen his eyes enough to see her clearly. She was slim, and small, with long dark hair, and a heart shaped face. He couldn't discern the color of her eyes, only that the color shifted as he watched, and her gaze was deep with sympathy when she met his stare. It had been so long since he'd seen a woman, she looked almost ethereal with her pale skin and fine features, but her cheek was badly bruised.

Easy to break. Viper could crush her neck with one hand, and yet she seemed angry, not afraid.

"You're alive." She reached out and stroked his cheek.

Holt jerked back at her gentle touch. Instinct. Borne of constant pain from every touch he'd endured since the last day he'd seen the sun.

"I'm sorry." Her voice was soft, throaty. He'd forgotten about the beautiful things in life. Soft things. Gentle things. Sights and sounds. Tastes and touches. She was all of them wrapped up in one sweet package.

"Viper thinks you're dead." Her brow furrowed. "I heard him talking with his men before he brought me down here. They're planning to get your . . . you and bury you somewhere."

He listened to the lilt of her voice, watched her lips move. Felt a stir of happiness that he had the chance to behold beauty one last time on the eve of his death.

She stepped closer, inspected his bare torso, the cuts and bruises, welts and burns. She choked when she saw the whip marks that crisscrossed his skin, and pain flickered across her face.

"Viper did this to you." A statement, not a question, and not one that he could answer, but this close he could see all the bruises on her face, a cut on her temple—Viper's handiwork on her beautiful skin.

Rage, the only emotion he had left, coiled in his breast, along with a curious desire to protect the beautiful woman from Viper's wrath. He jerked his hand, tugging against the manacles on his wrists, and the chain clanked, drawing her attention.

"He'll kill me if I let you go." She glanced around the dungeon, her gaze resting on the Sinner's Tribe cut pinned to the wall with Holt's dagger. "You're a Sinner."

Holt shrugged. Once upon a time he was a Sinner. Now he wanted nothing from the club except their destruction.

She stared at the cut, and then her gaze flicked to Holt. "No one hates the Sinners more than the Black Jacks. You're their only threat to dominance in the state. I'm surprised you're still alive."

So was he. After months of torture there was little about the Sinners he hadn't shared with his captors. But Viper was a sadist at heart, and he'd clearly taken more pleasure in Holt's pain than he would have in Holt's death. At least until he found another distraction.

"If I help you, the Sinners will owe me," she mused. "Maybe they can hide me or protect me. Maybe even work out a deal so Viper leaves me alone."

He shook his head, wanting to explain to her that he was done with the Sinners, but she was already searching the dungeon, her hands brushing over the racks and cinder block walls. "I don't suppose he left the keys."

Holt grunted and tipped his chin to the door. Of course Viper had left the keys to the cuffs. Just like he'd installed a light switch in the dungeon. Nothing drove home the hopelessness of the situation as well as leaving the tools for escape just out of reach.

The woman followed his gaze and grabbed the keys from the nail near the door. "Let's think this through . . ." She twisted her lips to the side, the keys dangling from her fingers.

What the fuck? This wasn't the time to think. It was the time to act. The guards might be back any minute, and freedom was within his grasp.

"Keys." He blurted out the word, gestured to the cuffs.

"Just wait." She held up a hand. "Would it be better to leave you like that so when they walk in, they see you chained, but I'm waiting behind the door to knock them out?"

Was she fucking serious? Had she seen the guards? There was no way a woman her size was taking out even Viper's smallest man.

"Keys. Now." His voice was hoarse with disuse and the abuse of constant screaming, but she understood him.

Without hesitation, she unlocked the cuffs. Her hair brushed over Holt's arm, sending a peculiar wave of sensation through his body.

"Can you stand?" She stared at him in consternation and Holt nodded. The chains gave him enough freedom to reach the metal toilet affixed to the floor and to stretch his legs—a freedom he had used to exercise when he was alone so that when the day came he would have the strength to exact his revenge. Except the last beating had been so bad, he hadn't managed to do more than crawl in days.

"So what's the plan?" She toyed with the ring on her finger. "Even if we get through the door, we still have to cross the clubhouse grounds, evade the guards, get through the electric fence, and find a way to town. Or out of town since the Black Jacks own Devil's Hills."

Holt pushed himself to stand, and his legs wobbled. Viper had fed him just enough so he would have the strength to endure the torture, but he'd had no food or water for the last few days. Now he knew why. Dead men didn't need to eat.

But he didn't need to walk far. Once he had the guard's gun, he just had to make it to the clubhouse and into Viper's lair. The woman would have to fend for herself.

"What do you think?" She looked up, and Holt sucked in a breath. Now that he was on his feet, she looked even smaller, maybe around 5'4", with gentle curves on a light frame. Definitely no match for any of the Jacks.

How could he leave her to fend for herself? And yet, how could he not? The thirst for vengeance had sustained him for the three long months he'd been imprisoned. Revenge burned bright in his chest.

"Dagger." His harsh tone startled her, and he felt instantly contrite, but she rallied quickly, fear giving way to curiosity.

"Where?"

"Wall." He gestured to the cut, and she reached up and worked the dagger free, then caught the cut before it fell.

Turning the cut, she read the patches in the faint light. "T-Rex. Is that your road name?"

"Was." He swallowed, trying to wet his swollen tongue. "Name's Holt."

"I'm Naiya." She returned with the cut, but Holt shook his head and took the dagger instead. He had plans for that cut. He had visions of tossing it on the bonfire that was the Sinner clubhouse after he'd made every last Sinner pay for their betrayal, for leaving him to rot in Viper's dungeon.

"Probably too painful to put it on," she said, misunderstanding.

"Help me . . . door." A plan formed in his mind as she gave him her shoulder to lean on, her body shaking with his weight. For a moment his conviction wavered. She was too small, too slight, to support him, and no doubt she would freeze the moment someone opened the door. And then what? There was no way he could make it across the grounds on his own.

"Come on, Holt." She straightened and took a step forward. "Pick it up. We don't have all day. I've got things to do, places to go, and Sinners to meet. And we still don't have a plan. We can't just rush into this without thinking. That's how people get killed."

A sound came from his mouth, and it took a moment before he recognized his own laughter. *Christ.* She was something else. Imprisoned in Viper's dungeon with a man who had been left for dead, and she was cracking jokes.

She half-walked, half-dragged him to the wall beside the door, and Holt sank down to the cold, stone floor. Damn legs. How the hell was he going to ride?

He turned the dagger over in his hand, and emotion welled up in his throat. In the first few weeks after his capture, he had imagined his rescue again and again, and always Tank was leading the charge. More than a friend, Tank had been like a brother to him, and his betrayal hurt most of all.

"So, how about I think of a way to lure the guard back in here, then you distract him so I can jump him and knock him out?" She squatted down beside him. "I read that in a romantic suspense book when the hero and his buddy are kidnapped and locked in a room. Of course, those books all have a happy ending. Not sure if it will work out in real life."

Even if Holt could have talked, he wouldn't have known what to say. Except for Arianne, Viper's daughter and now, after an incredible betrayal, the Sinner president's old lady, he'd never encountered a woman as cool and collected as Naiya. No screaming or crying or sobbing. No balking at the risk of trying to escape. She was calm, focused and determined to plan their escape out to the nth degree. As if life ever went according to plan.

Holt had learned that lesson the hard way. If life went according to plan, the Sinners would have beat down Viper's door the very day Holt sacrificed himself to save Evie's life. .

"I'll take care of the guard," he said with a confidence he didn't feel in the least. "Just stay out of my way."

"How are you going to jump him when you can't stand?"

"I'll lean." He braced himself against the wall and willed his legs to push. "Help me up."

Naiya came up under his arm and helped him up. "This is the last time I'm doing this until we get out of here," she said. "You smell worse than my grandfather's socks, and that's saying something because he boasted he only washed them once a year."

That sound again—laughter—erupted from his throat. Naiya looked up and smiled.

"I was worried about you for a while there. Thought maybe they'd done your head in. Viper likes his little mind games. He twisted my mom when she young, and she was never the same again."

Holt frowned. "Viper . . . your dad?"

"God no." Naiya recoiled. "One of the Jacks is my dad, but my mom never told me which one, and I don't care because I want nothing to do with them. I don't think she ever knew. I honestly don't understand it. She didn't want to have a baby. She told me all the time that I ruined her life, her body, her status in the club . . . I mean, if you're life's ambition is to be an MC sweet butt and your currency is your body, why not make the guy wear a condom so you don't get pregnant? No glove. No love. That's my motto. Well, it would be my motto if I slept around . . ."

Sex. She was talking about sex. He hadn't thought about sex since the day Viper imprisoned him in the dungeon.

In the daily fight for survival, sex was the least of his concerns. But now that she brought it up, a woman with her looks and that lush body should have men falling over themselves to be with her. Maybe she had a man. But then where was he? If she had been his, no fucking way would he let Viper near her. And if Viper did get his hands on her, he'd be moving hell and earth to get her back. Like he would have done for any of his brothers. Like they didn't do for him.

Lucky for the man who had her. Holt had long given up hope of ever being with a woman again after what Viper had put him through. And Holt loved women. He loved their softness and their curves. He loved the musical lilt to their voices and the silk of their hair. He'd been with many women, but he'd never had a woman of his own. Not since he'd failed his sister, Lucy. Not since the day she died. Even if he got out of here, that torture would never end.

"You okay?" Naiya touched his cheek, bringing him back to the moment.

What the hell? He had to focus. They had one chance to get out of here and one chance only. And it was all up to him.

"Maybe I should stab the guard." She ran her finger along the flat of the blade. "We learned all about stab wounds in one of my courses at college. Did you know that if the direction of the force is perpendicular to the skin, then it's considered a stab wound? But if the direction of the force is tangential or parallel to the skin, then it's considered a cut wound? If we want to slow him down, we'll need to stab." She made a thrusting motion with her fist. "Rather than cut." She drew the knife down, and Holt jerked away.

So, she was smart as well as pretty. "You ever kill someone, darlin'?" The more he talked the worse he sounded.

Hoarse, rough. So unlike himself. But then all he'd used his voice for over the last three months was screaming.

"No." Naiya paled, looked away, her hesitation belying her bravado. "I just . . . read about it. And study it. Death, I mean. And crimes leading to death. So really, it's just theoretical. And I was just thinking about wounding him, not killing him."

His tension eased the tiniest bit. Okay, maybe she wasn't crazy, but she wasn't living in the real world if all she did was read and study about death, or if she thought she'd have enough control to stab an enraged man without killing him. She certainly didn't have the life experience to put her plan into action.

"Can't let you do it." Holt tightened his grip on the dagger. "If it goes wrong, you'll never get over it."

"You've done it? Killed someone?"

"Yeah." Holt shrugged, feeling neither shame nor remorse. Like her, he'd done what it took to survive. First as a member of a street gang in Laredo, Texas, and then as a full patch brother in the Sinner's Tribe. He didn't enjoy killing. But if it came down to his life or the lives of his brothers, he had no hesitation pulling the trigger. "And I'll do it again." He gritted his teeth when his legs trembled, protesting their use after so many months of inactivity. "You gonna scream and give us away?"

"Do I look like a screamer?" Naiya let out an irritated breath. "I just offered to stab the guy. I'm not about to start jumping around and waving my hands in the air whimpering that I can't deal with the sight of blood. I lived in Black Jack party central from when I was nine years old. I saw all the things parents are terrified their kids will see. You name it, I was there. I just can't handle the dark. But other than that, I don't even scream when I see spiders or mice. In fact, I keep them as pets."

"Pets?"

"I'm messing with you, Holt." Her lips turned up at the corners. "Defense mechanism. Inappropriate humor. Maybe 'cause we're in Viper's dungeon and he's about to send his brothers down to kill you and chain me to his bed. And you're weak and beaten down and can't stand, and even if we get out, we still have to get through the yard and away from the clubhouse without a vehicle. But at least we have a plan. Things could be worse."

"Worse?"

"We could be naked."

He couldn't help it. His gaze travelled down her body, drinking in her curves, the crescents of her breasts beneath her black tank top, her narrow waist, full hips, and long lean legs. He imagined her naked, soft creamy skin beneath his palms, dusky rose nipples begging for his touch. His cock stirred, and for the first time he wondered if Viper hadn't broken him after all.

Naiya swallowed hard and dipped her head, and her sudden shyness aroused him even more. "Definitely worse," she mumbled.

He heard footsteps outside the door, the rattle of keys.

The door opened. Just a crack, and then wider.

★ TWO ★

"Let me out of here." Naiya threw herself at the guard, beating his chest to distract him from Holt who was leaning against the wall behind the door with the knife in his hand.

Dammit. Why didn't he move?

She grabbed the guard's cut and shook him, doing her best to feign terror. "I can't take it. I'm afraid of the dark. I'll do anything. Tell Viper. I'll be good. I promise."

"Jesus. Fuck. Get off me." The guard swatted at her, but Naiya held on, keeping his back to Holt.

Still, Holt didn't move. What the hell was he waiting for? An invitation? Goddamnit. This was what happened when you didn't have a plan. Clutching the guard's cut, she slammed her knee into his groin. He doubled over with a grunt and she caught a blur of motion behind him. Holt's knife flashed and the guard dropped like a stone, blood dripping from his neck onto the concrete floor.

Holt stumbled to the side and Naiya caught him before he fell.

"I was worried for a moment there. Thought you might not be up to the task." She felt curiously unmoved by the

guard's death. Maybe because his wasn't the first violent
death she'd witnessed—by the time she turned eleven
years old, she'd seen two stabbings, a shooting, and a strangling, all in her mother's apartment. Maybe she was in
shock. She hadn't really expected Holt to kill him, just
slow him down. Or maybe it was because the guard was
one of the Jacks who had held her down in Viper's office
that terrible night and part of her believed he deserved
what he got.

Holt snorted, wiped the knife on his jeans. "It's about
timing. Knowing when to act. Rolling with the punches."

"I'll remember that next time I have to slit someone's
throat." Nausea finally roiled in her belly, and she
pushed the sick feeling away. They had taken a life. And
although she wasn't the one who had wielded the knife,
she was complicit in the crime. A wave of panic washed
through her, and she was profoundly grateful Holt had
taken on the burden himself. For all that she studied death
and spent her free time reading suspense novels and watching crime shows, and for all the violence she'd witnessed in
her life, she was pretty sure, when it came down to it, she
couldn't have done the job.

Naiya peered out the door and into the night. "Step one.
Completed. Now for step two. Hopefully it can be accom-
plished without bloodshed." She couldn't look at the man
on the ground as Holt rifled through his pockets, but his
grunt of pleasure drew her attention.

"Bike key." He held up a black, circular key fob. "We'll
ride out of here in style."

Naiya fought back a groan. "Now we have the beginning of a plan. And an end. How about we work on the
middle?"

"We're gonna have to improvise the middle bit." He patted down the fallen guard, relieving him of his wallet, his
weapon and the holster around his waist. "Problem solved."

"Ah, it's the old shoot 'em as you go routine." Naiya couldn't keep the sarcasm from her voice. "Nice and discrete. Definitely won't draw the attention of the fifty or so Black Jacks partying inside."

Holt tugged the Black Jack cut over the guard's shoulders and yanked off his T-shirt. "Put these on me. He's got the same hair color as me. Pretty much the same size. I'll keep my head down. You hide your face in case they recognize you. I'll lean on you and you giggle. Make like we're drunk."

"I'm not a giggly drunk," she protested. "I'm not even a giggly person. I'm more the serious type. Maybe you didn't notice with all the dancing and singing I was doing." Naiya helped him on with the T-shirt and cut, catching his grimace as he slid the Black Jack colors over his broad shoulders.

Despite the beatings he had taken, and the lack of sustenance, he still had more muscles than the men she'd dated until she hooked up with her current boyfriend, Maurice. And Holt was tall—an inch or two over six feet, she guessed—and that face . . . she could imagine women falling over themselves for a taste of him. Even the bruises couldn't hide the chiseled planes and angles of his jaw, the wide, sensuous mouth, or those blue eyes . . . so piercing they shone in the dim light.

"And I'm not a fucking Jack. Pretend."

Naiya startled at his sharp tone, but when she saw the tremor in his hand as he tucked the gun into the holster around his waist, she forgave him. He'd clearly been a prisoner for a long time, and if they didn't make it out, Viper would finish the job he thought he'd finished days ago.

"Sorry. I'm not good at pretend either."

His face softened, and he stroked her cheek. "Let's just get out of here."

"Sure." She took up her position under his shoulder,

bearing his weight as they breached the doorway, her cheek against the cool leather of his cut.

No. A Black Jack cut.

Naiya slid out from under his shoulder. After spending years in the biker world, she understood the importance of a biker's cut. It meant more to him than his bike. His cut was his heart, his soul, his bond to his brothers and his club. "Your cut. I'll get it."

"No."

"It's okay. I'll just be a second." She ran back inside, balled up his cut, and tucked it under her arm.

"Good to go." She slipped back under his shoulder and Holt grunted.

"Just leave it."

"Really, Holt. It's okay. I know what the cut means. I've turned it inside out and folded it. No one will see your patches."

"Not my colors anymore," he muttered as he pulled the door closed behind them. "Not my club."

Before she could ask what he meant, he took a step forward, and Naiya slid an arm around his waist. Hopefully, they wouldn't draw the attention of the guards, ever present around a biker clubhouse to protect them from enemies, and especially from an enemy as formidable as the Sinner's Tribe.

The enemy of my enemy is my friend.

A friend that could assure her safety. And her future. Especially after her stupidity in Viper's bedroom this afternoon.

They crossed the compound with slow, halting steps, arms wrapped around each other, heads bowed. Naiya's heart thudded in her chest, and she pressed her cheek against Holt's side.

"How far?" he whispered.

"Their bikes were parked out front. About one hundred and fifty yards to go. There's a guard ahead."

"Start giggling." He dug his fingers into her side and she snorted a laugh.

"Stop. I'm ticklish."

"That's the idea." He tickled her again, and she laughed.

"Rafe?" A voice echoed in the darkness. Naiya looked up at the name patch on the cut Holt wore.

"That's you," she murmured, pulling him back a few steps. "Stay in the shadows."

"Yeah." Holt lowered his voice to a husky growl as footsteps approached from the direction of the clubhouse.

"You check on Viper's new bitch? He's getting impatient. He's waited a long time for another taste of that pussy."

Naiya choked back a breath and shoved her face into Holt's side. He smelled vile—sweat and blood laced with decay—and yet his body was warm and solid, his arm tight around her shoulders.

"She's still screaming and making a fuss. Knocked her around a bit and cut the lights. An hour in the dark with the rats and that dead Sinner, and she'll be ready for him." Holt's voice was thick, hoarse, and scratchy.

"Viper likes them broken." The biker stepped in front of them, and Holt ground to a stop, dipping his head. His hand slid to the gun tucked into the holster around his waist. Naiya could feel his heart thudding in his chest.

"Who you got there?"

"Piece of tail I found in a bar."

"Piece of tail?" she whispered, indignant.

Holt dug his finger into Naiya's side and she forced a giggle through clenched teeth. How could he be so calm?

"Gonna take her home. Too drunk to do much with."

The biker grabbed Naiya's hair and gave it yank. "They

don't need to do anything except lie on the bed and spread their legs. If you don't want her, I'll have a piece."

A shudder ran through Naiya's body, and she tightened her grip on Holt, pressing her forehead into his chest. Non-ononononono. Not again. She couldn't go through it again. A soft whimper of fear escaped her lips and Holt's body tensed.

"You don't want her bro. She's got . . ." He lowered his voice to a rough whisper. "Fucking STD, man. Doing the brothers a favor by taking her outta here."

The biker jerked back, and released her hair. "Fuck. Hate that fucking shit. Such a fucking waste of pussy. Go."

Holt nodded and tugged Naiya's shirt. She quickened her pace, almost dragging him after her.

"STD?" She hissed at him. "You told him I had an STD? I've never had sex without a condom except for . . ."

She cut herself off. Rape wasn't sex. Only fifteen, she'd been flattered by Viper's attention at a Black Jack party. He'd been charming, gentle, and seductive. But the moment he had her alone, everything changed. Too late, she realized there was no going back. No didn't mean no to Viper. It meant nothing at all.

"Shut it, darlin'," he murmured. "You wanted to be passed around? Handed over to Viper? Nothing turns a man off more than tainted pussy."

She stiffened in his arms. "I think I liked you better when you couldn't talk. Before, I was just an innocent and helpless victim of Viper's cruelty. Now I'm a drunk piece of tail teeming with STDs."

"I'm protecting you," Holt said. "And you don't seem to appreciate that I'm sacrificing to get you outta here. What I want to do is go back and shoot every fucking Jack I see, but there's no way you're gonna make it out of here on your own."

"I thought I was protecting *you*." She huffed. "After all, you're the one who can hardly walk."

"Don't need to walk to use a knife or a gun. Don't need a woman to protect me." They reached the edge of the parking lot, and Holt nodded at the two guards.

"Bitch's got a fucking STD. Gettin' her outta here."

"Christ, Rafe. You sure can pick 'em. Just toss her out and let her find her own way home." One of the guards grabbed Naiya's shoulder. "I'll take her to the gate. Bitches gotta learn not to bring that shit into the club."

Holt pulled Naiya against his side. "Got another chick already lined up. Gonna bring her back and share her around. I can drop this one off on my way." He took a step forward, and the second guard stepped into his path.

"What the fuck happened to your face?"

Desperate for a distraction, Naiya turned, hoping the guard wouldn't recognize her. There had been an endless parade of Black Jacks and sweet butts in and out of her mother's apartment when Naiya lived there, trading drugs for sex, or just hanging around. She had never felt safe at home, and often had to barricade herself in her room to keep out the Jacks who assumed she was her mother's daughter in every sense of the word, and didn't care that Naiya was underage or unwilling.

"You want a kiss, sugar?" she said. "Maybe a blow? I don't think the stuff on my lips is catching right now." God, she sounded like her mother.

"Fuck." The guard stepped back, his hands flying in the air. "Don't fucking touch me. Get her the fuck outta here, Rafe."

Naiya's pulse kicked up a notch, and she fought the urge to run as they stumbled forward and into a sea of chrome and metal. Dozens of bikes were parked in neat rows. Oh God. With the guards watching, how would they find the right one?

"You sure that's Rafe?" One of the guards muttered behind them.

"He was wearing his cut."

"When did he grow his hair? And what's with the beard?"

Holt pressed the key fob and she heard the beep of an alarm.

"Over there." He gestured to the far end of the lot, and Naiya picked up her pace, urging Holt to hurry.

"Rafe." The shout echoed in the darkness, and Naiya trembled.

"Can't you go faster?"

"That'll answer their question the wrong way." Holt kept his pace slow and even, his weight heavy on her shoulders.

"Rafe."

He raised his hand in the air, and waved just as they reached the dead Black Jack's bike, as if saying good-bye.

"Do you know how to drive it?" Naiya slid on the pillion seat the way she'd watched her mother slide onto countless motorcycles as she raced away leaving Naiya alone night after night.

Holt snorted as he straddled the bike. "It's a Harley, darlin'."

"Stop!"

She looked over as the two guards raced toward them. "Go, Holt. They're coming."

He flicked the throttle and the bike roared to life.

"The gate!" Naiya pointed to the chain-link fence as Holt peeled away from the lot.

"Automatic." He revved the bike, and the gate slid to the side. Holt raced through. Naiya clung to his waist, her cheek pressed up against his back. Behind them, she could hear the high-pitched rev of engines, and she clenched her fists against his stomach.

"Are we going to the Sinner's Tribe clubhouse?" she shouted.

But Holt didn't answer. Instead he leaned low over the bike, and they sped into the night.

★ THREE ★

"Holt, wake up."

Holt startled awake, bracing himself for a pain that didn't come. He stared up into the darkness and frowned. Usually, after he passed out, Viper would throw a bucket of water on him so he could continue with whatever torture he had planned for the evening. Even after Holt had told Viper everything he wanted to know about the Sinners, the sessions continued. Viper got off on Holt's pain, and only Holt's fantasies of retribution filled the void when hope fled.

"Holt."

The hands that shook him were small and gentle, the voice soft. He blinked to clear his vision and saw stars overhead, the dark shadow of branches, the silver light of a full moon, bats fluttering overhead. Taking a deep breath, he inhaled the scent of pine and the earthy fragrance of the forest. He was free.

"How do you feel?" Naiya leaned over, frowning. "You crashed the bike."

Fuck. He remembered feeling dizzy on the highway, the lines swimming in front of him, panic at the sound of bikes behind them, desperation, determination, turning onto a dirt road, slowing the bike . . . and then nothing.

"You okay?" He pushed himself up on his elbows, his gaze taking in the woman kneeling beside him.

"Just a few scrapes and bruises. I jumped when we started to wobble."

"Christ." He was supposed to be protecting her, not killing her. "What about the Jacks?"

"They drove past, so we can call it a successful escape. But I think you need food and water and medical attention. I was going to flag someone down on the road and ask them to take us to a hospital."

"No hospital." Definitely no hospital. The kind of injuries he had sustained screamed for police intervention, and even though he intended to leave the biker life behind after he exacted his revenge, he wasn't about to involve the police in biker affairs. Some lessons couldn't be unlearned.

"Sure." She kneeled beside him and brushed the hair off his face. "I guess the Sinners have their own doctor."

"No Sinners."

Her face creased in a puzzled frown. "But they're your club. They'll want you back. You must want to see them. They probably think you're dead."

Holt lay down again and stared up at the night sky and the stars he had never appreciated until they were gone. The Sinners probably hoped he was dead because when he did show up they would be faced with the repercussions of failing to rescue their brother.

"We'll grab a ride to the next town," he said, acutely aware he hadn't answered her question. "The guard had a couple hundred dollars in his wallet. Should be enough to get you a motel room. You just lie low for a coupla days until I take care of Viper. "

A curious look crossed her face, a cross between confusion and disappointment. "I don't need your money. And

I don't need to stay in a motel. I have friends in Missoula. And . . . a boyfriend. I can call them and they'll come and get me. I just thought it would be easier if the Sinners helped me out in case . . . you know . . . maybe you don't succeed. Viper's not going to let me go. He thinks I owe him a debt."

"You don't need the Sinners," he assured her. "I'll deal with Viper. You got my word."

Easier said than done. Now that he was free, he questioned his original plan to return to the Black Jack clubhouse and hunt Viper down. With all the guards patrolling the property, he'd never make it within five feet of the gate, much less get up close and personal with Viper in a straight-on assault. Plus he had no strength, no weapons, and no advantage.

"You're hardly in a position to go after him," Naiya said, as if she could read his thoughts.

Or maybe he did have an advantage. His gaze fell on Naiya, fiddling with the ring on her finger. She was right that Viper would come after her. Not just, as she said, because Viper thought she owed him a debt, but because she was smart, pretty, brave, and sexy as fuck. A real prize for a degenerate bastard like Viper. And his type of woman, given the similarities between her and Evie, whom Holt had saved from being raped by Viper in a bike shop. Plus, there was the matter of a dead Black Jack and a stolen bike—things Viper couldn't ignore.

If Holt kept her close, he wouldn't have to go to Viper. The Black Jack president would come to him.

"You're right," he said, dissembling. "I could use your help. Food. First aid." He rolled to his side and didn't have to feign a grimace. "We'll go to a motel, lay low until I've got my strength back." He gritted his teeth, forced out the lie. "Maybe call the Sinners if we need them."

"I don't have much first-aid experience," she said,

frowning. "We spent more time with dead people than live people in my course, but I can call my friend Ally. She's a nurse."

"No nurse." Holt groaned. "Just you. Don't think I could handle too many people right now."

"If you're sure." Her worried gaze travelled across his body. "I suppose if they're got a computer and Wi-Fi at the hotel, I can look things up. I dropped my purse in Viper's room when I . . . we were . . ." Pain flickered across her face and she looked away. "I don't have my phone. I feel kinda lost without it."

What the fuck did Viper do to her? Holt felt a twinge of guilt at his deception. From the way she kept twisting that ring on her finger, and the slight tremble of her hands, he could see she was scared. And, although she'd brushed off his question, she was hurt.

A surge of protectiveness rose up inside him—something he hadn't felt since he'd lived in Texas. Even if he didn't need her to lure Viper, he couldn't just leave her alone to fend for herself. Look what happened to his sister when he'd taken the fall for his street gang and spent two years in juvenile detention for a crime he didn't commit. Even now he couldn't forgive himself for her death.

"So I guess the plan is to hitchhike to the nearest motel and get you fed and cleaned up." Her voice wavered. "Then I'll call someone to come and get me. You can call me when the deed is done so I know it's safe to come out of hiding."

Fuck. What was with all the fucking plans? Why couldn't she just wing it and then he wouldn't have to keep thinking his way around her? "Don't involve anyone else," he said. "You don't want to put them in danger. Just stick with me."

Naiya's brow creased in a frown. "I'm not sitting around in a motel waiting for you to serve up poached Viper à la mode at your convenience. I need to find a job. I spent the last of my savings on my mother's funeral. That's where Viper caught me. At the cemetery."

Jesus Christ. Viper had no limits. But then Holt knew all about Viper, and not just from the time he'd spent in the dungeon. He'd heard stories from Viper's daughter Arianne, who had abandoned and betrayed her father years ago to become the old lady of her father's greatest rival, Sinner's Tribe MC President, Jagger. Viper had killed his old lady, Arianne's mother, when he thought she was having an affair. He had repeatedly beaten Arianne and her brother Jeff and paid off social workers and medical staff to look the other way. He had even given Arianne to one of his men against her will, offering her virginity as a reward. He was clever, cunning, ruthless and cruel. A formidable enemy. A monster of a man.

"I'm sorry about your mom." Although his mom was still alive and living with his dad in Laredo, she was dead to him after effectively abandoning Holt and Lucy to indulge her addictions and not being there to save Lucy when Holt was locked away.

Naiya shrugged. "I hadn't spoken to her in seven years. She was more interested in getting her next hit and being Viper's prize sweet butt than she was in me. And she betrayed me in the worst possible way."

They had something in common after all. He'd figured she had to have some connection to the biker world. A civilian wouldn't have known about the importance of a biker's cut, nor would she have stayed as cool as Naiya had when they'd been confronted during their escape.

Interested despite himself in the beautiful little spitfire, he leaned closer, his head brushing against her arm. "What work do you do?"

"I'm a forensic scientist. Well, I was supposed to be. I just finished my internship, and I was supposed to have an interview for a full-time position at a crime lab this afternoon. Looks like I missed it."

"A forensic scientist? No shit."

"No shit." She leaned back against a tree, her skin pale in the moonlight, her lips turning up in a smile. "Not the usual response I get when I tell people about my career. Usually they ask me if I'm doing the stuff they see on crime shows."

The question danced on the tip of his tongue. He and Tank used to watch all the crime shows together, making fun of the stupid criminals who left evidence behind, and the cops who took too long to put the pieces together. Although nothing topped the night one of the crime shows had featured an outlaw MC. They'd laughed so hard at the idiotic portrayal of bikers that Tank snorted beer out his nose.

Out of habit, Holt curled his fingers around the handle of his knife. He'd never said anything to Tank about the words engraved on the handle, but then he didn't have to. They understood each other so well sometimes words got in the way.

Longing gripped Holt hard, and he fought it away. He couldn't afford to indulge in memories of the Sinners or the man who had been closer to him than a brother.

"Once I find a job," Naiya continued, "I'll be doing blood and body-fluid analysis, DNA imaging, identifying genetic material on evidence, testifying in court . . . stuff like that. I've always been a bit of a science geek."

Holt pushed himself up on his elbow. Beauty and brains. The only scientists he'd met cut meth and other drugs in basements and underground labs. Maybe that's why Viper wanted her so bad.

She pushed herself to her feet. "I'll go flag down a truck. That bike must weigh at least one thousand pounds and there's no way you're lifting it in the condition you're in, and even less of a chance I can lift it. I do weights at the gym, but the most I've ever lifted is fifty pounds." She held out her arm, flexed her tiny bicep. "Check out these pythons."

Holt snorted a laugh. Fuck she was cute.

"Sorry." Naiya blushed and looked away. "That was stupid. The geek strikes again. You just make me nervous, especially when you don't talk, and I feel like I'm babbling. I'll go get us a ride."

Was she fucking crazy? "Hell no. It's not safe for you to be standing on the side of the road in the dark."

"I can tick off at least five reasons why we can't stay here." She held up her hand and tapped her finger. "First—

"I said no, darlin'. That's all the reasons you need."

She lifted an eyebrow, flicked her long hair back. "The very fact you can't get up and stop me is the very reason we need to go. You need medical attention. I need not to spend the night in the cold, dark forest with a strange biker."

Damn stubborn woman. "When the man says no, it means no." Holt forced himself to sitting and folded his arms, surprising himself with the vehemence in his tone. Where the hell had that come from? He was the peacemaker in the club, the negotiator. Rarely did he ever take a firm stand, or impose his will, preferring to resolve problems by finding a mutually agreeable solution. But something about Naiya . . . or maybe it was their situation . . . gave him a confidence and conviction he'd never felt before, a need to take control. Protect. Which made no sense since he planned to use her as bait.

"Maybe back in caveman times." Her hands found her hips. "And maybe that kind of thing works with your sweet butts and house mamas, but it doesn't work with me. I'm not part of the biker world anymore. I don't answer to bikers. I don't answer to anyone."

Holt's groin tightened as he watched her stalk down the road, the moonlight caressing her curves, smoothing over her ass, lush in dark denim. Used to women falling over themselves to bed him, he'd never met a woman quite like Naiya. Smart, confident, self-assured, and seemingly oblivious to the charm that made it easy for him to meet women and talk his way out of trouble, she was the most intriguing woman he'd ever met.

"Fuck." Holt fell back on the forest floor, leaves crackling under his stolen vest. He needed to keep his focus on the fight and his dick in his pants so he wouldn't risk discovering the damage Viper had done was permanent. She was a means to an end, and his interest was likely the result of months of isolation and a lack of female company. He would protect her until she'd lured Viper to him. After that, they would go their separate ways.

He had no idea how much time had passed when Naiya returned, the bottom of her T-shirt tucked into the neck in a way that exposed her smooth, toned midriff and the crescents of her breasts.

Holt's mouth watered, if that was possible for a man dying of thirst. Jesus fucking Christ, she was hot. And it had been so goddamn long since he'd had a woman . . .

"I got one," she said, as he tried to keep his gaze anywhere but on her chest. "He's a trucker. His name is Lucky Larry. He's waiting for us. I told him we were in a bike accident and the bike was totaled."

Someone had seen what he was seeing now? He pushed himself up to his haunches and took a deep breath as a wave of dizziness hit him. "You stood on the road like that? What the hell were you thinking?"

"You think he would have stopped if I was standing at the side of the road dressed in black?" She put her hands on her hips. "The best way to get a ride is to show a bit of skin. I always dreamed about traveling across the country, so I follow a couple of travel blogs. One of them had a post with hitchhiking tips. Not that I ever would have hitchhiked alone because statistically speaking it's dangerous for a woman, but I always like to be informed in case the situation arises, which it did."

Holt stared at her aghast. "You learned hitchhiking from a blog?"

"I remembered practically everything," she said, seemingly oblivious to his incredulous tone. "Where to stand, what kind of vehicle to flag down, how to be seen in the dark. Of course, it's always better to use a sign instead of your thumb, and not hitchhike at night, but we're doing it right since we're traveling together and you have a knife."

"Put your shirt down." Anger, unexpected and unwanted, sizzled through his veins. Did she have any idea what it did to a man to see something he wasn't meant to see? And those curves, her breasts, and . . . JESUS FUCK that sexy tat on her side . . . His cock hardened, straining against his fly. Good to know Viper hadn't damaged him permanently after all.

Holt unholstered his weapon and pushed himself to stand, leaning against a tree for support. If the trucker had any fucking ideas about touching her, he'd find himself with one extra hole in his body and one truck short.

Lucky Larry was clearly disappointed to see that Naiya hadn't made up the story about a boyfriend, and even more disappointed when Holt made sure he got a good view of his weapon. Still, he gave Holt a bottle of water and an egg-salad sandwich he'd picked up at a restaurant a few miles back. Holt had never tasted anything so good. He had to force himself to go slow, taking the water in tiny sips and nibbling on the sandwich, knowing his shrunken stomach wouldn't be able to handle the food.

Thinking Holt distracted, Larry chatted with Naiya, carrying on a conversation that bordered on flirtatious until Holt thought he'd have to either shoot the fucker or jump out of the damn truck and drag Naiya with him.

Lucky for Larry they reached the next town before Holt lost the last threads of his control. He dropped them off at a small motel on the outskirts of Benton, population 3,000, but not before brushing a kiss over Naiya's cheek before she slid out of the truck.

"Anytime, sugar." He slipped a piece of paper into her hand. "You got my number."

"Bastard had a fucking hard-on for three fucking hours." Leaning on Naiya for support, Holt snatched the paper as Lucky Larry's truck pulled away from the parking lot. He crushed it into a ball and flicked it away. "There. Now there'll be no calling Lucky Larry."

What am I doing? He stared at paper, shocked at the strength of his reaction to what was likely an innocent gesture on Larry's part, especially after the kindness he'd shown to Holt. But Naiya was his—his responsibility, his unwitting prisoner, his path to revenge, his to protect.

"Seriously?" Naiya stared at the balled-up paper on the ground. "You seriously think I was going to call him for a date? He's probably twice my age and three times my weight, and he smells worse than you. And even if I did want to call him . . ." She poked him in the chest. "You had no right to do that."

"I'm fucking protecting you." Holt wrapped his hand around her finger and drew it away. "Get used to it."

"I don't have to get used to anything. We've escaped. Tonight I'll look after you. Tomorrow Maurice and Ally will come to get me. And maybe then you'll feel like calling the Sinners for me out of the goodness of your heart. And if not, then you can go after Viper when you're feeling better, and let me know when it's safe again."

Holt felt a curious tightening in his gut. He was going to have to come clean about the Sinners. And then she would have to get used to the fact she'd be staying with him until he made contact with Viper and let him know he had Viper's prize.

"Can you stand for a minute?"

He nodded, and Naiya slipped out from under his arm and bent down to pick up the paper. Her jeans rode down and her shirt rode up and . . . fuck . . . he could see her panties, red and lacy with some kind of ridiculous bows around the edges. Hard on the outside, sexy and sweet on the inside. Why couldn't he have been rescued by a dude, or a grandma, or anyone who didn't make him think about just how long it had been since he'd been with a woman?

"Larry gave me some cash for the motel." She smoothed out the paper and tucked it into her pocket. "I asked for his address so I could repay him, and he added his phone number, too."

Holt bristled at the suggestion he couldn't care for the woman under his protection. "I told you. I got money from the guard."

"Now we have more money." She pulled a wad of cash from her pocket and waved it in front of him as she slid back under his shoulder. "You should be thanking me. And Lucky Larry. It only cost me a kiss."

She took a step forward, but Holt didn't move. Couldn't move. She kissed the bastard. Those soft pink lips had touched his grizzled cheek. And all so Holt could have a bed for the night like the fucking pussy he was.

Jesus Christ. He had been better off in Viper's dungeon. At least then he'd felt like a man. No matter what Viper did to him, he didn't break. But this . . . his damn emotions were all over the place. He wanted to steal a vehicle, chase after the truck, and show him just what happened when a man fucked with a Sinner's woman.

Except that he wasn't a Sinner. Naiya wasn't his girl. And he could hardly walk without her help.

"Let's get a couple of rooms," she said quietly.

"One room."

"I'm not sleeping with you." She pulled to a stop and he almost lost his balance. "I don't care how long you were in that dungeon. Or how nice you scrub up. Just so we're clear, I'm sticking around because you look like you need help, and I need your MC connections to get Viper off my back. I don't . . ."

"I'm the one with the gun, darlin'." He cut her off, irritated that she would think of sleeping alone. "And that's the only thing that will save you if Viper hunts you down. Not interested in anything besides food, a shower, and a bed that's not made of concrete and crawling with vermin." He also didn't think he could make it to the shower without her help, but damned if he would show any more weakness than he already had.

"Fine. One room. I'll ask for twin beds."

Five minutes later, she returned with a key and helped him along the walkway of the faded stucco building until they reached the last door. The room was small, but functional, decorated in yellow and orange with a queen-size bed, desk, dresser, small table and chairs, and a television. Bathroom to the left, painting of the forest to the right, window to the front, slight scent of mold and mothballs. Holt closed the plaid curtains and let out a breath when Naiya closed and locked the door behind her.

"They only had rooms with queen-size beds." She flicked on the lights, and Holt squinted, his eyes unaccustomed to the glare.

Until now, he'd only had glimpses of her, always in the shadows, but he could see clearly now, and his throat tightened as her hazel eyes shifted from brown to green under his scrutiny, gold flecks sparkling in the light. So beautiful. He drank in the soft glow of her skin, the dark, curly hair tumbling to her shoulders, and the clothes that clung to every delicious curve of her body. Christ. He'd been rescued by an angel.

"Gonna take a shower." A cold one.

"Okay." She swallowed hard. "Do you . . . need help?"

Yes, he needed help. Dehydrated, starved, beaten, and injured, he couldn't stop thinking about stripping her down to those sexy red panties and then talking her into a shower for two. But did he really want to find out how deep the injuries went? Performance had never been an issue for Holt. But what if it was now? Better to find that out with someone he would never see again.

"I'm good." He took a step, wavered, and forced himself to go on. Enough of the damn weakness. He had a woman to protect. A predator to lure.

A Viper to kill.

★ FOUR ★

TANK

James "Tank" Evans hated the dungeon.

He'd decided this after the call this morning that had taken him away from the club's newest sweet butt, Julie— the roundness of her body, the wetness of her pussy, and the constant stream of chatter, that should have been a warning sign it was going to be a long night. Most of his brothers liked their women chatty, but not Tank. Talking wasn't his thing. He'd been brought up in a family where children were seen and not heard, hit and not hugged. When he brought a woman to his bed, he wanted to get down to business without gossip or chitchat. For that reason, he stuck with the club sweet butts who knew his predilections. But Julie was new, and the only woman available to bring up to his room in the clubhouse last night.

He also hated the Black Jacks. Not just the ordinary kind of hate that he felt for watered-down beer, refried beans, and those small dogs that had to be carried around in handbags. He hated the Black Jacks with every ounce of his soul, every cell of his being. The Black Jacks had stolen his brother, ripped away the best friend he had ever had. T-Rex . . . no . . . Holt was dead because of the Jacks.

And now he had a piece of Black Jack scum in the chair in front of him, all ready to enjoy his new accommodations in the basement of the Sinner's Tribe clubhouse.

Tank punched Snake in the face, just a light tap to get him warmed up before Dax, the club torturer, arrived in the dungeon. The dark, windowless room the Sinners used for interrogations was well sound-proofed and located just off the clubhouse games room where the brothers could cool off between sessions with a couple of cold ones and quick game of pool.

The Black Jack idiot had been caught skulking around Sinner property. A stupid move considering the clubhouse was located in the far reaches of Conundrum, at the base of the Bridger Mountains, and there was nothing around them for miles except trees, scrub, and the odd wolf. No reason to be out here unless it was a bad reason. And bad reasons meant for good times, at least if you had put down your marker for being involved in anything that had to do with hurting the Jacks. If Tank couldn't have T-Rex back, he would spend the rest of his fucking life making sure every single Black Jack was wiped off the face of the earth.

Starting with Snake.

"How's that feel, Snake? You feeling warmed up? You don't want to meet our club torturer cold."

Snake spat on Tank's boots. Tank smashed his fist into the bastard's nose, enjoying the crack of cartilage when Snake's head snapped to the side. With his broad chest, wide shoulders, and thick arms, Tank had been pegged as a linebacker in high school, but sports cost money, and his family had none to spare.

T-Rex had a similar build, although he was blond where Tank was dark, his eyes blue where Tank's were brown. T-Rex had missed out on high school football, too,

spending time in juvenile detention when he lived in
Laredo, although he'd never told Tank why. Not that Tank
would ever ask. T-Rex did the talking. Tank did the listening. And yet T-Rex had understood him better than anyone
in his life. Maybe because they spent all their time together.
Tweedledee and Tweedledum, one of the sweet butts had
called them. Jagger had called them "the Twins." Tank
figured that was about right 'cause with T-Rex gone he felt
like half of him was missing.

And yet despite evidence to the contrary in the form of
a body found in the dungeon of the Black Jack clubhouse,
Tank hadn't given up hope. He couldn't shake that niggle of
doubt that had him riding as close as he dared to the
Black Jack clubhouse every week, scouring ditches and
forests where they'd been known to dump bodies, checking out hospital emergency admissions . . . T-Rex was
strong. Tough. No one could take him down in a fight. He
always had Tank's back, and Tank always had his. T-Rex
wouldn't go down this way. He had to be alive, and if he
was, he would need Tank's faith, his persistence, and his
dogged determination to find his best friend.

He heard T-Rex's voice in bars and in the executive
boardroom where he'd been called to fill T-Rex's seat as
the junior full patch member-at-large. He saw T-Rex's
broad back and his mop of hair on the mandatory Sunday
Sinner rides. So he kept looking. Hoping. Because he knew
T-Rex would never give up on him. If he could have just
one wish in his life, it would be to see T-Rex again.

Snake moaned and Tank tugged on the ropes, testing
them for give. He tried to focus on the task at hand, but
his mind was still on T-Rex. His buddy would have liked
Julie. He was always attracted to loud, bubbly, curvy
women; the ones who weren't afraid to go up to a biker
and drag him onto the dance floor; the ones who were the
life of the party, making everyone laugh; the ones who

were the loudest in bed. Tank went for quieter women, often with hidden depths or vulnerabilities, women who needed protecting and could handle his need for control in the bedroom.

"Let's get you tied up nice and secure," he said to his prisoner. "We don't want you hurting yourself while Dax is working. Nothing pisses him off more than self-inflicted injuries." He tightened the ropes as an image of Connie flitted through his mind. She was the only woman he'd lusted after who didn't fit his usual type. Short, cute, with an elfin face, a blonde pixie cut, and a sassy mouth, the motorcycle shop clerk had caught his interest the first time they met. But just when he'd started thinking things were going well, Sparky, the Sinner road chief, moved in on his territory, and Tank walked away. He wasn't into playing games. Not that it mattered now. She'd just up and left town one day to join her musician parents on tour without letting either of them know when she'd be back.

"It's too tight." Snake still hadn't figured out that he would be grateful for the ropes when Dax arrived. Dax didn't like irritating things like hands interfering with his work.

"You haven't felt pain until you've spent five minutes alone in a room with Dax." He heard the door open behind him, glanced over his shoulder and saw Dax walk in the door, but before he could greet the torturer, Snake snorted laugh.

"You're wasting your fucking time." Snake spat out as blood trickled down his temple. "If you think I'm going to rat on Viper and the Jacks, think again. Nothing that dude behind you can do to me will even come close to what Viper will do if he finds out I talked."

"You don't know Dax."

"I don't need to know him," Snake said. "Viper is a *master* torturer. Hell, he kept your damn Sinner brother alive in our dungeon for three fucking months so he could make him suffer over and over and over again. You should have heard that Sinner scream, man. You should have heard him beg. Even after he spilled everything about your club, Viper didn't let up. You know why? 'Cause he's a fucking sadist. He enjoys that shit. Gets him off. That's the difference between a real torturer and the pussy behind you. And that's why I'd rather be sitting here than spend a minute alone with Viper after he finds out I failed him."

Tank's breath left him in a rush. Three months? The dude had to be lying. T-Rex had been gone three months almost to the day. Gunner and Sparky found his body in the Black Jack dungeon only a week after Viper had taken him. Had they been wrong and Tank was right? Had T-Rex been suffering for three months waiting for his brothers to come for him while the Sinners mourned his death?

Nononononono. Pain sliced through his gut at the thought of T-Rex waiting for a rescue that never came, holding out hope that Tank would find him. His heart squeezed in his chest, and for a moment he wished it would stop beating, torturing him with each thud that meant he was alive and T-Rex had died alone. The bastard had to be playing him. The alternative was a hell beyond what Tank could bear.

"You didn't know?" Snake smirked. "You thought he was dead? He wished he was dead. He begged me to kill him more than once."

A sound escaped Tank's lips—a roar—pain, rage, frustration, anguish, and grief—accompanied by an almost desperate need for revenge. He lunged toward Snake, reaching for his neck.

"Stop."

He froze at the sound of Jagger's commanding voice—the only voice that could have stopped his raging need to avenge his brother. Powerful, formidable, and ruthless, the

Sinner president put a hand on Tank's shoulder, dominating the small room with the force of his presence alone.

"We heard him." He gestured to Gunner, the Sinner sergeant-at-arms, and Dax beside him.

"By the time I'm done with him, he'll be begging us to take him to Viper, although we won't be able to understand because he'll have no tongue." Tall, slim, and pale but with a shock of dark hair, Dax placed his black "toy" bag on the table beside the wall, deliberately paying no attention to Snake. He loved the drama of the moment, the slow reveal when he turned his black, soulless eyes on his victim for the very first time.

"Took you long enough to get here." Tank didn't understand why Jagger and Gunner had come to the interrogation room. Usually Dax worked alone with the assistance of a few junior patch members of the club.

Gunner reached for the door just as the new prospect, Benson, stumbled in. A former Conundrum deputy sheriff, Benson had asked to pledge to the club after his extracurricular activities on behalf of the Sinners had brought him to the attention of the Bureau of Alcohol, Tobacco, Firearms and Explosives (ATF). Instead of facing a grueling internal investigation, he had handed in his badge and begged the Sinners for a chance to prove himself worthy of the club and the protection they could offer.

"Christ. What the fuck is he doing here?" Gunner slammed the door and glared at Dax.

"I need an apprentice, and he's already shown some promise," Dax said. "Bruisers like Tank and Gunner are all about brute force and power. I need them for the heavy lifting. Benson understands finesse and the psychology behind what I do. He knows his torture implements. Plus, I've planned a nice, long session and we'll need someone to bring us snacks." A trained psychiatrist, Dax had become

interested in torture and human behavior while writing his
PhD thesis in university. His work had brought him to the
attention of several covert government organizations, but
Dax came from a biker family, and nothing could pull
him out of the life. He liked the freedom to experiment, to
come and go as he pleased, to have no one to answer to
but his brothers and his old lady.

"Fuck you." Benson, still unused to being on the receiving end of orders received a cuff to the head by an irritated Dax.

"Don't care what you did before, prospect, or who you
were," Dax snapped. "Learn your place or go face the ATF
firing squad."

"Fuck you." Benson's face tightened when Jagger lifted
an eyebrow. "Sir."

"What happened to our friend T-Rex?" Dax tilted his
blade saw to catch the light from the naked bulb overhead.
He kept his voice low, deceptively soft, forcing Snake to
lean forward to hear him. He'd told Tank and T-Rex over
beer one night how much he enjoyed the brutal betrayal
of that intimacy, saving some of his more vicious techniques for when his victims expected it the least.

Snake barely gave the blade saw a second glance. "Suck
my cock."

"Not while it's still attached." Dax waved Benson over.
"But that gives me an idea. Prospect, help the man off with
his pants."

"Jesus Christ." Benson swallowed hard and took a step
toward Snake.

"I'll give you something for free," Snake said quickly.
"But you promise not to touch the family jewels."

"Son, you're not gonna be needing those jewels anymore. They were forfeit the minute you stepped on Sinner
property." Dax glanced over at Jagger, and something

passed between them, an agreement made with the barest of nods. "Tell us what you know, and I'll make it clean and quick."

"Fucking Sinner bastards." Snake snarled. "I'll give you something just so I can watch you fucking suffer. He's dead. Day before yesterday, Viper finally decided he was finished with his play toy. Three fucking months he kept that bastard alive. But then he got himself a new distraction—one with a pussy. Never got to see her 'cause you caught me the day he was going for her, but she must have been one fine piece of ass 'cause he fucking loved beating on your boy and listening to him scream."

Red sheeted Tank's vision and he threw himself at Snake, fists thudding into the Black Jack's body. The chair toppled backward and Tank followed it down, raining blows as if the thunder of his fists could drown out the keening sound in his heart. This was for T-Rex, for every fucking hour of every fucking day he suffered, for every minute he waited for his brothers to come for him, for every second he doubted Tank's love. For the moment he lost hope.

Arms as thick as tree trunks wrapped around his chest, pulling him against a body as hard as concrete. Gunner. Six foot six of pure muscle. Not even Tank's rage could loosen Gunner's hold.

"Fuck." Jagger's voice was raw, thick with emotion. "Tank, stand down. Let Dax get as much information from him as he can, and then you can have him. And I promise you, T-Rex will be avenged. You have my word." He turned to Benson, his face tight with pain and anger. "Find Sparky. He and Gun found the body during our raid on the Black Jack clubhouse. I want to know if it's possible they made a mistake."

"Gimme twenty minutes." Benson headed for the door. "Sparky's at the shop."

Sparky, the Sinners' road chief, responsible for

maintaining the club vehicles, ran a garage at the edge of town with Jagger's old lady, Arianne, a journeyman mechanic.

"You got ten," Jagger bit out. "Maybe seven if I lose my patience with this Black Jack bastard."

"He's not gonna say anything different than we told you before." Gunner tightened his grip on Tank as if he knew Tank was still not in control. "We found T-Rex's medallion on the floor beside a body that was the same height and build as T-Rex. His face had been so badly beaten he was unrecognizable, but our sources had confirmed that T-Rex was in that dungeon."

"Bring him anyway," Jagger snapped. "I won't leave a stone unturned."

Now that he'd had a moment to cool off, and Snake was lying in a bloody heap on the floor, Tank's tension eased. "I'll stand down. You have my word."

Jagger nodded, and Gunner released him right away. A biker's word was his bond. And Tank had given his word only because of Jagger's promise to avenge his friend. Not that they hadn't attacked the Jacks already. After T-Rex was abducted they turned up the heat, going after the Jacks on all fronts, trying to break the Jacks' stranglehold on the lower-level clubs in the state. And although the executive board that ran the Sinner's Tribe MC had decreed their actions were for T-Rex, the attacks were politically motivated and strategically executed. Tank wanted something just for T-Rex. Something that would have made his friend smile.

Something personal.

★ FIVE ★

Should she stay or should she go?

Naiya looked from the motel room door to the bathroom and back again. With the shower going, Holt wouldn't hear the door close. She had enough money from Larry to pay for a cab and find another motel for the night. In the morning she could go to the bank, withdraw her savings, call Ally or Maurice, then jump on a bus heading across the state line. Away from Montana. Away from Viper. Away from Holt.

What would Holt do if she left? Despite the fact he'd crossed the room without her help, she could see the pain etched on his face with every step. He needed medical attention and she couldn't understand why he didn't contact his club. Not only that, she owed him a debt. No way could she have escaped the dungeon without him. And she didn't know anyone who could do what he did. Her loose association with the Black Jacks had taught her how ineffectual the police could be when it came to biker politics. Aside from leaving the state, if she wanted protection from Viper, she needed the Sinners and Holt was their man.

A man who'd gone to take a shower, although he could barely stand, and she still hadn't heard the water. She crossed the room and knocked on the door.

"You okay in there, Holt? You need a hand."

"S'good." His voice was faint, far away, and she felt a twinge of guilt at the thought of leaving him alone.

Sticking with Holt wasn't an entirely unpalatable idea. Yeah, he was battered, bruised, and broken. But that hadn't stopped him from doing what they needed to do to escape. He'd been resourceful, strong, and cunning. And she had to admit, riding behind him on the bike as they raced away from the Black Jack clubhouse had been just about the most thrilling experience of her life. At least until he'd crashed. She liked how he slapped Larry's hand away from her leg when he became a little too affectionate in the cab of his truck, and how he snatched Larry's phone number from her hand. Almost like he was jealous, although she was sure it was more about getting them to safety than anything else. Bikers and geeks didn't mix.

She needed advice, and there was only one place to get it. With one last look at the bathroom door, Naiya picked up the motel phone and punched in her bestie's number.

"I'm in trouble, Ally," she said quickly, although she doubted Holt could hear her over the shower. "Viper came for me at the cemetery."

"Bastard." Never one to hold back an opinion that needed expressing, Ally spat out the word. Naiya could imagine the look on her best friend's face. Ally was as expressive physically as she was verbally and more than once after they met at college in Missoula, Naiya had been on the wrong end of her flailing hands.

"You should have let me come with you to the cemetery," Ally continued. "It's not that long a drive from Missoula. He wouldn't have dared touch you if I was there."

"He probably would have taken you, too. And I didn't

want anyone there. I didn't even cry, Ally. I just felt . . . nothing." Even now she felt guilty. Who didn't cry at their mother's funeral? But then what mother would tell her daughter to go back to the man who had raped her to ensure her mother's drug supply?

"That's because your mother was a selfish bitch who only cared about getting her next fix and who she could sleep with to pay for it." Ally knew about Naiya's past and had been supportive and encouraging when Naiya decided to try therapy. She'd been the one to get Naiya back into the dating game, setting her up with sensitive, understanding men who didn't mind waiting to have sex. Men like Maurice.

A hard-working lab tech and devout Catholic who shared her interest in science, Maurice had been happy to put the sexual side of their relationship on hold, which saved Naiya from the usual charade of faking orgasms and focusing on her partner's pleasure to deflect attention from the fact she wasn't enjoying herself. Although Naiya wasn't sexually attracted to him, she thought Maurice was stable, fun, and comfortable to be with, and they rarely disagreed.

Ally's tone softened. "Are you okay? I mean . . . Viper . . ."

She filled Ally in on the details: the threats, the dungeon, Holt, their escape, and now her predicament—stuck in a motel room with an injured outlaw biker who felt obligated to protect her, when really, she needed to get away from Montana, as far and as fast as possible.

"He needs medical attention, but he refused to go to a hospital. I was wondering . . ."

"I'm there. And I'll bring the boy with me."

A smile tugged at the corners of Naiya's lips. Ally had been with her boyfriend, Doug, since she was sixteen years old. Although he was five years older than her, she often called him "the boy" because of his babyish face, easygoing nature, and his willingness to pretty much do anything she told him to do.

"I won't tell Holt until you're here. He's not very receptive to suggestions when it comes to his health."

"Is he cute?" Ally asked.

"Yes." She blurted out the word before she could stop herself. "Blue eyes. Blond hair—long since it hasn't been cut for a while. And he's got a beard, although I'm not sure if that's a normal look for him." She lowered her voice to a whisper. "He's breathtakingly gorgeous and that's with his face all bruised and cut up and his body doubled over in pain. He's also stubborn, and he's got a protective streak a mile wide. He's a big guy, too. Not fat, obviously, since he's been imprisoned for some time. But he's got a linebacker's frame and a lot of muscle. I can't imagine what he was like before."

"Annnnd . . . you're planning to run away?"

Naiya laughed. "And you're trying to set me up with a ruthless outlaw biker hell-bent on revenge who's been tortured for God knows how long and was going to just dump me off until he realized he needed my help. I have a boyfriend, thanks."

"Maurice is a nice guy," Ally said. "But, and I say this with all due respect to Maurice since he's Doug's friend, he's kinda dull. Certainly not as exciting as an outlaw biker on the run. You've spent years doing dull, and it hasn't worked out for you. Maybe you should try the wild side."

"I lived the wild side, Ally." Her chest tightened with the memory of the first time she'd gone to a party at the Black Jacks' clubhouse. "That didn't work out so well for me either."

"That was a one-off with the biggest, meanest, vilest piece of crap on the planet." Ally's voice sharpened. "You can't let it stop you from spreading your wings a little bit."

Naiya perched on the edge of the bed, reluctant to touch

any more of the bedspread than necessary. All the travel blogs she followed warned about contaminated bedspreads and how the first thing you were supposed to do in a hotel room was remove them. "I'm happy with Maurice. He's comfortable. He doesn't push."

"You're like an old married couple," Ally said. "The other day you said his kisses were soft and mushy and tasted like milk."

"That's 'cause he drinks a lot of milk. He's not into drugs or alcohol, or mind-altering substances."

Ally heaved a sigh. "You are in serious need of a mind-altering substance if you're planning on spending the night with a bad-ass biker and not taking advantage of the situation."

Naiya stood and pulled the orange plaid bedspread off the bed with one hand, tossing it over a nearby chair. "He's injured. I'm not about to whip off his clothes and . . . you know. He probably doesn't even like me. I got nervous around him and let my geek side show."

"So that's what you want?" Ally said as Naiya kicked off her shoes and settled back on the cool, white sheets. "A boring life with milquetoast Maurice? You need to have some fun before you settle 'cause that's my only regret in life. I love Doug to bits, but we got married too young and we never got to go out and do crazy things like go on the run from a psychopathic biker with a strange tortured biker in tow."

"Life isn't supposed to be fun," Naiya said quickly. "It's supposed to be hard work. If you want to have a good life, a decent and stable life, you have to be disciplined and focused. You have to have a goal and a plan and work hard to achieve them so you don't wind up as a forty-five-year-old meth-addicted biker club whore who hasn't spoken to her daughter in seven years and overdoses in a biker president's bed."

"Oh honey." Ally was instantly contrite. "I'm so sorry about your mom."

But Naiya was a on a roll, trying to justify her decision to stay with Maurice despite the very concerns Ally had just raised that had been in her mind over the last year. "Maurice shares my philosophy and my dislike of the free-wheeling, irresponsible, criminal biker lifestyle. This year he took a second job at night so he could increase his savings. And he keeps me on track. When he sees me reading those travel blogs, he reminds me how much money we'll need for a deposit if we want to buy a nice house in a nice area of town. And when I wanted to go to a motorcycle show, he calculated the depreciation of a motorcycle over ten years, then pulled up the statistics of motorcycle deaths on Montana's highways."

"He's a real catch, that one," Ally said dryly. "I am seriously wondering what I was thinking when I introduced you two."

"You knew he'd be perfect for me."

"So why haven't you called him yet?" Ally said softly. "Why isn't Maurice, the white knight, already in his white Volvo and driving out to rescue you?"

A good question. And not one for which she had an answer. Once Maurice arrived, it would be all over. Good-bye Holt and his tickling fingers, his searching eyes, his jealousy over a man who was not even remotely attractive. Good-bye heart-thumping escapes and breath-stealing motorcycle rides. But really. What was she thinking? Maurice would be worried sick when she didn't answer her phone. He would probably swing by her apartment and call the police when he realized she was missing.

"Maybe you should call him," Naiya said. "I don't have his number. It was in my phone."

"You sure?"

No, she wasn't sure, but calling Maurice was the right thing to do. "Yes, of course. He'll be worried about me."

Never one to give up without a fight, Ally said, "I'll take my time. Just in case you want to get some biker lovin' before we get there. What's there to lose? You're not having sex with Maurice, so technically it's not cheating. No ties. No heartbreak."

Naiya's stomach did a curious flip. But aside from the fact Holt was injured and clearly desperate to get rid of her, she couldn't imagine being with someone as dominant and controlling. Too much like Viper and the bikers she had worked so hard to leave behind.

"Maybe he can't," she whispered into the phone. "He was tortured, Ally. He's hurt pretty bad."

"I'll check him out when I get there. Give you the scoop."

"Very professional." She snorted a laugh. "I have a feeling he's not going to let you do a full examination. He's not like any biker I've met before. I think the pain and torture softened him up, and he'll be back to his no-good, ruthless, womanizing, murderous, misogynistic biker self in no time."

She gave Ally directions to the motel, warned her to make sure she wasn't followed, and then hung up the phone. Now what? Her stomach rumbled, giving her the answer. Maybe there was an all-night convenience store nearby or somewhere she could grab a few sandwiches. Holt clearly was in need of a good meal. She pulled open the door, only to freeze when she heard Holt call out behind her.

"Where are you going?"

"Food." She looked back over her shoulder at the badly beaten man wearing only a towel and a scowl. How long had he been standing there? What had he heard? "Maybe get you some clothes."

"My job."

"Get over it. You're injured. That means you rest, and I look after you. Grumble all you want, but there's not much you can do about it, and if you try to stop me I'll box your ears."

His lips quirked, amused. "Box my ears?"

"Yes." Her cheeks heated. "My grandmother used to say it. I didn't want to threaten real violence because you've been through enough." Her gaze took in the dark red wheals on his chest, the long thin marks of a whip, and the countless bruises, cuts, and burns. Softening her voice, she said, "You really need a doctor, Holt. I think some of those cuts are infected."

"I'll be fine. But you won't be if you go out there."

She supposed he was right. The Black Jacks had chapters and support clubs all over the state and a quick email or text with her picture was all it would take to alert them to be on the lookout. "I won't go into town. I'll just go to the restaurant attached to the motel and see if they've got anything left over from the day."

"I'll keep watch from the door." He walked toward her, taking slow, measured steps, and she struggled not to look down.

"In your towel?"

"Gotta gun. If I wave it around, no one's gonna be looking down." He leaned against the doorjamb. Maybe he wasn't concerned about her safety as much as he was worried about her leaving. After all, he'd been in that dungeon alone for a long time. And although he seemed okay, he had to be suffering the effects of the torture and isolation, maybe even fear. Just like her.

"I'm coming back, Holt."

His shoulders sagged just the tiniest bit, and he grunted his assent as he made his way across the room. "Still gonna watch from the door."

"If it makes you happy."

Curiously, it made her happy that he was concerned about her safety. This last year, Maurice had stopped walking her to her car at night or asking her to call him to let him know she'd gotten home safely. When she asked, he said he knew she was always cautious, and he didn't want to demean her by assuming she couldn't look after herself. Which had made sense at the time, but now she realized she'd missed that little show of caring.

He stood in the doorway as she walked through the parking lot to the reception desk, and he was still there ten minutes later when she returned with some Styrofoam containers, a bag of snacks and some Bolton, Montana, souvenirs: T-shirts, sweats, and hats.

"You get to advertise for the town." She handed him a bundle of clothes after he closed the door behind her. "Unfortunately, they didn't have any underwear."

Holt held up the navy blue sweatshirt with a yellow beaver embroidered on the front beneath a Bolton Beaver logo.

"Beaver Country?" He pointed to the slogan. "Christ. We're in the fucking sticks."

"I got you sweatpants and a couple of T-shirts, too." She pointed to the rest of the clothes. "And I got a T-shirt to put over my clothes in case there's a draft on the floor."

"You're sleeping in the bed."

"Floor."

"Bed." Holt sat on the bed and patted the mattress. "Beside me."

"You're injured. You need your rest. And they have a computer in the lobby with free Wi-Fi. While you're sleeping, I can do some research about bus schedules, and get back to job hunting. Anything you want me to look up?"

He stretched out on the bed, the towel loosening around his hips. "You're staying here. In bed. Won't be able to rest if you're lying on the floor, and I can't watch you if you're in the lobby. You don't gotta worry. I barely got the energy to stand much less try it on with you in your beaver shirt."

"You don't understand." Her voice sharpened. "I need to check my messages and do some research. I won't be able to sleep if I don't have a plan. There's no time to waste."

"Sleep isn't a waste of time." He folded his arms over his head, and she got a full, soul-destroying look at the abuse he'd suffered in Viper's dungeon. Cuts, bruises, whip marks, knife wounds, scars . . . Even with all her forensic-science training, she couldn't identify some of the implements that had been used on him. How did someone go through all that and come out emotionally unscathed?

"You had a shit day, same as me," he continued. "Gotta recharge the batteries."

Naiya twisted her lips to the side, considering. Although she was loathe to admit it, the prospect of sleep held some appeal. And she hadn't been keen on sleeping on the floor, which was no doubt as filthy as the bed spread.

But did she trust him? After the night with Viper, trust had been her biggest issue with men. Even more than her inability to enjoy sex. Although she'd come a long way with her therapist, she only dated men she knew first as friends, or who were known by her friends. Holt was the first man she'd been alone with whom she didn't know in some respect.

"You can trust me, darlin'," he said, as if reading her thoughts. "The last thing I would ever do is hurt you."

Clearly, some part of her did trust him, or she would have stayed in the truck with Lucky Larry to the next town instead of agreeing to share the motel room with a strange biker. And it wasn't like she'd be trapped here all night with him, the way she'd been trapped with Viper. The door was locked from the inside. The walls were paper thin, and the parking lot was almost full, which meant there were people who could hear—civilians who wouldn't ignore her screams the way the Jacks had done when Viper took her on his office desk.

Not only that. Ally was on her way with Maurice and Doug. And although Doug was a marshmallow, he was a cop, a big guy, and more than able to hold his own in a fight.

"Okay. But you have to put on the sweatpants. I've taken off the bedspread to protect us from germs, but we'll need to put towels over the pillows and check for bedbugs, too. I got you some socks. You should wear them to walk on the floor, but take them off before you get into bed."

"Bedbugs?" Holt pushed himself up, laughing. "The things that were crawling around that dungeon . . ."

"Don't." She held up her hands in warning. "I don't need to know."

While Holt ate the leftovers she'd managed to procure from the motel restaurant, Naiya covered the pillows and checked the sheets all under Holt's bemused gaze. She joined him at the table for a snack, and then went to the bathroom to change.

"Where's your sweatpants?" Holt, already in bed, glared as she hung her clothes up in the closet. She'd thrown on the biggest of the Bolton Beaver T-shirts and it fell to her mid-thigh, enough to cover what she didn't want to be seen.

"They didn't have any my size."

"So I gotta lie here beside you while you're wearing a shirt that says Beaver Country and nothing else but a pair of panties, after being alone in a dungeon for three months?" He cocked his head to the side. "You are wearing panties, aren't you?"

"None of your business. And if it's a problem, we can

go with plan number two, which is Naiya sleeps on the floor." She reached over and turned off the light, her body freezing until she reminded herself she'd left the bathroom light on. "That's probably better because I don't want to hurt you."

Holt rolled to his side, propping his head up with his elbow. "Yeah, I'm hurting. But I know you're hurting, too. You buried your momma, got slapped around, kidnapped, and now you're on the run after escaping Viper's dungeon. So come lie beside me and let me hold you and we'll hurt together."

Emotion welled up in her throat, and for a moment she couldn't speak. She'd locked the day away so she could focus on doing what it took to survive. Holt's words and his gentle tone threatened to open a door to feelings she couldn't analyze or understand. Feelings and emotions that scared her. "People don't hurt together. They hurt alone."

"Naiya." His deep voice rumbled through her. "I've been alone a long time. Lie with me."

Her breath left her in a rush, his command as much a permission to put aside her fears, as it was an invitation to share her burden, and behind it a plea. He needed her.

No one had ever needed her before. She lay down beside him, her head on his shoulder, keeping her body rigid in case she hurt him. With an irritated huff, Holt pulled her close until her body pressed tight against him.

"I'm sorry about your mom," he said softly. "I lost my sister. I lost lots of brothers. I know how it hurts. You lose your dad, too?"

His words. His touch. His warm embrace. She almost unraveled right then. "I never knew him. And now that my mom is dead, I'll never know who he is. I used to pretend he didn't know about me, but that if he did, he would have taken me away and protected me." She held up her left hand, showing him her ring. "All I have is this. My mother said he came to see me at the hospital the night I was born, and left it for me. It's the Phantom's ring. Do you know who he is?"

"Comic book hero." Holt chuckled. "You like comic books?"

"Yeah." She buried her face in his shoulder so he couldn't see her blush. "That's my geek side showing again."

"Like the geek side," Holt said. "We got a geek at the clubhouse. Hacker. Big into computers. He went to university and has a bunch of degrees, but he's pretty laid back and doesn't make a big deal about it. The rest of us, except Dax, don't have much education. Some finished high school or did a few college courses. Not me. Wound up in juvenile detention when I was sixteen and when I got out, I left town, and went on the road. Found the Sinners."

"I left town when I was fifteen, too." And only after her grandmother's priest had saved her from going through with her plan to shoot Viper by way of revenge. But that wasn't a story she shared with anyone. Not even Ally. She'd hit rock bottom that night. Lost to herself. Betrayed by her mother. Nowhere to go. No one to turn to. She'd bought the gun. Walked through town. And only a chance encounter with Father Doyle had saved her from a lifetime of regret. In that moment, she realized how far she'd fallen. It was the only time in her life she had ever asked for help.

"Well then the geek and the biker have something in common." He stroked a warm hand down her back, his touch soothing. "So tell me more about the Phantom. Does his ring have magical powers? Can it turn us invisible so we can just walk into the Black Jack clubhouse, take out Viper, and walk out again?"

Naiya smiled up at him. She rarely told anyone about the ring for fear they would make fun of her. But Holt seemed genuinely interested.

"He was a ghost with no superpowers so he defeated his foes using his intelligence. He wore two rings that could permanently mark everyone they touched. This one is the Good Mark, and people who touch it are under the Phantom's protection and the mark gives good luck. On his right hand he wears the Skull Mark and people that receive it, usually with a punch, are branded a victim of his wrath and bad luck follows them around. I used to imagine he gave me the Good Mark to protect me. Not that it did any good. I've had to look after myself since my grandmother passed away."

"Maybe it did," he said. "You found me. I'll protect you."

"Not the Sinners?" She bit her lip and then forged ahead. "You aren't going back to the club?"

"They fucking abandoned me." Bitterness laced his tone, and his fist clenched against her side. "They left me to die in that shit hole. After I've offed Viper and as many of the Jacks as I can take out at once, I'm going back to make the Sinners pay. Just like I did when I was just a teenager. My parents fucking abandoned me and my sister so they could get high or drunk or whatever they needed to help them forget their shitty life. A street gang became my family. I took the fall for the president when it all went bad and wasted two years of my life in juvenile detention. When I got out, I found out the first thing the president did was go after my sister because I wasn't there to protect her."

"Oh, God, Holt. I'm so sorry."

His voice caught, broke. "I had lots of time to plan while I was in Viper's dungeon. I got a new mission in life. Revenge. It's the only reason I survived as long as I did. It's what I lived for. It's all I want."

Naiya placed a gentle hand over Holt's heart. "I'm not the only one hurting inside."

★ SIX ★

Bang. Bang. Bang.

Holt jerked awake, blinking in the semi-darkness, his heart pounding in his chest. How long had he been asleep? Usually he timed his sleep by the light coming through the bottom of the door. Daylight was safe because Viper was busy with club business. Night. Darkness. That was the dangerous time. He tried to stay awake at night so Viper wouldn't take him by surprise. There was no light now, but there was something on his chest. Moving.

Rat.

Holt bolted up, brushing off his chest, his arm flinging to the side with enough force to smash the rat against the wall. After so many months, he had a system in place and a pile of decaying rodents in the corner of the dungeon as a measure of his success.

Except this time his hand met with flesh, not fur. And the rodent screamed.

Damn. Still alive. He rolled to the side, his hands outstretched to catch it.

Bang. Bang. Bang. Someone pounded on the door. Viper was here. The pain would begin again.

"Holt. No."

He reached, grabbed something much bigger than a rat. Smooth. Soft.

Another scream. A sob. Shouting outside the door.

"Holt. Please. It's me. Naiya."

"Naiya." A shriek came from outside. "Doug. Break it down."

Holt froze. Beneath his palms he could feel the thud of a pulse. Water dripped on his hand.

No. Not water. Tears.

Naiya.

He ripped his hands away, rolled off the bed. Naiya curled up on the mattress, her hands around her neck. Sobbing.

"Fuck." He reached for her across the bed as the door continued to shake. "I thought I was back in the dungeon . . . I didn't know. Did I hurt you?"

"Door." She pointed behind him, waving him away. "It's my friend, Ally."

Holt didn't move. "I hurt you."

"Please . . ." She swallowed, her voice soft, broken. "Open the door."

He unlocked the door and pulled it open. A woman pushed past him and ran into the room, leaving him face to face with a man only an inch or two shorter than him, but with at least fifty pounds on him in weight.

"On the ground." The dude pointed to the floor. "Hands behind your head."

"What the fuck?" Holt folded his arms. "You some kind of cop?"

"He is a cop," the woman—Ally—shouted. "So you'd better do what he says."

"Where's your uniform?"

"It's okay, Doug." Naiya said from the circle of Ally's arms. "He didn't mean to hurt me. He was half asleep."

The cop stared at Holt and he stared right back, each of them assessing the other. Any other day, Holt would have been confident he could take the bastard down, but today—tonight—he might have to work at it.

"Doug. Stand down." Naiya broke away from Ally, stepped between Holt and Doug. Even from where he stood, Holt could see the marks of his fingers around her neck. One more second and he would have choked her. He might be out of the dungeon, but it wasn't out of him. Maybe it never would be.

How could he keep her close if he was a danger to her? And what the fuck had he been thinking putting this innocent girl back in Viper's sights? But how else would he lure Viper and to exact his revenge? And how else could he keep Naiya safe?

Without thinking, Holt reached out and lightly stroked the marks on Naiya's neck. She shuddered, and Ally slapped his hand away.

"Paws off, biker bastard."

"Ally!"

"Look what he did to you," Ally's voice rose to a shriek. If not for the hulking presence of her man, Holt would have been tempted to gag the bitch. He'd never heard a woman shriek so loud.

"He thought he was in Viper's dungeon," Naiya said. "You're a nurse. You know about trauma and psychological distress."

"All I know is that a biker was strangling my best friend and if we hadn't got here when we did, she'd be dead."

Holt grabbed a shirt from the chair. "I'll go wait outside till you're packed up and ready to go."

"No." Naiya spun around to face him. "I asked them to come here to look after you. Ally's a nurse, and Doug had medical training for his police work. Since you won't go to a hospital, they're the best you're going to get."

"I'm not—"

Naiya cupped his face with her hands and drew him down. "I'm okay. I know you didn't mean to hurt me. I understand, Holt. I had a . . . traumatic event and I sometimes wake and think I'm still there. That's why I sleep with the light on."

Something shifted inside him as she held his gaze, clicking into place. Her hands felt right on him, her words resonated in his chest. In that moment he wanted nothing more than to wrap his arms around her and keep her safe.

But he kept his hands down and his desire at bay. "I'll get another room."

"You don't need to do that. We'll work it out." She slid her hand through his and squeezed, a soothing gesture that would have amused him if he hadn't found such comfort in her touch.

"So how about we start again," she said. "This is Doug." Naiya gestured to the cop. He had a round, smooth face and wide blue eyes framed by long blonde lashes. Christ. If he hadn't been six feet tall, with a good-size belly, Holt would have sworn he was staring at a kid.

"And this is Ally."

The short, curvy blonde with the bob and way too much makeup scowled. "Don't look at Doug 'cause if you hurt my girl, it'll be me coming for you."

"And my boyfriend . . ." Naiya looked to the door, and her brow creased in a frown. "Didn't Maurice come with you?"

Doug and Ally shared a glance and then Ally paled. "Um . . . he couldn't make it, but he was relieved we were coming out. Maybe we can talk about it later."

Holt didn't like the look Doug and Ally shared, or the pain that flitted across Naiya's face. Who was this loser of a boyfriend who didn't come out the second he heard his woman was in danger? And why would he have let her go to Devil's Hills alone if he knew Viper wanted her? The dude was a fucking moron and needed some sense pounded into him. Too bad he didn't have the balls to show because Holt was of a mind to teach him what it meant to be a man.

"Appreciated, but I'm good." He grabbed his shirt. "I'm glad she's got friends to take care of her. Keep her outta sight for the next week. If you give me a number, I'll text when it's safe again."

"You won't last a week if those wounds aren't treated." Ally gestured to his chest. "I might be pissed, but I made a promise to Naiya I'd look after you and I will. So on the bed, biker boy. Lose the sweats. Find a towel. And assume the position." She looked over at Doug, now sprawled in a chair. "I need my bag, babe.

Doug jumped up like the chair was on fire, and lumbered out the door. "Back in five."

Holt fixed the crazy bitch with a stare. Hard enough to accept her help, but no fucking way was he letting a chick boss him around. Either Doug had been born without balls or she'd stolen them from him when he was asleep.

"Please," Naiya whispered.

She'd deflated after hearing the boyfriend hadn't come, her shoulders sagging, the spark going from her eyes. Curious how that more than anything they'd been through since meeting in Viper's dungeon had affected her. He supposed a person who liked to plan everything didn't deal so well with unexpected change. It made her seem less assured, more vulnerable, and it roused in him a fierce need to protect her.

Which, of course, he couldn't do if he was injured, or if he walked out the door.

"Naiya will sit beside me," he said. Maybe if she had something to do, she wouldn't look so lost.

Half an hour later, as Ally tended his wounds, and Doug

ran back and forth to the bathroom for water and hot towels, Holt confirmed his Doug diagnosis. Pussy whipped.

Christ. How did the dude put up with it? Any woman tried to order him around like that, he'd put her in her place pretty damn fast. Ally reminded him of a sexy, young reporter he and Tank had met once in a bar, Ella Masters. Holt had tried to put the moves on her, but she was having none of it. For every step he made forward, she pushed him two back while Tank chuckled in the corner. Finally Holt went for broke, sliding his hand up her skirt as he whispered all the dirty things he wanted to do to her back at the clubhouse. His plan backfired big time. She dumped a beer over his head and told him exactly where he could stick his cock, and it wasn't anywhere near her sweet pussy.

He felt a pang of longing as he remembered the good times he'd had with Tank—the rides, the bars, the parties, the women, the jokes they'd played on each other, secrets they'd shared . . . Hell, Tank had been as close to him as a blood brother—the first true friend he'd ever had. But weren't friends supposed to be with you through thick and thin? If Tank had been taken, Holt would never have given up the fight. Not for a minute. He would have given his life to bring Tank home.

"You okay?" Naiya stroked his damp hair as Ally dabbed antiseptic into one of the more recent cuts on his back.

"Yeah." He liked having Naiya near, knowing he could touch her, protect her if Viper walked in the door. He'd always thought scientists were a cold, calculating bunch, but Naiya was all warmth and compassion.

"He's as a strong as an ox," Ally said. "And as thickheaded, too. I'm guessing he was concussed a couple of times, broken ribs, broken nose, broken fingers and toes, broken arm—some of the breaks haven't set right, by the way—internal bleeding, permanent scars and skin damage from whips, chains, cuffs and burns, infected lacerations, bruises upon bruises upon bruises, blunt trauma to the head, and the list goes on."

"No shit." Doug pulled up a chair, and Ally narrowed her gaze.

"Don't sit."

"You need something, babe?" He jerked to stand, and Holt wondered how he functioned as a cop. If he couldn't control his woman, how the heck did he keep criminals in line?

"I need you to take all this stuff to our room. I'll shoot Holt up with painkillers and antibiotics and let him sleep, then I'll check him over in the morning."

"The lady at the front desk told me there were no rooms free." Naiya's brow furrowed, making her impossibly cute. Some women were just not made to frown. But Naiya . . . hell, everything about her was cute, from her beautiful face to her curvy body, and from her innocence to her amusing quirks that she called her geeky side.

"Doug flashed his badge and suddenly we had the room next to yours." Ally walked over to the wall and gently shook a framed print of the Montana fall—trees and mountains and a blaze of color. "Convenient. This way, we'll be disturbing someone we know. Last time we were on vacation we broke the bed and knocked all the pictures off the wall in the room beside us. The people next door called the cops." She barked a laugh. "Good thing Doug had his badge with him, and we got off with a warning. Nothing better than hotel sex where you can really let go."

Doug gave a satisfied smirk, and he and Holt shared a male-bonding moment. Okay so maybe the guy had one ball. Or maybe he had two, and he liked them in a vice. At least he had control in the bedroom.

Holt glanced over at Naiya and his heart twisted. She wasn't laughing with everyone else. And the look on her face . . . not shock or disgust, but longing. What kind of man was this Maurice? Obviously he didn't perform well in the sack. Another strike against him because Naiya was made for sex. That body, those curves, her beautiful face, her kind heart. And Viper had hurt her. The fucker was going to die two painful deaths.

"Doug . . ." Holt addressed the man although Ally made herself out to be the boss. And yet, he had a feeling if the shit hit the fan, it would be Doug calling the shots to protect his woman. "You should move your vehicle round the back. If something goes down, get Naiya out and take the girls through the passageway that splits the two buildings and you'll buy yourself a good five minutes."

Ally spluttered and opened her mouth, but Doug put a warning hand on her shoulder. "He's right. Nothing we can do here if the Jacks track them down. We'll need to get out fast."

"I'm not a girl," Ally muttered as they left the room.

Doug looked over his shoulder and gave Holt a wink. "With those boobs and that ass, you're all girl all the time. Just wait until I get you tied to the damn bed."

Naiya locked the door behind them, and joined Holt on the bed. "Ally said that shot she gave you to help with the pain will let you sleep without nightmares."

"What you did . . . appreciated." He looked over, saw a tear trickle down her cheek. "You okay?"

"Yeah. Fine. Why wouldn't I be?"

Maybe because her asswipe of a boyfriend hadn't showed. Holt had a feeling there was more to the story than just his failure to be there for his girl.

Holt lay back and tucked Naiya into his side. Without protest, she curled up against him, her head on his shoulder, one hand resting lightly on his chest. Holt let out a breath and pulled her closer. She felt right beside him. Perfect.

Broken.

Just like him.

"So what's the plan?" Ally handed Naiya a box of donuts as Doug and Holt pulled chairs around the table in their motel room. Fresh from a night of very loud motel sex, Ally had been up early to find coffee and donuts so they could start their day on a sugar and caffeine high.

"She always has a plan," Ally said to Holt as he reached for a donut.

"I noticed." His lips quirked at the corners, and Naiya blushed. They'd slept together all night, and, good as his word, he hadn't tried anything. Not that she expected him to. A man like Holt probably had women falling over themselves to spend the night in his bed. Curvy science geeks wouldn't be on his radar.

Naiya plucked a Bavarian cream from the box and placed it in the center of her Styrofoam plate. Knowing her quirks, Ally had brought a plastic knife and fork, and Naiya carefully cut the donut into six equal pieces. She didn't notice the silence around the table until she lifted the first bite to her mouth.

"What the fuck?" Holt stuffed half a jelly donut in his mouth and talked while chewing. "What did you do to that donut?"

"I like to cut the filled ones up so there is an equal amount of filling in each piece." She placed a sliver of donut in her mouth and chewed, overly conscious of Holt's scrutiny.

"Seriously?" Holt finished off his donut with a second bite, and reached for another. "Darlin' you gotta live a little."

"I am living. Donuts aren't a healthy breakfast." She speared another piece of donut and Holt snatched the fork away.

"Hey."

He held the jelly donut up to her mouth. "Bite."

Naiya glanced over at Ally and Doug who were watching them, rapt and unusually silent. "Fine. If it means you'll let me eat my donut in peace." She leaned over and nibbled on the end.

"Bite," he said again. "Like you really want it."

Her cheeks flushed and she took a big bite of the donut, her teeth sinking through the soft dough and into a pool of sweet raspberry jelly. She licked the sweetness from her lips and swallowed, desire curling in her stomach. "Good enough?"

"Again." His voice dropped, husky and low. Naiya looked up and blushed at the intensity of his gaze.

This time when she bit, she kept her gaze on him, watched his eyes drop to her mouth, his nostrils flare. Her body heated, moisture pooling between her thighs. She'd never had a man look at her like that, never felt such a rush of desire, and the simple process of eating from his hand was almost . . . sensual.

"More?"

He fed her the last bit of the donut, his fingers brushing over her lips as he placed it on her tongue. He seemed fascinated by her mouth, his gaze never leaving her face despite Ally's less-than-discrete coughing beside him.

When she finished the last bite, he dabbed some excess jelly from the corner of her mouth with a napkin and smiled.

"Good?"

"Yes." She nibbled her bottom lip, tasting the lingering sweetness. "Every bite was a surprise. Some with lots of jelly. Some—" She cut herself off. God, she sounded stupid. Everyone knew how a donut tasted.

But Holt didn't laugh. "Some without," he continued for her. "Unpredictability is what makes life interesting. Kept me going in that dungeon. I'd spend hours trying to guess what Viper would do next, whether the next day would be my last, whether the Sinners would show up . . ." His voice trailed off and Naiya's heart clenched. She knew that feeling. When the trauma invaded even your happy moments. When it just wouldn't let go.

"How come you never feed me donuts?" Ally lightened the moment by giving Doug a nudge.

"'Cause you'd bite off my hand." Seemingly oblivious to Ally's mock glare, Doug lifted a honey-glazed donut from the box.

"After that comment, I'm definitely gonna be biting something off tonight," Ally huffed. "And it's not your hand."

With a laugh, Doug stood and gestured to Holt. "You want to come for a walk, stretch your legs? Then we can plan with the ladies where to go from here. I might have to come with you if the wife's gonna bite off my dick."

After they'd gone, Ally sipped her coffee, uncharacteristically silent, while Naiya tidied up their breakfast. By the time she finished, Ally was over at the window, watching Doug and Holt in the parking lot.

"I like him," Ally said. "A lot. He's very protective of you."

"He's been alone for a long time. It makes sense he needs a friend." She shoved the bedspread aside and sat on the bed. "What's going on, Ally? You're not usually so quiet."

Ally turned, drew in a deep breath. "It's about Maurice. I just don't know how to tell you. Doug thought I shouldn't tell you and let Maurice tell you himself, but I'd want to know and I think you would, too. And now that I've met Holt, I feel better about telling you."

"Tell me what." She twisted her ring around her finger.

"Doug couldn't get in touch with Maurice last night, so

he swung by his place. He was . . . " She bit her lip and a pained expression crossed her face. "With someone else. A woman. And she wasn't delivering pizzas. He was with her. If you know what I mean."

Naiya stared at her friend aghast. "Doug saw them together?"

"Maurice came to the door in his underwear, and she wasn't far behind. When he saw it was Doug, he came clean. He said it had been going on for a year. He cares about you, but—"

"But I wouldn't have sex with him." Her shoulders slumped.

"I'm so sorry, Naiya." Ally crossed the floor and wrapped her in a hug, but Naiya didn't need her comfort. She was disappointed, sure, but not particularly sad. Definitely not the kind of sadness she would have expected to feel at the end of a two-year relationship.

"I would have slept with him," she said, pulling away. "I told him that. In the beginning, I just wanted to go slow. But he said he was fine with waiting. He never pushed, never asked. And then platonic just became normal."

"He told Doug he didn't push because he didn't want you to do it just to make him happy. He wanted you to want him, and he never felt you wanted him that way."

Now that took the air from her lungs. "He's right," she whispered. "He's a nice guy, but he never made me hot. I never fantasized about him, never dreamed about him touching me. Even when we kissed, it was nice, but I didn't feel anything. I figured it was because of what happened to me because it was always like that with the guys I've been with until . . ."

Ally's face brightened. "Until?"

"Now." Naiya glanced over at the window. Holt leaned against a fence, his Bolton Beaver sweats riding low on his narrow hips, T-shirt tight around his chest. Even starved and injured, dressed as a tourist, he exuded strength, confidence, and a raw sexuality that took her breath away.

"When he fed me that donut . . ."

"Yeah." Ally pretended to fan herself. "It was better than some of the porn Doug downloads on a Saturday night."

"It made me hot," Naiya continued. "I've never felt like that before. And when I look at him . . . even all bruised and beaten . . . he's the most gorgeous man I've ever seen. But it's stupid. We just met. He's hurt—"

"Not where it counts."

Naiya snorted a laugh. Ally was nothing if not direct. "And he's on a quest for vengeance—not just against Viper and the Jacks, but the Sinners, too. I thought he'd go back to his club, and they would help me, but he's gone rogue, and I don't want to get dragged into something that's going to put me right back where I started. I need to hide from Viper and then I need to find a job so I can have a nice, quiet life and maybe meet someone stable to settle down with." She squeezed her hand around her ring. "Did Maurice . . . give Doug a note or did he ask me to call?"

"No, honey." Ally's nose crinkled in disgust. "He asked Doug to tell you it was over, the little shit. I always knew he had no balls, but that just proved it to me. He couldn't even tell you to your face, or at least do it over the phone."

"It's okay." Naiya grabbed a pillow off the floor and hugged it to her. "I'm not that upset, just . . . I didn't really expect it. Now I'm losing a friend."

"You don't need friends like that," Ally said. "You need friends who are there for you when you need them. Doug called in a favor to get someone to cover for him today. He didn't think twice about it. You need us. We're there. And a real boyfriend would have been here before us. Hell, he wouldn't have let you go to Devil's Hills alone."

The door flew open and Holt burst into the room, chest

heaving. "Jacks are coming. I heard their bikes coming down the mountain. We got seven, maybe ten minutes at most. Grab your stuff." He raced out of the room and Naiya followed him down the hallway.

"How did they find us?"

"Viper probably had someone watching your friends." Holt pushed open the door to their room and grabbed the duffle bag Ally had stuffed with clothes for both of them. "And your work, your gym, any hang outs . . . It's what we . . . the Sinners, would have done."

Dammit. She should have thought it through. Holt had warned her, and now she'd put Ally and Doug in danger.

Holt checked the gun holstered beneath his shirt, while Naiya balled up his cut. She'd stuffed it under her shirt when they escaped the Black Jack clubhouse and she wasn't about to leave it behind now.

"You go with Ally and Doug." He handed her the bag. "I got business with the Jacks."

She stared at him aghast. "But you can't fight. You're still injured. You barely made it into the parking lot with Doug. It's suicide."

"I got a gun, darlin', and today I'm gonna kill me some Jacks. I lived through those last three months for only one reason—revenge. And it starts right now."

Ally banged on the door, and Holt yanked it open. "She's ready to go. Get her out of here. Fast."

"What about you?" Doug took Naiya's duffle bag and stood to the side as she stepped into the hallway.

"Got shit to do," Holt said to him. "Not something I want to share with a cop."

Doug stepped into the room, pulling the door behind him, and their conversation dropped to a hushed murmur.

"We'll take you somewhere safe." Ally gave Naiya's arm a squeeze. "Let's go. Doug will meet us at the car."

If it had been yesterday, or any day in the last thirteen

years since her grandmother died, Naiya would have followed her friend. She had learned the hard way how to survive in the biker world, and those lessons included running from danger at the earliest possible moment and never looking back. Easy to do when it had only been her, but this time she had someone else to think about. Someone who was still suffering the effects of months of torment. Holt had saved her from the dungeon as much as she'd saved him. How could she abandon him now?

"He's going to kill himself, Ally." Naiya looked back over her shoulder. "He couldn't take on even one Black Jack in his condition much less the number I'm guessing Viper sent after us."

"You have to think about yourself." Ally tugged her hand. "Holt's a big boy. He knows the score. You have to respect his decision."

"He was tortured." Naiya gritted her teeth together. "And all he thought about was getting revenge. He says it was the only thing that kept him alive. He can't see past it. He can't see that he doesn't have the strength to make his dream a reality. His mind needs to heal as much as his body. The same thing happened to me after Viper raped me. I was blinded by hopelessness and revenge. I couldn't see beyond the moment I pulled the trigger. Father Doyle saved me from myself. Holt needs someone to save him."

"And I can't see why you're going to risk your life for someone you barely know," Ally snapped. "I like him. And I know you like him, but maybe you're just rebounding after finding out about Maurice. Holt's an outlaw biker. There are lots of hot guys out there who won't drag you back into the biker life you've been running from all these years or get you killed."

Naiya scrubbed her hand over her face, torn between the man who had helped her escape and held her in his arms so they could share their pain, and the fierce survival instinct that had kept her alive when she had no one to care for her.

Run. Run. Run. But she couldn't run and leave him to die. Not just because she felt a moral obligation to save him, but also because she felt a connection with him. When she'd curled up on the bed with his strong arms around her, she felt safe in a way she hadn't been since her grandmother died. She liked how he hadn't laughed at her quirks, and how he'd wanted to share her pain. Holt wasn't like any of the bikers she knew, and that alone was reason enough to help him. But dammit, there was no time to plan.

"Do you have something in your medical kit that will knock him out fast?" The words came out before she could catch them, uncharacteristically impulsive, driven by desperation and a desire to help the man who had helped her.

Ally's eyes widened, and she nodded. "I brought a sedative just in case he was difficult. It's an intramuscular injection. But it might take a few minutes to work. How will you get him to stand still?"

"Just give it to me."

The rumble of motorcycles grew louder, and Naiya's heart drummed in her chest. She never did anything without a plan. But Holt was a stubborn man, and she wasn't going to change his mind by banging heads with him. If there was ever a time for a rash decision, this was it. She needed to throw aside her calm, ordered, controlled life and live a little to save a life.

Ally fished around in her medical kit. She quickly prepared a syringe and Naiya palmed the needle just as Holt and Doug joined them outside the door.

"Come with us, Holt. Please." She gave him what she hoped was a beseeching look, praying he would make the right decision instead of forcing her hand.

"I'm not going anywhere when there are Jacks about. I got a mission. You gotta survive. Now go."

She slid the needle between her fingers until her thumb was on the plunger. Then she slid one hand around his neck and pulled him down toward her. "Do I get a kiss good-bye?"

Holt's gaze fell to her mouth. "Naiya . . ."

She licked her lips and leaned closer, so close she could feel the heat of his breath. "Please."

He leaned in, and she jammed the needle into his tattooed arm and pushed the plunger.

With a roar of anger, Holt shoved her away, ripping out the syringe. "What the fuck? What the fuck did you do?" He came at her, backing her up against the wall, and for the first time since she met him, she felt truly afraid.

"I'm sorry." She held out her hands in a placating gesture. "It will just make you sleep. They'll kill you, Holt. I can't let you die so soon after you got out of that dungeon."

His handsome face twisted into a curious mask of rage and despair, disbelief and betrayal. "Fuck, Naiya. This was all I wanted. A chance to get back at the Jacks."

"You want Viper," she said, struggling to keep her voice firm as the veins in his neck throbbed. "You know he won't come out on a mission like this. He's back at the clubhouse, and you won't get your revenge if you die now."

He reached for her, his hands just brushing the sides of her neck before he staggered back and into Doug's chest.

"Christ." His gaze never left hers as he struggled to stay upright. "You shouldn't have . . ." His eyes closed, and Doug caught him as he fell.

"That was so wrong." Doug heaved Holt over one shoulder. "So damn wrong. A man has the right to choose his own destiny. You can't take that choice from him."

"His destiny isn't to die right now before he gets what

he really wants," Naiya bit out, surprising herself with the conviction in her tone. "Now let's get him to the car."

Naiya and Ally supported Holt's other side and they carried him to the passageway that led to the back of the motel.

"He was a prisoner for three months." She heaved in a breath as she tried to take more of Holt's weight. "He's not thinking straight. He has no chance against a bunch of Jacks alone, barely able to walk, and with only one gun and no ammo. I won't stop him from going after them and having his revenge. But not now."

"I wouldn't want to be you when he wakes up." Doug tossed the keys to Ally and she opened the passenger door of their sporty green SUV. "I'll take you up to my brother's cabin. It's only a few hours away and very isolated. We can pick up some food along the way. No one will find you there. Ally and I will stick around until he wakes up. Run interference."

"No. I want you guys as far away from me as possible," Naiya said as they eased Holt into the vehicle. "If anything happened to you, I couldn't bear it. I made this choice. I'll pay the price."

★ SEVEN ★

TANK

Tank wandered into Big Bill's Custom Motorcycles and Artwork dazed and floundering, his senses numbed by alcohol and lack of sleep. In all his imaginings, he had always pictured himself picking up T-Rex's bike because his friend had come home. He had saved it from the original Big Bill's shop after Viper burned it down, and brought it to Evie after she'd rebuilt the business in a new location. He'd made sure it would be as good as new and ready for T-Rex to ride. And then Snake had ruined everything.

Dax had worked him over the way only Dax could, and Snake never changed his story. T-Rex had survived three months in Viper's dungeon. Three months in pain. Three months in agony. Three months alone and believing until the end the Sinners would come for him, that Tank would have his back.

Tank pulled out his flask and finished the last of his whiskey. Hope no longer burned in his chest, but the whiskey soothed his pain.

"Hey, Tank. How can I help you?" Evie looked up from the counter and Tank forced a smile. It wasn't Evie's fault that Viper had become obsessed with her, or that Viper had gone to the shop that day because her former boss, Big Bill, had tried to rip Viper off. And it wasn't Evie's fault that T-Rex had saved her from Viper by offering himself in Evie's place.

"I came for T-Rex's bike."

Evie's smile faded and pain flickered across her face. "I'll tell the guys in the garage to bring it round."

Tank checked out the bike gear as he waited for her to return. Evie had kept everything from the name to what was left of Big Bill's inventory when she rebuilt the shop. She sold everything from new and used bikes to gear and parts. Out back, the mechanics did fixes and tune-ups, and Evie did custom paintwork. He'd thought about getting some artwork for T-Rex as a welcome home present, but now he knew his buddy was never coming back.

"They'll have it for you in a few minutes." Evie came around the counter and held out a folder. "These are the designs I had worked up after we talked about artwork for the bike. I thought you might like to have them."

His hand shook as he took the folder and he held it against his chest. If he looked at them now, he'd embarrass himself and dishonor T-Rex's memory, just as he had done at the funeral three months ago. He sniffed, inhaling the scent of leather and the new bike smell that T-Rex loved. Tank had gone with T-Rex to pick out a bike the day after T-Rex had patched into the club, and T-Rex had cracked him up breathing in the new bike smell so deep he'd choked himself. That was the same day Tank had given T-Rex the knife his grandfather had given him, repaired, polished, and sharpened to celebrate T-Rex's patch-in. He'd had a message engraved on the hilt. Something straight from the fucking heart.

"I heard about Snake," she said softly, pulling him back into the moment. "I'm so sorry, Tank. I knew from the fact you hadn't picked up the bike that you still hoped."

Fuck. He wished she'd stop being nice. Zane's old lady was T-Rex's type, slim and pretty with dark hair and green eyes. T-Rex had tried to hit on her when they were first assigned to protect her, not realizing she'd been the woman Zane had held a torch for all the years they'd known him.

He nodded his thanks, unable to speak for the lump in his throat, and headed outside where Shooter, the newest full-patch member of the Sinner's Tribe, was loading T-Rex's bike into the trailer under the guidance of Shaggy, the oldest member of the club.

Stocky, and broad-shouldered, with a short blond buzz cut, Shooter looked like he should be playing high school football instead of running with an outlaw MC, but he knew his way around a gun and was one of the best marksmen in the club, albeit a little out of control.

"Careful," Tank shouted. "Don't scratch the paint."

"What are you going to do with it?" Shooter grunted as he pushed the bike up the ramp.

"Not up to me. It's club property now that . . ." Tank choked on his words. He couldn't say it. He couldn't say that T-Rex was gone because he still didn't believe it. T-Rex had been closer to him than a brother. They had a bond, and that bond was still there. He could feel it, taste it. If T-Rex were dead, he would be dead, too, like those old couples who died within days or hours of each other because they couldn't bear to live without their partner. Not that he and T-Rex were together in that way, but they were as close as friends could be. Closer.

What the fuck was he doing? His head said it was over, but his own damn heart was still beating. He couldn't give up. Until he laid his eyes on an actual body, he just wouldn't accept that T-Rex was dead.

"You gotta let it go, man." Shaggy clapped him on the shoulder, the ring on his finger digging through Tank's shirt. "I lost a lot of brothers over the years and at some point, you gotta tell hope to take a hike and move on with your life."

Gray and grizzled, with a bushy silver beard, Shaggy had been with the Sinners almost since the club's inception, and yet he had never run for any of the executive positions, preferring to remain a member-at-large. As far as Tank knew, Shaggy had no kids or old lady, although he enjoyed the attention of the sweet butts, and would take two or three to his bed at a time. Jagger often bounced ideas off him and he was well respected in the club. But his biggest claim to fame was that he hadn't cut his beard in twenty-two years. Tank didn't know how long a beard would be after twenty-two years, but it sure as hell smelled like it had never been washed.

"Not giving up yet." He shook off Shaggy's hand and shouted at Shooter who had lost his battle with gravity and dropped the bike on its side. "Jesus Christ. I don't know why Jagger gave you that patch if you can't even push a bike up a ramp without dropping it. Take it back inside and ask the mechanics to touch it up. Then I want you to detail it like your fucking life depends on it. Make sure there isn't a speck of dust on T-Rex's bike. I want it to shine like the goddamn sun, so when I bring it to him he's blinded by the fucking light."

"Hold up, brother." Shaggy's hazel eyes shifted from green to brown, unnerving Tank who always looked to a man's eyes to take his measure. "Much as I hate to defend Shooter, he was trying his best. The ramp isn't even."

"Then he shouldn't have pushed the bike on it," Tank spat out, grateful to have a focus for his grief and anger.

Shaggy shook his head. "This won't bring him back."

Tank clenched his fist so tight his nails dug into his palm. "I'm not doing it to bring him back," he bit out. "I'm doing it because he's coming back, and when he does he'll need his bike. If it's clean, he'll know I never gave up on him, that I had faith, that I knew he'd be back."

Shaggy held up his hands palms forward. "Hey, man. Whatever makes you happy."

"T-Rex's bike. Clean. Waiting for him to ride. That makes me fucking happy." He turned away quickly so they didn't see his damn eyes water.

★ EIGHT ★

What the fuck?

Holt stumbled along the wood-paneled corridor, his brain still hazy from sleep. Last thing he remembered was Naiya shoving a damned needle in his arm. Anger. Swearing. Frustration. And a curious fear that he wouldn't be able to protect her. Then fucking nothing.

A wall of windows greeted him as he emerged into a spacious living room overlooking a thick forest with the glimpse of a lake beyond. Even without the log furniture, antler lighting, and rustic decor he would have guessed they were in a cabin. The mixed scents of cedar and pine filled the air, and something else . . . something delicious.

His stomach rumbled as he followed the smell to a cozy kitchen. The donuts Ally had brought to the motel room had barely made a dent in the hunger pangs that had been his constant companion for the last three months.

He jerked to a stop in the doorway, trying to get a grip on his anger. After what he'd been through in the dungeon, he wasn't emotionally equipped to deal with the loss of agency her little trick had engendered, or the vulnerability. He never wanted to be helpless again, and back at the motel . . . when he felt the drug pulling him down . . . only anger had saved him from the grip of fear.

Hand tight on the doorframe, he shouted her name. At least that's what he thought he did. Instead, his mouth dropped open and he just stared at Naiya stirring a pot on the stove, her back to him, her body bathed in the warm orange light of the setting sun as she sang Led Zeppelin's "Ramble On."

Jesus fucking Christ. He loved that song. The greatest fucking geektastic song by the best band of all time. He remembered the first time Tank played it for him. They'd been trunking with Cade one night and the drug dealer they'd stuffed in the trunk was making a helluva lot of noise. While Cade called the dealer's buds and arranged a payout for his freedom, Tank turned up the radio just in time for the first few beats of "Ramble On." Holt had always thought it was about a girl and wandering around, but Tank made him pay attention to the lyrics. Mordor. Gollum. The whole song took place in Middle Earth. Holt never forgot the grin that split Tank's face. After that, every fucking time they drove around together, Tank pulled the song up on his phone and blasted it through the speakers. And he always had the same grin. Ear to fucking geektastic ear.

Holt had never made the connection, but as he listened to Naiya's soft voice, watched the sway of her hips, and the sun play over her hair, he realized she had a lot in common with Tank—from her love of comic books, to the music she enjoyed, to the way she stayed calm under pressure and did what she thought was right despite Holt's views on the matter.

His gaze drifted down to her perfect, heart-shaped ass outlined in dark denim, the flare of her hips, and then back up to the curve of her waist, hugged by a tight red T-shirt. Maybe not exactly like Tank.

He liked that her feet were bare, and that she sang as she cooked when she thought no one could hear her. After the hell he'd been through, the entire scene was surreal, peaceful. Domestic. Sweet. Not something that had ever been on his radar. He almost didn't want to have words with her about what she had done.

"Are you just going to stand there, or are you going to sit down and eat?" She looked back over her shoulder, cheeks flushed, the light dancing in her eyes. "I've made lasagna, garlic bread, and salad. I like red wine with dinner, but Doug thought you were more of a beer or whiskey man, so I bought both. I've also made soup in case real food is too much for you."

Holt's mouth watered, not just at the prospect of eating a meal, but also at the fact it was home cooked. Before his capture, he lived at the Sinner clubhouse with a few of the other unattached brothers who hadn't saved up enough money to buy their own place. Food was grabbed on the go unless one of the brothers with an old lady invited him home for dinner, or one of the sweet butts did some cooking instead of doing what they were supposed to do—what they often did for him, what he was thinking about doing now that Naiya had bent down to pull something from the oven.

Christ. She had a sweet ass. And it had been a long time since he'd had a woman.

A woman who had knocked him out when he was about to take down a few Jacks.

"What the fuck did you do?" His gaze dropped to the dish of pasta in her hands, and he reeled from the delicious aroma of melted cheese and tomato sauce. If he didn't hurry up this conversation, his stomach would rule his head, and he would miss the opportunity to lay down the line.

"Saved you." She placed the dish on the table. "There

were six Jacks, fully armed, none of whom appeared to have been chained in a dungeon for months. I get that you want revenge. But that wasn't the time or the place. A shoot-out would have landed you in jail, or worse, dead, and you have a Viper to kill. He's who you want. Not them."

She was right. Every fantasy of retribution he nurtured in that dungeon had Viper in the starring role. But damned if he would admit it to her. "You had no fucking right. What you did . . . if we were in the club, a kick out would be the least of your punishments."

"But you're not in the club," she said quietly. "And neither am I. Although I'm not sorry I got you out of there, I am sorry about how I did it. But I didn't think you would listen and we didn't have time to talk."

"How long was I out?"

"Eight hours. Ally said the shot should only have lasted one or two, but your body needed to heal. She stayed until a few hours ago to make sure you were okay, but she and Doug had to get to work. She left stuff for me to treat your wounds."

Holt grabbed the nearest chair and yanked it out from the table then sat heavily on the wooden seat, his harsh movements rattling the cutlery and plates. He wanted to be angry with her, should be angry, but she'd saved him from his own stubbornness, and now she was standing barefoot in the kitchen after cooking for him, singing his favorite song, looking so fucking lost and beautiful he thought his heart would break.

"Don't do it again," he mumbled.

Her shoulders dropped, releasing a tension he hadn't realized she'd been holding "Only if you promise not to try and get yourself killed too soon. I have a vested interest in seeing Viper dead, too." Naiya placed a basket of garlic bread beside him and a bowl of tossed salad, the vegetables so brightly colored he almost wondered if they were real.

"Ally said to go slow and easy with the food. Drink lots of water. She didn't think alcohol was a good idea but . . ."

"Whiskey. Neat." He looked up when she startled, mentally kicking himself for his abrupt tone. "Please."

"I didn't know bikers said please." She headed over to the counter, covered with bottles, cans, and shopping bags.

"It's been known to happen when beautiful women drug them, take them to cabins in the mountains, save them from their own pig-headed stupidity, and then cook for them."

Naiya laughed, a light bubbly sound that made him smile. "I'll keep that in mind."

She returned with the drinks and joined him at the table. "Cheers to revenge." She held up her glass and Holt did the same. Then he shot back the whiskey in one gulp.

"Son of a bitch." He wheezed out a breath as the bitter liquid burned its way down his throat and into his shriveled stomach. His head spun and he wondered if it was possible to get instantly drunk.

"Eat something." Naiya handed him the bread basket, and he shoved a piece of warm garlic bread in his mouth. *Oh fuck.* The taste, the tang of garlic, salted melted butter. Texture. Warmth. He'd never tasted anything so good in his life.

"More." He reached for the basket, and Naiya pulled it away.

"Slow."

Holt grunted his annoyance. "Pushy little thing, aren't you?"

"Actually, no." She picked up the spatula and served him a steaming slice of lasagna before filling her own plate. "I've never had anyone to boss around. When I was little, I lived with my grandmother and after she passed away I lived with my mom, which basically was like living with half the Jacks since they were in and out of the apartment all day, doing drugs, selling drugs, shooting up, and . . ." Her face tightened, and she toyed with her ring. "While my mom did what drug-addicted sweet butts do."

"In front of her kid?"

"Unless she had a boyfriend. Some of them didn't like to share. The sharing types wanted to share me, too, so I spent a lot of time at the library or staying late after school to help the teachers so I didn't have to go home. I read a lot of books, found places to hide . . ."

Holt's stomach clenched at the image. She talked about it so casually, yet he saw her tremble when she put down the spatula. And when she sat down, she put her hands on her lap instead of picking up her fork.

He recognized her pain. Understood it. Hell, she'd been abandoned just like him. And yet there was more she wasn't telling him. The real reason she needed to plan and control every aspect of her life.

Naiya was full of secrets. Painful secrets. Beautiful secrets. If they'd met her in a bar, Tank would have been all over her, and Holt wouldn't have stood in his way. Holt went for assertive women who would speak their minds— women who laughed loud and enjoyed being the center of attention. He liked a woman who knew where she wanted to be touched and how. Tank, on the other hand, liked the quiet women, deep, the ones with hidden passion. Tank liked to explore, seduce, unlock, and uncover. The more secrets a woman had, the better. Except, right now, the thought of Tank anywhere near Naiya made Holt's stomach clench. If anyone was going to tease out Naiya's secrets, it should be him.

"Looks like I'm hiding again," she said, "Except this time I'm not alone."

Guilt speared through his gut. How could he go through

with his plan to use her to lure Viper from his den when she had dragged him out here to save him instead of escaping with her friends?

"Not while Viper is still walking this fucking earth." He lifted a fork full of lasagna, and his taste buds exploded. Christ. Had food ever tasted this good? The combination of tangy sauce, rich ground beef, and sharp cheddar stole his breath away, and for the next five minutes he couldn't speak. Instead, he savored—simple pleasures that had long been denied.

"Fucking delicious." He reached for the spatula, and Naiya shook her head. "I think you should stop. It's not going anywhere. If you feel okay you can have more later."

"Bossy." He put down the spatula, reached for the bread.

"Only around you, it seems." She tilted her head to the side and laughed.

Damn cute. If they'd been anywhere else, any other time, he would have flirted with her, started the slow dance that would eventually lead to the bedroom where he would strip her down and make her moan. He suspected she hid her true emotions, and once he cracked those inhibitions he would find deep passion beneath the orderly facade.

"Ally, Doug and I were talking about where I should go." She sipped her wine, the red staining her lips. He wanted to lick it off, kiss her lips until they were plump and pink, just like he'd imagined when she kissed him before the needle hit home.

"You don't need to go anywhere." He stood, poured another whiskey, leaned against the counter. "Once I kill Viper, you'll be safe. You can get back to your normal life." He sipped the whiskey, slowly this time, letting the liquid burn and warm his tongue.

"Yeah." Naiya toyed with the salad on her plate. "I'll find a good job, save up some money to buy a little house, maybe I'll meet a nice guy with a good job—"

"What about Maurice? You gonna dump him because he didn't show?"

With a sigh, she stood and carried her plate to the sink. "He dumped me. Doug caught him with another woman, and he asked Doug to tell me it was over."

Holt thudded his glass on the counter. "He's a fucking piece of shit, and he'll come crawling back 'cause you're a real class act, and he's gonna realize what a mistake he made."

Her eyes warmed, and a smile spread across her face. "That's the nicest thing anyone ever said to me."

"It's the truth, although I gotta admit I hope he doesn't come back 'cause you deserve better than a man who isn't there when you need him."

She put her plate in the sink and turned on the water. "There weren't a lot of good men around when I was growing up, which is why I was so desperate to get out of the club. I wasn't safe."

"So you're not with the Jacks?"

She gave him a horrified look. "No. Absolutely not. I don't want to wind up like my mom. Most of the women at the club are drug addicts or sweet butts or both. That's not a life. I might have had it rough as a teenager, but when I lived with my grandmother, she encouraged me to work hard so I could have a future outside the MC. She never minded that I never really fit in."

He pointed to the tattoo on her shoulder, bared by the short-sleeved tee. He'd missed it before, but in the evening light it stood out, a black stain on her otherwise perfect skin. "You got the Black Jacks mark."

Naiya yanked on her sleeve, and her face crumpled. "Not by choice."

He barely caught the words she whispered, but when he did the food stuck in his throat. Jesus H Christ. She'd been inked against her will?

"Viper?"

"Yeah," she whispered. "Viper."

Holt felt a strange tightening in his gut. Viper had claimed her, not just for the club, but also as his own. No wonder he'd sent the Jacks to hunt her down. And yet he'd never met anyone so ill-suited to club life. Why did Viper want her so bad when he had a club full of women willing to satisfy his every whim? Maybe for the same reason Holt found her interesting. She was different, smart, ambitious, and beautiful. And yet, just like all bikers, she didn't fit in.

A fierce wave of protectiveness crashed over him, the likes of which he hadn't felt since Lucy was alive. He wanted to gather her into his arms, hold her close, and promise her no one would ever hurt her again. He wanted to grab his gun, drive until he got to the Black Jack clubhouse, and shoot until every Jack was dead and he'd blown so many holes in Viper's body there would be nothing left to bury. And then he wanted to take her away. Keep her. Claim her as his own.

Just as Viper had done.

"Lie still."

Naiya patted antiseptic over the wounds on Holt's back. Getting him into the bedroom so she could check his dressings had been no easy task. After they finished eating and washed the dishes, he prowled around the cabin, checking out every window, door, nook and cranny. Then he'd walked the grounds, charting out the property in slow, halting steps before returning to the kitchen to polish off the rest of the food. Only the promise of chocolate-chip cookies—albeit made from a mix—had lured him to the bedroom. Even then, he had grumbled as he stripped off his T-shirt, telling her he didn't need any more "fixing."

"What the fuck is that stuff?" He tensed when she ran the cotton ball over the freshest of the stripes across his back, pushed himself up, twisting his head to look over his shoulder.

"Keeps the germs out." She pushed on his shoulder, biting back a smile. "Lie down. You're worse than a kid."

"You don't need to put it everywhere." He twisted his head again and Naiya stroked a soothing hand through his thick, soft hair.

"He hurt you everywhere."

He growled softly as she stroked, a deep rumble of pleasure, so she kept up the rhythm as she cleaned his wounds. His hair was long, just brushing his shoulders. Did he always wear it like that, or had it grown while he was in the dungeon? He had trimmed his beard after his shower, and although she'd never been a fan of facial hair, it suited him. Made his handsome face just a little more badass, hinted at the wildness in him, coiled tight and ready to spring. She would be a fool to forget it.

For now though, she had soothed the savage beast. She could feel the tension ease from his body, and when she ran her nails over his scalp, his growl of approval sounded almost like a purr.

"I like your tats." She ran her hand gently along his right arm, and then down his left shoulder and along his ribs. "Did you get them all at once?"

He sighed, his body sinking into the bed. "Got the shoulder piece when I was in the street gang and the body piece when I was wanting to show the Sinners I was as badass as them. The sleeve I got with Tank when I got patched into the club. We got them together. Me on the right. Him on the left, so when we walked together we were like one person, not two. It was his idea. I couldn't say no to him. If he'd wanted to get our faces tatted, I woulda done that, too."

Laughing softly, she massaged his head again. She'd never had anyone to look after other than herself. Her mother was rarely alone and every time she overdosed, someone else called the ambulance. Naiya visited her in the hospital each time, wished she could feel something other than anger when the doctors said she was slowly killing herself, and one day her body wouldn't be able to take it anymore. And when her mother was lucid enough to ask her to bring her drugs, she left desolate in the knowledge even the near-death experience hadn't been enough to turn the tide. In the contest between Naiya and narcotics, the narcotics always won.

She felt safe now. Secure. Despite what she'd done to Holt, he hadn't even raised his voice. And when he'd pulled out the chair and told her with only a grumble not to do it again, she carefully laid down the knife she had clenched in her hand, ready to defend herself if he flew into a rage. For the briefest of moments, she had allowed herself to wonder what would have happened if the kiss in the motel had been real.

Still lost in the daydream of that kiss, she leaned over and pressed her lips to the one section of untouched skin beneath his shoulder. "He missed this."

Holt tensed beneath her, and she jerked away. "I'm sorry."

He rolled to his back, seemingly unconcerned by the undressed wounds. "You kissed me."

"I wasn't thinking."

"This morning, before you jabbed that needle into my arm, you kissed me." He traced his thumb over the bow of her lips.

Naiya's face heated and she crumpled the soft cotton bedspread in her hand. "I . . . needed to distract you."

"Soft lips," he whispered, his gaze searching her face. She looked down, trembled, wanting more, afraid to ask. For years after that brutal night with Viper, she'd stayed away from men, and then she met Ally who had gently encouraged her to start dating again. Naiya had gone from one extreme to another, trying to reclaim herself by sleeping with as many men as she could to erase Viper's mark on her soul. After that soul-destroying experience, she'd dated casually, men who were quiet and unthreatening. Men unlike Viper. Even then, intimacy had eluded her, as had the ability to enjoy sex. And when feelings began to emerge that she couldn't understand, she ended it.

Holt pushed himself up and cupped her jaw with his hand, tilting her head back until she was lost in the depths of his piercing eyes, a blue so clear she thought she could see into his soul.

"Soft," he murmured. "Sweet."

Her heart pounded, blood thundering through her veins. She'd never felt desire like this, never let a man touch her in a way she hadn't directed, never been held so firmly she could do nothing but stare. He'd already pushed her boundaries in the motel, and yet she sensed that was nothing compared to what would happen if she let him in. Despite her fear, she wanted to touch him, taste him, and make her fantasy real. Drawing in a shuddering breath, she leaned closer.

Holt's fingers tightened on her jaw and his gaze dropped to her lips. Then he gently pushed her away and fell back on the bed with a groan. "Get out, darlin'. Go."

Shock swept through her, followed by a sickening wave of humiliation. The one and only time she'd put herself out there, she got the door slammed in her face.

Well, she wouldn't give him the satisfaction of seeing her pain. She'd been stupid to even think he'd be interested in someone like her. Bikers went for the girly girls, with big boobs and bigger hair, tight clothes, high heels, and snappy comebacks. She'd never seen a sweet butt at the clubhouse dressed in jeans and a T-shirt, her hair in a pony tail, face clean of makeup, nails bitten to the quick, and her feet bare.

Know thyself. Her grandmother had cross-stitched a tea towel with that saying, and Naiya had taken it to heart. She wasn't girly or particularly pretty. She would never achieve glamour or excitement, or play the games she'd watched her friends play, but she could make a difference in her own way. Once she got a job, she could make the world a better place, help catch the criminals who sold drugs, ran guns, and committed murder. Criminals like the bikers. Like Holt.

"Let me know if you need anything else." She kept her voice calm and even as she pushed herself off the bed, remembering the first aid kit only when it hit the floor with a soft thunk. Unable to face Holt again, she kept walking. She'd pretty much dressed all his wounds. If he wanted more treatment, he could damn well do it himself.

"Naiya. Wait."

But she didn't wait. Couldn't wait. A black hole had opened in her chest and was sucking her in. She needed to keep moving, make a plan. No more of this impulsive bullshit. It wasn't her, and it definitely wasn't how she wanted to live her life.

"Night, Holt." She closed the door behind her and made her way down the hall. Maybe a few hours on the Internet to check bus routes out of the state and places she could go while she job-searched online would calm her down. She'd never left Montana before, but California appealed. Warm. Sunny. She could sit by the ocean and listen to the surf. Ally had given her some money to tide her over until she could arrange things with her bank—without her ID and bank cards, she would have to jump through several hoops to access her accounts and that would take time.

She looked back at the closed door and sighed. For a

moment she'd been lured into thinking she could lean on someone else, that she wasn't alone. But that wasn't the lesson she'd learned at the Black Jack clubhouse.

And she would be a fool to forget it.

★ NINE ★

Holt woke up in a bad mood.

No, scratch that. Worse than bad. And it wasn't helped by the fact he had woken up alone after spending the night with a hard on that just wouldn't quit. He'd beat that puppy into submission enough times that his dick was chafed and sore, but damned if he hadn't woken up in the morning in the middle of a hot dream about Naiya, and he had to deal with the situation all over again.

Maybe it was the three months of forced abstinence. Or maybe it was the relief of knowing that vital appendage was in full working order. Or maybe it was the woman who embodied all his fantasies, and called to his deepest protective instincts. He still couldn't believe he'd told her to leave. When had he ever asked a woman to leave before he'd fucked her silly? But he wanted her so bad, he needed to be firm to keep her safe. Thank fuck she'd got the message because the things he wanted to do to her . . .

He found Naiya in the living room, stuffing clothes into her backpack beside a neatly folded pile of blankets and a pillow.

"Why the fuck did you sleep on the couch?"

"I didn't want to disturb you." She didn't look up, but he could see her tension in the rigid line of her neck, the set of her jaw, the waver of her voice. He'd been too harsh, ruined what little trust had grown between them. The irony wasn't lost on him. He'd pushed her away to save her from the side of him that could hurt her far more than she was hurting now.

"What are you doing?" He gestured to the bag as understanding dawned.

"I'm going to catch a bus in town and head out of state. Maybe take a vacation until the whole Viper thing is sorted out, and apply for jobs from a beach somewhere. I've never had a vacation before. Ever since I left home, it's been work, work, work." She shoved her Beaver Country shirt into the bag. "You look like you'll make a full recovery. And you've got a mission to fulfill. Since you aren't going to take me to the Sinners, I need to look out for myself and priority number one is getting out of town."

"Is this because of what happened last night?" Holt wasn't usually so direct. He had never been a confrontational kind of guy. Usually, he would go with the flow, but right now he was seized by an urgent sense of desperation. He couldn't let her go, and it wasn't just because he needed her to lure Viper.

"No, of course not." She turned away, tightening her grip on the bag, her hair swinging over her cheek, hiding her face.

Yes.

"It was good you . . . stopped." She stared out the floor-to-ceiling windows over the valley spread out below them. "I mean, you have things you have to do, and I have things I have to do, and they aren't things we need to do . . . together."

Together. Fuck. She'd thought about them together.

Although he was pretty damn sure she hadn't thought of them together the way he had all fucking night long.

"Naiya."

"I made breakfast. It's on the stove." She slung the bag over her shoulder. "Happy revenge."

No fucking way. "It's not safe out there."

"It's not safe in here."

"I couldn't be gentle with you," he said. "I'm a hard man, Naiya, and the shit I just went through just made me harder. I don't have sex. I don't make love. I fuck. And when I do, it's hard and it's rough, and that's not what you need."

"You don't know me." Her face tightened. "You don't know what I need."

The hell he didn't. He could read the longing on her face; he could hear it in her voice. It was the same longing that had gripped him since he met her. The old Holt would have let her walk out the door because it's what she wanted to do, and who was he to rock the boat? He didn't know where that Holt had gone, but the man he was now was not letting her get away.

Without taking his gaze off her, he ripped the bag from her fingers and tossed it on the couch. Then he cupped her face between his hands and covered her mouth with his.

Ah God. Her lips were as soft as he imagined, her mouth as lush. Her lips parted on a sigh, and he touched her with his tongue. She tasted of honey and coffee, warm and sweet. He wanted her, wanted this woman with the broken soul, wanted to fix her, show her the beauty of trust and surrender, open her up and fill her with joy. Yeah, he wanted to fuck her bad.

"Holt." She pulled back, her chest heaving. "I don't want this. I just broke up with Maurice. We were together two years. It just feels . . . wrong."

Didn't feel wrong to him. In fact, nothing had ever felt

so right. He slid an arm around her waist and crushed her against him, the way he'd seen Jagger and Cade do with their women, the way he'd seen Tank with Connie. Dominant. Controlling. And damn it felt good. Taking what he wanted. Being in charge.

And yet at the back of his mind, he was assessing her responses, the way she leaned into him, her soft sigh, the flutter of her lashes, and the little hints that told him she was on board and that he wasn't stepping over the line. He had a strong feeling Viper had crossed that line, and if he caught her, he would cross it again.

Naiya leaned in, melted against him. Pleasure rippled through his body, and his cock hardened in an instant. He dipped his head, drank her down, delighting when she moaned and tangled her tongue with his.

She broke away again, her lips plump and swollen from his kiss. "I should go . . . I was just leaving . . ."

Deeper. Rougher. He slid one hand through her hair, tugged her head back, and held her still as he fed off her hidden desire. Her hands came up, pressed against his chest. Holt tensed, thinking she would push him away. Instead, her arms wrapped around his neck and she pulled him closer, straining upward as she kissed him back with a passion that belied her words. She wasn't leaving. Not now.

Not ever.

Holt backed up to the couch, pulled her down with him until she straddled his lap, her knees on either side of his hips, the curve of her sex pressed tight against his aching shaft. One hand on her nape, holding her to him, the other around her waist, he plundered her mouth, brutalizing her lips as his need spilled out in a deep groan. His cock strained painfully against his fly, and his fingers tightened against her ass, her jeans rough against his fingers as he rocked his hips, grinding against her pussy.

"Oh God, Holt. You're so hard," she breathed. "So rough. I like it. I want more. Give me more."

His control began to slip, his kisses became deeper, harder, his hands on her body tighter, clutching. Rough. Wild. Good for the skanky bitches he met at the clubs, or the club whores who knew what he liked and were happy to give it. Not good for a woman whom he was beginning to suspect didn't know what the hell kind of box she'd just opened.

Fuck me.

"Darlin'," he gritted his teeth, released his grip on her body. "Last chance. Unless you want to take this further, you'd better get off my lap. It's been a long fucking time . . ."

"Not as long as me." She pulled away, her face flushed, lips pink and swollen. "Maurice and I were waiting."

"Waiting for what?" He cupped her breast in his palm, gently squeezed the soft weight, brushed his thumb over her nipple peaked beneath her clothes. She moaned and leaned forward, pressing her breast into his hand. What man could lie beside this woman night after night and not want to fuck her multiple times?

"I guess . . . for things to be right. Serious. But they never were, and after awhile it just stopped being an issue."

"Sex isn't an issue, darlin'. Not for a man. And not if he's got a beautiful, curvy woman like you lying beside him in the bed. Only issue is how many times he's gonna make you come and how loud he's gonna make you scream."

A smile tugged her lips. "More compliments."

He slid his hand under her shirt and flicked the catch of her bra. "Not saying it to be nice. Saying it so you know how this is gonna play out, if that's what you want."

Her breath caught when he pushed her bra up and

stroked a finger along the curve of her breast. So soft. So warm.

"I don't know if this is what I want. I just broke up with Maurice. You're a biker. And you're injured. Maybe it's not right."

He brushed his lips over hers. "Then why are you still sitting on my lap?"

The roar of a motorcycle shattered the silence.

Naiya slid off Holt's lap, her heart pounding now for a different reason. Holt ran for the window. "Jesus H Christ. How the fuck do they keep finding us?" He saw her reach for her bag and shook his head. "Leave it, darlin'. We gotta run."

"We'll have no clothes, no food. And your cut . . ." Heart racing, Naiya grabbed the backpack and shoved Holt's cut inside. Then she raced to the kitchen and grabbed a bottle of water and a few apples. As an afterthought, she grabbed a kitchen knife. Not that she would ever stab anyone, but it was good to be prepared.

"Leave the fucking cut. I'm done with the Sinners." Holt holstered his gun and tugged on his shoes. "Whatever is missing, we'll have to wing it."

"The whole winging it thing is starting to get to me." Naiya fastened her bra and slid the backpack over her shoulders. "Ever since meeting you I've been more impulsive than I've ever been in my life."

"Gimme the pack." Holt held out his hand.

"You're barely able to walk, much less run." She tightened the shoulder straps. "You don't need the added burden of the pack."

Holt scowled. "Pack. Now. I'll not have a woman carrying anything for me that I can carry myself."

"Seriously?" Naiya clipped the chest strap above her

breasts. "This isn't the Stone Age. I go to the gym. I work out. What's the point of lifting weights if I don't use my muscles?"

"What muscles?" Holt stalked toward her, his hand outstretched. "You're small. Soft."

"Statistically speaking, men are generally stronger than women," Naiya said. "However, right now, given your current condition, I suspect I have more stamina than you, and you'll need all your energy just to keep up with me. As a result, it makes sense for me to keep the backpack and for you to get your ass in gear."

"Christ. Gimme the damn pack!"

The cabin vibrated with the rumble of motorcycles, and Naiya's heart drummed in her chest. She yanked open the back door and looked over her shoulder. "Come and get it."

She took off down the path leading into the forest, Holt close on her heels, shouting directions as they pounded their way along the dirt trail. She heard the high-pitched rev of an engine and caught her breath.

"They're coming down the trail on their bikes. We'll never outrun them."

Holt passed her at a run, reached back, and grabbed her hand. "I walked the trails when we got here. A couple of them are too narrow for their bikes. This way."

Chest heaving, she ran behind him, struggling to keep up with his long strides. If this was Holt injured, she couldn't imagine how fast he could go if he were well.

The rumble of bikes vibrated through the forest, silencing the birds. Holt veered off the main path to an overgrown trail, barely visible through the underbrush. After fifty feet, the trail angled down, and Naiya stumbled, dropped to her knees in the dirt.

"Up." Holt yanked her arm, and pulled her up. Sweat soaked her back beneath her pack, dripping off her forehead as she stumbled behind him. Every breath burned in her lungs. Although she ran three or four mornings a week, she had never run like this—full on, flat out, every muscle in her body straining—it almost made a joke out of her morning jog. Part of her thrilled at being pushed to her limit, and yet this wasn't recreation. She knew what was waiting for her back at the Black Jack clubhouse and she couldn't go through it again.

She kept her head down and followed Holt's feet, stepping where he stepped, jumping when he jumped. Despite his injuries, he kept up a good pace, although he was breathing as hard as she was.

Holt skidded to a stop when they reached the lake at the end of the trail. "Boat launch." He pointed along the shore.

Naiya groaned, wavered on her feet. "I don't think—"

Holt unclipped the strap across her chest and tugged the pack off her shoulders, heaving in his breaths. His hair was plastered to his face, his face red with exertion. "Go."

"You can't . . ."

He shoved her gently toward the dock. "Go, Naiya."

"What about you?"

"I'll hold them off."

Damn stupid man. Clearly, he couldn't go on, and he was planning to sacrifice himself after she'd gone to so much trouble to save him. She put an arm around his waist and braced herself to take his weight. "I'm not going without you."

Holt looked down at her, and his lips quirked, amused. "What are you doing?"

"Helping you."

"Even if it might cost you your freedom?"

Naiya shrugged. "The bikers I know would either have abandoned me or taken advantage of me in the same situation. But here you are."

"Maybe I'm using you," he said softly.

"I thought of that." She took a step, urged him forward.

"I make good bait if you want to lure Viper out of his den. But even if you are using me to get to him, I have a vested interest in the outcome, and so do you. But more than getting Viper off my back, I want you to have your revenge. That's why I drugged you at the motel. You deserve justice, Holt, and even I can see that you won't get that from the law." She tugged on his shirt. "Now come on. We don't have time for all this talking."

He stared at her like she was some kind of exotic creature, wondrous and curious at the same time. Uncomfortable beneath his scrutiny, she jogged ahead, only to feel his hand clasp hers. He picked up the pace, tugging her forward, where only a few moments ago she thought she'd be supporting him.

"I'm not worth that kind of loyalty," he said as they raced along the beach to the boat launch. "But you are safe with me."

Warmth curled in her belly, spread out to her fingers. Maurice wasn't the protective type. He explained away his reluctance to walk her home at night, or meet her at the bus stop in the dark, as a dislike for the antiquated conventions of chivalry. In fact, he claimed to be honoring her feminist beliefs by lying on the couch watching sports when she came to visit at night, overcoming his primitive urges to protect his woman and mark his territory. He was a modern man of modern times no longer ruled by biology. Of course it made logical sense, and yet a tiny, betraying part of her wished he would put an arm around her and beat back the shadows of the night.

They hit the boat launch at a run and turned into the parking lot, the acrid diesel fumes overpowering the fresh pine-scented air.

"Let's check if that one's open." Holt gestured to an SUV on the far side of the lot. The empty trailer attached to the hitch suggested the owner was out on his boat, but when Naiya looked out over the water, there was no one in sight.

"You're going to steal a vehicle?" She pulled up short, stared at him aghast.

"You wanna live? You gotta take risks. You gotta be prepared to break some rules." He scanned the beach behind them, checking for pursuit. "I think we're clear for a bit. Their bikes won't make it down the beach, and there's no way they'll leave them behind. There's nothing more important to a biker than his ride."

"Not even having to face Viper's wrath?"

Holt shook his head. "A biker is nothing without his bike. They'll have to backtrack and come after us on the main road. That means we need wheels to put some distance between us. We'll dump the vehicle at the nearest service station and pick up something else."

"I'll never get a job if I have a criminal record, Holt. The security checks they do for crime labs . . ."

"I'll do the driving, and I'll take the rap if it comes to it, darlin'."

Just like he'd done for his sister. He may have been an outlaw, but at heart, he was a good man.

"I'll tell them I kidnapped you to lure Viper out of hiding." He ran toward the vehicle and Naiya followed behind him.

"I couldn't let you . . ."

"Survival," he said. "That's what it's all about."

His words were like a punch to the gut. She'd survived those first few years living with her mom by doing what it took to keep safe, whether than meant breaking into empty houses to find a place to sleep at night, or lying to teachers about why she wanted to stay after school. But after that night with Viper, survival had given way to fear—fear of winding up back in Viper's clutches, fear of becoming like her mom, fear of breaking any rule in case she was dragged so far down she couldn't get up. She had set about controlling every aspect of her life so she didn't have anything to fear, and yet fear was the one thing she couldn't control.

She'd been afraid to live. But right now she had to make a choice. Live or die.

Holt stepped toward the vehicle, and Naiya's training kicked in, making the decision for her. "Don't touch it. Your prints will be all over it. And take off your shoes. They'll be able to trace everywhere you've been from the dirt in the treads, and they'll be able to tell your height and weight, unusual aspects to your gait, whether you walked or ran . . ."

Holt laughed and wrapped his hand in his shirt before rounding the vehicle to the driver side door. "Very useful skills. You'd be an asset to the club."

She opened her mouth to tell him she hadn't spent all those years in school to wind up right back where she'd started, when a hand wrapped around her neck.

"Look what we got here. Viper's new bitch."

Her breath caught when the cold barrel of a gun pressed against her temple. She didn't have to turn around to see who had found her. She knew the voice of Viper's second in command, remembered every detail of his sharp, angular features, pale skin and thin slash of a mouth. But more than his face, she remembered the enormous cruel power of his muscular body. That night in the clubhouse, Leo had been one of the men who held her down.

"Yo, Sinner," he shouted as he pulled her away from the vehicle. "Look what I caught."

Holt looked up, and his face tightened. He whipped out his gun and stalked toward them, his gaze fixed on Naiya and not the Black Jack behind her.

"That's far enough." Leo shouted when Holt was only

a few yards away. "Put down the weapon and maybe I'll let you watch me fuck this bitch before I put you to ground."

"Don't be stupid," Naiya snapped. "I belong to Viper. You can't touch me."

Leo smashed the butt of his gun against her head. Naiya's vision blurred and pain lanced through her skull.

"What the fuck, little mouse?" he murmured in her ear. "Never heard you mouth off before. I liked you better when you were quiet, hiding in the bedroom at your momma's place, thinking no one could see you. Except with that body and that sweet face, we all saw you. Only reason you didn't get to taste a whole lotta Black Jack dick is 'cause Viper laid claim to you. Told us all your virgin pussy belonged to him and he was gonna have it when you turned fifteen. That's why he sent Jeff to get you on your fucking birthday."

No. She couldn't imagine Jeff bringing her to the clubhouse knowing what Viper planned to do. Viper's son had no love for his father. For the first few years after her grandmother died, she had hung out with Jeff and his sister, Arianne, and the other Black Jack club brats at the clubhouse when her mother was off on road trips with whatever biker she was sleeping with at the time. Although Jeff had turned to drugs after Arianne left the clubhouse, he'd always been friendly and kind to Naiya. She had no reason to doubt his motives when he called her up on her fifteenth birthday to invite her to a clubhouse party. Alone at home, and feeling sorry for herself, she'd made the mistake of accepting the invitation despite her misgivings.

"Jeff wouldn't do that," she spat out.

Leo laughed. "Well now he's dead, so you'll never know. But I'll give you one piece of advice. Never trust a biker." With the gun still at her temple, he yanked her hair, forcing her head back. "And as for touching you, I can do whatever the hell it takes to bring you back. Viper likes his women bruised and broken. I may not be able shove my dick in that sweet pussy, but there's other places it can go."

"You're not gonna shoot her," Holt closed the distance between them. "So there's no point holding that gun to her head. Aim it at me. I'm the one you can kill. Viper'll probably give you a reward for getting rid of me."

Leo's hand tightened on Naiya's hair, and then he pointed his gun at Holt. "Your funeral, Sinner."

"Her funeral." Holt aimed his gun at Naiya's chest. "What are you gonna do now? I kill her. You kill me. You go back to Viper empty handed, and you'll be taking my place in the dungeon."

Damn Holt was good with the mind games. Or was this for real?

"You're not gonna kill her. You want her, too." Leo's heart drummed in his chest so hard she could feel it through her body. He was scared. But then, so was she.

"I needed her to get the fuck outta that dungeon." Holt's gaze flicked to Naiya and back to Leo. "Then I decided to stick it to Viper by using his bitch and sending her back to him full of my cum. But this is better. I'll put so many holes in her, he won't know which one's for his dick."

A shudder ran through Naiya's body at his brutal words, his harsh tone and his cold, hard stare. She saw nothing of the man who had promised to protect her, but instead, a Sinner intent on revenge. She'd suspected he might be using her, but she never thought he would take it this far.

Leo must have seen Holt's resolve, too. In one swift move, he shoved Naiya to the side and fired. "You don't fucking touch her."

His shot went straight through the space where Holt had been standing only moments before. Too late, Leo realized his mistake. Out in the open, he had nowhere to go when Holt returned fire from the cover of the bush. A shot cracked the silence, and Leo dropped to his knees, firing blindly into the trees. Holt fired again and again until Leo crumpled and fell to the ground.

Shocked, Naiya couldn't move, couldn't breathe. She'd spent the last few years analyzing dead bodies, watching autopsies, and staring at pictures that would make ordinary people cringe. She'd hung out at the Black Jacks' clubhouse and various biker hangouts. And yet, she'd never seen anyone actually shot before. Bile rose in her throat. How had she thought of Holt as anything other than the violent, ruthless outlaw he was? How had she let her guard down?

She pushed herself to her feet and took one step back, then another. Holt seemed oblivious to her presence, his gaze focused on the unmoving man in the dirt. Taking a deep breath, Naiya turned and ran.

A bullet thudded into the tree beside her head. She froze mid-step and slowly turned around, blood rushing through her ears so fast she could barely hear her own rasping breaths.

"You're not going anywhere." Holt's voice was flat, savage, dark like the gun aimed at her heart.

Naiya swallowed hard. "I know you want your revenge on Viper. But please don't use me."

"Get on the bike." Holt gestured to Leo's Harley Davidson, partially hidden in the trees.

"Let me go," she said softly, pleading. "I won't tell anyone about Leo or the guard at the Black Jack clubhouse. I'll leave the state. You'll never see me again."

"On. The. Bike." He enunciated each word, his voice increasing in pitch.

"Holt. Please." Naiya heard a rustle in the bushes behind her. Holt's gaze snapped over her shoulder, and he continued his steady pace.

"Jesus Christ, Naiya. Get on the fucking bike." He walked toward her, holding his gun level with her chest.

There was no point running. She had no chance against a bullet. But she wasn't getting on the damn bike either. No way was she making this easy for him, even if her knees shook and she had to fight back the wave of nausea that gripped her stomach. She shivered and his expression darkened.

"You think I'm gonna hurt you?"

She wrapped her arms around her body, hugged herself tight. "I think you're going to do what it takes to bring down Viper, regardless of who gets in the way."

"Damn right I am." He lunged for her, slid his hand around her nape, yanked her into his chest . . . And fired.

Holt tightened his grip on Naiya, as the Black Jack who had been watching them from the bushes went down. Fucker made more noise than a bunch of bikers at a patch-in party. Hell, when Jagger had given him his cut, the Sinners cheered so loudly he thought the roof would fall in.

"Shhhh. I'm not shooting at you." He brushed his lips over her ear when she tried to back away, but tight in his grip, she wasn't going anywhere.

"Let me go."

He slid his hand down to her waist, pulled her trembling body against him. "Gotta make sure there's no more Jacks about."

Naiya's hands slid between them, and she leaned back and thudded his chest with her fist. "You were going to kill me. You were going to use me to get back at Viper."

Holt scanned the forest around them. "Keep it down. No telling who else is around."

"Good. I want them to find us. Viper might hurt me, but at least I'll be alive."

He looked down at her face, twisted with anger. For one fleeting second, he had considered the possibility of offing her to stick it to Viper. The bastard wanted her bad if he was sending his top brass out this far out to track her down, especially when the Jacks were in the middle of a war with the Sinners. But almost immediately the thought disappeared beneath the overwhelming urge to protect her. She was intimately tied to his quest for vengeance. But more than that, they were connected in a way he still didn't understand. He couldn't bear the thought of her in danger, or at the mercy of the Jacks. He would never allow it. They had rescued each other. Now, she belonged to him.

"I said I'd protect you. If I killed you, I'd be breaking my word."

"Let me go." She shoved hard, forcing him back a step. His pulse kicked up a notch. Although he hadn't heard any bikes or any rustling in the trees, the Jacks would be coming soon and there was always a risk of the guy who owned the SUV returning with his boat and seeing them near the dead bodies.

"We don't have time for this," he snapped. "Look who he sent after you." He gestured to Leo's body on the ground. "His fucking VP. You're not just another piece of tail to him, probably because you aren't like the women in his club. Even if you leave the state, he'll track you down. Your only chance of staying alive and living the life you want to live is to stick with me. I'm not going to hurt you. You'll have to trust me on that."

She pushed against him, glared when he didn't let go. "I don't trust you. Not anymore. I saw your face, Holt. For a moment there you thought about shooting me. I'll take my chances on my own."

Her body was warm against him, soft despite her agitation. He lowered his mouth to her neck and kissed the hollow at the base of her throat. "Part of you already trusts me 'cause you're still in my arms."

"You have a gun," she snapped. "And you're holding me so tight I'm going to have bruises."

"Where would you go?" he challenged. "How would you hide? Who would protect you?"

"The Sinners." She stared up at him, her eyes defiant. "If I tell them where you are, they'll owe me. And if you are thinking of doing something to me, you should know I took a picture of you with Ally's phone when you were sleeping. If something happens to me, she'll send the pictures to the Sinners. They'll know you're alive, and they'll hunt you down. We both know what happens to brothers who betray the club. Call it an insurance policy."

"Jesus Christ." He pushed her away, torn between anger and admiration. How had he misjudged her? She wasn't the soft civilian she appeared to be; she'd been forged in a Black Jack hell, and although she professed to be done with that life, it wasn't done with her.

"I'm beginning to think you don't need protection," he said, his voice gruff.

"I need Viper off my back, so it seems we have a mutual goal," she said. "But I'm not up for being part of a kill-team, or being used as bait, or sacrificed to stick it to Viper. So how about you make a new plan to bring him down that doesn't involve me?"

"You don't want justice?" His forehead creased in a puzzled frown. "You don't want revenge for what he did to you?"

"Like this?" Her voice cracked, broke, and he caught a glimpse of just how hard she was struggling to contain her emotion, her fear. "I can't handle this. Guns. Shooting. Death. Crime. I just want to go back to my normal life and—"

"Hide."

"There's nothing wrong with hiding," she said.

"There is if it means you're not living." He released her

and stepped away. "You're so focused on getting your life in order, you're forgetting to live it. Donuts don't need to be cut up. Motel beds don't need to be made. You don't always need a plan. People aren't always going to act the way you expect them to act. Guns aren't always bad, especially when they save your life. And sometimes crimes are committed for good reasons."

"Are you trying to justify what you're planning to do to the Sinners?"

Holt frowned, shifted his weight. "I don't need to justify it. They betrayed me."

"Or so you think." She folded her arms, surveyed the scene. "You know them. They were your brothers. Your friends. Would they really abandon and betray you? All of them? Every single Sinner? Would you have abandoned them? How can you stand there and accuse me of being narrow-minded when you're acting the same way? You're so focused on looking back, you're forgetting to look ahead. And it's a long road to nowhere if you've got no one to share it with you."

Fuck. He didn't want to be having this conversation. Not here. Not now. And not with someone who clearly didn't understand the ties of loyalty, honor, and brotherhood that bound bikers together, and how devastating the betrayal of the biker code could be.

"We gotta get out of here before more Jacks show up," he said curtly, making it clear that conversation was over. "We'll take Leo's bike."

Naiya looked around the parking lot. "I know we don't have a lot of time, but this is a crime scene. We've left a lot of evidence. No point running from the Jacks if we just wind up with the police on our tail. At the very least, we need to get rid of our footprints, fingerprints, fibers, and any mud we may have tracked from the path. If we have to commit a crime to survive, we might as well do it in such a way that we don't get caught."

He would have laughed at the irony if he hadn't been so pissed off. "So does this mean you're planning to stick around?"

She tilted her head to the side. *Cute as fuck.* "Are you going to let me go?"

"No."

"Then I guess I'm sticking around."

★ TEN ★

TANK

Tank parked his bike outside Joey's Fish'n Chips in the sleepy little town of Still Water. Gunner and Sparky pulled up beside him. Benson drove past on his way to the gas station to fill up the SUV.

"What the fuck are the Black Jacks doing out here?" Sparky adjusted the bandana over his thick, brown hair. Usually, he spent his days in the Sinner garage with Arianne but Jagger needed men on the road keeping tabs on the Jacks so Sparky had left the shop in Arianne's capable hands to follow up on an unusual Jacks sighting with Tank and Gunner as his back up.

"Any local clubs in the area they might be trying to recruit?" Tank texted Benson, telling him to watch the bikes after he was done filling up the cage. As the only junior patch member of the group—both Gunner and Sparky were senior patch and executive members of the board that ran the MC—Tank was responsible for keeping Benson busy and out of trouble.

"Nah." Gunner shook his head. "Most of the cabins out here are for rich city folk, and the local businesses are all about serving their needs."

Tank had often dreamed about having a cabin. Fishing, hunting, off-roading, canoeing . . . There weren't many outdoor activities he didn't enjoy. As a kid, he'd always wanted to do the father-son things his friends always did with their fathers. But Tank's dad didn't have time for his kids. Except to beat them for being bad.

And then Tank met T-Rex, who loved the outdoors just like him, and all the shit he'd gone through with his dad didn't matter.

They ordered lunch and spread out a map on the worn wooden table, dividing up the small roads in the area for a thorough search. The strong fishy scent of the restaurant reminded Tank of the weekend he and T-Rex had hiked into the mountains to fish. It had been a perfect day. Warm, sunny, the mountain lake clear and still. They took a rental boat into the middle of the lake, chilled out with a cooler filled with beer, and shared stories about their youth. They agreed the Sinners were the best thing that ever happened to them, and they would be Sinners until the day they died. It had been a perfect day, at least until T-Rex caught a forty-pound trout and fell out of the boat trying to bring it in. Despite losing the catch of the season, Tank had never laughed so hard.

After lunch, Gunner and Sparky headed out to check the side roads, leaving Tank and Benson in town to ask local business owners if they'd seen any Jacks. Tank left Benson to pay the bill while he checked a small grocery store with a stuffed deer head over the front door.

"Only bike I've seen here in the last few days is the one at the gas station across the street." The owner pointed across the road in response to Tank's question. "But they aren't the bikers you're looking for. Young couple. They were in here twenty minutes ago buying groceries. Looked like tourists. Not wearing any leather vests or stuff."

Tank thanked him for his time and headed across the

road to the gas station. He spotted the bike at once and whistled low. The top-of-the-line, 2015 "super premium" CVO Road Glide Ultra slathered in chrome and custom Radioactive Green paint with a luxury pillion seat and Harley-Davidson's strongest motor, was one of the most expensive Harleys currently available. Only an MC president or VP would ride a bike like that, as much a show of power as it was of wealth.

He positioned himself behind a plumbing van to keep watch. Only five minutes passed before he was rewarded with the sight of a pretty chick with long dark hair and the sweetest heart-shaped ass he'd ever seen.

She headed over to the bike and unbuckled the saddle-bag. Tank let out a sigh. Off limits. Any man who rode a bike like that wouldn't be happy to see another man sniffing around. Hell, if he had a woman like that, he wouldn't let her out of his sight.

As if on cue, the door to the gas station opened, and a man stepped out and called her. His long hair obscured his face, but he was wearing a Bolton Beaver T-shirt that matched the girl's hoodie. Tourists. Probably just weekend warriors who took the bike out only on sunny days. What a fucking waste. He turned to leave when the man stepped forward and partially into the light.

One step. So familiar. Something niggled at Tank's brain, and he turned back and took another look.

The dude was around Tank's height, but much thinner. His broad shoulders and chest, and the way he carried himself suggested a bigger guy, more muscular. Someone who could ride that Ultra Glide with ease. He waved to the woman, and Tank caught sight of a tat sleeve on his right arm, although he couldn't make out the details. A memory seized him, and he looked down at the tattoo on his arm. The day after T-Rex was patched into the club, he and

Tank had gone to the top tattoo shop in Conundrum to celebrate with matching tats.

His skin prickled and he stared harder at the man who had now retreated into the shadows. The way the dude held himself, the way he moved, his height, the sleeve, all reminded him of T-Rex. And yet T-Rex had at least fifty or sixty pounds on this guy, his hair was always short, and he would never be caught dead in tourist gear or without his cut. And T-Rex would never have been able to afford a bike like that. Hell, he doubted any of the Sinners except maybe Jagger or Zane would be able to drop that sort of cash on a bike.

As if he knew Tank was watching, the dude looked up and stared straight at him. But damned if his hair didn't hide his face.

Tank's phone buzzed, and he checked the text. Sparky and Gunner had seen two Jacks just outside of town and needed him to come right away and help chase the bastards down. Tank looked up again, but the man and woman were gone.

"I think T-Rex is alive."

Tank paused, letting the Sinner executive board take in the revelation. He'd thought about the dude at the gas station as he and Sparky and Gunner chased and lost the pair of Black Jacks on the mountain pass. He'd thought about him when he returned to the gas station to ask about the couple on the bike. He'd thought about him on the ride home, and while he rolled around in his bed at the clubhouse, remembering the good times he and T-Rex spent together, and how well he knew his best friend.

Maybe not well enough.

"No fucking way." Zane, the Sinner VP and Jagger's

best friend, folded his arms and glared, his eyes dark. "Dax tortured that Black Jack in our dungeon for three days. There was nothing coming out of that bastard's mouth that wasn't the truth. Yeah, it was hard to hear that the body Sparky and Gunner found in the Black Jack dungeon wasn't T-Rex, and that he was still alive when we had the funeral, but Tank, man, now we know for sure he's gone. You gotta let it go."

Why the fuck did everyone keep telling him to let it go? If it had been him in the Black Jack dungeon, T-Rex would never have let it go. Never.

"I pulled the tapes from the gas station." Tank spun his laptop around so everyone could see. The entire board was present: Jagger and Zane, Gunner and Sparky, Cade, Dax, and the senior member-at-large, Shaggy. T-Rex and Tank had shared the club's junior member-at-large position and T-Rex's empty chair was a reminder that someone would soon have to step into his shoes. "The owner wasn't too happy," he continued. "I had to pull my weapon and pay a heavy price so he wouldn't call the cops."

He pushed PLAY and showed the grainy footage to the board, although even he had to admit it wasn't convincing. The cameras didn't capture the things that had made Tank so certain he was looking at T-Rex—the way he held his shoulders and cocked his head when he was talking to the cashier, his stride and his constant fiddling with what Tank was sure was a knife under his shirt. But that damned hair hid his face, and the camera angle made it impossible to see the details of the tat on his arm. "He was buying pizza by the slice," Tank offered into the silence. He stopped the tape on the best image—a full frontal of the dude, face obscured, but holding a pizza box in his hand.

"Doesn't even look like him," Shaggy said. "Wrong body type. Wrong hair. And where's his cut? Can you imagine T-Rex going anywhere without his cut? Or being free and not high-tailing it back to the Sinners? That boy was born to be a Sinner. He lived and breathed for this club. He's dead or he's here at this table, and since I don't see his face, then he's not coming back."

"It's him," Tank said, his voice rising in desperation. "Look how he moves . . ."

"Tank. Brother." Jagger held up his hand. "It's hard to lose a brother, but T-Rex was special, and we all know he was your closest friend. You're gonna see him in so many faces. You're gonna hear his voice again and again. And always you turn only to find out it's not him, and you feel like someone's just punched you in the gut. I've been through it. We all have. And although it's hard to hear it now, it will get easier. Just give it time."

"I just want to go back up there and check it out, maybe ask a few questions, drive around . . ."

"I hear you, brother," Jagger said. "But if the man you saw was T-Rex, then he's not in danger and he'll be making his way home. If we weren't at war with the Black Jacks, I'd drive up there with you to check it out, but these are dangerous times. I can't let you go alone, and I can't spare the men to go with you." He thudded his fist on the table. "I'm not losing another brother to those goddam bastard Jacks."

Tank turned the laptop around and threw himself down in his seat. Jagger didn't know T-Rex the way he did. Hell, none of them did. That was T-Rex at the gas station. And damned if Tank wasn't going to find him.

Zane stared at him while Cade gave this treasurer's report, gloomy as usual because of the war with the Jacks. Cade had even pulled his new old lady, Dawn, from club finance duties because he was worried about her and their kids. Tank couldn't blame him for that.

But Jesus Fuck he wanted Zane to stop staring at him. The VP had mellowed since he'd hooked up with his old flame, Evie, and discovered he had a son, Ty. But mellow for Zane was one hundred degrees of intensity for a normal guy, and Tank felt like Zane's eyes were burning into his soul, reading the betrayal Tank was only thinking about.

He tightened his fist under the table. Of all the Sinners, Zane should have been the one giving Tank his support. T-Rex had sacrificed his life to save Evie. Zane owed T-Rex a life debt, and if T-Rex was in need of saving, Zane should have been by Tank's side.

"Something is up with the Jacks," Jagger said. "Something big. Even our mother chapter is worried. Our man Mario, who we had inside Viper's house for a couple of weeks, skipped town after he buried a knife in Viper's back to save Evie, and National isn't willing to risk any more lives or the resources."

"We should focus on offense. Not defense." Shaggy stroked his beard. "What about Viper's cabin up in the mountains where he held Ty and Evie? Now that we know the location—"

Jagger cut him off with a wave of his hand. "I sent Dax and Sparky up there to take a look. The place is deserted."

"He had another dungeon in his basement," Sparky said. "Never saw anything like it. He's one sick bastard. The place was Dax's fucking wet dream. It must have been where he kept T-Rex when we thought he was in the Black Jack dungeon."

Dax snorted his derision. "Viper tortures for pleasure. I torture with purpose."

"Don't fucking pretend you don't enjoy it," Shaggy said. "The minute you hear we got someone downstairs you start drooling and get a fucking hard on that won't quit."

"That's cause I'm twice the man you are." Dax grabbed his crotch and jerked his hips in his chair. "I got five boys at home and a damned happy old lady. If that's not a fucking show of virility I don't know what is. How many kids you got? All these years and you're still fucking sweet butts 'cause none of them will have you permanent like."

"Variety, my friend. That's the way I live my life." Shaggy's thick, gray brows furrowed, hiding his eyes, and his voice dropped so low Tank had to lean in to hear him. "No old lady to tie me down or nag me about staying out late. No sprog to drain my bank account. I live free and I live large. Couldn't ask for anything more."

"If we're done trading insults," Jagger interrupted, "I want to know what the Jacks are doing up in the mountains. They've been lying low for the past few weeks, and suddenly they're buzzing around tourist resorts. I got reports of them in Bolton, and now we know they've been up in Still Water."

Bolton.

Tank cocked his head to the side. The couple on the flashy Harley were wearing Bolton shirts. But the place was a tourist town, and the shop owner said that he thought they were tourists. Was it a coincidence, or something more? He wanted to raise the issue again with Jagger, but now wasn't the time.

"I say fuck National and plant another spy in the Jacks." Gunner thumped his fist on the table. "We got the best intel we've ever had when we bribed Mario to go inside."

"Send Gunner." Shaggy gave him a sly look. "He needs to go into hiding. Every damn weekend some chick's husband is hunting him down. He's moved on from twins to married women, and his extra nine lives are the only reason he's sittin' here today."

"You're fuckin' jealous 'cause your dick shriveled up twenty years ago." Gunner folded his arms over his massive chest. "And yeah. Married women. That's the way to go, man. They're not looking to be tied down 'cause they already are. But they're not getting any lovin' at home so when I get them in my bed . . . Christ . . . they're hot. And they'll go all fucking night long 'cause they don't know when they'll get it so good again."

"You didn't go all night long last weekend." Shaggy laughed. "Most fun I ever had, watching you running with your jeans undone, and your dick hanging out when that Skull Splitter MC dude drove into the parking lot behind Rider's Bar and found you fucking his woman for information about the Jacks. Next time I'll come along. Give you a hand."

"Christ. We're gonna fuck our way into winning the war," Shaggy grumbled. "Never would have happened back in the day."

"That's 'cause back in the day, you couldn't find your dick," Gunner retorted.

If it had been back in the day—three months earlier when T-Rex was still alive—it would have been Tank and T-Rex joking about women, offering to hunt down and bed some Black Jack support club chicks, placing bets, then meeting up at Rider's Bar to share their experiences.

But it wasn't back in the day. Life hadn't been the same since T-Rex went missing. The world was duller, quieter, and bleaker. He didn't go to the gym where they'd trained together anymore. He never ate pizza at T-Rex's favorite restaurant, Papa Joe's, where Tank had always given T-Rex a hard time for ordering ham and pineapple. Seriously. Who the heck put fruit on a pizza?

He stared at the image on the screen and his eyes focused on the pizza box, the words barely visible on the side: Ham and Pineapple.

T-Rex. That's who.

★ ELEVEN ★

"I'm a bad girl." Naiya trailed her hand over the sleek, shiny surface of an AK-47. "I've never been an accessory to murder, stolen a motorcycle, or broken into a weapons shed before."

"And you'll never do it again if you're not quiet." Holt lifted the gun and shoved it in his pack, his face an expressionless mask. "Jagger knows about this cache, and I wouldn't put it past him to have someone on watch."

Naiya sighed. Her attempt to lighten Holt's mood had fallen flat. Something had broken between them at the boat launch—the stirrings of intimacy and trust she'd felt at the cabin were gone. And she'd made it worse with her fake story about the message that would go to Jagger if she died. But when she'd looked into Holt's eyes and saw nothing there but cold, steely determination, she had to find some way to shift the power balance. Maybe Holt hadn't really intended to use her against Viper. Maybe she'd let fear cloud her vision. But what was she now? A prisoner? Would Holt really stop her if she walked away?

"How do you know about this cache? I thought bikers kept their weapons in heavily fortified facilities. At least

Viper always did." She pulled another weapon from the box, smaller, but with a wider handle. Naiya had never held a gun. Although there had been plenty of weapons lying around her mother's apartment, she had no interest in touching them, and even less interest in taking up any of the Jacks on their offers to teach her how to shoot.

"Mad Dog Sanchez, VP of the Devil's Brethren, stole the guns from another club and hid them in his sister's house. Long story short, he's dead. His sister went into witness protection. Jagger sent me to have a chat with her before she left to make sure she understood we'd find her if she said anything or did anything that hurt Cade's old lady, Dawn or her kids. Dawn was Mad Dog's old lady. Cade is the Sinner Treasurer. Mad Dog's sister told me where Mad Dog had hidden the guns as a show of good faith. I told Jagger. He said to keep it quiet. The fewer people knew about them, the better."

"Sounds like a soap opera. I'm not even going to pretend I followed all that."

"Once you're in the life, it's in your blood. The brothers are your family." His voice tightened. "You try to leave and you get sucked back in."

Naiya aimed the gun at the window, her gaze focused on the woods beyond. Evening light filtered between the branches, bathing the forest in an orange glow. "You're trying to leave. Why do you think you won't get sucked back in?"

" 'Cause there won't be anybody left."

Holt came up behind her and covered her hands with his to reposition the weapon, but the warmth of his body couldn't melt the chill in her blood. Was he really going to kill his brothers? What about their old ladies and kids? Who was this man she was travelling with, and how deep did his hatred go?

His hands lingered on hers, and or a long moment Naiya

couldn't move. She couldn't believe he would hurt her. From what she'd seen of Holt, he didn't seem the type. In fact, he didn't seem the type to engage in the mass slaughter he kept talking about. Although he had suffered in that dungeon, at heart he was protective and caring. Revenge had been his crutch, and he couldn't see that he didn't need it any more.

"Holt?" She looked over her shoulder. He'd been distant since they'd stolen Leo's bike and headed into the mountains. And after they'd filled up at the gas station, he hadn't spoken at all. In fact, he threw out his pizza and hurried her out of the gas station only moments after calling her in, his face taut with what she could only describe as anguish.

"You'll need to learn how to shoot." His lips were only inches from hers, his breath warm and sweet. If she leaned up only the tiniest bit she could have a little taste.

"Okay." She drew in a ragged breath, her body heating at the memory of his kiss back in the cabin, the slow glide of his hands on her body, the unfamiliar rush of desire through her veins.

"I won't always be around." A tremor ran through his body, and he clenched his jaw. "Even after Viper's gone, it's a good skill to have. Fighting, too. If you're walking around at night, you need to know how to defend yourself." His body tensed, his fingers threading through hers, forcing her to tighten her grip on the gun. His strength and dominance both aroused and frightened her, and her pulse throbbed between her thighs.

"I took a self-defense class at college," she offered.

"What would you do if someone came up behind you like this?" He stepped closer, plastered his chest against her back, the bulge in his jeans pressed tight against her ass, his lips brushing her nape.

Arousal surged through her, a potent combination of

fear and desire that pushed everything from her mind except for the heat of Holt's body and the ache deep in her core.

"Drop the gun." He released her hands and she let the unloaded weapon fall to the floor.

"Tell me, Naiya." He circled her waist with one arm, held her so tight she could barely draw in a breath, his voice hard and low. "What would you do?"

She struggled for the memory, the training that had been drilled into her head when she and Ally had taken Doug's self-defense class together. "I'm . . . supposed to step back."

With his free hand he gripped her jaw, pulled her head against his shoulder, the gesture at once intimate and threatening. Arousal gave way to fear and she bit back a whimper.

"Let me go."

He tightened his grip, holding her immobile. "I trusted you."

"And I trusted you." Anger surged through her, sending strength to her limbs. She lifted her knee and bashed her foot down on his instep, then elbowed him in the ribs where he'd suffered the worst of the bruises. She spun to face him as he doubled over in pain.

"I protected you. I looked after you. I trusted you, Holt, and you were going to shoot me. And now, I thought you were . . ." Her face flamed. "I'm done with this. Get your weapons and drop me at the nearest town."

"Don't be stupid," he growled. "The Jacks are still around which is why the Sinners were up at Still Water. I saw Tank at the gas station. I should have fucking shot him when I had the chance, but I couldn't do it."

Despite her anger, her heart squeezed in her chest at the pain in his voice. God, that's why he'd been so abrupt at the gas station. His best friend had been standing only fifty yards away. Except for her grandmother, Naiya had never had a real family, had never been part of something bigger than herself. What would it feel like to have it all ripped away? To have the people you cared about betray you?

"Of course you couldn't. He was your friend." She crossed her arms over her chest, clenched her T-shirt in her palms. "Maybe it wasn't what you thought."

"It was exactly what I thought." The self-loathing in his voice sent a chill down her spine. "If it had been Tank missing, I would never have given up. Every minute of every day I would have looked for him. I would have told Jagger to fuck himself if he tried to stop me. I would have armed myself and blasted my way through the fucking Jacks' clubhouse. I would have been happy to die if it meant he could be free. But he didn't do the same for me. None of the Sinners did. No one had my back. I just gotta get it together. Get the job done without any distraction or worrying about someone stabbing me in the back."

This was the Holt she'd seen down by the lake. Cold, determined, his eyes unnaturally clear. It was like a mask he put on that didn't sit quite right, one that he didn't want to wear. And it couldn't hide his pain.

"If you really believed that, then you would have shot him, Holt. But part of you doesn't believe it. That part held you back. He's your friend, and you knew him well, so maybe deep down you know there's a reason he didn't come for you. Doesn't he at least deserve a chance to explain? After what you had together, can't you at least give him that?"

He took a step toward her, and she stumbled over the gun. Her body blocked the light from the window, casting him in darkness.

"Pick up the weapon," he snapped. "I'll fill the pack.

Mad Dog left some cash with his sister, too. Viper's cash. I put it in the boiler room out back. I'll grab it and meet you here, then I'll drop you off like you wanted."

"I think that would be best."

He jerked as if she'd slapped him, and then he turned and walked out the door.

"Hey baby, you lookin' for a good time?"

Holt pulled his bike over to the side of the road and gestured the hooker closer. Except for the bright red dress and matching heels, there was nothing to make her stand out from the other prostitutes on the street, except that she happened to be standing near the traffic light when he slowed the bike. He'd dropped Naiya off at the nearest town and then headed into Missoula to stock up on supplies and do something about the fucking ache in his balls that just wouldn't go away.

His stomach clenched, and he pushed away the memory of Naiya outside the cheap motel in Trenton, wearing her Bolton Beaver T-shirt, the red neon motel sign flickering on and off behind her. She'd refused to take the weapon he offered her or any of the money he'd taken from the Sinner cache, saying Ally had loaned her some cash to tide her over until she could figure out how to access her bank account without her ID. Her face crumpled when she said good-bye, but it was nothing compared to the emptiness he felt as he drove away.

By the time he'd reached Missoula, he'd thoroughly cursed his damn luck at always hooking up with people who abandoned and betrayed him. He resolved never to trust anyone again. After he got his revenge, if he was still alive, he would spend the rest of his life as a nomad, riding from town to town. Just him, his bike, and the open road.

"Man like you. Girl like me. I think we could find a way to spend the next hour that would make us both happy." She slid her hand down his arm, her fire-red nails glinting in the streetlight.

Naiya didn't wear nail polish. Or makeup. Or at least he thought she didn't. He supposed she wouldn't have dressed up to go to her mother's funeral, and makeup wouldn't have been her first priority once they were on the run. He couldn't imagine her in makeup, not with that fresh, natural beauty. And damn, she'd looked beautiful standing in the kitchen at the cabin, her hair damp, feet bare, chilled and relaxed after fucking drugging him to save him from his own stupidity. He wanted to see her smile again. Hear her laugh. It didn't make any sense. He'd only known her for a few short days.

"I'm doing a hot-guy discount tonight." The hooker had a high, thin, childlike voice that made the hair on the back of his neck stand on end. "And you look like a hot guy in need of some loving."

Maybe that's what he needed. These confusing feelings, unfamiliar emotions, were a need for release. He hadn't been with a woman for over three months. If he just got back in the saddle, he would stop thinking about Naiya, and how soft she felt in his arms, and how desperately he wanted to unlock the passion he only glimpsed when he kissed her.

"You got a room?"

She smiled and flicked back her long, blonde hair. "Just down the street."

Holt parked the bike and grabbed the packs. He wasn't worried about the Jacks calling in the plates—bikers didn't involve the police no matter what the situation—but leaving two bags filled with weapons on the bike was just asking for trouble.

He followed the woman to a low-rise, stucco apartment

building and then up one worn flight of stairs. He dumped his bags near the door once they entered the bachelor apartment. Typical hooker hangout. Old, run down, sparsely furnished except for a bed, couch, and TV, no doubt owned by her pimp and rented out for use by his stable of girls. She reached for the light and Holt shook his head. He could see well enough with the streetlights shining through the cracks in the curtains. He wanted only one thing, and he didn't need the reminder that he was getting it from the wrong girl.

"How much?"

"Sixty for oral with a condom. One hundred without. One hundred for sex with a condom. One fifty without. If you want something else it's an extra fifty per act. You want me to call you 'daddy,' I'll throw that in for free."

Holt pulled a wad of bills from his pocket and threw three twenties on the counter beside him. Last thing he needed was her commenting on the marks all over his body. Naiya had given him the first-aid kit and instructions on how to care for his wounds, as if he would do anything about it. His groin tightened at the memory of her gentle hands on his body, and the soft press of her lips on his skin.

Fuck. Stop thinking about her.

"You want to sit?" She gestured to the bed.

Holt shook his head, his nose wrinkling at the sharp scents of sex and sweat in the claustrophobic apartment. Maybe this wasn't such a good idea. Now that he was here, he just wanted to get this over with.

"You look tense." She leaned up and pressed a kiss to his throat, twined her arms around his neck. "I don't bite." Her lips curved up. "Unless you want me to."

He slid his hands down her body. Christ she was tiny. Usually hookers that thin were druggies, forgoing food in favor of their next fix. He cupped her jaw, tilting her head back and his thumb slid through a layer of makeup, revealing a bruise on her soft, plump cheek. Too soft.

"How old are you?"

Her eyes widened, flicked to the ceiling at the corner of the room, then back. "Twenty-one."

Naiya was twenty-two, and this girl looked much, much younger than her. He flicked on the light and stared at the smooth lines of her face, the rounded cheeks, the small perfectly white teeth nibbling at her lip. Then he looked up at the corner, spotted the camera. Her pimp was watching, protecting his girl.

Just like he should be protecting Naiya.

What the hell had he been thinking leaving her alone? The Jacks were in the area and Viper would stop at nothing to find her. A woman as beautiful as Naiya wouldn't be able to hide for long. But more than that, he ached for her. Needed her. Maybe it was some kind of psychological shit since she'd helped him escape. Maybe he'd imprinted like a fucking baby chick because she treated his wounds, and looked after him. Or maybe she was the first woman he'd met who needed him—really needed him—although she couldn't admit it. Broken. But still strong. Just like Tank had been when they first met. And just like Tank, she understood him in a way no one else did.

Unlike this girl in front of him.

Holt pulled the weapon tucked under his shirt behind his back. Before the girl could even gasp, he shot out the camera. When she shrieked, he slapped his free hand over her mouth to muffle her scream.

"I'm not gonna hurt you."

Tears welled up in her eyes, streaking the makeup on her face. Christ. Now she looked her age. Like a kid playing dress-up.

"Any more cameras?"

She shook her head and Holt took his hand away. "You choose this life, sugar? Or were you forced into it?"

"You can't interfere," she whispered. "Davy will find me. He says I owe him for taking me off the streets. Last time I tried to run, he beat me so bad I almost died."

"If you could get out, would you?"

Her eyes dropped and she nodded. "It was a big mistake. Huge. I ran away from home 'cause there was all sorts of bad shit going on, but I ran out of money, and I couldn't find a job. Davy found me. He was so nice at first. I thought he loved me. And then he locked me in a room and . . ." Her voice broke. "This."

"Where is he?"

Her eyes widened. "Two doors down."

"Wait here." He yanked open the door and strode down the hall. At the second door, he didn't bother testing the handle. He just kicked it in.

A tall, bald dude with an ear full of rings jumped up from behind a table full of screens, pulling one hand out of his sweats while he aimed a high performance .357 at Holt with the other. Fucking pimp got off watching the girls. He was also making a lot of money off them considering the size of the duffle bag of cash on the table beside him. Holt didn't waste any time. He shot the bastard in the chest, and blew out all the monitors.

Not one to waste an opportunity, Holt made a quick search of the apartment. Dude had some nice clothes, and they were about the right size. He'd left too much evidence at the lake and it was time for a change.

Holt stripped off his Bolton Beaver shirt and threw on a plain black T-shirt before stuffing a handful of clothes into the duffle bag, along with the cash, a box of ammo, and the pimp's weapon. He kicked off his shoes and squeezed his feet into a pair of the pimp's cowboy boots—fucking pointy toes. Christ. If Tank ever saw him, he'd never laugh it down.

He wiped down his weapon and rolled it in the dead pimp's hand before dropping it beside him. One last check of the apartment turned up a worn leather jacket. If the cops ever traced the gun or any fibers from Holt's clothes or shoes like Naiya said they'd could, they'd find Leo's killer here—stone-cold dead.

He found the girl huddled in the corner of the hallway and pulled her up. "He won't hurt you now, but we gotta go. You got a name?"

"Skyler."

She followed him down the stairs, breathing hard as she tried to keep up. They had to move fast in case someone called the cops, although he doubted anyone living in a building like this would be ratting out anyone else. "Guys like that don't work alone," he said when they reached the street. "I'm gonna put you in a cab and pay your fare to Conundrum. When you get there, you call the Deputy Sheriff. His name is Benson. You tell him you met a Sinner and he called in a favor. He'll look after you."

She stumbled after him, her eyes still wide with shock. "Don't you . . . I mean . . . if you still want . . . I don't have anything to give you to thank you."

Holt turned when they reached the front door, shook his head. "You're a pretty girl. You got a nice body, but you don't need to use it to get ahead. Get off the streets, or you'll wind up on drugs and never get out. Go home. Finish school. Get a good job so you can look after yourself. Find a nice guy who'll look after you."

"I can't go home," she said. "My stepdad . . . I ran to get away from him. If he finds out where I am, he'll hunt me down."

"How old are you really?"

Her eyes filled with tears. "Nineteen," she whispered. "But I've been here for four years since my mom died and I was left alone with my step-dad."

Christ. She'd been a kid when she started out. So young and all alone. If he went ahead with his plan to off his Sinner brothers, he'd leave a bunch of kids with only one parent to care for them—kids who might wind up on the street like her. How could he fuck up all those kids, most of whom he'd known since they were born? He had no grudge against them or the old ladies. Maybe he'd give the brothers with kids a pass.

"If Benson can't help you sort something out, you tell him to take you to the Sinner's Tribe MC. He's in good with them. When you get there, ask for Tank. He'll introduce you 'round and you can decide if that life is for you. You can trust him. He won't take advantage. But don't go to the clubhouse alone or they'll get the wrong idea."

Not that there would be many Sinners left after he paid them a visit. Although now that he thought about it, a lot of them had kids. Jagger, Gunner, Sparky and Shaggy were single, although if he offed Jagger, Arianne would hunt Holt down for the rest of his days. And what if those single brothers had kids they didn't know about or kids they supported but kept secret from the club? And what about the old ladies? He'd eaten dinner at their houses, talked with them at parties. Hell, he'd even gone to a christening or two.

"Fuck." He thudded his hand on the wall. He wasn't cut out for revenge if it meant innocent people would get hurt—people he knew and cared about. Maybe Naiya's suggestion was a good one. He would capture one of them and ask what the hell had happened and who was involved, give them a chance to explain. Then he wouldn't have innocent deaths on his conscience. He would go after the right men, and leave the others to rebuild the club.

He wrote Benson's contact details on a twenty-dollar bill and handed it to her. "Let's find you a cab."

"Could I stay with you?" She looked up at him, her eyes wide, pleading.

"I got a girl," Holt said. "Left her behind. Now I gotta go back and find her."

"Nice shirt."

Naiya groaned inwardly and plastered a fake smile on her face before looking over at the man standing beside her at the bar. With Guns N' Roses', "Appetite for Destruction" playing in the background, and the scents of stale beer and pot filling the air, Rick's Bar and Grill at the edge of Trenton wasn't the kind of place she would normally go without a friend. Too many men assumed she was looking for a hook-up, and after three hours, she had a standard response down pat. However the shirt comment threw her off, and for a moment she didn't know what to say.

"I passed through Bolton once," he said. "I remember the beaver shirts. Never thought anyone would actually wear one, but it looks good on you. Cute." He sat on the stool beside her and asked the bartender for a jug of water. In his dark suit, crisp white shirt, and muted blue tie he looked like a city banker or a businessman, certainly not the type of person to patronize a seedy bar in a small town in the middle of nowhere.

Pleasantly surprised, Naiya shrugged. "I didn't buy it thinking it would be an invitation, but apparently that's what it is when you're in a bar full of drunk juveniles." She mocked one of the many male voices she'd heard that evening. "Can I see your beaver? Nice beaver. Can I pet your beaver?"

He laughed, the smile softening an otherwise hard face, all sharp lines and angles. "It could be worse. My sister went to fairy tale theme park and came back with a shirt that said PUSS IN BOOTS. She only wore that one to a bar once and never again."

Naiya's tension eased as he talked about his sister, and she sipped her third Mai Tai of the evening. With a fierce sweet tooth and a dislike of strong alcohol, she was a cocktail girl all the way. "You don't look like you belong here either." She gestured to the suit, and then waved vaguely over the collection of rough drunks seated at the tables behind them. "Or at a place like Bolton."

"My line of work takes me all over." He poured a glass of water from the jug the bartender had left for him. "I could say the same about you. This bar isn't the safest place for a woman alone, especially in a beaver shirt." He offered Naiya the water and she shook her head, held up her glass.

"It's a drown your sorrows kinda night. And I'm not here for long. Just waiting for the bus." Although she had no idea where she was going. After Holt had driven away, she'd felt more lost and alone than she'd ever felt in her life, and the prospect of going on the run by herself made her stomach twist. But she didn't want to put Ally and Doug or any of her friends in danger. And Maurice had found someone else. She took a bigger sip of her drink, wondered what kind of girl Maurice was with and whether he made her moan when he kissed her, the way she had done with Holt.

He sipped the water, his movements slow and deliberate. Although he seemed friendly and hadn't overtly hit on her, something about him didn't seem quite right. Maybe it was because he was so different from everyone else in the bar, or maybe it was the way he watched her when he thought she wasn't looking.

"I'm Michael, by the way," he said, breaking her train of thought.

Naiya shook the offered hand. His skin was soft, smooth, so unlike Holt's calloused palms. In fact, he was almost Holt's complete opposite. Slim where Holt was broad, with short-cropped dark hair, brown eyes so dark they were almost black, and a lean body. No visible tattoos. No cuts or bruises on his face. No character.

Holt was all character. From his scars and tattoos to his understated sense of humor, and from his biker swagger to his ability to dominate a room, he was the most intoxicating man she'd ever met.

"N—" She cut herself off. Better not to share her real name. Years of hanging around bikers had taught her to be wary of strangers. "Nora."

"Can I buy you a drink, Nora?"

"No, thank you. I'm just about at my limit." She gestured to the pitcher of water. "You aren't drinking?"

He shook his head. "I'm working. I'm investigating two murders not too far away. A high-profile biker was found at Gull Lake. He was shot at close range along with his buddy."

She sucked in a sharp breath. "Are you a police detective?"

Michael pulled out his wallet and flashed his ID. Bureau of Alcohol, Tobacco, Firearms and Explosives (ATF). Everyone in the biker world knew and hated the ATF. No one could take down an MC faster, and if they were in the area, looking into Leo's death, it wasn't just a simple shooting between rival biker gangs; it was a very big deal.

"Usually the local police would handle the case," he said into the silence, "But they were from one of the biggest outlaw clubs in the state, and there has been a lot of unusual biker activity in the area, so they called us in."

"Oh." She lifted the drink to her lips and forced down the sickly sweet liquid. Her heart thudded to the bass of Black Sabbath's, "Paranoid." "So . . . do you have any leads?"

"Curiously, no." He cocked his head, stared at her. "Whoever did it knew how to cover their tracks. All we know is that the shooter took the high-profile victim's motorcycle. We were able to identify the make and model from the tires, and we're trying to ID the body. Bikers wear their road name on their leather vests, but when we contacted his club, they weren't minded to tell us his real name."

"I guess not." She forced a laugh. "And are you supposed to be telling me all this? Won't people be afraid if they know there's a killer on the loose and you have no leads?"

"Won't be for long," Michael said. "I have a nickname at the ATF. They call me the Bloodhound. I can sniff out clues in the most unlikely places. I haven't had one unsolved case yet."

"I'll rest easy tonight then, knowing you're on the case." She tipped her glass to him and drank the rest of her cocktail in one gulp.

"Actually, I came over here because of your shirt." Michael gestured to her sweatshirt. "There were reports of outlaw bikers in Bolton. They shot up a couple of rooms in a motel. One was rented out under a fake name. Just wondered if you were there at the time. Maybe you saw something . . ." He sipped his water, watching her over the rim of the glass and it was all she could do to stay in her seat.

"Um . . . no." She curled her hand around her empty glass, her knuckles whitening. "I haven't been there for a long time. This is an . . . old shirt. But it's comfortable, so I wear it when I travel."

"Ah." He nodded, but his eyes narrowed almost imperceptibly, and the skin on the back of Naiya's neck crawled.

"I should get going." She glanced up at the clock, desperate to get away from Michael and his searching gaze.

"Where are you headed?"

"Um . . . Idaho Springs." She blurted out the name of the first Colorado town that came to mind since the bus was headed that way.

He waved to the bartender and pointed to Naiya's glass, gesturing for a refill. "You have lots of time then. The next bus doesn't leave for an hour. I'll buy you another drink."

Damn. She faked a smile and glanced over her shoulder. The bar had quieted down since Michael walked in the door, no doubt because most of the customers were the kind of people who could smell a cop a mile away. So what had happened to her well-honed senses? Probably the same thing that happened the night Viper had lured her to his office at the back of the Black Jack clubhouse. She'd let her guard down. Time to get the walls back up and go on the offensive or the next thing she knew, he'd be carting her off to jail.

"So are you on duty twenty-four seven, or do they give you time off for good behavior?" She tapped her foot to Bon Jovi's, "Livin' on a Prayer" and tilted her head to the side in her best imitation of Ally when she was at a bar trawling for fun. A woman with something to hide wasn't going to hit on the man who could cuff her for real. Or so she hoped.

Michael startled at her sudden change in demeanor, and his brow creased in a frown. "Well I'm pretty much on duty all the time." He lifted his glass. "Hence the water."

Hence. Who talked like that? She couldn't imagine Holt ever saying hence. She couldn't imagine him in a suit. Although he'd looked damn sexy in that Black Jack cut. And even more sexy without it.

She gave herself a mental shake. Holt was gone and he wouldn't be coming back. She'd burned that bridge twice over.

"Are you going to buy yourself an Idaho Springs shirt when you get there?" He gestured to her shirt again.

"Seems tourist shirts are gaining in popularity. The owner of the gas station near the crime scene saw a man and a woman wearing Bolton Beaver shirts and riding a motorcycle not long after what we estimate to be the time of death."

Run. Run. Run.

"Popular place, I guess." Sweat trickled down her back, but she knew better than to give into her instincts. There was nothing that excited a predator more than fleeing prey. Not that she'd done anything wrong. Well, maybe she had. She'd been an accomplice to murder, an accessory after the fact, and she'd stolen a motorcycle, money, and weapons. This entire situation had thrown her carefully ordered life into chaos, and she couldn't see a way out. "I'm sure there are lots of people riding motorcycles around here. I can imagine bikers would like the windy roads."

Michael sighed and rimmed his water glass with his finger. "We'll never know. Another biker showed up after they left, held a gun to the owner's head, and took the video surveillance tapes."

This time her surprise was genuine. "Why would he do that?"

"I thought at first they were working together, but the couple weren't wearing biker cuts, and I don't know any outlaw biker who would be seen dead without his cut." He hesitated, his smile fading. "The owner of the gas station had a good memory for details, though. I have to say, you match his description right down to the shirt."

Naiya's heart pounded so hard she thought she would break a rib, and not just from fear. He was toying with her. Like a cat with a mouse. Or a Viper with a fifteen-year-old girl who was flattered by his attention. Well she wasn't fifteen any more, and she was damn tired of his game. During her internship, she'd hung around with plenty of police and detectives. She'd partied with them, listened to them talk. If he had any evidence other than the vague re-collection of a gas station owner, she would be cuffed and in his car already. But since he was clearly fishing, maybe she could turn the situation to her advantage.

"You still owe me a drink." She patted his knee. "How about you order it while I freshen up?"

He covered her hand with his, trapping it against his leg. "How about you tell me what you were doing at that gas station and where your friend with the motorcycle has gone?"

Game over.

★ TWELVE ★

TANK

"Hey, biker. I remember you."

Tank's head jerked up and he tried to focus his bleary eyes on the woman standing at the bar beside him. But after eight beers and too many hours drinking at Rider's Bar alone, it took him a full minute to place the fucking hotalicious babe, her curves spilling out all over the place. In her tight suit, her blonde hair in a sleek bob, a briefcase on the floor beside her, she stood out in the rough, dimly-lit biker bar, with its worn, stained tables, polished wood bar, and bike memorabilia scattered about. If she hadn't been on the Conundrum news every night at six p.m., and if her face hadn't been plastered on buses and billboards all over town, he might not have recognized her at all.

"Ella Masters. I've seen you on TV." He held out a hand, hoped it was steady. What the hell was Conundrum's top news reporter doing in the Sinners-owned Rider's Bar? And what the hell did she want with him?

She shook his hand and almost broke his fucking bones. Crap. That was some handshake, but she was a tall, athletic woman with breasts a match for even Tank's large hands.

She lifted a quizzical eyebrow. "You don't remember the night we spent together?"

Holy shit. Had he slept with Ella Masters one of the many drunken nights he'd spent partying with T-Rex? "Uh . . . Sure I do." Tank sipped his beer and prayed she would go away. He wasn't in the mood to talk. For the last few hours, he'd been pulling in favors from all over the state, calling all the local businesses in Still Water, but so far no one had spotted two civilians in Bolton Beaver shirts on a shiny new Ultra Glide.

Ella laughed, her hair swinging along the soft edge of her jaw. "Your friend, Holt, spent an entire evening trying to get into my pants about a year ago at some dive in East Conundrum while you sat and watched. Now does it ring any bells?"

Fuck. Everything came back in a rush. T-Rex calling dibs on the cute blonde who was laughing it up with the bartender. Tank watching him chat her up wishing he had the balls and charm to go after a woman as famous as Ella. Startling when she dumped a beer on T-Rex's head. And then his surprise when T-Rex told him he'd insulted her so she would chase him away. *She's dangerous*, T-Rex said. *Steer clear.* Tank had figured he was pissed 'cause she was the only woman who had ever shot him down. But now, with his hand aching from her bone-crushing hand-shake, he wondered if T-Rex had been right.

"Not sure if I remember that night in particular. T-Rex tried to get into every chick's pants." He sipped his beer, tried to play it cool. He'd had no problem when T-Rex had called dibs on Ella. She wasn't Tank's type. Too tall, too curvy, too confident, too loud, and way too much of an ice queen. He liked the quiet ones, shy, reserved—women with a dark secret or hidden vulnerability that called to the damned protective streak that had seen him punch his dad the first and only time he'd hit Tank's mom.

Her brow creased in a frown. "Tried?"

"He's dead." Tank downed the rest of his beer and nodded to the bartender, Banks, to give him another bottle. But instead of serving, Banks jerked his head toward the end of the bar.

What the fuck? Banks wanted to talk? Now? Ex-military, tatted and hard, Banks ran the bar jointly with the Sinners, although he had refused Jagger's attempts to bring him into the Sinner fold. He was taciturn, reserved and generally surly, but his sharp mind, underground connections, and military training made him one of the Sinners' most trusted allies.

"I'm sorry." Ella placed a gentle hand on his arm, and Tank jerked away. The last thing he needed was sympathy. Hard enough to keep it together without some chick breaking down his walls.

"Tank." Banks barked his name and Tank scowled. Why the fuck was Banks bothering him? Couldn't he see Tank was talking to Conundrum's equivalent of a celebrity? Women like Ella Masters didn't talk to guys like Tank. She was so far out of his league he would never have approached her if she hadn't spoken first. He still couldn't believe they were having a conversation since the bar was heaving tonight, and a woman as famous and pretty as Ella could have any man she wanted.

"Fucking busy talking to a lady here, Banks," he growled.

"Saw someone sniffing around your bike out back," Banks said. "Thought you might care since you are a damn biker. "

"Son of a bitch." Tank pushed away from the bar. "Anyone touches my bike, they're gonna fuckin' die."

"I'll wait for you here." Ella sipped her drink. "I get queasy at the sight of blood."

Banks snorted in derision, and led Tank through the

stockroom door. But when Tank headed for the back exit, Banks clapped his hand on Tank's shoulder.

"Hold up. There's no one around your bike. I needed to talk to you, and you're so damn thick-headed you didn't take the hint."

Thickheaded. Numbskull. Dimwit. Lout. Tank's dad had an endless supply of insults for his son, and after years of being told he was stupid, Tank began to believe it. Even after he joined the Sinners, he stayed in the background, taking on missions that required brute force instead of those that involved strategy and planning. After years of being told he wasn't the brightest light bulb in the box, he knew to keep his mouth shut and just do what he was told to do. At least that was the case until T-Rex showed up.

T-Rex never made Tank feel stupid. He came to Tank for advice. He listened when Tank talked. He followed Tank's suggestions. He made sure the brothers knew that Tank had good ideas, and if anyone tried to put Tank down, T-Rex was right in their face. With T-Rex by his side, Tank began to speak up and earned the respect of his brothers. Tank could never repay T-Rex's faith and friendship, but he could give him his loyalty and have his back. There was nothing he wouldn't do for T-Rex. And there was nothing T-Rex wouldn't do for him.

Tank looked at the back door, then back to Banks. "What the fuck is this all about?"

Banks gave an exasperated sigh. "Ella Masters has been here all week asking questions. When I pulled her aside, she said she's got a thing for bikers. Well, I got thing against reporters, and something about her sits wrong with me. She reminds me of those female black widow spiders that eat the males after sex."

Tank's face twisted in disgust. "I'm a fucking Sinner. I'm not afraid of that tiny blonde bitch."

"She's a sinner, too," Banks said. "The kind that fucks

with the Devil and then eats his head. You don't have T-Rex anymore to watch your back. I'm trying to do you a favor. You're a good guy, Tank. Probably one of the most loyal, trusting guys I know. And that's not always a good thing when you're alone."

Christ. This was all he needed. Yet another reminder that T-Rex was gone when he'd come to the damn bar to forget. "Are we fucking done here?"

Banks nodded. "Said my piece. Can't do more than that."

Tank returned to his seat. Ella smiled when he sat down, like she was happy to see him again. Tank's stomach knotted. It was damn hard to believe this beautiful woman could do anything more than smile for the camera and read the news off cards someone held in front of her, like he'd heard all reporters did.

"Was your bike, okay?"

A poor liar at best, Tank froze for a heartbeat and then quickly recovered. "Uh . . . Yeah. Must been a cat he saw or something."

"Sure." She gave him a warm smile. "I was worried I'd said something wrong when I brought up your friend. I didn't know he'd passed. I'm so sorry. I'd forgotten about it, but I remember now one of my colleagues reported on his funeral. It was a huge affair. He must have been well liked. What happened?"

Tank's reticence after Banks' warning warred with his desire to share his pain with someone—anyone—not inside the club. But it wasn't like the funeral was a secret. There had been all sorts of reporters there. "Jacks got him. Tortured him for months in their dungeon."

To her credit, she didn't gasp or cover her mouth with her hand, or do any of the things people did when they heard a horror story like he'd just told. But then she'd reported the death of Wolf, president of the Devil's

Brethren from the scene of the crime, among other grisly murders in Conundrum, so he shouldn't be surprised.

"He seemed like a good guy," she said, and then she gave him a rueful smile. "Now I kinda wish I hadn't dumped that beer on his head. I could tell you two were close."

"He's not really dead." He lifted the bottle, startled when he saw it was empty. That sure had gone down fast. How many had he had since coming to the bar? "They got it wrong. I saw him the other day in Still Water. I know it was him."

Her face softened, and she slid a beer over to him. "I ordered another one from the waitress for you in case you came back. Looks like you need it."

"Appreciated." Tank nodded and lifted the beer to his lips. The taste was slightly off, flat and bitter, but maybe that was because it had been sitting while he talked with Banks.

"Maybe you just imagined seeing him," Ella said.

"No!" Tank slammed his beer on the counter, drawing a scowl from Banks at the other end of the counter. "I know T-Rex. I know him like I know myself." He thudded his fist against his chest. "Nothing has hurt as bad as losing him. I can't fucking sleep at night for the fucking pain, but I always knew it wasn't right. I knew he couldn't be dead."

He shuddered, realizing he had never really spoken about T-Rex's death to anyone. Not to the brothers or any of the sweet butts. Not even to the club doctor when he'd gone to him for sleeping pills. But now it had spilled out, and to a fucking stranger who didn't even know the life, a woman both Banks and T-Rex had warned him about. Hell, she'd probably call the cops on him for the things he'd already told her.

"I lost someone close to me, too," she said. "Years ago.

And it still hurts. You never stop thinking maybe some-one got it wrong. That maybe he's still out there and he can't come home, or he has amnesia or he's lost his way. You think because you hear his voice in coffee shops and bars, or you turn a corner and you're sure he was just there. You think maybe they buried the wrong guy. Maybe it was someone else in the plane that crashed and not the man I'd loved since I was fourteen years old."

Tank wasn't good with words, but he understood her pain. "You sure you don't want a drink?"

"Actually, I do." She dabbed her eyes with her napkin. Fuck. He hadn't even noticed any tears.

"Patrón," she said. "Neat. But only if you're having another beer. I don't like to drink alone."

He ordered the drinks from a scowling Banks, tossing him a few bills when he returned a few minutes later.

"Hard liquor," Tank said when she took her first sip. "My kinda girl."

That got him a smile and the mist cleared from her eyes. "Why are you so sure your friend is alive?"

"I saw him." He fingered his phone, itching to show her the video. But he wasn't stupid. T-Rex had taught him that. He'd stolen that tape at gunpoint, and he knew better than to serve up that kind of story to a reporter. And, although Banks' warning had ruffled his feathers, he respected the bartender enough to be careful around Ella, especially when he had a real serious buzz going after an evening of drinking. "It was at a gas station, and I played the scene over and over in my head. It was the little things—the way he moved, the tat on his arm, the pizza he was eating—it's hard to explain."

"Sounds right up my alley." She smiled—a real smile, and not the fake one she used on TV—her eyes crinkling at the corners. Damn she was pretty.

"I thought you were a news reporter."

"My big dream was always investigative journalism." She sipped her drink, leaving a pink lipstick print on the glass. Ella had nice lips, full and lush. Tank imagined Ella in her tight suit on her knees, looking up at him with those big, blue eyes, those beautiful lips wrapped around his cock. His blood rushed to his groin, and he tried to pay attention to her words and not the images in his head of him with this classy chick, showing her a bit of rough and making her scream with pleasure.

"Unfortunately, the powers that be needed a new face for the evening news, and they liked mine," she continued.

"You're good." Tank didn't usually throw out compliments, but Ella was good. Damned good. And he would know since he had watched her on the news every night for a couple of weeks after T-Rex's big strikeout. Who knew she'd turn out to be so nice and easy to talk to, or that she'd even want to share some of her personal life with a guy like him? Even if they didn't wind up in bed together, he was just happy to share his grief with someone who understood exactly how he felt, and the fact that she was attractive made it that much more enjoyable.

"Thanks." Her face lit up with her smile. "I actually think you mean that instead of just saying it to get into my pants."

"I do mean it." His body warmed with the knowledge he had pleased her. "And I wouldn't try to get into your pants 'cause you're wearing a skirt."

She laughed, her eyes sparkling, like he'd said the funniest damn thing in the world, and Tank felt the first stirring of something akin to pleasure, a feeling he hadn't had since T-Rex disappeared.

"I have ambitions beyond the local Conundrum news." She drummed her thumb on the counter. "Getting the scoop on one of the country's biggest outlaw MCs would open those doors. What if I help you find your friend?

I meet a lot of people doing what I do. I've made a lot of contacts . . ."

Aha. So this was what she wanted. He felt a stab of pride at the thought he'd so quickly discovered what Banks had been dying to know, and he imagined Banks's face when he told him Ella Masters was after a story about the Sinners. But his imaginary pride quickly faded when he thought about telling Jagger and the executive board. No doubt they would do something to ensure that kind of story never made the news, and after hearing about Ella's loss, he didn't want her to get hurt.

"Sorry, love. Club business stays in the club. If Jagger ever caught me sharing club information, friend or not, he'd have my head."

Her beautiful lips turned down at the corners, and she stroked her finger over his knuckles. Damn she had soft hands, and her nails were painted the same hot sunglow red as T-Rex's bike.

"Not even something small?"

"I'm not the talker T-Rex was . . . is," he said, his brain fuzzed by the gentle stroke of her hand and the knowledge that Ella Masters was touching him. "Never had his ability to charm women into my bed."

"His charm didn't work with me." She finished her drink, licked her lips. Tank's gaze followed her little pink tongue, imagining the things her tongue could do in the same place he wanted her lips to be.

"He wasn't my type." Her words came out in a soft murmur that he could feel in his cock.

"What is your type?" T-Rex was every woman's type so he couldn't figure out what kind of dude Ella would want.

She leaned closer, and he inhaled her perfume, sharp, bold, intoxicating. "I like the strong, silent type. The ones who sit back and watch. The ones who talk little and feel deep. The ones who see things other people don't see, who know when their friend is alive even when no one believes them."

Holy shit. Was she saying what he thought she was saying? What had started out as a bad night had just taken a turn for the better. "How do you know no one believes me?"

"It's my job to read between the lines. It's what makes the difference between a good reporter and a great one." She nudged his beer toward him. "Drink up. You don't want it to go to waste."

Tank finished his beer and closed his eyes as a wave of dizziness threatened to topple him off the stool. Damn. It had been a long time since he'd had so much to drink. "Yeah, well it doesn't matter what people think. I'm going to find him on my own."

"Sounds to me like you need a friend. My offer is still open. No strings attached." She finished her drink, licked a drop of Patrón off the corner of her mouth. Tank's gaze rested on her lips where the drop had been, and he wished he'd been the one to lick it off.

Tank gave her an apologetic smile. "That's nice of you, but like I said, it's biker business. We don't involve reporters."

Ella's cheeks reddened, and she dropped her gaze, her voice wavering. "You seemed so sad. I just wanted to help because I know how it feels, and if something comes of it that makes a good story and doesn't get you in trouble with the MC, then that's a bonus for me. If not, maybe we'll just get to know each other better, and I'll get to indulge my secret love for investigative journalism and maybe get you the happy ending I never had."

Longing gripped him so hard he could barely breathe. He'd sell his soul to see T-Rex again. And yet he'd be stupid not to heed Banks' warning—the same warning T-Rex had given him so long ago. Tank wasn't stupid—T-Rex had cured him of that belief—but he was picking up some signals that Ella might be interested in taking their conversation out of the bar, maybe even to bed. And that's what he needed right now. A little distraction. He could play along, pretend he was considering her offer, and after they'd had their fun, he would gently turn her down.

"So what could you do to help?"

Ella squeezed his hand and leaned in close. "Why don't we go to my place and talk about it some more?"

Hell, yes. He was going to score.

Tank's gaze dropped to her chest where her current position gave him a perfect view of her ample cleavage, the crescents of her creamy breasts, and the edge of her red-lace bra. His cock hardened, and he growled deep in his throat. He must not have had that much to drink because performance clearly wasn't going to be an issue. Oh, yeah. He could play this game.

"Does that growl mean yes?" she whispered, her lips brushing over his ear.

"Let's go." He stood, staggered a step, and then righted himself when she grabbed his hand.

Something about her hand triggered a memory from earlier in the evening, a painful memory, but damned if he could remember what it was.

★ THIRTEEN ★

Holt knew there was trouble the moment he walked in the door.

And it wasn't just because of the black sedan parked outside, or the fact Rick's Bar and Grill was unnaturally quiet given the rough crowd. No, it was the stench of law enforcement; the pungent odor of power that created an invisible barrier around the undercover cop that only those who lived on the wrong side of the law could detect. Which, from the looks of it, was pretty much everyone in the bar.

Except Naiya.

As quickly as he had stepped in, he stepped out again. He wouldn't be able to do any good if he gave that damn cop even the slightest reason to suspect them of Leo's death—and he was damn sure that's why he was talking to Naiya. After three months in Viper's dungeon, Holt was off his game, or he would have ditched the damn Bolton Beaver shirts right away. Thanks to the pimp's clothes, he was safe, but the cop was sniffing too damn close to his girl and he had to get her out of there.

But first he had to ditch the weapons and the bike. No

doubt the cops had taken the CCTV tapes from the gas station in Still Water and run the plates. Even if they hadn't, the bike was conspicuous for both its size and the fact there weren't many like it on the road. *Stupid. Stupid. Stupid.* He'd killed Leo in a public place and stopped too close to the scene of the crime. But that was Leo's fault for running the bike down to empty.

He glanced through the window at Naiya and the cop. She didn't appear to be distressed. In fact, it looked like they were just having a friendly chat, like two people who'd just met in a bar. But after years living on the wrong side of the law, Holt knew just how tricky cops could be, and this guy was after Naiya. No doubt about it.

"Fuck." He didn't want to leave her, but the bike would give them away, and the money and weapons would put them in jail for a very long time even if the cops couldn't pin Leo's death on Holt. Could Naiya hold out until he got back? She was sharp and savvy, and so far she'd managed to keep it together. The minute he walked into the bar, the cop would be on the hunt. He had to get rid of any evidence that could tie him and Naiya to Leo's death.

He drove the bike out of town and dumped the weapons, clothes, and money in the woods fifty yards off a turnoff. Then he drove the bike in the opposite direction and into the middle of a field. He wiped it down with a rag, dipped the rag in the gas tank, then set the rag on fire, brushed his footprints away while the rag smoldered, and took off as fast as he could go.

When he was two hundred yards away, the gas tank exploded with a loud boom, consuming the bike in a ball of flames. Hopefully, by the time someone reported the fire, there would be nothing left of the bike and no prints on the ground. He jogged down the road and flagged a ride to the bar with a trucker who was passing through. At most, he'd been away twenty, maybe twenty-five minutes. If the cop had taken Naiya, Holt would give himself up and make sure they knew she wasn't involved.

Steeling himself for the worst, he slammed open the door to the bar and walked in as if he had every right to be there. As if he was looking for his woman, and he was damned pissed she'd run away.

Naiya turned at the noise and her eyes widened. She shook her head and mouthed at him to run. Damn woman was trying to save him when it was his job to save her. He was the man. The protector. And she was in this position because of him.

"Babe." He sat on the seat beside her, threw his arm over her shoulder, ignoring the cop who was no doubt salivating at the thought of getting his hands on Holt. "Gettin' damn tired of you running away every time we have an argument."

She froze for only half a second, and then she pressed her lips together and glared. "Me run? You're the one who pushed me away."

"Needed some space, babe. A man needs a little peace and quiet after a day on the road, especially after you crashed the vehicle."

He hoped she got the message and could let him know what her plan had been if it was something she'd shared with the highly attentive prick seated beside her.

"I wouldn't have crashed if you'd kept your hands out of my damn pants."

Holt fought back a smile at her quick thinking. If they weren't in so much danger, the banter would almost be fun. "You said you had an itch, and I wanted to be there for you."

Naiya's nostrils flared, and her face reddened. "You chose a bad time to scratch it."

"You coulda said no."

Her face turned three shades of red. "Maybe if I wasn't

so desperate I would have." She narrowed her eyes and glared at the cop. "Seriously. Look at me. Do I look like the kind of woman who could survive only getting some once a week? That's what he means when he says he's there for me. Once a week. And even then it doesn't always happen because he's tired after work, or there's a game on television, or he can't get it up because of his problem."

Holt sucked in a breath. Did she think she was going to get away with calling his masculinity into question? Even if it was a damn ruse, a man could only take so much.

"Maybe you should put a bit of effort in, babe. I mean that ratty old sweatshirt and ponytail don't scream, 'I want my man to do me bad'. How about you make an effort? Put on some lingerie, do your nails, brush your hair, maybe some makeup, shave your legs, and how about you trim the bush so a man can see where he's going?"

Naiya spluttered and clutched her glass so hard her knuckles turned white. "I'm supposed to dress up for you when you get home? As if I haven't put in a long day at work, too? You want your meal all cooked and served to you? A couple of cold ones waiting by your chair? A foot stool all ready so I can massage your feet while I suck you off all dressed up like the fifty dollar hookers you think I don't know you go see?"

Ouch. Now that hit too close to home. He felt a stab of guilt, although he hadn't done anything wrong. Holt shared a glance with the now totally engrossed cop and winked. The cop laughed. There were some things that bonded all men, regardless of which side of the law they were on.

"Every man's dream, babe. And it's sixty dollars for a blow in Missoula. You charge fifty and you're underselling yourself. You give decent head. Not sixty dollars worth, but twenty for sure, maybe twenty-five."

The cop spluttered his water, grabbed a napkin, and dabbed his lips.

"Pig," she spat out, her tone and face so convincing he almost wondered if she was acting or incensed by what wasn't really a joke. The image of her dressed in a skin-tight dress, kneeling at his feet with his cock in her mouth while he sipped a cold beer and watched the game held serious appeal.

"I'm going to get on that bus to Idaho Springs and bury my grandmother alone."

Ah. Now he knew the plan. Damn she was smart. He just hoped he could keep up with her.

The bartender placed a drink on the counter in front of Naiya. Although Holt was pretty sure they'd thrown the cop off the scent, he didn't want the moment to end. He had never seen this side of Naiya before. She was beautiful in her anger, her face flushed, eyes glittering. Her sharp mind and quick wit were almost as arousing as her heaving breasts and plump, moist lips.

"Babe." He patted her stomach. "I told you. No drinking while you're pregnant with my boy."

How he managed to keep a straight face as she choked on her words, eyes wide and filled with the promise of retribution, he didn't know.

"I didn't buy it." She gestured at the cop. "Michael did."

Michael's hands shot up, palms forward in a defensive gesture that made Holt want to fist pump with both fists. "I didn't know she was pregnant. My mistake."

Temptation curled inside him. Words he shouldn't say. They'd played the game long enough and it was high time they got out. Now that he knew she hid a little spitfire inside, he had no doubt she would kill him the minute they left the bar. But how could he not? He'd never met a woman with this kind of fire. And maybe they could use it as an excuse to get away.

Digging his fingers into his left palm so he could play out the rest of the scene without dissolving in laughter, he patted her stomach and scowled at Michael. "Seriously? You didn't know? You think she got a belly like this from eating too many pizzas?"

"What?" Naiya shrieked and jumped up so quickly her stool toppled over. "I am getting on that bus, and you are not coming with me."

"You'd better have that drink." Michael pushed the glass over to Holt, his silver ring tapping on the glass. Something twigged at the back of Holt's mind. A memory. Faint. Something about that ring. Many rings. But he couldn't place it. He took a grateful sip of the drink. Although not a fan of girly drinks, right now any kind of alcohol was good.

"Appreciated." Holt stood and gave Michael an apologetic shrug. "Sorry about this." He leaned in and whispered loud enough for Naiya to hear. "It's the pregnancy hormones. She was like this with the other four kids, too."

"Four?" Michael's eyes widened. "She doesn't look *that* old."

"She wears a lot of makeup to hide all the wrinkles."

"Shoot him," Naiya said to Michael. "Put me out of my misery."

"Afraid I can only shoot criminals." Michael stifled a laugh. "He doesn't seem like a criminal to me."

"He is a criminal," Naiya muttered. "Criminally insane." She stalked out of the bar and Holt threw a few bills on the counter. "Sorry about the trouble. Thanks for looking after her for me."

He inspected the fed's car as he exited the building. Typical black sedan with blacked-out windows and the usual oddities on the plates: non-random lettering, reflective sheeting and a hologram of an American eagle. Resisting the urge to slash the vehicle's tires, he made his way to the side of the building where Naiya was waiting, but he didn't get the welcome he'd expected.

"You said I was fat." She slapped him on the chest. "I don't care if it was all pretend. I hate it when men dismiss a woman's anger as hormones. It's . . . sexist."

Slap.

"And demeaning."

Slap.

"And patronizing."

Slap. Slap. Slap.

Fuck. All his life he'd gone for the loud women. Brash, confident and outgoing. Naiya was different. Quiet and gentle. Smart and quirky with a sense of humor that matched his own. But hell, when she was riled she had a fire inside that blew his mind. She needed protecting but she was no victim. She was broken but needed no glue. She'd held her own against that cop, and she'd planned to leave Holt and travel alone across the state. And now she was slapping him on the damn chest, pissed off at a fight they hadn't really had, about something that wasn't even true.

He'd never been so turned on in his life.

Holt grabbed her hands and pushed her up against the wall, pinning her wrists to the cold brick surface. "Fuck woman. It wasn't real."

"Oh it was real. I saw it in your face. But I'm so not the kind of woman who is going to dress up for you every night and cook your supper and blow you while you drink your beer."

"But you are the kind of woman I'm gonna fuck until she screams." Unable to restrain himself any longer, he kicked her legs apart and ground his erection against her hips. "'Cause fuck me, babe, I have never been so damn jacked. You in there. Your fire. Your smarts. The fucking adrenaline pumping as you played that cop. It was all

I could do not to push you over the counter and take you right in front of the whole damn bar."

"You left me." She bit out. "You left me in a parking lot, and I almost got arrested for something I didn't do."

"I fucked up, darlin'." He leaned in and nuzzled her neck. "I fucked up bad. But you said you wanted me to drop you off, and at the time I thought it was a good idea. You need to get out of the state. I need to go back to Conundrum. We're not seeing eye-to-eye on Viper meeting his maker. It wasn't until that hooker was on her knees . . ."

Only a lifetime of sharp reflexes saved him from a world of pain when her knee jerked up, hitting his thigh instead of the family jewels.

"So that's how you knew how much a hooker cost. And now you want to fuck me right after you've been with her? I am so done with you, Holt. I meant it when I said I was getting on that bus alone."

He gritted his teeth, pulled himself up. "I left you once, and look what happened. You need me. That cop saw you in that beaver shirt. He knows what you look like. You're on his radar now, and I'm sorry for it. But if you leave the state you'll have the feds and Viper after you. I'm your only hope for keeping your name clear of this mess and keeping you safe. And now you showed me a side of you that makes it so I will not be leaving you again. You showed me your fire. Moth to a flame, darlin'. I'm sticking around even if I get burned."

"Misogynistic, chauvinistic, patronizing," she muttered. "That's the side you showed me in there."

"You insulted my manhood." He pressed his hips against hers, his cock so damn hard it hurt. "A man's gotta defend himself when the essence of his being is attacked."

"Your cock is the essence of your being?" She glared, but her body arched against him, taut nipples brushing against his chest.

"It's gonna be the essence of your being very soon if you don't stop turning me on."

She rocked her hips against him, grinding against his aching shaft. "You're already turned on."

"So are you." He whispered kisses along her jaw. "You want me to do something about it?"

"Yes." The word dropped from Naiya's lips before she could catch it, and before she could even consider taking it back, Holt tugged open her jeans.

Naiya glanced quickly to the side to make sure they were alone, but there was nothing to see in the semi-darkness at the back of the building but trees, a few toppled garbage cans, and the hull of a burnt out car. The air was thick and moist, scented with pine and cedar and the faint odor of grease from the kitchen vent above them.

Holt slid his hand inside her panties, feeling his way over the soft down covering her mound, and then along her folds, slick and wet. A whimper escaped her lips. She hadn't felt arousal like this since . . .

Shame flushed her cheeks at the memory. Viper had made her come. Before he took her to his office, he'd spiked her drink, sat her on his lap, and kissed her as the drug took effect. She remembered feeling semi-dazed, thrilled by his attention, lulled by the soft croon of his voice and the gentle stroke of his hands on her body, as he told her how pretty she was, how innocent, how he couldn't resist her, how he wanted to make her feel good. It was only when she felt his hand under her skirt, fingers pushing aside her panties, that her mind shrieked a warning. But it was too late. Her body betrayed her under the touch of Viper's skilled fingers. And after she'd come on his hand, Viper had laughed. Told her that her body clearly wanted what he intended to give her. That she was a slut. Just like her mother. And that was just the beginning.

She shuddered and Holt froze. "Did I hurt you?"

"No."

"What's wrong?"

Naiya bit her lip, considering. She'd never wanted a man like she wanted Holt and even that simple desire confused her. After the assault, she'd shut down, finally hitting rock bottom when her mother kicked her out, choosing the club over her. After Father Doyle saved her from pulling the trigger and damning her soul, he helped her relocate to Missoula, and she slowly began to heal. But sexual pleasure eluded her. She faked orgasms and gave blowjobs until she was tired of pretending. And then she met Maurice and he didn't seem to mind having a relationship based solely on friendship and mutual respect, without the complications of intimacy.

"I'm not used to being on the receiving end." She dropped her hand to his belt. "Maybe I should . . ."

Holt studied her, his head tilted to the side. She was beginning to hate that gesture because it usually meant he could see right through her, and there were things she didn't want him to see.

"One day you're gonna tell me what he did to you," he said. "But only when you're ready."

Naiya dropped her hand, ready to go, but Holt didn't step back. Instead he leaned forward and traced his tongue over her lower lip. Her mouth opened, but he didn't press inside. Instead, he brushed kisses over her cheek, her jaw, and down her neck, cool on her heated skin.

"Shouldn't we go?" She wasn't used to a man changing tracks. The men she'd been with would let her take over when she froze up, and a few had walked away. But Holt wasn't in any hurry to leave, and he was still in control.

"You in a rush, darlin'?" He nibbled her lip, sucking on

it gently. Naiya moaned and only then did he move, slanting his mouth over hers to kiss her. His arms slid around her, pulling her into his chest, and he brushed kisses down to the sensitive spot between her neck and her shoulder. Easing the neck of her shirt aside to reveal her bare skin, he bit down gently, sending a shiver of pleasure down her spine.

Hard yet gentle. Firm, but not brutal. Dominant but not forceful. It was exactly what she needed to let go. "No," she whispered. "I kinda like it out here."

He returned to her mouth, and this time she opened for him, tangled her tongue with his, trying to push him just a little bit further.

Holt reacted quickly, fisting her hair, holding her in place as his kiss turned savage, hungry. He ravaged her mouth, yet she had no doubt he would stop if she asked, that he would never hurt her.

For the first time since the assault, she felt arousal instead of fear. Excited. She twined her arms around his neck, pulled him closer.

"Been wanting to touch you for so long," he murmured in her ear as he cupped her breast in his warm palm. "When I saw you with that cop, his hands on you, I almost lost it. You're mine, and no one is gonna hurt you. Ever."

When he rubbed his thumb back and forth over her nipple, she gasped, her head dropping back against the wall. How could it feel so good? She'd been touched before, faked her moans when the men she dated squeezed her breasts. Once when Maurice tweaked her nipples in the shower she'd even felt a short stab of pleasure. But never anything like this.

He cupped her other breast, pressed them together, and dragged his thumbs over her nipples at the same time. Naiya bit her lip when her nipples hardened. She wanted more. She wanted his fingers on her clit, his mouth on her nipples. She wanted it here. Now. But it was crazy. They hadn't thought it through. What if someone came around the corner? Was she desperate? Rebounding from Maurice?

Holt's hands slid over her bare skin and he pushed her shirt over her breasts. With a gentle tug, he eased her breast over the cup of her bra. Her body trembled as he bent down and drew her left nipple into his hot, wet mouth. Oh God. So good. A moan rose in her throat, and she choked it back, shocked that it had slipped out uncontrolled. But nothing had ever felt as good as the gentle pressure of his mouth, the slow slide of his teeth, the lap of his tongue.

Her body flamed, her pussy quivering with awakening. No one had ever made her wet. Not since . . . She pushed the thought from her mind, focused her attention on Holt and his clever tongue, his gentle fingers, the heat and strength of his body . . .

"You've got beautiful breasts, darlin'. Been wanting to taste them for a long time." He slid one hand between them, brushing it over her stomach to rest at the open fly of her jeans. "Been wanting to taste something else, too."

Swallowing nervously, she glanced around. She wanted this. She wanted it so badly she ached, and it wasn't just lust, but the hope that maybe Viper hadn't ruined sex for her after all. "Yes," she whispered.

Holt eased her jeans over her hips and she sucked in a sharp breath. "What if someone comes?"

"What if they do?" He slid his hand into her panties and Naiya jerked back, hitting her head against the wall.

"We could be charged with indecent exposure. And Michael is still inside the bar." Her mind struggled for reasons he should stop, but her body swayed toward him, and Holt's naughty fingers continued their descent to where she wanted them most.

"Gonna touch you, Naiya. Gentle this time. You tell me

if you need me to stop." Two fingers caressed her sensitive flesh, stroking along her folds, light as butterfly wings. "Don't worry about Michael. He was torn between wanting you for himself and doing his job. I made the choice for him. I claimed you. He knows you belong to me. He knows I'm the one who's gonna give you pleasure. I'm the only one who's gonna touch this sweet pussy, keep you safe, and make you come."

She whimpered as he teased her with his fingers, but when he touched her wetness, she stiffened. Not because his touch didn't feel good, but because she was so wet, embarrassingly wet, like she'd never had sex before. But then, she never really had. Not like this. Not with a man who was focused entirely on her pleasure.

"Shhh, darlin'. Relax. Spread your legs. You're so damn wet; it's killing me. I want to watch you come. I want to feel your pleasure on my hand."

Relax? With a cop on the other side of the wall? Her breast exposed, and his hand down her pants? But, oh God, she couldn't resist the exquisite sensation of his finger circling her clit.

"Good girl." He pressed one finger into her wet heat, and Naiya went up on her toes, her inner walls clenching around him. Holt tightened his free hand on her waist, holding her in place. "So tight." His voice dropped to a husky growl. "So fucking hot and wet. I'm gonna make you come so hard you'll never look at another man again." He drew out his finger, thrust in again. Slow and gentle, coaxing her pleasure even as his body shuddered. She sensed he was fighting for control, fought a moment of panic. But he never changed his pace, never rushed her, and when he added a second finger, she gave into sensation and groaned.

"Love that sound." He brushed his mouth over her neck, his body taut and trembling. "Next time you decide to get me all wound up, make sure you're wearing a skirt. I wanna fuck you so bad. I want my cock in your tight, wet pussy. But I'm not gonna risk stripping you down with a cop inside who is probably still trying to figure out what just happened."

"Oh." She hadn't meant to sound so disappointed. After all, she was always thrilled to have the sex part of her evenings out of the way. But not this time. She wanted more. More Holt pressed against her, his magic fingers working her to a fever pitch. More Holt who had come to save her, his mouth hot and wet on her breasts.

"Shhhh." He thrust his fingers deep inside her. "I'm gonna take care of you."

"But, I never . . ." Her hands found his shoulders, her nails digging through his shirt and into his skin.

"Never what?" He added a third finger, stretching her, increasing the pace, his fingers curled to hit the sensitive spot inside that had only ever come to life with her vibrator.

"Never fucked a biker outside a bar?" He moved in closer, pinned her against the wall, and leaned down to suck her throbbing nipple.

Something inside her snapped—all her tension, her fear, and her anxiety were swallowed up in a rush of desire. She sagged against the wall, giving in to the unfamiliar sensations pulsing through her body. Her hips rocked against his hand, and she ground her clit into his palm in a wanton display of need such as she'd never imagined before.

"That's it. Give it to me." Holt groaned, released her nipple. "Jesus Christ, you're so fucking hot." With his free hand, he tugged on his jeans and freed his cock from its restraint. Naiya's breath caught when she looked down. He was huge, thick, the head of his cock pink and glistening.

"Stroke me."

Well, this was more familiar territory. She knew all

about giving pleasure, just not how to receive it. Without hesitation she wrapped her hand around his shaft and worked him from base to tip.

His cock hardened beneath her hand, and he let out a long, low groan against her breast, one arm tightening around her waist, while he continued the slow, torturous slide of his fingers inside her.

"Harder." His voice had gone dark, guttural. His shaft hot and throbbing in her palm. She tightened her fingers, pumped harder, even as she felt a deep, erotic pressure build in her womb.

"Oh God, Holt. I'm going to come." All her blood rushed downward, swelling the tissues in her sex. She bucked against him, losing all her inhibitions in the burning need for release. "Don't stop, Holt. Don't stop."

"Come for me, darlin'." He ground his palm against her clit, driving his fingers inside her.

Her climax overtook her, wiping her mind of everything except the wet, pounding, clenching, all-consuming pleasure that pulsed through her body in wave after wave of electric heat. Her eyes shut at the frightening intensity, a pleasure like nothing she'd ever felt before. Her back arched, and she released his cock, buried her face in his shoulder, and screamed.

"Hell, that's the fucking hottest thing I've ever seen." He held her against him, drawing out the last quivers of her orgasm, and then he withdrew his hand and pressed gently on her shoulders. "On your knees, darlin'. I wanna see those beautiful lips wrapped around my dick. I want to fuck your sweet mouth."

"I want to taste you, Holt."

Naiya dropped to her knees as he pulled a condom from his pocket and sheathed himself. When he was ready, she wrapped her hand around him and squeezed tight licking over the head of his shaft. This she knew: After she started dating again, she'd quickly discovered a man could be put off sex if he got regular oral pleasure, so she'd researched, studied, and perfected her technique, combining her love of science and her knowledge of anatomy with the best porn the Internet had to offer.

She took him all in, fast and deep, dragging her tongue along the underside of his cock, longing to taste him free of the latex sheath. Still, his musky scent of arousal made her pussy clench with need all over again.

"Yes. Fuck. Yes." His shaft swelled, and she pumped her fist in counterpoint to her mouth as she withdrew, and took him in again. Holt bucked against her, his hand fisting her hair.

"You're so fucking sexy and it's been so damn long, you do that again and I'm gonna come so hard." He panted his breaths, as she took him to the back of her throat, his body coiling tight. "Harder, Naiya. Fuck. Fuck. Fuck. Suck my cock. Take me as far as you can in that sweet mouth."

She sucked, and licked as she pumped her hand, but she didn't need any of her tricks. On her last stroke, Holt threw back his head and let out a guttural groan, his hand tightening in her hair, holding her still. Naiya relaxed her throat as he thrust deep and climaxed hard, his orgasm going on and on, his cock pulsing against her tongue. Finally, he shuddered and pulled out.

"You okay, darlin'?" He pulled her up and let out a ragged breath.

"Been awhile?"

With a groan, Holt fell forward, palms to the rough brick wall, his forehead pressed against hers. "Three months or so. I thought maybe Viper had made it so I could never be with a woman again."

"Apparently, you're in good working order," she said with a soft laugh.

Holt pressed a kiss to her temple. "But it's never been like that."

"For me either." She cupped his jaw, bristly with a five o'clock shadow. "But now I can add fuck a biker outside a bar to my list of skills on my resume."

He kissed her lightly and they straightened their clothing. He disposed of the condom in a nearby garbage can and returned to kiss her again. "Seeing you with that cop drove me fucking crazy. I woulda happily gone to jail to get his hands off you."

Shoes crunched on the gravel around the corner. Holt spun around, pushing Naiya behind his back.

"Oh, there you are." Michael's voice rang out in the semi-darkness. "The bus driver said you hadn't boarded yet."

Holt held her firm behind him with one hand, while the other slid beneath his leather jacket to the gun holstered at this back.

"I forgot to give you my card." Michael held out his hand as he walked toward them. "Just in case you remember anything that might help. I'm giving them out to everyone who was in the area at the time."

"Su—"

"Neither of us was in the area," Naiya said quickly, interrupting Holt. She stepped out from behind his back. "And we won't even be in the state after tonight. Sorry we can't help."

Michael stared at her, his eyes narrowing every so slightly. "My mistake." He tucked the card into his jacket pocket, and looked around. "Not much to see back here in the dark."

Naiya put her hand on her stomach. "Still in the throwing-up stage of the pregnancy, and the restroom was occupied."

Beside her, Holt choked back a laugh.

Michael's gaze flicked to Holt and then back to her. "Ah. I guess with five kids it's old hat for you."

She pressed her lips together and met his challenge head on. No one would ever trip up a scientist on details. "Four kids. Tim, Fiona, Pat, and Louis." She rattled off the names of her co-workers at the science center where she volunteered during the summer. All one year apart. We didn't want to waste any time."

Tension crackled in the air between them. Holt slid one hand around her waist, the other resting at his hip near his weapon. "Good luck with your investigation."

Michael hesitated and then nodded. "Good luck with the baby."

Naiya's heart thundered in her chest, and she focused on slowing her breathing as Michael walked away.

"Kinda like the idea of gettin' you knocked up," Holt murmured when they were alone. "Then there'd be no doubting you were mine."

Naiya let out the breath she didn't know she'd been holding. "There would also be no mission of revenge because you'd be too busy changing diapers and rocking your daughter to sleep. Doesn't really fit with the big, bad, outlaw biker image." She pulled away and gave her clothing one last check.

"Lots of Sinners got kids," Holt said. "Dax has five boys and he goes to the school and their sports games wearing his cut, not hiding who he is or what he does. And Cade's got three kids. They moved to a house on Dax's street 'cause the people there were accepting of Dax's biker ways. Zane's got a boy he didn't even know he had, and there's rumors Shaggy's got kids all over the place with different women, but he never sees them 'cause his life is about the club . . ."

His voice trailed off and Naiya caught a flicker of

sadness in his eyes. "You're talking about them as if they're still your family," she said gently.

"They were my family. Not any more." He shook himself and slid an arm around her waist. "Guess we gotta get on that bus. He'll be watching. I think we put him off, but guys like that don't give up easy."

"Where will we go?"

"Conundrum."

"Isn't that where the Sinners are based?"

He leaned down, nuzzled her neck. "It's the only place you'll be safe. Black Jacks can't cross the border without risking death. Sinners own the cops since we got Deputy Sheriff Benson on our payroll and a coupla others, so they don't do much except handle civilian problems and petty crime. We'll lie low until I'm ready to move. I got some ideas about how we can spend the time."

"I thought your plan was using me as bait," she said dryly. "That's not going to work if the Black Jacks can't get to me."

Holt's face tightened, and he pulled her into his chest. "I got a new plan. One that doesn't put you in danger and keeps you close."

"Lucky me."

A slow smile spread across Holt's face. "You are lucky, 'cause once we find a place to stay, we're gonna pick up where we left off, and this time no one's gonna interrupt us."

★ FOURTEEN ★

TANK

"What the hell happened to you the other night?" Banks handed Tank a beer, raising his voice above the roar of the crowd as Rider's house band took to the stage. "Never saw you drink so much before. I went to find someone to take you home, but when I turned around you were gone."

Tank put the bottle to his lips trying to come up with a suitable lie. After being warned off Ella, he could hardly tell Banks he had spent the night with her, albeit he couldn't remember anything. He'd been drunk before. Hell, he'd spent the years before he met T-Rex half cut. But he'd never passed out. Never lost his memory. Never fucked a woman and not remembered it the next day. Something was definitely off about that night. And the worst thing was, he didn't even know if he'd said anything that could get him into trouble with the club.

"Don't remember much." The cold bitter liquid slid over his tongue, grounding him in the moment, a contrast to the surreal feeling of waking up alone in an utterly pristine, ultra modern white room. At first he thought he'd died and gone to fucking heaven, but T-Rex wasn't there, and given all the bad shit he'd done in his life, he knew the place he was going would be colored red. And yet, it had to be hell, 'cause why didn't he remember doing such a hot babe, why were his clothes still on, and why was he all alone?

Maybe that's how it was with smart women. They didn't get all emotional about sex. They were busy with their work, and although they enjoyed cutting loose, it didn't mean they were looking for more than a good time. Although he didn't know if she'd enjoyed their night together because he'd drunk himself into a fucking coma.

"Well, at least you got away from Ella," Banks said. "I heard some shit about her that would make even the toughest dude turn and run. She's fucking merciless when it comes to getting a story. There's nothing she won't do."

"Yeah, lucky me." He took another sip of his beer. If she was only after a story, why the hell did she invite him home after he'd made it clear he wasn't about to share any information about the club? Had he missed something? He'd never been with a smart woman before. Maybe because smart women were attracted to smart men. Tank loved mechanics, tinkering with engines and machines, and fixing his bike, but he had no formal training or education. Sure he was loyal, strong, brave, and a damned good shot, but he had nothing to offer a woman like Ella.

Jagger joined them at the bar, and Banks poured him a shot of Scotch.

"Good to see you kicking back, brother." Jagger lifted his glass to Tank. "These are hard times, and sometimes you gotta step back and have a bit of fun." His glaze flicked to former Deputy Sherriff Benson, now a lowly prospect, wiping tables in the corner, and an evil smile spread across his face. "Prospect." He waved Benson over, and Tank's mood lifted as Benson hauled ass across the bar. He hoped Jagger kept Benson as a permanent prospect. There was nothing as entertaining as watching the former Deputy Sheriff doing all the grunt work for the club when only three months earlier he had the power to lock them up.

"Sir." Benson pressed his lips together in grim anticipation of the humiliating task Jagger had in store for him.

"Hold the bottle. Fill my glass—" Jagger cut himself off and frowned. "Why did Gunner let that girl into the bar? No way is she legal."

Tank looked up as Gunner led a pretty, young blonde with fire-red nails through the bar. He figured she was eighteen at the most, but her eyes suggested someone much older.

"What the fuck?" Banks grumbled. "I'm gonna be fucking shut down before I get this place going."

"Girl's looking for Benson." Gunner gave her a gentle shove in Benson's direction. "Here he is but he's not Deputy Sheriff anymore. Now he's our slave."

Jagger lifted an eyebrow. "Didn't think you were the type to go for teenagers, prospect."

"I'm not," Benson said. "I've never seen her before in my life."

Tank joined in the raucous laughter. How many times had women come to the club or the bar and a brother threw out that line? Hell, even he and T-Rex had used it a couple of times when a few skanky bitches tracked them down after a wild night.

"What do you want with our prospect, sweetheart?" Jagger finished his drink and nodded at Banks to pour him another.

"I met a guy in Missoula." She stared at the floor, twisted her hands as she talked. "He . . . rescued me from a bad situation and told me to come to Conundrum and look up Deputy Sheriff Benson. I was supposed to ask him to take me to the Sinners. I went to the address he wrote down, but when I got to the police station, they got angry and told me I'd probably find him here."

"Well you've found him." Benson pointed to his chest. "But what business do you have with the Sinners?"

Her voice dropped, almost to a whisper. "He said I should ask for Tank, and he would hook me up at the club."

"He knew Tank?" Jagger turned his full attention to the girl. "Did he tell you who he was?"

She shook her head. "Didn't know much about him. He was about his height." She pointed at Tank. "But a lot thinner. Long, blond hair. He was wearing a shirt with a beaver on it."

Tank's heart skipped a beat. "Dark blue? Yellow beaver?"

"Yeah. I think so," she said. "I mean it was kinda dark when I met him, and I wasn't paying much attention. He had a kick-ass bike though. It was huge. All chromed up. I think it was green."

"It's him. It's T-Rex." Tank's body shook as if he'd just been shot with adrenaline. "Fuck. Jagger. That was him I saw in Still Water. Same bike. Same shirt. Same description. He knew my name." He grabbed Jagger's cut in his fist. "He thought Benson was still a Deputy."

"Tank." Jagger's voice was low with warning. "Hand."

Tank jerked his hand away as if he'd been burned. "It sounds like T-Rex. He's got a big heart. This is exactly the kind of thing he would do. We gotta go get him, Jag. Now. We need to send a team to Missoula . . ."

"Tank." Jagger cut him off with a bark. "Slow it down. This could be a trap. If it was T-Rex, and he got out, why isn't he here? Why is he driving around Missoula dressed in a sweatshirt picking up hookers instead of giving you a call?" He lifted the girl's chin with his finger. "Isn't that right, sugar?"

Tank startled when tears spilled down her cheeks. "I didn't want that life," she sobbed. "He got me out. He said Benson and the Sinners would help me."

Jagger gave her a sympathetic look. "Benson's not in a position to help you any more. It's me who decides what happens to you, and I'll be needing a lot more information about your meeting with that guy on the bike before I make any decision." He stared pointedly at Tank as he emphasized the word "any."

Tank felt the refusal like a punch to the gut. "But—"

Jagger shook his head. "I'm not saying we don't go check this out. If T-Rex is out there, I want to find him as much as you, but we need to know what we're up against. My job is to keep my brothers safe. There are pieces to this puzzle that make sense and pieces that don't. Snake said he was dead. Now I got a girl who met a guy who knows your name, rides a fancy bike, got long hair and a beaver shirt. Maybe she's making it up. Maybe she's a Black Jack rat. I'm not sending anyone out on the road until I know for sure what's going on."

"Let me go," Tank begged. "Just me. I'll take the risk. If it's a lie, I'll find out. If it's a trap, I'll spring it. If he's lost, I'll find him and bring him home. If someone's gonna die, let it be me."

He couldn't go against Jagger or the club. But how the hell could he stay here when T-Rex was out there? Needing him. Just the thought of T-Rex alone and hurting made him feel sick inside.

"Christ." Jagger scrubbed his hand over his face. "If you feel that strongly about it, then go. But you're not gonna find him in the dark. Wait until morning, so I can talk to this girl and make some calls so you got some support clubs behind you if things go wrong. And I'll want your word that if anything feels off, or you see any Jacks about, you turn around and come home."

Tank let out a relieved breath. This is why he respected and admired Jagger, would follow him no matter what. He listened, not just to a brother's words, but also to his heart. He was firm but fair. And he cared about his brothers.

Tank's phone buzzed, and he pulled it out and checked the message from the unidentified number.

Watch the ten o'clock news. See you at midnight. Ella.

Ella? He hadn't given her his number. Damn bitch must have been in his phone while he was asleep. How did she get past his security? He scrubbed his hand over his face. What else had she seen? And what the fuck was going to be on the ten o'clock news?

★ FIFTEEN ★

"I've never stayed in a place like this."

Naiya toyed with the ring on her finger as Holt pushed open the door to the penthouse suite of the Conundrum Park Lane Hotel. For a man who professed to hate planning, he'd thought of everything. From ditching the bike to hiding the money and weapons, and from paying off the bus driver to make a pit stop outside of town so he could pick up their bags, to paying him again to drop them off in Conundrum.

"Me neither, but no one was complaining when I paid in cash." He closed and bolted the door behind them, and Naiya drank it all in. Blending an Art Deco–inspired interior with modern luxury style, the room contained a massive, dark-wood four-poster bed, white-and-cream furnishings, period furniture, and a marble bathroom as big as her living room. Floor-to-ceiling windows took up an entire wall, framing the bright lights of Conundrum spread out below them.

"You can barely see the Bridger Mountains in the dark," she said. "It looks like the lights just end, and then there's nothing."

"The Sinners' clubhouse is right at the base of the mountains," Tank said coming up behind her. "If you look real close, you might be able to see a light or two behind the trees. There's nothing else out there except us, which makes it easy to catch anyone who comes near the clubhouse."

Us. Unconsciously, he still thought of himself as a Sinner. What would happen to him if he went through with his plan for revenge? Naiya's life had always been about survival. No one had ever needed her the way Holt needed her. He was lost, alone, confused, and in pain. He was, at heart, a good man, and his plan for revenge—the crutch that had helped him survive in the dungeon—was now tearing him apart. He needed to hear the truth from someone he trusted because if he was wrong about Tank and the Sinners, he would never be able to live with himself. A protector who went against his nature would be destroyed.

"So the Sinners are based outside Conundrum?"

"Technically, we're still in the border, and everyone understands that it's our town," he said, again unconsciously including himself when he referred to his club. "We've got a lot of businesses operating within the town limits—strip clubs, night clubs, restaurants, garages, bars . . ." He pointed to a collection of buildings near the center of town. "That's Rider's Bar. It's a Sinner bar, and when the brothers aren't at the clubhouse, that's where they'll be. Tank and I had our own table at the back. You only get that when you get appointed to the board. Tank called it a chick magnet. The girls were always hanging around those tables."

Naiya looked back over her shoulder and huffed. "Not that I'm jealous or anything, but I'm not really interested in hearing about all your other women."

"She's jealous." He pressed a kiss to her nape. "I like it."

"You can like it alone." She slid away from him and walked toward the bathroom, needing some time alone to think through what she needed to do. "I'm going to take a bath. It's been too long, and I'm feeling too grungy to be in a place like this."

"Good idea. I'll join you."

Naiya stopped him with a hand in the air. "You're staying out here to watch the door. I feel like an imposter in this hotel in my dirty beaver shirt, with a duffel bag, a giant bag of cash and two bags of guns. I'm terrified someone is going to burst in and haul us out of here and throw us on the street, or worse, in jail after our little brush with the ATF."

"Anyone comes through that door, I'll shoot them." Holt pulled out his weapon and brandished it at the door.

"That's sweet in a fucked-up, outlaw-biker kinda way." She pushed open the bathroom door. "I'll leave you to it."

After a long soak in the tub and a scrub with the most expensive toiletries she'd ever had the pleasure of using, Naiya joined Holt on the bed in front of a sixty-inch television.

"What are you watching?" She tightened the belt on her fluffy white bathrobe, giving serious consideration to adding it to their collection of stolen goods when they left the hotel.

"Nothing yet. Three hundred channels so far and nothing appeals." He tugged on her belt and pulled her against him. "What do you like to watch?"

Naiya nibbled her bottom lip. "Um . . . you probably won't be interested."

"Tell me."

"SyFy." She buried her head in his chest and Holt laughed.

"Tank's favorite channel. It's fucking scary how much you two have in common. I thought I'd finally get away from being forced to watch shows about aliens, guys with pointy ears, and big-ass space ships. Let's give it a go." He flipped at rapid speed to SyFy and Naiya shrieked in delight.

"Oh. My. God. It's a cult classic. The 1980 version of *Flash Gordon*. It's so good, Holt. You'll love it. It's about a football player who goes into outer space and faces down a super villain named Ming the Merciless. It's the ultimate in camp." She snatched the remote from his hand and turned up the volume. So what if it was the ultimate in geekiness. Some pleasures were just meant to be shared.

"You weren't even born in 1980." Holt settled on the bed, tucking Naiya beside him, her head against his shoulder. "Neither was I, so I'm guessing the special effects are gonna leave a lot to be desired."

They watched the opening credits, and Holt stiffened. "That sounds like Queen."

"It is Queen. They did the soundtrack."

"What a damn waste of good music." He stroked her hair as if he knew she was about to rear up and lambast him for putting down one of the classic science fiction movies of all time.

"Shhhh. You're ruining the mood." She snuggled into his chest, toying aimlessly with his belt.

Holt shifted on the bed, his arm tightening around her. "You keep playing down there and the mood's gonna change real fast to something that doesn't involve some pansy ass prancing around. Seriously. That's the hero? I could kick his ass in less than thirty seconds. Who talks like that?"

"It was the 1980s." Naiya poked him in the stomach. "Now hush up. It gets better."

But what got better was Holt's reaction to the movie. Every few minutes, he huffed or snorted, interrupting her with his running commentary about the stilted way the characters said their lines, the cheese ball drama, the retro set design, the special effects, and . . . his favorite, the over-the-top costumes.

"A real man wouldn't dress in red spandex," he said laughing at Flash Gordon's first costume change. "Anyone tried to put that on me and I'd shoot them."

And then, after seeing yet another scantily clad woman—"Jesus Fuck!" he shouted. "It's one fetishistic costume after another. I want to see you in something like that. Especially pink."

Thoroughly enjoying his commentary, she wasn't ready when he shot up, spilling her off his chest as he roared with laughter.

"Jesus Christ. What are the Hawkmen wearing?" His chest heaved, and his eyes teared. "I wish Tank could see this. I'll bet he knows this movie. Next time I see him, I'm gonna give him fucking hell for not telling me about it."

Naiya smiled, her pleasure at his laughter bittersweet. She wondered if he realized how often he talked about Tank, how Tank was still a part of his life. How much he loved him. He would never get over losing Tank, especially if he was the one to pull the trigger.

"What are you smiling about, aside from this disaster of a movie?" He pulled her up between his legs, her back to his chest, the bulge of his erection unmistakable against her ass.

"You," she said. "I've never heard you laugh before. Really laugh. I'll have to show you some more of my favorite geek movies so I can hear you laugh again."

"Like my geeky girl." His lips whispered over her ear, his breath warm on her skin. "And her comic-book hero fetish."

Naiya glanced down at her ring, twisted it around her hand. "I never thought of it that way, but it's true. My favorite heroes are from comic books."

"What about me?"

She turned in his lap, slid her hands over his shoulders, her knees on either side of his hips. "If you put on a pair of those black leather Hawkman Speedos, you might just make the cut."

With a low growl, Holt pulled her closer until she could feel the beat of his heart against her breast. "Pathetic earthling," he teased. "No one can save you now." He nuzzled her neck, and desire sizzled through her veins.

"I've created a geek," she said with a laugh.

He cut her off with a kiss, his lips soft and warm, and his arms holding her tight. "You saved one." His mouth moved over hers, and she gave herself over to the moment— the pounding of her heart, the ache between her thighs, the spiral of heat curled low in her belly.

Holt rolled them until she lay back on the bed. He straddled her hips and smiled. "Gonna see my soft, sexy geek girl now." He tugged at her robe, pulling it open. "Gonna go slow and taste every last geektastic inch."

Naiya froze when he bared her completely, her nipples beading as cool air rushed over her heated skin. "Maybe we should . . . you know . . . get down to business." She didn't do slow. Or soft. Or gentle. Sex was hard and fast and then over. It was about the act, not the feeling. Something to endure, not savor. And yet behind the bar, Holt had focused on her pleasure, and for the first time, so had she.

"Maybe I want more than business." He traced a warm finger over the curve of her breast. "Maybe I want to see you, touch you, make you lose control and come over and over again until you're so wet and ready for me you're begging for my cock."

"That won't happen." She'd never asked for sex. Never wanted it except to wash away Viper's stain. And then it hadn't been pleasurable. It had been necessary.

A smile tugged at the corners of his lips. "You should know by now I'm not one to turn down a challenge."

"You're not one to turn down anything."

"Especially not when she's all I think about," he said.

Naiya's cheeks flushed and she dropped her gaze, but there was something sinfully arousing about the fact he'd been looking at her, thinking about her that way when she'd been totally oblivious to his interest.

"Like it when you're shy." He cupped her breasts in his warm palms. "I like that my strong, independent woman is vulnerable inside. I like that she needs something from me."

"I need a lot of things from you, it seems." Her nipples hardened under his touch, and he rolled them, tugging gently until her breaths came in short pants.

"Just like I need a lot of things from you." His hands slid down, and he traced one finger along the elastic of her panties. "I want these off."

"Maybe I'll just . . . keep them on." She drew his hand away. "Or I could . . . look after you."

"Then I'll be missing the best part." He leaned over and tore the panties away.

Naiya gasped and her hand flew to her hip, fingers splayed in what she hoped he took as a casual gesture.

But, of course, Holt missed nothing, and particularly not her attempt to hide the long, thin white scars, angled down to meet in the middle.

"What's this?" Pushing himself to sitting, he tugged her hand away. Defeated, she looked away, a lump forming in her throat.

"V for Viper." Her voice dropped to a whisper. "He did it after the tattoo so that every man would know I was his."

She squeezed her eyes shut, wishing she'd turned off the lights like she usually did when she had sex to avoid the inevitable questions.

The bed creaked. She heard the rustle of clothing. A soft groan. And then Holt's warm tongue on her stomach.

"H for Holt." He licked the letter over her scar, and Naiya trembled, clutched the soft silk sheets in her hands.

"Don't."

"N for Naiya." He licked again, and emotion welled up in her chest.

"Please, Holt. Stop."

"B for beautiful." This time he traced the letter with his lips, his breath warm on her skin.

"You don't have to do this," she whispered, stroking his hair.

Sliding lower, he kissed her scar again. "M for Mine." And then he slid down, kissing his way over the soft skin of her abdomen to her mound.

"Open for me, darlin'. I got more writing to do."

"Holt." She threaded her fingers through his hair, undecided about whether she wanted him to keep going or stop. She'd never let any man go down on her, finding the act too intimate, leaving her vulnerable.

"You've never been tasted?"

"No," she whispered.

He paused, studied her, then he pushed himself up, dropped his weight over her body. "Let me taste you. Let me be the first one to give you that kind of pleasure. I'll go slowly. I'll be gentle. You hold on and stop me if I do something you don't like." Then he grinned. "But I guarantee that's not gonna happen."

The smile did her in. He didn't smile often, but when he did his face lit up and she caught a glimpse of what she assumed was the man he used to be—the man he had been before Viper took him. Kinda like the girl she had been before that terrible night at the party. "Okay."

His smile broadened and he slanted his mouth over hers, caressing her lips with his tongue. Such a gentle, tender kiss, as if they were starting all over again. She touched her tongue to his, wanting more than gentle, wanting the kind of kiss he'd given her before, hard and hungry and full of passion, but he pulled away. "I'll start here." And then his mouth brushed against her cheek, her jaw, down the column of her neck, his lips cool and smooth, the rasp of his beard deliciously erotic.

Naiya trembled, her body heating with every nip and lick. He moved carefully, sweeping down over her shoulder and then back up to her mouth, then down the other side, biting this time, a light pressure on the sensitive spot between her neck and shoulder blade that made goose bumps rise on her arms.

When he returned to her mouth, his lips firm and smooth, she threaded her hands through his hair and pulled him down, thrusting her tongue between his lips. She wanted more. Hard. Sensation. Obliteration.

"Ah ah ah." Holt pulled back. "You don't get to be in control, darlin'. This is about me making you feel good." He sat back and smoothed his hands up her forearms to her wrists. "Should I restrain you? Tie these pretty wrists together so you can't try to run the show?"

Her pulse kicked up a notch and she shook her head violently, unable to voice her fear.

His face softened. "How about you fold your arms under your head and give me a promise not to move them no matter what I do?"

She bit her lip, considering. No restraints. Her legs were free and her hands if she chose to use them. And she'd let men touch her before, although only where she told them. "I promise." She folded her arms and tucked her hands behind her head.

The lines at the corners of his eyes crinkled and his gaze heated. "You're beautiful, darlin'. When I was down in that dungeon I thought I'd never touch a woman again, tried to remember what it was like. But you are more than I ever imagined. I'm gonna take my sweet time enjoying your body, and you're just gonna lie there for me and feel good."

His hand covered her breast, his fingers circling her nipples one at a time until they were hard and peaked. She arched into his touch, needing more.

Holt didn't oblige.

Instead, he twisted her nipples, squeezing hard. Naiya gasped as a stab of excitement shot down her body, straight to her core.

"She likes that," he murmured, half to himself. He alternated between breasts, cupping and squeezing the soft flesh, then pinching her nipples until her pussy throbbed and she had to thread her fingers together behind her head to keep her promise.

"Should I keep going?" Satisfaction glimmered in his eyes, and Naiya nodded. She didn't just want him to keep going. She wanted him never to stop.

Holt leaned over and closed his lips around one swollen nipple, swirling his tongue around the peak. Heat sizzled through her veins, and she could feel herself get wetter. He sucked her nipple deep and then nipped with just enough pressure that she let out a low groan.

Naiya stiffened. That groan was real, not faked. For a minute there she'd lost control. Just like she'd lost control with Viper when he'd made her . . .

Holt drew back, his sharp eyes on her face. "Did I hurt you?"

"No." She unlocked her fingers, and then forced them together again, remembering her promise. "But maybe I should look after you. This must be hard for you after so long."

He stroked her cheek. "After so long, I want to take my time, and nothing gets me off like the sexy noises you make when you're enjoying what I'm doing to you."

Enjoy? She endured sex for the few moments of intimacy that came after; the feeling of being held, imagining she was safe and no one could ever touch her. Sex was a price to be paid.

Holt slid his hand between her legs, dipped a finger into her wet, slick center, and then wiped his finger along the inside of her leg. Although she knew she should be horrified, she found his actions incredibly erotic.

"You were enjoying yourself."

Hard to deny it with her wetness glistening on her thigh. "Yes."

"Then let me keep going. I haven't even gotten to the good part yet."

Her body wanted more, even though her mind was balking at the thought of giving up more control. Holt wasn't like any of the bikers who had come to their apartment to give her mom drugs in exchange for sex; or the bikers at the Black Jack clubhouse who would take the first sweet butt they saw when the need struck; or Viper who just took. But what if he was? What if this was all an act, and the minute she let down her guard . . . ?

And what if he was for real? Maybe the Sinners weren't all like the Jacks.

As if he could read her thoughts, he gave her a reassuring smile. "I got a lot of anger in me," he said softly. "Always have, although nothing like I got now. Sometimes I'm afraid it will consume me. But when I'm with you, it . . . just . . . fades. I'll never hurt you. Never push you farther than you want to go. You're safe with me. You got my word on that."

Safe. It was the one thing she had always craved. The word she needed to hear to let herself go.

His mouth covered hers again, and her anxiety faded. He tasted sweet and faintly of . . . what she could have sworn was lipstick.

Before she could ask, his hand settled on her stomach, then trailed over her hips. He eased down the bed and feathered kisses along the sensitive skin of her inner thighs.

"Open for me, darlin'."

The low rumble of his voice rippled through her, and she did as he asked. Holt stroked a finger through her folds, a barely there touch that had her angling her hips for more.

Holt chuckled. "You're so wet, but I think we can make you wetter." His finger circled her clit, up and around, but never touching, and then through her folds until her pussy felt swollen, aching for release.

God, he was nothing like the bikers she'd watched at the Black Jack clubhouse as she hid with the other club brats, learning the facts of life too early and in the most brutal way. Until Ally had set her up with regular guys, she had assumed sex was about taking, the focus on the man's pleasure, the woman a means to an end and nothing more. Even after she'd started dating, it wasn't hard to push men into that mold, forgo her own pleasure to get it over and done.

He leaned down and licked her clit, every so lightly, his tongue warm and wet. She jerked at the exquisite sensation, and Holt placed his hands over her hips holding her down. "Don't think about going anywhere. Not until I'm done."

His tongue slid down through her wet heat and back up again, circled her clit, stroking, lapping, so soft . . . relentless. Tension coiled inside her with every lick, her body tightening. A flush rose in her cheeks, but when she bucked against him, he held her still, his control giving her more assurance than fear. He slid his fingers along her folds, stroked along the sides of the little nub, and then pushed inside.

She sucked in a breath at the sensation of rough skin sliding over sensitive, swollen tissue. Fisting her hands behind her head, she dug her heels into the bed as he stroked in and out, driving her higher and higher.

Holt added a second finger, pumping them slowly as his tongue flicked over her clit, and she gave up on worrying about who he was or what he was doing, how she was re-acting, or her need for control. Instead, she let go, gave her-self over to his soft tongue and his gentle fingers and the damn relentless drive of her body toward release.

Holt hummed his approval, increasing his pace, alter-nating his fingers and tongue. Every sensation coalesced into one hot, urgent ball of need, her nerve endings raw and waiting. Another lick. Another slide. Her inner mus-cles contracted around him; her fingers dug painfully into her scalp. She angled her hips, arched into his mouth, tak-ing what he offered. Wanting more.

"There she is," he whispered, and then his rough tongue slid directly over her clit.

Her ecstasy released like an arrow, shooting white-hot lightening through her in relentless spasms of blissful heat. She loosened her hands and threaded her fingers through his hair, holding him still as wave after wave of pleasure crashed through her body. He licked again, thrust again, drawing out her orgasm until she sank into the bed, her body limp and languid beneath him.

"I never . . . no one ever . . ." Her bottom lip quivered.

"Another first." He gave her a warm smile. "And not the last. I'm not done with you, darlin', unless you want to stop."

She liked that he didn't assume. That he kept asking if she wanted to keep going even though he was very clearly aroused. That he offered instead of taking. She wanted to give something back, not to get it over with, but because she wanted him, wanted to give him the kind of pleasure he'd given her. But more than that, she wanted to feel close to him. Intimate. Even naked, exposed, and emotionally raw, she felt safe with Holt.

"I don't want to stop. I want you."

He stroked her hair back from her face, and gently pulled her to sit. "Might need some help off with the clothes."

"Of course." She pushed herself up and slid her hands under his shirt, carefully pushed it up over his chest, avoiding the bandages. Although his injuries were healing, the marks of his ordeal were still clearly visible on his skin. On impulse, Naiya leaned close and pressed her lips over one of his scars.

Holt drew in a deep breath, and his hand slid through her hair. "Something to remember him by."

"Like me."

His jaw tightened, and his hand fisted her hair. "I'm gonna give you good memories so that when Viper and I are both gone, all you'll remember is the feel of my lips on your skin."

Emotion welled up in her throat at the brutal reminder that the path he'd chosen to follow didn't include her. And although he'd never been anything but clear about where he was headed, she knew in her heart, she didn't want to let him go.

Steeling herself, she pushed his shirt up, and kneeled on the bed to tug it over his head. Despite his ordeal, he was still well muscled albeit thin, his shoulders broad, and his biceps thick. She slid her hands down his torso, over the cuts of his obliques to his narrow waist and tugged open his belt.

"Where did you get these clothes? You smell of cheap perfume."

"Pimp." He stilled, and Naiya looked up for more explanation, but the firm line of his jaw told her it wouldn't be forthcoming.

"Oh." She didn't want to think about the pimp who had given Holt the clothes or the kind of women Holt would have encountered during that meeting. She didn't want to think about his comments in the bar or how he knew the cost of a blowjob in Missoula. Just like she hadn't wanted to think about why Maurice stopped coming to her place every night or why he suddenly thought his place was too small for them both to hang out or why he sometimes smelled of perfume. Willful blindness was sometimes a blessing in disguise.

"I saved a young girl who was walking the streets," he said into the silence. "Took out her pimp, gave her some money, and sent her to find a cop I know here in Conundrum so he could take her to the Sinners for help."

"More killing," she said, heart sore.

"That's the world I live in." He cupped her jaw in his hand. "The pimp was a piece of shit who'd forced her into prostitution when he found her on the street. The world is a better place without him in it."

Naiya sat back on her heels. "Did you . . . and the girl . . . ?"

"No."

She breathed out a relieved sigh. "It's not like I was jealous or anything. It's just a . . . safety concern."

Holt chuckled. "You were jealous. You want me all to yourself." He cupped the bulge in his jeans and gave it a squeeze. "I don't blame you, darlin'."

Naiya snorted in derision. "I see nothing is wrong with your ego."

"Nothing is wrong with any part of me." He lifted her hand to his fly. "But let's test it out to make sure."

Without hesitation, Naiya ripped open his jeans and eased his clothing over his hips. His cock, thick and hard, bounced gently in her direction. Holt's hand found her head and he gripped her hard.

Sensing his need, she shoved his clothing down, pushing his jeans carefully over the bandages on his ankles, injured by the cuffs Viper had used to tether him on the wall.

"Now I have you naked and available for my pleasure," she teased to hide her dismay at the damage Viper had done to his beautiful body. Scars, slashes, bruises, and cuts marred almost every inch of his skin.

"Endless pleasure coming your way. But we need a condom." He left her on the bed and walked across the room to the dark, lacquered dining table near the window where he'd dumped one of the bags. Naiya took in his lean, muscular body, and his perfect ass. He was breathtaking now. How had he looked before Viper got his hands on him?

"Come over here, beautiful girl." He ripped open the condom with his teeth and sheathed himself. "I got a need to see you laid out on this table so I can fuck you overlooking Conundrum."

"Is that supposed to turn me on?" She slid off the bed and walked toward him, swallowing back all the small dissatisfactions with her body as he drank her in with his heated gaze.

"You're already turned on. I can see your wet pussy from where I'm standing."

Her cheeks flamed, and she scrambled to find something to say to cover her embarrassment. "Did you get the condoms from the pimp, too?"

He lifted an eyebrow. "They were in the bag of clothes Ally left for us. I thought you'd asked for them."

"Me?" She stared at him aghast. "I wouldn't assume . . ."

"Ally did." He pulled her into his chest, his erection pressed hard against her stomach, his body hot against hers. Naiya ground her hips against him, and Holt groaned.

"Don't think I can take much more, darlin'. I've been wanting you, seems like forever." He slid his hands beneath her ass and lifted her so his cock was poised at her entrance.

"Yes?"

There it was again. Asking. Not taking. What would he do if she said no? His cock was thick and hard, swollen with arousal. Was there a point at which a man could be pushed too far? When he wouldn't be able to stop?

As if he could read her thoughts, he brushed his lips over her cheek. "Whatever you want. However long you want to take."

Maybe another man wouldn't be able to stop, but Holt was different. She trusted that he would, and that trust gave her the courage to go on. Gritting her teeth, she braced her arms on his shoulders and lowered herself down.

"Christ." His hands tightened on her ass, the cords in his neck straining. "Oh Jesus. Fuck. Naiya, darlin', you feel damn good."

Not as good as the feeling of his thick, hard cock pushing through her swollen tissue. Her breath hitched, and she levered herself up, then eased back down. Up and down, with Holt's hands firm around her, his eyes blazing with sensual passion.

Her clit throbbed, and she increased the pace. Holt's biceps strained, and his hips rocked, meeting her rhythm, but it wasn't enough. Not hard enough or deep enough. She wanted to feel his power, his passion. She wanted him to be in control.

"Holt . . ." She didn't know how to ask, had never asked for what she needed. But this time, with him, she fought for the words. "I want you . . . to . . ."

She didn't have to finish. Gritting his teeth, he released her, spun her around, and pushed her down on the table. One hand in her hair, the other on her hip, he kicked her legs apart and thrust hard into her wet center.

Oh God. So perfect. He filled her completely. She trembled, her breasts pressing against the cool wood, hands white-knuckled on the edge.

Holt groaned and slid deeper. "You're so fucking tight, and hot and wet, darlin'. I've been waiting a long time to take you like this." He squeezed her ass cheeks, and she quivered under his hands. Then he slid his fingers over her clit, making her moan.

"Not gonna forget about you," he murmured, leaning over her back, his lips warm against her ear. "You're gonna come with me."

He started slow, letting her stretch to accommodate him, then he went hard, plunging into her, letting himself go. With one hand in her hair, he yanked her head back, forcing her to arch up, his fingers skimming over her clit, building her higher and higher, until finally, she came, her inner muscles tightening around him. As if he'd been waiting for her, Holt roared and thrust deep, his cock erupting in forceful jerks that drew out her own orgasm, ripping a moan from her throat.

When his cock stopped pulsing, Holt collapsed over her back. She could feel his heart pounding against her, his breaths rasping in her ear.

"You okay, darlin'?" he whispered.

"Yeah." She shivered, and he lifted her off the table and wrapped his arms around her. For the longest time they stood, looking out over the city. They were safe up here where no one could find them, but nothing good awaited them below. Death. Destruction. Jail. The loss of all her dreams and everything she had worked for since the night she'd left home.

"I don't want to leave here, Holt." She leaned back against him, sinking into his solid warmth. "I don't want you to go after Viper and the Sinners. I don't want anything to happen to you."

Holt tightened his arms around her waist. "I was kinda thinking that myself. When I left that dungeon, I was prepared to die for revenge 'cause I had nothing to live for. I never imagined I'd wind up here. Now I got you, and I want to keep you safe. I don't feel like the same man who walked out of that dungeon, but I'm not the man who went into it either. Only thing that still makes sense is that Viper's got to die."

"When I was standing in the cemetery saying good-bye to my mother," Naiya said, "I never imagined I'd wind up here, either. I thought after the funeral I'd go back to my normal life."

Holt cupped her breast, gaze it a lazy squeeze. "What was your normal?"

Naiya shrugged. "A steady partner, a good job, friends, and maybe one day a house and if I could get over my issues, kids. Now I've lost Maurice and my job opportunity. I can't contact my friends or access my bank account. I've only got the clothes on my back, and I can't go home because I'm on the run from Viper. I've committed crimes that mean I likely will never work in a crime lab. But I've had sex—real sex, and I've met someone who makes me feel safe and who makes me laugh and makes me eat donuts in bites. I've lived more in the last week then I've lived in the last seven years. How can I go back to my regular life?"

"How can you not?" Holt released her abruptly, leaving her bereft. "There's no future with me."

She turned to face him. "There is if you go back to the Sinners and hear them out."

"Not gonna happen." His face tightened, and his lips pressed tight together.

"Holt." She reached out to touch him, but he was already walking away.

★ SIXTEEN ★

TANK

To Ella's credit, she didn't even look scared when Tank kicked in her door.

Nor did she look surprised. In fact, she seemed to be waiting for him.

And that just pissed him off even more.

"Goddamnit, bitch." He kicked over her coffee table and yanked her off the white leather couch. Her white-silk dressing gown slid softly over her body, the front gaping wide, revealing the crescents of her lush, creamy breasts, and the barest shadow at the apex of her thighs.

Tank forced his gaze away, focused on his anger. "What the fuck were you thinking saying that on the fucking news? Now the fucking cops are gonna think the Sinners did the hit on the Black Jacks up in Still Water. The ATF will be all over the clubhouse with warrants coming out their wazoo." His voice rose to a shout. "Jagger's going to go out of his fucking mind, and he's gonna come for you."

He didn't know if Jagger had seen the news, but no doubt he would get word about it soon. Ella had been up in Still Water, reporting that the police had found two Black Jacks down by the lake, the victims of what they believed to be a biker-related shooting. Ella had referred to "a source" who had suggested the murders had been carried out by members of a rival MC, the Sinner's Tribe.

Ella tilted her head to the side, and the silken strands of her hair brushed over his hand. "Hello, James," she said coolly. "Nice to see you again."

Tank drew in a ragged breath, inhaling the rich, sultry scent of her perfume. All his blood rushed to his groin and he cursed inwardly. *Son of a bitch*. He was here to deal with this fucking mess, not fuck the woman who threatened to bring down his club.

"Shut. The. Fuck. Up. You put my club at risk." If she'd been a dude, he would have resorted to violence. Punches. Kicks. A few broken bones. Then he would have pulled out his weapon. But he couldn't hit a woman. He saw no point in using his strength against someone weaker than him, despite the fact his dad had not hesitated to use his fists on Tank.

As if she knew he wouldn't hurt her, Ella smiled. "I was helping you. I did a little digging, talked to a couple of my friends in the police department. It looks like the dead biker's bike might have been the same bike you saw at the gas station. I checked the gas station video on your phone when you were sleeping and made a few notes. The bike you saw matches one of the bikes on the list forensics drew up from a partial track on the main road and was registered in the dead biker's name. If the Jacks tortured your friend, it makes sense that he would go after them. He is a Sinner after all. So it was a win win for both of us. I got a story, and you got your man."

"I told you no story. You're gonna get me kicked out of own fucking club. Now sit the fuck down so I can think." He paced her living room as she settled on her couch. How could he get out of this? If Jagger kicked him out of the club, he wouldn't have any support if he went after T-Rex, and what would he do without his brothers? Where would he go? The club was his goddamned fucking life.

"James . . ."

"Don't call me that," he barked. "Name is Tank." The name the club gave him when he'd earned the cut, not because he was built like one, which he was, but because he'd stolen a tank from an army base one night on a drunken dare from T-Rex just so they could take pictures of themselves in a tank. He'd taken a lot of heat from Jagger for his stupidity, but he wouldn't have traded that moment for anything. He still had the selfie he took of him and T-Rex, leaning back on the tank, grins on their faces, beers raised in a "fuck you" salute.

A selfie she had probably seen when she went through his phone. What else had she seen and how the hell had she unlocked it?

"Okay . . . Tank." She crossed one leg over the other and her gown slid up revealing the creamy expanse of her thigh. Fuck, she had nice legs. And nice tits. But then he knew that about her 'cause he'd watched her that night T-Rex warned him away. He probably knew more than that about her, but damned if he could remember their night together.

"I didn't mean to get you into trouble with your club." She loosened her belt, letting the gown fall to the sides of her hips. Now he could see her cleavage, the soft skin of her stomach, and . . . Fuck. Her pussy was bare. Tank bit back a groan. Nothing he liked better than smooth, soft, bare pussy.

"I didn't disclose my source, and really, you didn't give me the information. I deduced it. And I might be wrong. Maybe it was a drug deal gone bad, or a mafia hit, or even another club. If the Sinners weren't involved then you have nothing to worry about." She trailed her hand down her body, between her breasts, parting the white silk until she got to the juncture of her thighs. Her hand rested on her mound, her fingers dangling over what he most wanted to see, hiding it from his now throbbing cock.

Christ. She was like one of those mythical Sirens who lured sailors to their deaths. He couldn't tell whether the pounding in his veins was fury or lust. No wonder T-Rex had warned him about her. And Banks. He had to get out, and yet he couldn't look away. Something niggled at the back of his mind. A question. There was a question he wanted to ask her, but he couldn't remember what it was.

As if she could read his thoughts, she drew in a deep breath, her breasts rising, the silk slipping until he could just see the blush of a nipple. "I'm so sorry, Tank. Let me make it up to you."

Tank swallowed hard. How long had it been since he'd had a woman—and remembered it? One? Two weeks? Maybe more. But tumbling a sweet butt in his bed was never the same as fucking a woman he really wanted, a woman he had to work to get, a smart, classy woman the likes of whom never usually looked twice at a guy like Tank.

Unbidden, an image of Connie flitted through his mind. Connie was smart, too. She had a master's degree in music. He'd thought she would be soft and sweet in bed, but she'd gone fucking wild for him, clawing at his back, screaming his name. He'd never had that kind of sex with a woman. Hell, he'd never had that kind of connection. But Connie was gone, and Ella was here. Ella with her silky robe and her lush lips. Ella who had gone through his phone and put his club at risk. He couldn't hurt her, but maybe she could pay him back another way. She was offering after all. His mind wandered, and his cock rose to follow.

"Tank." She raised her voice, pulling him out of the beginning of a fantasy about the famous Ella Masters on her knees between his legs with her lips wrapped around his cock, wearing those damn glasses she wore on TV and nothing else.

"Yeah." He grunted, not wanting to risk any telltale huskiness in his voice, although if she looked down, the boner straining against his fly would be a dead giveaway.

"I can do more for you than access police reports." She pulled the belt on her robe, and the two sides parted, her perfect body on display.

His mind split in two, half of it focused on Ella, sitting half naked swathed in white silk, the other half focused on his club and what they would do to him when the ATF came beating down the club door wondering what the Sinners were doing in Still Water putting bullets into Leo's brain.

"Don't talk about the fucking police. They're gonna be all over the club 'cause of what you did." He struggled to put his thoughts together. "What I told you about the gas station was between you and me. I didn't say the Sinners were involved. If that was T-Rex and he offed Leo, he did it on his own and not as part of the club."

"Don't you get it?" She stood and the gown slid down her body and pooled at her feet. Christ, she looked like those marble statues he'd seen on TV—Greek goddesses with lush bodies and perfect faces, smooth skin, and bare pussies.

She walked toward him, her heavy breasts swaying, pink-tipped nipples hard and begging to be touched. "That little tidbit got me a boost up the rankings, which means I have more pull. I can stay on the story, and my boss is giving me more resources to investigate, resources I can use to help you. He's even sending me to the bike rally on the weekend. I'd say that's a win win for us all." She stopped only a few inches away, slid her hands over his chest. "The

Sinners are a powerful club. I'm sure they can handle the police."

Her soft words, the gentle lilt of her voice, her hand roaming his body, the sweet scent of her perfume, and her lush naked body all ripe for the taking eased his tension, assuaged his fears. He reached for her and pulled her against him, ground his erection into her hips. "You better not be fucking with me, Ella."

"I would never do anything to hurt you, James," she whispered, leaning up, her breath soft in his ear. "I want you too much. I always have." She clasped his hand, drew it down to the juncture of her thighs, slid his finger through her wet, slick folds.

Ella Masters, one of southern Montana's top reporters wanted him. She wined and dined with governors and senators. She was on the fucking news every night. She was smart and rich and beautiful and talented and she wanted him, really wanted him. Tank. An outlaw who had never even finished high school. She was wet for him, and he hadn't even touched her.

His phone buzzed in his pocket. Ella reached into his cut and pulled it out.

"Let's put this away," she whispered. "Right now it's just you and me."

The sight of her slim white fingers wrapped around his phone broke through the haze of his lust. Images tumbled through his mind: T-Rex, Banks, Connie, Sirens, Black Widow spiders with their heads bitten off, and the button on his phone that he pressed with his thumb to unlock it. And through her fingers he could see the flash, flash, flash of Jagger's name.

"Jesus fucking Christ." He ripped the phone from her hand and stepped away.

His president needed him. His club needed him. There

was only one way she could have accessed his phone when he was sleeping and the thought she'd used him that way made his skin crawl.

Ella opened her arms and his betraying cock throbbed. "Come," she beckoned him forward.

He went. But not in the direction she was expecting.

★ SEVENTEEN ★

Naiya slid off the bed, careful not to wake Holt. After the movie, they'd watched a crime show, and made love two more times before falling asleep. Holt had woken twice already with nightmares about his time in Viper's dungeon, but he calmed quickly when she held him, so she'd given up sleeping anywhere except curled tight against his body.

He was in a deep sleep now, his breathing slow and regular. Restless, Naiya walked over to the window, her mind going over what Holt had said. He was having doubts about his plan to go after the Sinners, but he still intended to follow it through. How could she save him from himself? Save the bikers who were his closest friends? She knew how overwhelming the desire for revenge could be. She'd been there, ready to pull the trigger, without any thought about the consequences other than an end to the man who had caused her so much pain.

Holt didn't have a priest to save him. But he did have Naiya, and the answer was out there. Rider's Bar wasn't far away.

She dressed quickly and left a note for Holt, telling him she'd gone for a walk. As an afterthought, she stuffed his cut in her bag before heading downstairs. Although it was nearly midnight, the lavish hotel lobby was busy with people chatting in the huge overstuffed chairs and clinking glasses in the hotel bar.

A cool breeze blew through the pink cotton sweater she'd bought during a rest stop on their way to Conundrum. She pulled it tighter around her as she raced through the streets, dodging pedestrians on their way home from the bars.

By the time she reached Rider's Bar, her hands were white from the cold. Taking a deep breath, she pushed open the door and stepped into a proper, old school biker bar that smelled strongly of beer with a hint of leather. The dark, cherry-stained wood walls and warm colors gave it a comfortable, yet masculine, appearance. Rough-hewn wooden tables were scattered throughout, and the walls were decorated with pictures of whiskey bottles, motorcycles, Harley symbols, fancy cars and, of course, women.

Conversation ground to a halt when the door closed behind her, and it took Naiya a moment to realize she had walked into a sea of biker cuts with not a civilian in sight.

"What do we have here?" A burly giant of a man wearing a padded "Security" vest cracked a toothy smile. "You get lost on your way to a wedding, sugar?"

Naiya gave him what she hoped was a winning smile, or at least a smile that would convince him to let her into the bar. "I'm looking for someone."

"Don't think the kind of someone a girl like you would be looking for would be in a biker bar." He took a step in front of her, blocking her way. Yeah, he was intimidating, but so were all the Black Jacks she'd encountered. And look what she'd done to Viper, who was the most intimidating biker of them all. Although her penknife had barely scratched him, she'd dared to stab the man many called untouchable.

"I'm here for a drink." She looked up, met his gaze head on, her hands dropping to her hips. "So unless this is a private bar, I suggest you let me in, or does the owner not want paying customers?"

A grin spread across his face. "Why don't you ask him?" He gestured to the bar. "His name is Banks. He's the dude in camouflage who looks like he just came back from a Black Ops mission. Tell him Gunner's buying your drinks tonight. He can put them on my tab."

Gunner. Holt said he was the club's sergeant-at-arms, responsible for internal discipline at the club. And she could see why. His arms were like steel pipes and, despite his smile, he was clearly not a man to be crossed.

"Thanks." She stepped to the side, and looked back over her shoulder with a genuine smile. "You're lucky I'm not a big drinker."

"You're not a big anything." Gunner gave her a wink. "But I like my girls small, cute, and curvy."

She made her way through the tables and sat at the counter. The bar had a good vibe going, busy but not buzzy, with the Moonshine Bandits', "For the Outlawz" playing through the speakers, and the murmur of conversation punctuated by the soft click of pool balls, the thud of darts, and the occasional bang of a fist on a table.

Banks looked up from the bar and folded his arms. "You legal?"

"I'm twenty-two."

"Everyone's twenty-two." He held out his hand. "You got some ID?"

"My purse was . . . uh . . . stolen."

He snorted a laugh. "When I hear 'uh . . . stolen,' that tells me right there you're lying. And if you're lying about that, you're lying about your age. And if you're lying about your age, you shouldn't be here. Already had an underage girl in the bar the other night. Don't want another one. Got enough trouble with these bikers. Not keen on being shut down for serving minors."

"I'm not here to drink. I'm looking for someone."

He raised an eyebrow. "Then do your looking outside. You ladies know better than to bring your business into my bar."

Naiya stared at him aghast. "I'm not a hooker."

"Suppose not looking all pink and pretty. But you don't look like you're twenty-two either. And if your purse was stolen, you wouldn't be sitting at my bar."

"I'm surprised they didn't name you Cerberus," she muttered.

"The three-headed dog who guards the gates of Hades?" Banks laughed. "I'll take that as a compliment. Maybe one day if I ever join an MC, I'll tell them I want that as a road name. I gotta be fucking on guard for these boys twenty-four seven, even if they don't realize it." He poured her a glass of water and slid it across the bar. "No alcohol unless you produce some ID or a good story about how you lost your purse."

God. All she wanted to do was find Tank. "You wouldn't believe the truth if I told you."

Banks threw back his head and laughed. "Sweetheart, after the shit I've seen since the Sinners started coming to my bar, I'm pretty much open to anything."

"Fine." She licked her lips. "I'm from Missoula. Originally from Devil's Hills. I went home to bury my mother, and Viper grabbed me and threw me in his dungeon under the Black Jacks' clubhouse." She paused, tilted her head to the side. "You know who Viper is?"

Banks' eyes narrowed. "Mighta heard of him. Go on."

"I escaped, but without my purse or my phone. I can't go home because he's after me to pay off my mother's debts with my body as currency. I might also have stabbed him with a penknife but not hard enough to do anything more than piss him off. Anyway, I met someone who helped me. Now I want to help him, and the only way I can do that is by talking to a Sinner named Tank. I'm not here to cause trouble or stir things up. I heard the Sinners come to this bar, and I figured someone might know where he is. I'm not armed. I don't even know how to shoot a gun. I just really, really want to talk to Tank."

Silence.

Naiya bit her lip. "Will you help me?"

"You a Black Jack bitch?"

She recoiled, and her nose wrinkled. "No."

"That's one hell of a story." Banks poured a shot of vodka in a glass and added some soda and lime. "And you're leaving a lot out." He pushed it across the counter, and Naiya took a grateful sip of the drink, sweet and tart with just the faintest kick of vodka. Perfect.

"Yes, I am, but only to protect someone, and because Tank should hear the rest of it first." She heaved a sigh. "I'm telling you the truth, and if you don't help me I'll stand outside the door and ask everyone who comes out where he is."

"Looking the way you look, dressed the way you're dressed, talking sweet the way you talk, that's tantamount to suicide." He looked over her shoulder then back to her.

"Tank was here earlier, but I think he's gone. Jagger's in the back room. He's the president of the Sinners. He'll know where you can find him."

Naiya sucked in a sharp breath. Now here was a part of the plan she hadn't thought through. Jagger was with Arianne, and Arianne knew her from the few times her mother had dragged her to the Black Jack clubhouse, and the weekends she'd played with Jeff. In fact, Arianne only knew her as a club brat, and she didn't want to think about what might happen if Arianne outed her as a Black Jack in a Sinner bar.

Bank stilled, assessing her. "You got a problem with Jagger?"

"No," she said quickly, thumbing the ring on her finger. "I've never met him. It's just . . . talking to the Sinner president sounds kind of scary."

"Who's scary?" A grizzled biker with a long, unkempt beard joined them at the bar. He had hazel eyes and a face weathered from years of riding.

"You are with that rat's nest attached to your chin. Fucking thing is a health hazard." Banks poured a shot of whiskey and shoved it across the bar. "This here's Shaggy. Oldest member of the Sinner's Tribe. His claim to fame is that fucking beard he hasn't cut in twenty years."

"Twenty-two and counting." Shaggy stroked his beard, his fingers lost in the tangle.

"Our sweet rose here is looking for Tank." Bank gave her a wink. "You seen him around?"

"He was out for a bit, but he just came in." Shaggy nodded to the door, and Naiya turned to see a tall, heavily built biker crossing the floor toward them. He was about the same height and build as Holt, but dark where Holt was fair, his eyes chestnut brown, and his hair thick, but closely cropped to his head, bringing his wide jaw and defined cheekbones into stark relief. Handsome but rough.

"There's a girl here," Banks said when Tank joined them at the bar. "Wants to talk to you."

Tank's gaze flicked to her, and he frowned. She could almost see the wheels turning in his mind. Who was she? Had he slept with her?

He glanced over at Banks, shook his head. "Another fucking night I don't remember. You'd better start cutting me off at two."

Naiya's mouth opened and closed again. This was Holt's best friend; the one person in the world he missed most of all; the man whose betrayal hurt him beyond anything

Viper had done to him. And now that she was standing in front of him, she didn't know what to say. What if Holt was right and Tank and the Sinners had abandoned him? What if Tank was the bad guy? What if he used her to find Holt and . . .

"You're scaring her," Shaggy said. "Lookit her eyes turning green. I think I remember a sweet butt whose eyes did that, or maybe it was a waitress . . ."

Banks snorted a laugh. "Or maybe you looked in the mirror one morning and scared the shit out of yourself 'cause your beard looks like it's swallowing your face."

Shaggy cursed at Banks and the banter continued. For a moment, she felt like she was in the Black Jacks' clubhouse all over again. But she'd had enough hiding and feeling scared, running away again and again. If she didn't do something now, Holt would never know the truth and he might kill an innocent man.

She swallowed hard, looked up at Tank. "Could I talk to you outside?"

Tank gave her a curt nod and gestured her toward the door. "After you."

"Congrats in advance if you're gonna become a daddy," Shaggy called after them.

Tank shot him a withering stare, then guided her out of the bar with one hand against her lower back. A gentleman biker. Kinda like Holt.

Once outside, Tank leaned against the brick wall fronting the bar, arms folded, his muscular body casting a large shadow on the sidewalk beneath the streetlight. Cars zipped down the street in front of them, and a biker pulled up beside the row of bikes to Tank's left and waved.

"What's this all about?" Tank asked.

Naiya unzipped the backpack and handed him Holt's cut.

Tank unfolded the leather vest and his face contorted in pain. "Where the fuck did you get this?"

"Viper's dungeon."

He fisted the leather, and a shudder ran through his body. "So you came all the way here to bring it back to the Sinners? You some kinda Good Samaritan? Why me?"

She shivered in the cold. "You were his best friend."

Tank's face tightened, and he leaned over her, glowering. "How do you know that?"

"He told me."

The pulse on his neck throbbed, and his voice, when he spoke, was harsh. "When?"

"Tonight. Holt . . . er . . . T-Rex is alive."

His breath left him with a moan, and he pressed a closed fist to his mouth. "How do you know?"

"I've been with him," she said, feeling braver. "We escaped Viper's dungeon together. You know I'm telling the truth. You saw him. At the gas station in Still Water. We were there."

Tank staggered back to the wall, scrubbed his hands over his face. "Christ. I knew it was him. I fucking knew it, and no one believed me. I knew he wasn't dead. I would have felt it. Just wait till I tell—"

"No. You can't tell anyone." Naiya held up her hands, keeping him back. "He thinks . . . you betrayed him. He thinks the Sinners left him to die in Viper's dungeon."

"Jesus fucking Christ." Tank groaned and wrapped his arms around his middle, clutching himself. "We came for him. A week of recon, a massive attack on the Black Jack clubhouse, explosives, trucks driving through the building, ambush . . . the works. Two brothers got into the dungeon and saw a body. Same build, same hair . . . they even found the medallion he used to wear. But they couldn't see his face." He thudded the wall with his fist. "They couldn't see his damn face, but they assumed it was him."

Naiya backed up a step. "I think it would be better if you don't tell anyone and come with me to see him first. But you should know he's here for vengeance, not just against Viper, but the Sinners, too."

"Three months being tortured by Viper, waiting for your brothers, losing hope." His voice cracked, broke. "I'm surprised we're still alive. Take me to him. And if he shoots me before I get a chance to talk, then I'll die a happy man 'cause I'll know he's alive and he's free, and that's all I ever wanted."

Holt startled awake, his heart pounding.

Viper coming. Must have fallen asleep. He clenched and unclenched his fists, trying to prepare himself for what was to come. But he didn't hear the chains. He tested one arm, then the other . . .

Reality hit him in a rush. He was free. In a hotel. And vengeance was close at hand.

He reached for Naiya, felt the empty bed beside him, the cool sheets, pillow barely dented.

"Naiya." He pushed himself up, looked around the room. Waited. Called again. His skin prickled, and he left the bed to search. First the giant marble bathroom, then the living area, the balcony, and finally the hall. Her shoes were missing. And her bag. And her new sweater was gone.

A black hole opened in his chest, sucking the air from his lungs. Had she left him? Had he been too rough? Too hard? Had he done something wrong? Was she still angry he'd left her behind?

He pulled on his clothes, reached for his weapons. On the table beside his gun and holster, he found her note.

Gone for a walk? At midnight? With Viper and the ATF

hunting her? What if she was hurt? Lost? What if they found her? What if she needed him?

Too agitated to wait for the elevator, he took the stairs two at a time down to the lobby. He checked with the night clerk and yes, she'd seen Naiya leaving about an hour ago, but no, she didn't know where she'd gone.

Holt ran out the door and into the darkened street. A taxi driver waved to him, but he shook his head. Where would she go? Why the fuck would she walk around alone at night? Panic gripped him hard and he staggered against the wall. He couldn't lose her. She was the only person who knew him when he didn't even know himself, accepted him for the way he was now, not knowing how he was then. She was the only woman he had ever truly wanted—a woman he couldn't imagine himself without.

She was Tank's type of woman—small and beautiful, deeply passionate, quirky and funny—and yet she made Holt feel things he'd never felt before; she made him feel whole again, and he couldn't go on if a piece of him was missing.

He looked left down the street, wondering if she would have headed toward the city. Or would she have gone right toward the residential area of town? He took a step to the left and he heard a sound. A voice. Laughter. Low and deep. So familiar. His heart skipped a beat, and then he saw them.

And in that moment his entire world imploded.

Tank. He would have known him anywhere. The same walk, the same set of his shoulders, the flash of the tattoo that matched Holt's own. And Naiya. His once best friend with his girl. Laughing as if they'd known each other forever.

Maybe they had.

Maybe the joke was on him.

He slipped into the nearest alley, pressed his back up

against the wall and took a deep breath. Tucked into his belt, he had a Glock 17 and a SIG P226. He'd holstered a Ruger P Series across his chest, along with a .22 on his left leg and an assortment of blades.

Vengeance would be his tonight.

He waited for the footsteps, the lilt of Naiya's voice, Tank's loud murmur. And yet vengeance was not his first thought as he stepped out of the alley, the Glock pointed at Tank's chest. "Get away from her."

Tank froze mid-step. The night air stilled around them. Time stopped. Holt looked into the eyes of the man he had called brother and saw himself. Walking dead.

"T-Rex." Tank let out a ragged breath. "Fuck. I almost didn't believe her. It's so good to see you, brother. So fucking good."

Holt's mouth opened and closed again as emotion balled in his chest. Memories assailed him. He and Tank trawling the bars, polishing bikes, riding through the mountains, watching TV, playing vids, covering each other in shoot-outs, backing each other in fights, fishing, talking, laughing . . . so many memories. So much pain.

"Into the alley."

Tank lifted his hands, palms forward. "Don't shoot, brother. We were coming to see you. To explain."

"Move." He gestured them both into the dark alley with his gun, and checked the street for witnesses. When he was certain the coast was clear, he backed them up to the brick wall, fighting a wave of nausea from the heavy stench of decay coming from the garbage cans behind him.

"So was this all a set-up?" His gaze flicked to Naiya. "You knew him?"

"No." Her face softened. "You said the Sinners hung out at Rider's Bar, so I went there and asked for Tank. He's come to explain what happened. They didn't leave you behind, Holt. Just hear him out."

Holt's hand trembled, his finger on the trigger, his muscles tight, ready to fire. This was it. This was what he had lived for in the dungeon. Revenge. Justice. Payback. And yet Tank did nothing to defend himself. There was no fear in Tank's eyes, just relief, joy, and goddamned tears.

"We came for you," Tank said, his voice wavering. "From the moment Viper took you, all we did was to try to get you back. And you know who was out there every fucking day doing recon? Zane. He staked out the Black Jack clubhouse, shot hundreds of pictures and videos, brought it back so we knew everything . . . the timing of the guards, the layout of the compound, where you were and how to get to you. He pulled in every mark he had. Disobeyed Jagger and took a fucking beating for it."

"Zane?" Holt couldn't believe Zane gave a rat's ass about him. The Sinner VP kept to himself, and never socialized with the brothers. Holt didn't think Zane had ever said more than two words to him in the entire time he'd been at the club.

"Yeah, man." Tank took a step forward. "He's mellowed now that he's got a kid. You saved Evie, brought their family together. Zane said he owed you a life debt. He even gave a speech at your funeral."

His funeral. Because they thought he was dead after they'd left him in the dungeon. He raised the gun, gritted his teeth. "There wouldn't have been a funeral if you'd come for me."

Tank's shoulders dropped. "Shoot me if that's what it takes for you to go on, but you should know we were there. Thirty Sinners and Evie, too. Benson—he's a prospect now if you can believe it—drove a truck filled with explosives into the Black Jack clubhouse. Sparky and Gunner blasted the door to the dungeon. They found a body. Same hair. Same build. But cut up so bad they couldn't see the face. They found your medallion, too."

"That wasn't me." It was stupid to say, he knew. Obviously, it wasn't him. But still, how could they not know their own brother?

"I know," Tank said gently. "If it had been me in that dungeon looking for you . . ." His corded throat tightened when he swallowed. "Anyway, it was an ambush. The Jacks had been tipped off about the raid. They had to leave the body behind. But I always knew . . ." He clenched his fist, smashed it into his palm. "I knew you weren't dead. I never gave up. I chased every lead . . ." He heaved out a breath, dropped his hands to his knees. "Fuck. I never gave up. I never gave up. Never."

Holt holstered his gun. Maybe it was all a lie, but it was a good one. And he knew who they'd found in the dungeon . . . a Devil Dog who'd tried to cheat the Jacks.

"Looks like no one is getting killed tonight, so I'll . . . just go back to our room." Naiya made a discrete exit, leaving them alone in the alley.

"Fuck it." Tank closed the distance between them in three easy strides of his long legs. He wrapped his arms around Holt and hugged him. "Shoot me if that's what you gotta do. Punch me. Stab me. I don't fucking care." His voice cracked, broke. "I thought you were dead, and here you are and I never felt so fucking happy in all my life."

Tank broke. Sobbed. His body shuddering. Holt swallowed past the lump in his throat, his arms dangling uselessly by his sides as emotion threatened to consume him.

This.

Words could be twisted, actions misinterpreted. But true emotion—where a man as strong as Tank would cry in his arms—couldn't be feigned.

His vision blurred. Holt never cried. Not when he'd spent two years in juvenile detention. Not when he found out what happened to his sister. Not when Viper had beat him or when he gave up hope the Sinners would come. But nothing had hurt as much as the thought Tank had betrayed him, and to see him again, know Tank had been looking for him all this time . . .

I never gave up. Never.

Holt wrapped his arms around Tank's shoulders and let himself go.

★ EIGHTEEN ★

Naiya had only a few seconds warning—the faint rasp of the key card in the lock—before Holt slammed open the door to their hotel room.

She shot up in the bed, pulled the sheet around her, and braced herself for the oncoming storm. She'd spent the last two hours alone in their hotel room, emailing resumes and figuring out what to do next. Holt was back with the Sinners, and Conundrum was a safe haven from the Jacks. They didn't need each other any more, and she had to get on with her life. So why did it hurt so much?

"You had no right to get involved." Holt burst into the bedroom, flipped on the light.

He looked wrecked, his hair mussed, face haggard, eyes red, cheeks streaked. Almost as if he'd been tortured all over again.

"You were going to kill an innocent man." Her heart pounded in her chest, the urge to run almost overwhelming. But this was Holt. She trusted him like she'd never trusted anyone before.

"You should have come to me after you found him. You should have given me the choice about what to do." He scraped his hand through his hair, paced the room, distraught.

"He's your best friend, Holt. Did you not want to see him? Didn't you want to hear the truth?"

"I don't know." He pounded his fist on the window. Again and again. "I don't fucking know."

Naiya wanted to go to him, hold him, but she'd never seen him so agitated—not even in the weapons shed when he thought she intended to betray him. "What happened? When I left, I thought things were good between you."

Holt pressed his forehead against the glass. "At first they were. We talked about the club. He filled me in on what I missed. The Sinners and all their support clubs are going to hit the Jacks at the Sandy Lake rally on the weekend, try to end the war. I should be happy, us going after Viper together. But I can't erase what's in my head. Three months of thinking they abandoned me. Three months of hating them. Three months of living solely for revenge. I told Tank not to tell the brothers he saw me until I got my shit together. I'm not the same man. I don't feel the same about them. It's like those ties broke, and they can't be fixed." He bashed his forehead against the glass and Naiya slid off the bed and ran over to him.

"Stop. Don't hurt yourself." She slid under his arm, and pushed him away from the window. He was cold, inside and out, and she shivered against him.

"I understand. Not many people would, but I do. I almost shot Viper after what he did to me. Even after I left Devil's Hills, I couldn't let it go, and it took me a long time to come to terms with the fact I wasn't the same girl anymore."

"Let what go? You never told me what happened. What did Viper do to you?"

She'd never told anyone except Ally. Not even Maurice. She didn't want anyone to treat her differently, like she was made of glass, or, worse, in need of sympathy. She'd become adept at hiding her lack of arousal, so the issue never came up. And Maurice had never asked. Looking back, she realized that should have been a warning something wasn't right with their relationship, but at the time she'd been happy not to feel pressured.

Holt was different. He was live to her issues even though he didn't know why. Now he wanted to know. And she wanted to tell him.

"He raped me," she said into his chest. "I was fifteen, alone on my birthday. Arianne's brother Jeff invited me to the Black Jack clubhouse where they were having a party. I knew better, and if I hadn't been feeling sorry for myself I wouldn't have gone, but Jeff had always been kind and he said he'd look out for me. But he was high when I got there, totally out of it. I was about to leave when Viper started talking to me. I was awed and flattered he even noticed me. He spiked my drink and touched me. He was gentle. Seductive. He said sweet things. I let my guard down and went with him to his office. The minute the door closed, everything changed. I don't remember that much about what he did to me. I'd never . . . It was my first time and he knew it."

"Son of a bitch," Holt muttered. "Son of a fucking bitch."

She stumbled over her words, not wanting to tell him that she remembered a lot more than she was letting on: terror, horror, torn clothes, hard desk, frantic pleas, begging, screaming, crying, slaps and punches, pain—so much pain, the sting of the blade on her skin, the burn of the tattoo gun on her arm, disgust, humiliation and utter despair. But worse had been waking naked, cold, and alone on his office floor, marked, discarded, and filled with self-loathing for her innocence and stupidity.

"My mom was at the party." Her voice wavered. "She

saw him with me. She knew what he wanted. She never stopped him. Never came into the office when I screamed. And afterward, when I went to her apartment for help, she told me to go back to him or he'd take out his anger on her. I refused, so she threw me out. I had nowhere to go, no one to turn to. They owned the cops and social services. They owned everyone in Devil's Hills."

"I got no words, darlin'." Holt hugged her tight.

Warm in his embrace, she found the strength to go on. "After a couple of weeks on the streets, I hit rock bottom. I used the last of my cash to buy a gun to kill Viper. My grandmother's priest saw me at a crosswalk. He must have seen something in my face because he convinced me to go the rectory with him. I told him everything and he got me out of town, found me a place to live with a family in Missoula where I could babysit in exchange for rent and food. They were good people. They encouraged me to finish high school and when I got my first job, I paid the priest back . . . every cent. He saved me, not just from Viper, but from myself."

Holt let loose a string of curses, his body going rigid. "Goddamn bastard is gonna fucking pay for everything he did to you. I'm not going to kill him easy. I'm gonna drag it out. Make him suffer the way I suffered, the way you suffered. I'm gonna make him wish for death, and it won't happen until there's nothing left to kill."

"Do it for yourself," she said. "I'm done with it. I'll never forgive him for what he did, but I don't want blood. I've worked too hard to make a new life for myself. I don't want to dredge up all those old memories. What he did affected me, but it didn't destroy me like killing him would have. If I'd gone down that road, I don't think I would have come back."

"You saying I shouldn't go after him?"

Naiya shook her head. "I'm saying it's not the right

thing for me, but it's taken me seven years to get to move on and accept I am not the same person anymore, even though I didn't pull the trigger. I had to settle in my skin, see the world through different eyes. Now I just want to live my life in peace."

"Do you?" Holt held her lightly, sighed. "You aren't living, darlin'; you're hiding, and until he's dead you'll always be hiding, looking over your shoulder, waiting for the next time he comes for you. And he will come unless you make him pay. Justice is for civilians. Revenge is for bikers, and you got biker blood in you. I saw it when we were in that dungeon and you were pounding on the door and cursing the living daylights out of Viper. I saw it when you kept your cool when we were escaping and when you fucking drugged my sorry ass. I saw it in the bar when you didn't back down from the ATF agent on the hunt. And I'll bet the brothers saw it when you walked alone into a one-percenter biker bar wearing your pretty pink sweater and looking like you just stepped out of a *Good Home* magazine."

"So I should just join the club and have my revenge?" Her voice rose in pitch. Secretly she'd always wanted Viper to pay for what he'd done. But more than that she wanted to know he would never hurt her again. It was wrong to want a man dead; wrong to condone violence, yet hearing Holt voice her secret desire sent a thrill through her veins. "As what? A club whore, like my mother?"

"Nah. You got too much class to be a club whore," he said, entirely missing the sarcasm in her tone or the point she was trying to make. "You could be a house mama or someone's old lady."

Naiya didn't know whether to be insulted or flattered. Yes, an old lady was the highest rank a woman could achieve in the biker world, but she hadn't pulled herself out of the gutter just to throw herself back into another one.

She had gone to college to make something of herself, and that didn't mean taking orders, cooking meals, cleaning guns, and sitting on the back of her old man's Harley on Sunday rides.

"I think I stick with my plan to be a forensic scientist, if that's okay with you." She hadn't missed the fact that he'd said "someone's" old lady. Not his.

"You gonna be happy working for the man?"

This time she laughed. "'The man' will give me a steady job that pays very well and is intellectually challenging and interesting. Plus I have another reason for choosing forensic science. One day, I'm going to find my dad." She held out her hand, flashed her ring. "There's a biker out there wearing the Skull Mark ring and DNA that matches mine. You found your family. I'll find mine."

"Lots of bikers have skull rings," he said, his voice gentle. "Hell, I'll bet most of the Sinners have one 'cause we got a skull in the center of our patch." His arms slid around her, and she thought that was a good thing. He needed comfort, and she could give him that. No one had ever needed her before, and she'd never had anything to give.

"So, what are you going to do?" She tensed, didn't dare breathe as he formulated his answer.

"No Sinners." His lips whispered over her hair. "I didn't want to meet them. Tank said he'd come back in the morning. He said he'd sit in the lobby all fucking day, sleep on the floor, until I came back."

"I've never had a friend like that," she said. "Ally's a good friend, and she's done a lot for me, but you and Tank have something that goes beyond friendship."

"We're not gay."

Naiya laughed. "I kinda guessed that from the way you . . . know your way around a woman. I just meant it's a very close friendship."

"We just got each other, always had each other's backs. The day we met, I was just hanging around the MC, helping out, hoping they'd ask me to prospect. Tank came over and gave me some tips. Told me what I needed to do."

"So he's senior to you?"

Holt stroked a hand through her hair. "We're both junior patch, but yeah, he's been with the club a year longer than me."

"I would have guessed you were older."

"That's what happens when life fucks you over." He pressed a kiss to her forehead. "So that first night they sent him out to watch the bikes, and this chick comes and just sits on Zane's saddle just to get some attention. Tank didn't want to hurt her, but when he tried to get her off, she kicked him and he fell back, knocked over the row of bikes. Even I knew that was the end for him, so I took the fall. Took one hell of beating, and then the brothers tossed me a bunch of cleaning stuff, told me to detail every bike. Got the first bike done, turned around and Tank was beside me with a rag. It's been like that ever since."

"And it will be like that again. Go with him tomorrow and see the Sinners. Give them a chance."

He twisted his hand in her hair, gently tugged her head back. "If I go, you're coming with me."

"I don't want to go to a biker clubhouse," she said, pulling away. "It was hard enough going into a bar. You don't need me. The Sinners will help you get revenge. And since I'm safe in Conundrum, I can stay here until you do what you have to do, or I find a job in another state. I checked my email when I came back and I've got interviews at crime labs in Florida, New Mexico, and Rhode Island. There are lots of options."

"You don't leave." He gripped her shoulders in his massive hands, his face contorted in a mask of pain.

Startled by the vehemence in his tone, she pulled away. "We don't need each other. You have your club back, a revenge mission to see through. I need to get back to my regular life. We're different people. We want different things. We live in different worlds, lead different lives. The things you do: stealing, and shooting people, running guns—even if you're doing them to keep me safe—they aren't okay with me. I can't live that kind of life. I'm starting a career where I fight crime. I can't be a criminal or hang around with a criminal organization."

"You're scared," he said firmly. "And that's why you should go. You can't keep hiding. You gotta confront the things that scare you. Nothing's gonna happen to you when you're with me. The Sinners aren't like the Jacks. All bikers aren't the same."

Holt was right about one thing. She had spent the last seven years hiding. She'd hidden physically and emotionally, burying all memories of that night so she could forge a new life for herself, untainted by the past. But, of course, it had caught up to her, and she was on the run again. Hiding. Not just from Viper, but also from herself and who she longed to be—a woman free to make her own choices, to live without fear. She wanted to be the Phantom of her own damn story.

"Don't leave." He reached for her, pulled her into his chest, leaned down and kissed her. Angry and desperate, his kiss was as much a claiming as a plea, a ravaging of her body and her soul.

She pulled away, gasped for breath, her breasts rising, pressing against the hard muscle of his chest. "Holt. What are you—?"

"I need you," he said. "You're mine, and I'm not going to let you go. Whatever I have to do, whatever it takes, however long . . . If you can't live the biker life after I'm done with Viper, then I won't live it. But you can't leave me. I am nothing, Naiya, if I don't have you."

Adrenaline pulsed through Holt's veins, followed by a surge of panic when Naiya tried to pull away. He felt right with her, complete, the way he felt with Tank, but this feeling was deeper, more intense. He'd felt lost without Tank. But if Naiya left, he would be destroyed.

With a fierce hold, he cupped the back of her neck and kissed her deeply, trying to tell her with his actions what he couldn't say in words. He was totally and utterly raw, emotionally exposed, flayed by Tank's revelation and Naiya's threat to walk away.

Naiya smoothed the damp hair from his temples. "Is that a request?"

"It's whatever you want it to be. Just so long as it means you aren't walking out that door." His future was no longer neatly laid out, his plan for vengeance no longer clear. All he knew for certain was that he'd been looking for something all his life and he'd found it with her. She was the only thing that made sense in the world. She was sweet in his arms but strong enough to defy him, beautiful and brave, stubborn and sexy. He had been through hell and survived, and his reward had come in the form of a woman who could bend but not break, challenge but not conform, submit but not surrender. Naiya was his. Totally, utterly, and irrevocably. And he would never let her go.

She gave him a slow, sensual kiss that sent all his blood rushing to his groin. "I have a feeling even if I did leave, you'd follow me."

"To the ends of the earth."

Naiya knew him in his new skin. Cared about him even though he didn't know what it was about this new Holt that would attract a woman like her. He didn't need to flirt or tease or seduce. He wasn't the "good guy," mediating his way through disputes, playing jokes, or being everyone's best friend. The new Holt was demanding and controlling. Impatient. Serious. So far removed from the self he knew, he would be lost without Naiya to anchor him to the ground. He needed her now. Needed to claim her, body and soul.

As if she could read his mind, Naiya drew his head down, brushed her lips over his ear. "Show me. Show me how much you want me. Don't hold back. Don't stop. You have my permission to take what you need from me, do what you want with me. I trust you, Holt."

As if a dam broke inside him, Holt crushed her mouth to his, driving away all his fear and panic as he gave in to the primitive instinct to conquer and claim. His tongue swept over every inch of her mouth, touching, tasting, drowning in her sweet surrender.

Naiya slid her hands under his shirt, pushing it up. She pressed a soft kiss to his chest and he yanked the shirt over his head. Licking her lips, Naiya placed her palms flat against Holt's chest and stroked over his pecs. "I want to feel you against me. Skin to skin."

Holt's brain fuzzed with lust. Desperate to undress her, he shoved her shirt and bra up over her breasts, almost tearing them off her as she pulled them over her arms. When she was bare before him, he wrapped his arms around her, crushing her taut nipples against his bruised, scarred chest. She felt so right. Perfect. His. With a low groan he sank his teeth into the sensitive spot between her neck and her shoulder, sucking her skin between his teeth.

"I need to mark you," he murmured against her skin. "I want the world to know you're mine."

* * *

Naiya sucked in a sharp breath as Holt left his mark, pain and pleasure mixing in a cocktail of lust that made her tremble in anticipation. For the first time in forever, she had opened up to a man—baring her deepest secrets. And now she was going to open to him another way— she was going to give him her body, uninhibited, unre- strained, without fear or regret—and trust that he wouldn't hurt her.

Her heart thundered as her hand dropped to his belt. "Is that all you've got?" She yanked open his fly, shoved his jeans down, freeing his cock from its restraint. "I said don't hold back."

Holt's voice dropped to a husky growl. "Damn. You might not believe it, or even want it, but you've got biker in you, right to the core."

He kicked off his jeans and dropped to his knees in front of her. Naiya slid her hands through his thick, soft hair as he trailed his hand down her stomach to the waist- band of her jeans. For a moment she thought—feared— he was going to slow down, but in five seconds flat her jeans were open and their hands were tangling as they shoved her clothing over her hips. Holt stood as she stepped out of her jeans and panties. With a deep, erotic growl, he cupped her ass and ground her hips against his.

Throwing aside her inhibitions, Naiya wrapped her hand around his thick cock, gliding her thumb over the smooth, moist head. "I want you. Inside me. Now."

He jerked his hips, pumping into her hand, and his voice thickened. "There's a condom in my pocket."

She slid her hand up his cock from base to tip. "I'm on the pill. Are you . . . ?"

Holt stilled. "Yeah. I'm clean. Never gone bareback

before, but get checked out once a year just the same. And the last three months—"

"I trust you, Holt."

The next thing she knew, she was spun around, pushed over the back of the couch. Holt kicked her legs apart.

"Yes. That." Her breaths came in short pants. "More. Take me. Hard."

He grabbed her hair, twisted it in his hand, and pulled her head up, making her back arch, her ass lifting in invitation.

She shivered in delicious anticipation as Holt slicked his fingers through her folds.

"Christ, you're wet," he murmured. "So ready for me."

Before she could respond, he thrust into her, his cock sliding deep into her channel, parting the swollen tissue to accommodate his girth.

Heaven.

With one hand on her hip, he pulled out and thrust in again. Naiya moaned, pushed back against him. Her hands fisted on the soft, beige cushions, her body taut, straining for release. But in this position, she had no control. She could take only what he would give, the way he wanted to give it. And yet she knew if she asked him to stop, he would. With Holt, she held the power, and knowing that, trusting him, she was able to let it go.

"That's right, darlin', I got you." Holt reached around and stroked her clit. Ripples of pleasure shot through her as she climaxed, her pussy tightening around Holt's rigid shaft. With a soft grunt, he pushed deep inside her, drawing out her orgasm with slow, measured thrusts.

"Fuck. Gotta have you. Gotta move." His hands clamped around her hips, and he hammered into her. Hard. Fast. His cock slid over her sensitive tissue, and another orgasm overtook her. Holt joined her, his cock thickening and swelling before he climaxed with a low, guttural groan.

He collapsed over her back, pressed kisses to the damp skin on her nape, and licked the bite on her shoulder where he'd marked her. Finally he pulled out. Semen trickled down Naiya's inner thigh. She stiffened as the sensation triggered a brutal memory of the morning after Viper's assault. Cold. Alone. Naked. Body marked. A gush of wetness . . .

Bile rose in her throat and she stood, hugged herself tight.

Holt's forehead creased in alarm. "Did I hurt you?"

"No." She edged away, grabbed her clothes from the floor. "I'm just going to . . . clean up."

She made it to the washroom before her knees gave out. Sinking down to the cold tile, she bit back a sob. What a mistake. She'd never let a man come inside her after that night; never agreed to rough sex. Why did she think it would be okay now?

After washing up and pulling on her clothes, she splashed water on her face and twisted her hair back in a ponytail. Holt was dressed when she came out, standing by the window. He turned to greet her, but she couldn't meet his gaze.

"What's wrong?"

"Nothing." She grabbed the remote and sat on the edge of the bed, flicking through the channels without really seeing the screen, looking for something to fill the black hole that had formed in her chest.

But Holt wasn't so easily put off. He knelt in front of her and gently took the remote from her hand.

"Talk to me," he said softly. "If I hurt you, I need to know. If it was too much . . ."

"I thought I could handle it, but I can't." She bit her lip, trembling. "I wanted to know Holt the Sinner. I wanted to know how far you would go and how rough you could be. I wanted to give you what you needed, but it was too much.

You'll never be able to let go with me. It all came back . . . Viper . . . the assault."

He cupped her face in his hands, stared into her eyes. "There is no Holt the Sinner. The only Holt is the one you know, and I want you in any way I can have you. If that was too much, we don't do it again."

Naiya covered his hands with her. "It's not just that. I'm not a biker chick. I don't want to be around bikers again. You need your brothers. You need a woman who loves the life and can give you what you want. That's not me. I don't want to be part of the club. When you go back to the Sinners, to Tank, I can't go with you."

"Then I won't go." He settled on the bed beside her and picked up the remote, casually flicking through the channels as if he hadn't just decided to turn his back on a life he clearly loved and the brother who had openly wept when he found him.

"Seriously?" Her voice rose in pitch. "You're just going to turn your back on them? For me?"

Holt shrugged. "You're the best fucking thing that's happened to me. The only thing in my life that makes sense. Tank said the brothers came looking for me, but I don't know if I believe him, and even if it's true, I don't know if I can go back. I'm a different man now. I got different goals. Viper's after you, and I'm gonna protect you with my last dying breath."

She shook her head, her momentary despair fading away beneath a mix of concern and exasperation. He needed to go back to his club, reconcile with his brothers, hear them out. That's how things were supposed to go. After hating them for so long, he needed closure. How could he make a decision about the future when he hadn't dealt with the past? How could she?

"Did anyone ever tell you that you have a flare for drama and a very irritating stubborn streak?"

"Tank."

Naiya twisted her ring around her finger. "Tank who is even now probably sitting downstairs waiting for you to show? He was so excited about taking you back to the club. He loves you Holt. If you don't go, it will tear him in two."

Holt lifted an eyebrow. "Then come for Tank if you won't do it for me."

Naiya stared at him, considering. Maybe she could deal with her past and help Holt at the same time. She could hang for a bit in the clubhouse, deal with her fear. She didn't have to stick around. And she wouldn't be alone. Despite their rough encounter, she trusted Holt more now, not less. His assurances and his willingness to just walk away for her, a geeky girl with a troubled past, made her want to reach inside and find the strength he seemed convinced she had.

She reached out and stroked a finger along his bristly jaw, more of an excuse to touch him than an invitation to start something new. She hadn't made a mistake opening up to Holt. He made her feel wanted and cherished, even after she tried to push him away. But sharing her pain and her body were not the same as sharing her heart. She needed to keep her walls up, protect herself. Despite his protests, Holt was a Sinner. What would happen if he decided to stay?

★ NINETEEN ★

TANK

T-Rex was alive!

Tank mounted his bike outside Rider's Bar and accelerated down the street. If he went back inside, he would be tempted to share his secret, and he'd promised to give T-Rex time.

He'd never broken a promise and he didn't intend to start now. Especially when T-Rex was involved.

Christ. That moment when he saw T-Rex on the sidewalk . . . Never in a million years would he have guessed that today would end with T-Rex coming home.

With his bike on full throttle he hit the highway and blasted down the road. He couldn't go back to the clubhouse because he was burning to share his secret, his joy, and the absolute thrill of discovering his searching, his hope, and his faith hadn't been in vain.

This night deserved a toast, but T-Rex didn't want to go for a drink. He was worried about Naiya.

Sweet girl. Beautiful. Spine of steel, walking into Rider's Bar the way she did and going behind T-Rex's back to save him. But Tank didn't get that relationship. She was the opposite of the loud, brash, chatty girls T-Rex usually went for—women who were the life of the party, aggressive, confident, and a challenge to get into bed. Ironically, Naiya was Tank's type, and Ella was T-Rex's type.

Ella who had hacked into his phone.

What the fuck was he going to do? He couldn't face the humiliation of telling his brothers, and there was always the risk they would tell Jagger, and he would be kicked out of the club. T-Rex would have kept his secret, but he couldn't burden his brother on the eve of his return. He would have to sort out the problem himself. Tank had been played, and now it was his turn to do the playing. He had to find out what Ella had learned from going through his phone and what she intended to do with the information. Failure wasn't an option.

After fuelling up his bike and buying a good bottle of whiskey as an excuse for his visit, he drove to Ella's house in a fancy suburb of Conundrum. He parked at the end of the block and walked past the assorted BMWs, Aston Martins and Bentleys, pausing to admire what had to be one of the coolest fucking bikes he'd ever seen: a Harley Sportster bobber boasting ape hangers and custom paint on the tins, all black and red to match the painted rims. It had been totally modded out and polished to a high shine. Someone had dropped some serious cash and some serious time into that bike. It was all about power and show, the kind of bike a president would ride.

With the bagged whiskey in one hand, he knocked on Ella's door. She hadn't answered the text he'd sent her, but he'd taken a chance she was at home, and he was glad he did. Her car was in the driveway, and the lights were on. Party time.

He heard swearing, the thud of feet, and then Ella pulled open the door.

Tank had never seen her look anything other than impeccably groomed. Even when she'd tried to seduce him the other night, she remained perfectly composed. But now, she was totally disheveled, her lipstick smeared, her hair tangled, and the pristine white silk robe she had teased him with the other day was dirty and torn.

"Ella? You okay?"

She stepped forward, blocking the door, and fixed him with what could only be an exasperated stare. "What are you doing here, James?"

Tank held up the bottle. "Thought you might want to have a drink with me. T-Rex is back." He didn't have to feign his enthusiasm. His joy at having T-Rex back was almost overwhelming.

Her eyes widened almost imperceptibly, and she cocked her head to the side. "He's back with the Sinners?"

Tank's shoulders dropped the tiniest bit. Naiya had given him T-Rex's cut, explaining that T-Rex refused to wear it. But now that Tank had explained everything, tomorrow they would go to the clubhouse, and T-Rex would wear his cut, and they would sit side by side at the boardroom table, and they would drink together, and laugh together, and everything would be right with the world.

Not that he could share any of this with Ella. He had to very careful about what he said. She was a reporter and they were all about taking small pieces of information and making them big. "Yeah. That's right. Let me in, and we can toast him together. I wanna thank you for offering to help me and believing me, and I owe you an apology for the other day when I had to leave . . . unexpectedly."

"Of course I believed you." Her voice dropped to a sultry purr, and she pressed a kiss to his throat, her robe falling partway open. "I guess that was him down by the lake, too. With his girl. Taking care of that Black Jack VP . . . ?"

Say nothing. Say nothing. Say nothing. This was his game, not hers. He just had to remember how much trouble he'd gotten into already by thinking with his dick.

"Dunno. We didn't talk much. I'm gonna organize a welcome-home party—the best damn party the MC has ever seen."

"He's lucky to have you," she said.

"And you're lucky to have me here tonight so fucking jacked with happiness I'm gonna give you the time of your life."

She bit her lip, sighed. "I can't, baby. I was just on my way to the studio. There's a breaking news story tonight, and I got called in."

"Dressed like this?" He slid his hand over her robe, soft and silky to the touch.

"No, silly." She smiled her TV smile, all teeth, and no warmth. "I was sleeping when the studio called, and I was just on my way to the shower when you knocked."

"Just one drink." He squeezed her ass, buried his face in her neck. But his nose wrinkled when he breathed her in. Instead of the heady scent of Poison, she smelled of smoke and leather, and something musky, manly . . . like cologne.

She stiffened in his arms. "Really, James. You need to go. I don't have time."

Tank jerked back, scowled. "You got a man in there, Ella?"

Her eyes widened, and she swallowed hard. "No."

The skin on the back of his neck prickled. She'd been so keen to get him inside before, but now she was pushing him away, and that scent . . . maybe he could work with it. Fly into a jealous rage like he'd seen Cade, Zane, and Jagger do when someone was sniffing around their old ladies.

"Out of my way." He shoved her roughly aside, pulling up short when he saw the state of her normally pristine living room—beer bottles and cigarette butts littered the tables, cushions were strewn across the floor. His gaze fell on the shards of glass, balled-up tissues, and empty pizza box on the thick, white carpet.

"It looks like a bomb went off in here. What happened?"

"I had a party," she said, dismissively. "It got out of hand."

Tank heard the creak of the door. A thud. He followed the sound to the kitchen where the back door swung open on its hinges. Pushing it open, he heard the unmistakable roar of a Harley in the distance.

The Harley.

Who the hell was on that bike? And was it the man who had been in Ella's house? He didn't buy the party story. Not with the lingering scents of sex and cologne, her disheveled appearance, and the fact there was only one pizza box on the floor.

He took off around the corner, belting it for the road. When he spotted the Harley in the distance, he jumped on his bike and punched the throttle. And although he was fast, he wasn't fast enough. The distinctive rumble faded, and by the time he hit the highway, it was gone.

Determined to find out what was going on, he returned to Ella's house, only to find the lights out, the doors locked, and her car gone.

Something didn't sit right about the whole situation.

But damned if he knew what it was.

★ TWENTY ★

If Tank hadn't been waiting in the hotel lobby, Holt would have skipped town with Naiya, never to return. He still hadn't managed to get his head around the fact that his brothers hadn't betrayed him. They had come and Viper stole him away.

"I knew you'd want your bike," Tank said, leading Holt and Naiya outside. "So I had Shooter and Benson drop mine off this morning so I could bring yours into town." He hesitated, grimaced when Holt frowned.

"We saved it from the fire. After Viper took you, he burned down Evie's shop."

"I knew about the fire." Holt put a hand on Naiya's back as they stepped out onto the street, part of him involved in the conversation, and the other part searching the street for danger.

"I kept it cleaned and polished and safe in Evie's new shop." Tank stopped and gestured to the bike. "It's good as new. Maybe better 'cause I had the mechanics give it a real good work over, and I detailed it myself this morning."

Emotion welled up in Holt's throat as he drank in the

sight of his ice and teal Heritage Softail Classic. He and
Tank had gone to the local Harley dealer to buy the bike
the day after he'd been patched into the club. Honest.
Clean. Uncluttered and unaffected by passing fads, the
Softail Classic dripped nostalgia, from the horseshoe oil
tank to the classic lines of a vintage frame. This bike was
all about class and tradition.

Holt nodded. "It looks good. Real good." Damn he'd
missed Tank. He was always doing little things that meant
a lot.

Tank smiled. "I filled it up, too."

"Appreciated, brother." He mounted the bike, sat for a
moment remembering the feel of saddle between his
thighs, the hard rubber grips, and the weight of the bike.
Naiya slid onto the pillion seat behind him and even she
felt right—her arms around his waist, her breasts pressed
up against his chest, her soft whisper that it was going to
be okay.

"Something's missing." Tank jogged over to his bike,
parked in front of Holt. His black denim Fat Bob took its
styling cues from the barrel of a tommy gun and was one
sweetheart of a ride. Tank pulled a cut from the saddle-
bag and held it out to Holt.

"Naiya gave this to me last night. You'll—"

"Not ready for that yet." Holt held up a hand. "You keep
it for me."

Tank's face creased in consternation. "You can't go into
the clubhouse without your cut."

"Jagger can make an exception for me." Holt had no
idea if Jagger would, in fact, make an exception for him.
Three months ago he wouldn't have even considered challenging Jagger or breaking the rules. But things had
changed—he had changed. And if Jagger kicked him out
for not wearing his cut, after all he'd been through, he
would be glad to go.

He followed Tank through Conundrum, but when they hit the open road heading north out of the city, he flicked the throttle and went flat out, blasting past Tank, a grin on his face. Tank whooped with delight and accelerated, easily matching Holt's speed since he wasn't carrying any extra weight. For the next twenty blissful minutes Holt let everything go—Viper, revenge, the Sinners, the uncertainty of his future. He gave himself over to the thrill of the ride, the freedom of the open road, the wind in his face, and the beautiful woman tucked against his back who easily rolled with the flow of his riding style and never second-guessed his decisions.

His respite lasted until they hit the gravel drive leading through the trees to the Sinner clubhouse. Almost immediately, his pulse kicked up a notch and tension tightened his brow. Tank directed him to his old parking spot and then ushered them toward the clubhouse.

Although he had only been away three months, Holt saw everything through new eyes. The former country house they had appropriated from a drug dealer who tried to cheat the club had been renovated to become the new Sinner clubhouse, but little attention had been paid to the exterior. As they climbed the worn, wooden steps up to the porch, Holt saw little things he'd never noticed before: loose boards, rotted railings and a broken screen door. He noticed the blue siding had faded to gray, and the huge front windows were dirty and streaked. Inside was no better: a sea of clutter covered the worn, wooden floors; the chandelier overhead had lost a few pieces, and the red carpet leading up the grand staircase had seen better days. And had the clubhouse always smelled of stale beer and pizza?

He ushered Naiya inside and closed the door behind them. "The place looks like a fucking frat house after a party."

Tank gave him a curious stare. "Whaddya you care? You never gave a shit about how it looked before."

Why did he care? Holt didn't know, but he felt embarrassed by the state of the clubhouse and ashamed to be part of a club that had no respect for its surroundings.

"This is pristine compared to the Black Jack clubhouse." Naiya squeezed Holt's arm and smiled. "They had so many pizza boxes lying around, they used to have competitions to see who could build the biggest stack, and there were things living in the corners—all sorts of critters."

Holt knew what she was doing, appreciated her effort. She was like Tank in so many ways.

"It's early," Tank said, his face falling as they walked through the empty living room. "No one's around, but the executive board is due to meet in ten minutes so you can meet the big guns first."

Holt stared at the worn brown couch where he and Tank had watched crime shows and played video games with Hacker. His gaze traveled to the multitude of pictures of girls, bikes and girls on bikes on the walls. He and Tank had put up many of those pictures, given carte blanche by the senior patch to decorate in any manner they saw fit. But now, with Naiya at his side, those choices seemed crass, almost juvenile.

He heard voices in the meeting hall, a huge room that they had created by knocking down most of the walls on the main floor. Tank's face lit up and he raced ahead.

"It's Jagger and Cade, and I'll bet the rest of the board is with them. Wait here and I'll tell them I've got a surprise."

"I'll stay here," Naiya said after Tank disappeared into the next room. "Give you some space to meet your brothers."

"I want you there." He threaded his hand through hers, pulled her to his side.

Pain flickered cross her face. "I don't belong here. I'm sure the Sinners are all good guys, but being in a clubhouse again makes my skin crawl. What if someone recognizes me?"

Holt cursed under his breath. He hadn't even thought about how hard it would be for Naiya to come to a clubhouse after what had happened to her. But he couldn't imagine seeing Jagger and the rest of the brothers alone. He needed her to ground him, to keep the beast that still hungered for revenge at bay, to shake some sense into him if he lost track of who he was now and what he needed to do.

"Anyone touches you, threatens you, hurts you in any way, I'll gut them like a fucking fish. And that will be the warm-up."

She gave him a resigned smile. "Okay, but if I'm in the way, just let me know. I'm more than happy to wander around outside or guard your bike."

"You will never be in my way, darlin'. You are the way."

He took a deep breath and waded through the debris toward the main hall.

Show time.

"Hold up, everyone!" Tank burst into the meeting room, barely able to contain his excitement. Jagger and Zane stopped mid-conversation and Gunner scowled.

"Watch your mouth when you're talking to the president, junior patch. Unless someone's dead, dying, or come back from the grave, it's bad manners to interrupt, even if the board's not in session yet."

"Cut him some slack." Cade looked up from the table where he was tallying the accounts. "Not too often our Tank gets excited about something. Maybe he's finally figured out what his dick is for."

"You would know," Zane said. "Weren't you the winner of the 'Most Sweet Butts in the Bed at One Time Prize' and 'Biker Manwhore of the Year' five years running?"

Cade raised an admonishing eyebrow. "I handed those titles over to you after I got myself an old lady."

"And I handed them to Sparky after I got an old lady and a son," Zane shot back. "So far he's not lived up to the title."

"Maybe we should pass it on to Tank." Dax gave an uncharacteristic smirk. "So what is it, junior patch? You got yourself some pussy?"

"Someone's back from the dead."

"You making fun of me?" Gunner took a step toward him. At the distinct sound of a cough, his eyes lifted, and he stopped dead in his tracks. "Son of a bitch. He wasn't lying."

Although he had been with the club for well over five years, Tank still admired the club's senior patch members. No matter what the situation, they kept their cool. Ambush, shootout, or ATF raid—they never broke a sweat. But when T-Rex walked into the room, their mouths went slack, their eyes went wide, and for once they had nothing to say.

"He escaped," Tank said into the silence. "He was in Viper's dungeon for three months."

"Fuck, T-Rex, it's good to see you. Welcome home, brother." Jagger took a step forward, hand outstretched, but T-Rex didn't move to greet him.

There was another awkward silence. Naiya whispered something to T-Rex and pushed him forward. Finally, he shook Jagger's hand. Hardly the reunion Tank had expected, but maybe it was just shock at seeing the brothers again.

Ice broken, Cade swooped in and pulled T-Rex into an awkward hug. Sparky clapped him on the back. Gunner punched his shoulder. The rest of the brothers greeted him warmly, but Zane held back until the end.

"What you did for my Evie . . ." His voice caught. "That's a debt that can't be repaid. You got my mark, brother. Anywhere. Anytime. Anything you need."

Tank swallowed hard, disconcerted by seeing the club's most recalcitrant member close to tears. But then he'd shed a few tears last night, too.

T-Rex introduced Naiya as a forensic scientist who had been the unfortunate object of Viper's attention. Tank caught a hitch in T-Rex's voice, knew he wasn't telling them the whole story, but maybe it wasn't his to tell.

The brothers peppered T-Rex with questions until Jagger called for silence. "Let's give our brother a chance to tell us what happened so he's not answering the same questions again and again."

T-Rex clasped Naiya's hand, pulled her against him, as if they were one person, not two, as if she was all the support he needed. Tank had the unsettling feeling of being the odd man out, and for the first time since he'd seen T-Rex again, he wondered if things could go ever go back to being the same.

"Not much to tell."

Tank frowned. Not much to tell? Kidnapped by Viper? Three months in the dungeon? An unheard-of escape? T-Rex was the talker in the club. He loved a good story, especially when it was about him. He'd never held back, especially when he had something exciting to share. Maybe he was just off his game and needed a little nudge.

"Evie told us about what happened at Big Bill's motorcycle shop," Tank said quickly. "She said she was detailing a bike and Big Bill showed up. He'd been skimming weapons off his shipments for the Black Jacks. He figured they were on to him, and he needed to pick up some stuff and get out of town. But the Jacks showed up before he could get away and Evie walked in on them . . ." He trailed off, hesitant to repeat the details of Bill's death in front of Naiya. She looked so sweet and innocent, and just a bit geeky in her black Space Invaders shirt. He had a feeling not many people would recognize the subtle silver block image on the front, but any retro gamer knew about Space Invaders. Her shirt gave her a hall pass to geek acceptance. And he would know. He had a Space Invaders shirt, too.

"Maybe Zane should tell this part." He cast a hopeful glance at Zane and got a scowl in return. Of course Zane wouldn't want to talk about the day he almost lost his girl.

When no one stepped in, Tank continued, more for T-Rex's benefit than for anyone else's. "So, yeah, Evie walked in, and Viper was fucking stoked to see her 'cause he wanted her so bad. But Evie wanted to try and save Bill so she took a small knife and stabbed Viper when he thought she was gonna give him some lovin'."

Tank swallowed hard, looking over at Zane again. Did he really want Tank to repeat the story about how Viper had beat her up and tried to rape her in front of his men? Tank sure as heck wouldn't be okay with anyone talking about what happened to Connie. She'd been there that morning, too, and Viper had torn her clothes and bruised up her beautiful face. Tank had spent the night with her, soothing her pain, keeping her safe as she cried in his arms, making love to her so she would know how much he cared. A lump welled up in his throat at the memory of the only woman he'd opened his heart to, and he coughed as he struggled to regain his composure.

"That's when I walked in," T-Rex said, saving Tank from an awkward situation and Zane from having his old lady's private horror shared in public again. Tank let out the breath he hadn't realized he was holding. This was the T-Rex he knew. The peacemaker. The good guy. The man who could smooth over any situation, diffuse any tension, or stop any fight. The friend who always knew when Tank needed him and always had his back.

"I'd been tailing Evie, keeping her safe for Zane." T-Rex stared at the window, his eyes vacant as he talked, as if he was lost in the memory. "I saw Viper and his men go into the shop, so I sent a text to Jagger and watched through the partially open shop door. There were too many of them for me to take alone so I was gonna wait for back up, but when Viper pushed Evie over the counter, I had to do something. I couldn't just stand there and let him . . . hurt her, so I offered myself in her place."

"Jesus Christ," Zane muttered from the corner.

"Viper took the trade," T-Rex continued. "Then he killed Bill and burned down the shop. I saw Evie and Connie escape as the Jacks pushed me into a cage, so I had no regrets. I figured since the Sinners had kidnapped Viper's old lady, you'd make a trade and get me back."

T-Rex drew in a shuddering breath. Naiya slipped an arm around his waist, and T-Rex leaned into her ever so slightly. Tank frowned. Why was he turning to Naiya for support when Tank was standing right here?

T-Rex's gaze fell on Jagger, his anger almost palpable. "At most I figured I'd have to go through a couple of bad nights in their dungeon." His voice caught, broke. "But one night became one week become one month and you never came."

Protests rumbled through the room as everyone tried to explain at once. Viper had refused the trade. He didn't give a damn about his old lady. And they had searched for him. Every brother had gone out to find him. They'd pulled every mark, used up every favor, blew up the Black Jacks clubhouse. Through the cacophony of sound, the message was loud and clear. *We didn't abandon you.* Did T-Rex hear it? More importantly, did he believe it?

"We blew up half their fucking clubhouse and a

semi-trailer to find you." Jagger silenced the protests with
a wave of his hand. He repeated the story Tank had told
T-Rex last night about the rescue operation and the body
in the dungeon.

"There was a Devil Dog in the dungeon when they
brought me in," T-Rex said. "After he died, they left his
body and took me to another dungeon. Musta been in a
forest 'cause it smelled like pine."

Tank stuffed his fist in his mouth to stifle the groan that
threatened to explode from his chest. They'd heard a rumor
that Viper had a dungeon under his house in the mountains,
but not until after they'd been there to rescue Evie's son.
Just the thought that they'd been so close made the entire
situation infinitely worse. Should they tell him?

As if he heard Tank's unspoken question, Jagger caught
Tank's gaze and gave an almost imperceptible shake of his
head. Yeah, Jagger was right. What good would it do to
tell him they'd been even closer than he knew? He was already hurting. Why hurt him more?

"What did the Jacks do to you?" Sparky asked.

Tank's head jerked up and he glared at Sparky, the bastard who had stolen his Connie away. Did the fucking
moron not realize T-Rex was already emotionally stripped
bare? "Shut the fuck up." He barked at the senior patch,
stepping in front of T-Rex as if to shield him. "He was tortured. You don't ask a man to live through the fucking
details. All you need to know is you wouldn't have lasted
a fucking day."

"Penalty for disrespecting a senior patch is an ass-
kicking from me." Gunner folded his arms over his massive chest.

"You lay a finger on Tank and I'll put a bullet through
your brain, brother or no." T-Rex didn't move and yet
somehow his power and presence filled the room. Tank
had no doubt he would do exactly as he said.

"Stand down. Both of you," Jagger said. "Emotions are high. People are saying things they might not mean. Let's cool down and hear about T-Rex's escape."

Tank looked over his shoulder and T-Rex nodded, the barest hint of a smile on his lips. This was how it was supposed to be. T-Rex had his back and he had T-Rex's back, although Naiya had his side.

"Viper threw Naiya in the dungeon with me." T-Rex put his arm around Naiya's shoulders. "She was able to distract the guard, and I took him out. I put on his cut and we bullshitted our way across the yard and stole a bike."

"He told them I was a hooker with an STD," Naiya said indignantly.

Chuckles filled the room, lightening the mood.

Jagger's face tightened with emotion. "What you did for Evie, for the club, what you went through . . . thank you is not enough. I don't know many brothers who could have gone through what you did and walk out the same man. But damn we're glad to have you back."

When the clapping and cheering finally died down, and everyone had a chance to say a few words to T-Rex, Jagger dispersed the crowd and gathered the board members together.

"Well, we got a board meeting to get to. T-Rex, your seat is still at the table. Looks like we'll need to get you a new cut."

Tank reached for the saddlebag he had brought with him, but T-Rex caught his eye, shook his head. Tank clutched the saddlebag strap as a growing sense of uneasiness intruded on his joy.

"Naiya can wait here unless she wants someone to take her home," Jagger continued. "Or she can wait up in your room. It's still there for you, brother. Same as you left it."

"I'll join the meeting, but Naiya comes with me."

And in that moment, Tank knew something was very wrong.

"Only full patch are allowed in the boardroom. You know that." Jagger's firm tone left no doubt about his position on the matter. "I can bend the rule about wearing a cut, but not the rule about closed meetings. Part of my job is to keep the brothers safe, and that won't happen if we compromise the security and confidentiality of the club."

T-Rex met Jagger's gaze head on, and there was no mistaking the challenge. "Then I won't be at any meeting, and if you or Gunner want to kick my ass for missing the meeting, I'll tell you right now I got enough ass-kickings in that dungeon to last me a lifetime. The marks on my body go through to my soul. So don't waste your fucking time."

A wave of panic flooded Tank's system. What was going on? T-Rex didn't cause trouble. He didn't challenge the rules. He was a mediator, and the person everyone went to when they had an irreconcilable dispute. He diffused tension; he didn't create it. Had he made a mistake bringing T-Rex here so soon? Should he have given his brother more time?

"You go with them to the meeting," Naiya said gently. "I'll be fine. I'll wait out here."

"You're coming with me. Wherever I go." T-Rex didn't even look at her. He didn't look at Gunner. Nor did he look at Tank. He fixed his unwavering gaze on Jagger and stood his ground.

Sweat beaded on Tank's brow. This wasn't the T-Rex he knew. He respected Jagger. Admired him. Hell, the night T-Rex thought Jagger had been caught by the Jacks, he'd been so distraught he hadn't even seen Jagger sitting at the boardroom table. But his quick thinking had saved Arianne's life.

Tank caught movement behind T-Rex and Naiya, but he paid it no mind. The other brothers would have to wait.

Right now he had to sort out this misunderstanding. Get things back on track.

"Viper is after Naiya." Tank addressed his comments to Jagger and Gun. "The Jacks have been chasing after them. He's concerned about her safety so he doesn't want her out of his sight."

Jagger's shoulders dropped the tiniest bit. At least Tank hoped they dropped. And was that a slight softening of Gunner's face? They just had to understand that T-Rex needed more time. He'd been away from the brothers, tortured, lost. And all he had was Naiya. She had brought him home. Of course T-Rex was protective of her and would want to keep her close. But soon he would realize he had Tank and the brothers to stand by his side. Everything would go back to normal.

"It's okay, Gun." Jagger made a placating gesture with his hand. "T-Rex only just walked in the door. We shouldn't expect him to just jump into the politics again. Hell, I wouldn't mind a break from the politics myself. Let's give him some time to meet with all the brothers, find his feet again. We'll keep his seat at the table. He can join us when he feels ready."

Tank's heart swelled with pride. This is why everyone loved Jagger, why he was such a good leader. He always knew the right thing to say, the right thing to do. He understood. T-Rex wasn't ready yet.

But he would be.

Dammit. What were they thinking?

Naiya dried her hands in the tiny washroom behind the clubhouse kitchen. She was certain the hand towel was supposed to be white, and not dark gray, and likely had never seen the inside of a washing machine, but she couldn't bring herself to care. Holt was waiting for her outside. After that fiasco of a reunion he'd declared their visit over and he was impatient to leave.

Poor Holt. He hadn't wanted to come to the clubhouse, and now she knew why. Although his brothers had been genuinely pleased to see him, there had been an unmistakable tension in the air. What had Jagger been thinking when he suggested Holt sit in on their meeting the day he returned? And would Gunner really have threatened to kick his ass after what he'd been through? And the whole damn fiasco with the cut? Sensitivity was clearly not a requirement for the Sinner's Tribe MC. The more she thought about it, the angrier she got. Holt needed support and understanding. Instead he got . . . bikers. Acting as bikers did.

Tank, Jagger, and Zane, the dark, brooding VP, were talking in the hallway outside the restroom, but their conversation stopped when she tried to slip past to get to the front door.

"Did he tell you what happened to him?" Tank asked.

"I saw what happened to him." Naiya bit out her words. "I was in the dungeon. They had him chained to the wall. He could barely walk or talk. He was starved and dehydrated, and his lips were cracked from thirst. After we got out, I called my friend Ally to come and look after him. She's a nurse. She'd never seen anyone treated so badly. You name a weapon, and he'd been beaten with it: whips, chains, canes, blades. There wasn't a part of him unmarked. She thought he'd had bones broken that had healed on their own. He had infected wounds, and some that needed stitches." She drew in a ragged breath. "But that was just outside. Inside . . . I don't know because I didn't know him before, but he's changed since we first escaped. He's . . . harder now."

"Tank says he has his cut, but he won't wear it," Jagger said, clearly inviting her to explain.

"No." Naiya pressed her lips together. Although she was willing to share the details about Holt's injuries so the Sinners would understand some of what he'd been through, she didn't feel it was her right to share Holt's reasons for not wearing the cut. She didn't owe anything to the Sinners, and after the way they'd treated him, she was even less inclined to be forthcoming.

Jagger lifted an eyebrow in censure, and Tank rushed in with an explanation she didn't need.

"Until he puts on the cut, he's not really back."

"He may never be back," Jagger said quietly. "I know men in the army who went through what he went through. They never got over it. And if they did, they weren't the same."

"What's your role in all this?" Dark and dangerous looking, Zane scowled. "Why is Viper after you?"

Naiya twisted her ring around her finger. "My mother owed him a debt. He decided to collect it from me. He kidnapped me from my mother's funeral and took me to his clubhouse. He—" Her throat tightened and she clenched her hand into a fist. "He dragged me to his room and I stabbed him in the chest with a pen knife to fight him off. He threw me in the dungeon to teach me a lesson. At first, I thought if I helped Holt, he would take me to you, and you would owe me a debt and protect me from Viper. I didn't know he was going to go after you for abandoning him. When I got to know him better though, I realized his heart wasn't in it. Revenge was a crutch, at least as regards the Sinners. But now that he knows the truth, he's got only revenge against Viper to keep him going."

"He can't go after Viper on his own," Jagger said. "Viper knows we've got a mark on him. He's tightened his security. He never goes anywhere without at least eight bodyguards. The bike rally coming up is our best chance to get close to him, but we need to work as a team."

Naiya shook her head. "Holt needs his revenge."

"He'll have it, but not alone." Jagger gave her a measured look. "I don't want to lose him again, and we've put a lot of time and planning into the hit on Viper at the rally. We need you to keep an eye on him. Let us know what he has planned so we can stop him if we need to."

Betray Holt? After he'd spent three months feeling betrayed? When he felt like he had no one to trust? Take away the one thing he had lived for all those months? The one thing Naiya secretly desired but had never been able to admit, not even to herself?

She stared at Jagger, stiffened her spine. Aside from Viper, he was probably the most intimidating man she'd ever met, and only a few weeks ago she would have agreed to his demands, desperate to get away and hide, afraid to stand up for what or who she believed in.

"I won't betray him. He needs this. And he needs to do it his way."

Jagger's eyes narrowed. "I'm trying to protect him, Naiya."

"You're trying to protect your club," she said. "And he's not alone. He has me, and I want revenge, too. For both of us." She felt the truth of her words as they dropped from her lips. She wanted Viper to pay for what he'd done to her and her mother, and locking him away wouldn't be enough. Most of the Jacks had been in jail at some point in their lives, and except for the fact they couldn't go beyond the prison walls, life for them continued as it had before: they ran their illicit operations, enforced their dominance, enjoyed their vices, and expanded their territory.

"And you'll have it," Holt said from behind her. "By my hand."

Naiya's eyes widened as she looked over her shoulder and met his cool, dark gaze. How long had he been there? How much had he heard?

* * *

It had been a mistake coming back to the club.

Holt reached out and clasped Naiya's hand, drawing her to his side. Far from being reassured after hearing the efforts his brothers had made to find him, he still thought they hadn't done enough. Why had no one made an effort to check for identifying marks? What about the tat on his arm? And leaving a body behind? Was that a story Sparky and Gunner made up because they didn't want anyone to know all they cared about was saving their own skins? He gritted his teeth, squeezed Naiya's hand.

"You okay?" she whispered.

"We're outta here." He'd heard enough. The brothers were set to betray him again. But Naiya—his Naiya—had refused to help them.

Even if he could have accepted that they did everything to find him, he couldn't accept what happened in Viper's house in the forest. He'd caught that look between Tank and Jagger. There was something they didn't want him to hear. But he had a secret, too. He'd heard them from the dungeon. Chained to the wall, his body bruised and broken, hope had flared in his chest, burned so bright he found the strength to bang his fists, rattle the chains, scream and shout, "I'm here. I'm here. Brothers, save me."

But they didn't come.

Nothing Viper had done to him had hurt as much as the moment his last hope fizzled and died.

And now, not only had his brothers left him to rot in Viper's dungeon, but they also planned to take away the only thing that had kept him alive. Revenge.

"We want the same thing, brother." Jagger and Zane shared a glance, and Zane slid his hand beneath his cut. Holt's skin prickled in warning. So they thought he was a threat. Well, he'd make sure they understood just how dangerous he could be if they tried to stand in his way.

"Then we'll do it my way."

"Come to the meeting and hear us out," Tank pleaded, shooting a desperate look at Naiya. "We've been setting this up for months, paying off the locals, planting bugs in the hotels. We haven't left anything to chance."

"Except me," Holt snapped.

"And we're glad to have you back." Jagger leaned against the wall. Outwardly, his posture was casual, relaxed, but Holt could feel the tension rolling off him, see the anger pulse in the veins of his neck. Once, he would have been cowed by Jagger's anger, but nothing scared him anymore. There wasn't anything Jagger could do to him that Viper hadn't already done.

"But we're not going to let you fuck this operation up or get yourself killed when you've only just come back to us," Jagger continued. "We aim to end this war and Viper is the key. We'll take him out and you'll have your revenge."

Holt bristled. "Viper is mine. No one is going to stop me from going after him. It's what I lived for in that fucking dungeon when you gave up on me."

"You heard what we did to find you. We didn't give up." Cold and distant, Zane was as intimidating as Jagger in his own way, simply because there was no line Zane wouldn't cross for the club. And yet when Holt looked at him now, he saw a man, not a monster—a man who had his woman at the cost of Holt's soul.

"I heard something else." Holt turned on Zane, letting out his pain and anger in a rush. "I heard the Sinners in Viper's house. You didn't want to tell me you were there, but I knew. I thought my brothers would finally come for me. Did you think to look? Did you think to ask? What about Mario? You remember the restaurant owner we planted in the Jacks? Our own Black Jack rat? Did anyone talk to him? He knew I was locked in the basement of Viper's house because he brought me food."

The room stilled and then Tank let out a tortured groan. "Oh fuck. Jesus fucking Christ."

So that was it. They truly had given up on him. No one had even bothered to ask the one person who had the information that would have saved Holt from months of torture.

"Viper kidnapped Evie's son, Ty, and took him to his house in the mountains." Tension—and was that a flicker of guilt?—lined Jagger's face. "He took Mario and a handful of guards with him, and we lost contact because Mario couldn't get a phone signal through the trees. Evie went on her own to rescue Ty. We stormed the house, and Mario knifed Viper then took off. We couldn't find him, and I didn't send anyone to hunt him down because he'd paid his debt to us. We couldn't search the house until later because Viper's guards called the Jacks and about thirty of them showed up to only six of us."

Holt's body shook with emotion. He'd heard the gunfight. Waited. Waited. Prayed, although he wasn't a praying man. He didn't know how much time had passed when the door finally opened. Hope flared for the last time and died in an instant when Viper walked into the room. And then hell began again.

Caught in a maelstrom of memory, torn by emotion, something inside Holt snapped. He loved them. He hated them. He had been through hell and back, suffered through hope and despair. He had lived to kill them and it was damn hard to throw it aside and accept they hadn't abandoned him because if he knew one thing about himself, it was that he would never leave a man behind. He needed to finish this. He wanted the torment to end. Although part of him warned that he wasn't thinking clearly, he reached beneath his cut and drew his weapon on Jagger. "It was easier to assume I was dead than make the effort to find me, wasn't it?"

"No." Tank moaned; his distress etched in the lines of his face. "No, brother. Don't do this. It killed us. Every one."

Zane moved swiftly, interposing his body between Holt and Jagger. He always had Jagger's back, had risked his life countless times to save him. Jagger was untouchable unless Zane was dead.

"Whatever you do, whatever you think, you should know that Tank didn't give up," Zane said, drawing his own weapon. "Even after the funeral. Even after we told him to let it go because we didn't have a shred of evidence to suggest you were alive, he looked for you. Days, nights, he was on his bike searching forests and ditches and alleys. He even fucked a coupla Black Jack sweet butts to get information. We didn't give up easy, T-Rex, but know that Tank didn't give up at all."

Nausea roiled in Holt's stomach, and his hand wavered. Was he ready to do this? To kill the men he had called brothers? To lose the only man he'd considered a friend?

"Don't do it," Naiya murmured, as he pushed her to safety behind his back. "You aren't thinking straight. You've been through hell, and meeting your brothers like this was a bad idea. They aren't the enemy. I wasn't there, but it sounds like they did everything they could do. And yeah, maybe they could have tried even harder, and maybe they fucked up, and you suffered terribly for it, but what I saw when you walked in the door was that they were overjoyed to see you. Viper is the enemy. Viper made you suffer. He took a lot from you. Don't let him take this, too. You all want the same thing. You want Viper dead. They just want to do it a different way."

"So you're with them, now?" His voice was rough, harsh. Broken.

"No. I'm with you."

The front door creaked open. Holt glanced back over his shoulder and saw Arianne in the hallway, her gun pointed at Naiya. Jagger's old lady was the best shot in the club thanks to her old man, Viper, who had given her a gun when she was three years old. She'd left him after years of abuse and slapped him in the face by becoming Jagger's old lady. But she was Viper's daughter through and through. No one fucked with Arianne or the man she'd risked her life to have.

"T-Rex!" she shouted. "You pull that damn trigger and I'll pull mine."

Holt struggled to contain the tidal wave of anger that surged through his body, turning the world into a red haze. "You get that fucking gun out of my girl's face or I'll shoot every damn person in this room!" Holt roared, desperate to turn, but knowing the minute he dropped his weapon, Zane would be all over him.

"Last time I saw her, your girl was a Black Jack brat," Arianne spat out. "Is that what this is all about? You're with the Jacks now? You thought you'd just walk in here and take out Jagger? The Sinners? Not on my damn watch, you won't."

Naiya cursed and reached under Holt's jacket to grab the weapon holstered at his back. Before Holt could stop her, she yanked it out and plastered her back against his. "I'm not with the Jacks. I never was. And this is getting out of hand. Holt and I are leaving. Everyone is going to lower their weapons and let us pass. No one is going to hurt Holt. He's been through enough."

"Darlin', are you pointing that weapon at Arianne?" Holt asked, his gaze still on Zane and the weapon pointed at his heart.

"Yes. You want me to point it somewhere else? Like at Zane? Because if he hurts you . . ."

"I want you to put it down," he murmured, struggling

to keep his voice even. Damn brave woman had his back, even though she didn't know how to shoot a gun. But with her inexperience, she was now the most dangerous person in the room, and that meant he had lost control of the situation. "I get that you want to protect me, but I think there's a bigger risk of someone getting hurt if you don't."

"Zane lowers his gun first," she said.

"I'll drop." He lowered his weapon, and Zane did the same. Holt holstered the weapon and raised his hands in the air, turning to show Arianne he was now unarmed. She nodded and holstered her gun.

"You can drop the weapon now." Holt gently pressed Naiya's arm down and pried her fingers off the gun.

"I wasn't really intending to shoot her," Naiya said. "I just got angry at how they were treating you."

"You gotta keep a cool head when you're handling a weapon." He tucked the gun back in its holster. Ironic that he was chastising her for being emotional when he could barely contain his own anger. "Otherwise the wrong people get hurt."

He'd almost lost Naiya back there. Yes, she'd been trying to help, but she'd put her life at risk and taken away his one chance to avenge himself against the MC. No way would Jagger let him anywhere near the clubhouse again. He was surprised Jagger was even letting them walk out the door.

Fuck. How had he got it so wrong? He'd thought the best way to protect her was to keep her with him, be there for her the way he hadn't been for his sister. But he was a danger to her. If not for him, she wouldn't have been in a situation where she had to put her life at risk, and the longer he stayed with her, the worse it would be. He was going down a path she couldn't follow.

A path he had to take alone.

★ TWENTY-ONE ★

Naiya tightened her grip on Holt's waist as he took a sharp corner, his motorcycle leaning so far to the side she was surprised they didn't tip. She'd ridden with Jeff and a few of the Black Jacks when she was younger, and they'd taught her what was expected of a pillion rider, but except for the ride out to the clubhouse, it had been a long time. Still, she trusted Holt, and the key to a safe pillion ride was trust. If he leaned, she leaned with him. Second-guessing his actions and shifting her weight in the wrong direction could be disastrous to them both.

She glanced over her shoulder at the thicket of trees that hid the clubhouse from view, half-expecting Arianne or Tank or some of the Sinners to come after them. Even she knew you didn't pull a weapon on the president of an MC and his old lady and walk away. Viper would have killed them both in a heartbeat. That Jagger let them go said a lot about how he felt about Holt.

Holt slowed the bike. Without the cool rush of pine-scented air, her hair fell over her face and she brushed it away, tightening her legs around his hips as he turned off on a gravel road. About one mile off the highway, where the grassy foothills gave way to trees, he stopped the bike and turned off the engine.

"Why did we stop?" Naiya slid off the bike, grateful for the chance to walk off the strain on little-used muscles. A cloudbank had rolled in while they were at the clubhouse, and she shivered in the cool air.

"I can't fucking believe you pulled on Arianne." Holt dismounted and flipped the kickstand. Naiya startled at his tone. She knew he was angry when they left the clubhouse, but she hadn't realized it was directed at her or that he would feel the need to stop on their way back to the hotel.

"She was going to kill you."

"You don't ever fucking put yourself at risk again." He thudded his fist on the seat. "And especially not for me."

"If not for you, then who?" Naiya folded her arms, annoyed that he would question her choices. She'd saved his damn ass back there. The least he could do was say thanks. "I've spent my life hiding in my books, watching the world pass me by. I saw all sorts of bad things happen, but I never did anything. I didn't tell the police or social services what happened at home with my mother, or about the men the Jacks killed, or the drugs they sold from my mother's apartment, or how Viper kept her addicted so he could control her. I didn't try to get her help—"

"You were a kid."

"I was fifteen when I left. I could have done something. Instead, I pretended it wasn't happening. Just like I pretended Viper didn't hurt me or that I was fine after what he did. I pretended there was nothing wrong with Maurice and me and that I was happy living a life where I was empty inside."

She dropped her gaze, stared at his bike, not recognizing her reflection in chrome. "And then I met you," she continued. "And you were so real. Bad things happened and you dealt with them. Everything about you is up front and honest. And when we were in there, and I knew you were hurting, and they weren't understanding, I suddenly got tired of pretending. That situation wasn't right, and for once in my life, I wanted to do something about it."

"It was the wrong fucking thing to do." His face darkened. "You almost got yourself killed. How can I protect you if you're gonna do crazy shit like that? That's not who you are. That's not what you do."

"Well, obviously, I didn't get killed," she huffed, kicking at the rocks on the road. "And it was the right thing to do because we're both still alive, which was iffy from the moment you pulled your gun on Jagger. And it is who I am and what I do because I just did it." Her voice rose in pitch, and she glared. Who was he to tell her who she was, when she didn't even know herself?

"Christ." He scraped his hand through his hair. "It wasn't a fucking game. I lost control of that situation because of you. People could have been hurt. You don't belong in this world anymore, Naiya. You don't understand the rules. You don't have the experience to survive."

A ball of disappointment lodged in her throat. Ever since she met Holt, she'd done things that scared her, things that took her out of her controlled, comfortable world and thrust her back into the biker craziness she'd been running from for the last seven years. She'd started living life instead of reading about it. She'd let her inner wild child out, and it had been fun and reckless and scary and exciting. And at the Sinners' clubhouse, she'd stepped out of the shadows and taken control of a situation that she knew was wrong. She'd felt confident and brave. For once, she'd felt like she mattered, like there was something she could do aside from tagging along with Holt on his quest for revenge. But he'd just ripped that all away, and now she felt stupid and foolish for thinking she could be part of his world.

She opened her mouth to retort, to tell him the Naiya

he met in the dungeon wasn't the Naiya who stood with him now, and closed it again. Why bother? She'd been wrong about Holt. She thought he'd seen her as she truly was, but clearly he hadn't seen her at all.

"Fine. Take me back to the hotel." She didn't need him and his stupid quest for revenge that was going to get him killed, especially now that he'd alienated his club. And she'd never wanted to be involved with bikers. She had a career to establish, rent to pay, car payments to make, and student loans to pay off. She wasn't going to do that riding around on the back of Holt's bike on the run from Viper and the ATF. Holt didn't need her, and she clearly wasn't cut out for this life. What the hell had she been thinking when she pulled that gun on Arianne? Holt was right. That wasn't her. She abhorred violence, followed the law. Hell, she didn't even know how to use a gun. Time to get back on track and make a plan to move forward; she'd been living without one too long.

He gave a satisfied grunt. "You stay there until you get the all-clear either from me or the Sinners."

Stay? No way was she sticking around. She had an interview in Florida next week. Might as well head down there early, get some sun, and forget about the hot biker with an over-protective streak who didn't think women could look after themselves.

"You go do your thing, and I'll do mine." She was giving him what he wanted—a chance to go after Viper, unfettered and unencumbered by her or the need to protect her. And she was doing what she wanted—pursuing a normal life, away from bikers and everything they represented.

So why did it feel so wrong?

Six hours later, Naiya sat in front of the computer in the hotel's business center, with a prepaid cell phone pressed to her ear, listening to Ally talk about the police visit to their house and how easily Doug put them off. Although the room looked out over the street, the brown-and-green decor gave it a dark, dreary appearance, fitting with her mood. She'd already filled Ally in on everything that had happened from the time they parted ways at the cabin to Holt's abrupt departure a few hours ago.

Other than a quick good-bye, she and Holt hadn't talked after their heated off-road discussion. He'd picked up his stuff at the hotel, left her with a bundle of cash she didn't want, kissed her cheek and walked out the door. She didn't know where they stood. Was that the end? Was he leaving her to find Viper and get himself killed? Or was he planning to come back?

Naiya didn't like uncertainty, and the only way to deal with it was by having a plan. She'd used the last of Ally's money to buy a cell phone and spent the afternoon responding to interview requests—two in Colorado and one in Hawaii—while wallowing in the ache of missing Holt. How had it gone so wrong?

"Maurice has been calling ever since Doug caught him with his new . . . that girl," Ally said. "Doug met up with him for a drink, and Maurice told him he'd made a huge mistake. He wanted to see you to explain, so Doug told him what was happening. He's worried about you on the run with an outlaw biker. Do you want to see him?"

It took Naiya a second to realize Ally had asked her a question. The minute she'd mentioned Maurice, Naiya had switched off. "I'm in Conundrum."

"And I'm heading your way as soon as I get off work," Ally said. "I'm not leaving my girl alone in a strange town when she's hiding out in a hotel, all broken up over her biker walking out on her, and she's being chased by cops and psychopaths. The question is: do you want me to bring

Maurice? He wants to come to see you. He says you can stay at his place and he'll look after you."

Naiya leaned back in her chair, fiddled with the computer mouse on the table. "Maurice who lay on his couch as I walked through the streets in the dark wants to look after me?" She couldn't imagine Maurice shooting someone like Leo or facing off against an ATF agent or pulling a gun on the president of an outlaw MC, but then she and Maurice had led a pretty sedate life. They both worked hard, went to the gym, met up a few evenings a week and usually spent the weekends watching movies and walking in the park. Calm. Predictable. Safe. Just what she needed after stabbing a biker, going on the run, becoming an accessory to murder, stealing motorcycles, and threatening to shoot someone with what she was pretty sure was an unregistered weapon.

"Doug thought he sounded genuine," Ally continued. "Maybe you should just hear him out. Even if you don't get involved with him again, you need friends right now, and although I still want to poke out his eyes for what he did to you, he's definitely not involved with the kind of people who could hurt you."

"Bring him along." Naiya sighed. "I'll hear him out. Frankly, I wouldn't mind feeling like a normal person again, having a normal conversation and just hanging out with people I know who aren't going to shoot someone or steal something or ride a motorcycle at one hundred miles an hour and almost get me killed."

"Does that mean it's totally over with Holt?" Ally hesitated. "I kinda liked him. He was an over-the-top hunk of alpha loving, and he was totally into you."

"He's a biker, Ally." Naiya rolled over the bed and picked up Holt's shirt. "I like him—more than like him, but I can't go where he's going. He had a falling out with his biker brothers, but I don't think it's a forever thing. They let him walk out of there unharmed because they care about him. I'm sure he'll be back with them at some point, and there is no way I'm ever getting involved with a club again. I'm a science geek, and I'm planning to spend the rest of my life in a crime lab. I need a secure future and a stable guy. I've already got three job interviews lined up, and I've just been offered—"

"Science geeks don't shoot guns," Ally said, cutting her off. "They don't go on the run with outlaw bikers, jab them with needles, steal weapons, and pull the wool over the eyes of an ATF agent. They don't fuck a man they barely know who is the total opposite of Maurice."

"That's pretty specific for an over-generalization." She pushed away from the desk and walked over to the window.

"When I saw you at the motel, you looked different. You looked alive . . . like you'd just woken up. Your eyes sparkled, and, although it was a scary situation, you looked like you were excited and having fun."

"Being chased by Viper isn't fun." She stared at all the normal people living their normal lives—shopping, walking, eating, and laughing. One day, that would be her. One day she would be free. "It's the last thing I ever wanted."

Ally's voice rose to the wheedling the tone she used when she was trying to convince Naiya to do something she knew Naiya wouldn't want to do. "But it was fun when you were with Holt 'cause he wasn't scared of Viper. And he made you not scared either. You took risks and survived. You hung with a biker and didn't turn into a crack whore, if you'll pardon my disrespect, but I'll never forgive your mom for abandoning you like she did. Holt would never do that to you. He wanted to protect you. If he's gone, it's 'cause you pushed him away."

"I didn't push him away." She lowered her voice when

a man in a business suit walked into the room. "He said he was going to do what he had to do, and I wasn't going with him because it was too dangerous and I didn't belong. That's when I suddenly realized I'd gone off the rails. I mean, what the hell was I thinking?" Naiya frowned when a black sedan with blacked-out windows pulled up in front of the hotel. Something twigged at the back of her mind. She'd seen that vehicle before.

"Isn't that his choice?"

A man stepped out of the sedan. Tall and lean, with dark hair, a black suit and a blue tie. Her heart skipped a beat.

Michael.

"Ally, I have to go." She raced over to her computer, logged off, and grabbed her stuff. Sweat beaded her forehead as she made a last visual sweep of her workspace.

"I'll call you later."

★ TWENTY-TWO ★

TANK

A woman shrieked, and Tank missed his shot.

"Fuck." He looked up at Gunner chalking his cue on the other side of the pool table. "That doesn't count." He glared at the group of women sitting beneath the flashing neon sign that read "Rider's Bar." What the hell was so funny? Didn't they know this was a place for serious drinking and not a place to party?

"Every stroke counts." Gunner snorted a laugh and made a lewd gesture with his hips. "That's what I tell the ladies." He looked over at Shaggy who was their fourth for the game. "Take notes, old man. Now that Zane's outta the game, I'm the new Sinner chick magnet."

Leaning over the pool table, to take his shot, Zane cracked a smile. He'd been doing that a lot since Evie had walked back into his life with the son he never knew he had. Tank didn't think he'd ever seen Zane smile before Evie, and he still couldn't get used to it. But it seemed to happen to the brothers who hooked up with an old lady. Even Jagger had been caught smiling once.

"You talking smack 'cause you forgot how to shoot, Gun?" With T-Rex's return to the club still uncertain, Tank felt obliged to try and fill T-Rex's role as peacekeeper, but it didn't come easy.

"Fuck you." Gun grabbed his cue and sent the cue ball careering wildly into the far bumper.

"Looks like you need some help holding your stick." Tank made a pumping gesture with his hand and everyone laughed. "You need some pointers, I'll be happy to show you how it's done."

"Yeah 'cause you're that hard up," Gun snapped, never one to enjoy being the butt of Sinner jokes. "Can't get a woman, so you spend your time with your hand down your pants."

Damn. They were always talking him down, never taking him seriously. Ever since T-Rex disappeared, they hardly noticed Tank anymore. He'd never realized how he'd stood in T-Rex's shadow until the light was gone. And now that T-Rex was back, he would disappear again.

"I got a girl," Tank said bristling. "A civilian. And she's famous. Classy. Smart as fuck. Not the kind of girl that would ever look twice at you." He regretted the lie as soon as it was out of his mouth. His brothers weren't going to let that one go, but if he let slip he'd been with a reporter, he'd be kicked out of the club.

"Yeah?" Shaggy lifted his thick brows. "Like movie or TV famous? Who is she? When are you bringing her to the club?"

"Jesus H Christ," Gunner muttered. "He's shitting you. What would a chick like that want with Tank? Movie and TV stars, society girls . . . they go for the big money or the big players. Maybe if he was president, he'd have a shot. But a fucking junior patch who lives in the fucking clubhouse and drives a piece of shit Fat Boy? Come the fuck on."

Tank opened his mouth for a snappy retort, when he heard someone call his name. Frowning, he looked through the crowd in the direction of the voice and caught sight of Naiya, a bag over her shoulder, her chest heaving, and her hair in disarray. She looked around, caught Tank's gaze, and relief spread across her face as she came toward him.

"Do you know where Holt is?"

Tank shook his head. "I thought he was with you."

She glanced over at the brothers and lowered her voice. "We kinda had a fight. He dropped me at the hotel and took off. But there was an ATF agent who was asking us questions in Trenton, and I just saw him outside the hotel." She leaned right up and whispered in his ear. "Holt shot Leo, Viper's VP, and then we took his bike. The attendant at the gas station where you saw us told the ATF he saw two people in Bolton Beaver sweatshirts on a fancy bike, and when the agent saw me in the sweatshirt he got suspicious. But without the CCTV tape, he couldn't link us directly."

"I took the tape," Tank said. "I told Holt when he told me about Leo. You're safe 'cause I won't let anyone get it."

"But the agent is at the hotel." Naiya's voice rose in pitch. "It can't be a coincidence. I need to warn Holt. We have to get out of town."

"This is a Sinner town," Tank assured her. "And you're a Sinner's girl in a Sinner bar. Nothing's gonna happen to you here."

She bit her lip, looked away. "I'm not a Sinner's girl. Holt and I . . . we kinda parted ways."

Tank laughed. He'd only spent a few hours with T-Rex since his return, but he knew his best friend inside and out, and he'd never seen him the way he was with Naiya. Intense. Protective. Head over fucking heels. She was his girl. He'd all but claimed her. Tank knew deep inside that T-Rex would do anything to protect her. And that meant when Holt wasn't around, Tank would look after her as if she were his own.

"He may have gone for a ride to cool off, but he'll never leave you." Tank put his arm around her and gave her a reassuring squeeze. "I know him like I know myself. He may have lost a part of himself in that dungeon, and he may need some time to come back to the Sinners, but there is nothing that will keep him away from you."

"He won't know where I am." She leaned against him with a worried sigh. "And what if he goes back to the hotel? He'll walk right into their arms."

"I'll call the clubhouse, get some brothers to keep watch around the hotel for when he comes back. They'll let him know where you are."

Shaggy gestured to her bag. "I'll take that and put it in the back. You can wait at the bar. Banks will take care of you while we get things sorted."

Naiya handed Shaggy the duffle bag, and he frowned. "Where did you get that ring? Looks like a man's ring. You got a man? You messing around with our T-Rex? He's been through enough."

"Leave her the fuck alone." Tank said before Naiya could answer. "She's Holt's girl. If there is another dude in the picture, he's as good as dead. And right now finding Holt is our number one priority. Last thing he needs is to wind up in another kind of jail."

Shaggy stared at Naiya's ring a second longer and shoved his hands in his pockets. "I'm gonna check out Sandy Lake. That's where I'd go if I was hunting Viper 'cause that's where Viper will be when the rally is on, and that's where he'll be the most vulnerable."

"Sounds good. I'll ride local." Tank gave Naiya a comforting squeeze. "That way I can be nearby to keep an eye on Naiya."

Shaggy grabbed Naiya's bag and hustled out the back door. Naiya looked up at Tank who had turned his attention to the local news on the television above the bar. "Why are you doing this when Holt hasn't really come back to the club? He's not even wearing his cut."

"Until he hands that cut to Jagger, he'll always be a Sinner." Tank had been carrying T-Rex's cut with him since last night. It might be a long and rocky road, but T-Rex would find his way back, and when he did, Tank would be the one to put that cut on his shoulders.

"We have to find him," Naiya begged. "I don't know what I would do if Holt wound up in jail. I don't know what he would do. He still has nightmares about being in the dungeon. And he killed Leo to protect me. I couldn't live with myself."

Warmth spread through Tank's chest, as Naiya's words made her feelings clear. She cared about T-Rex as much as he cared about her, and after what T-Rex had been through, he deserved a little happiness.

"You stay here," Tank said. "I can't go looking for him if you're on the streets unprotected. I'll check in every half hour, but you're safe at Rider's. Don't worry. I'll find T-Rex. I'll bring him home."

★ TWENTY-THREE ★

"What the fuck am I doing?"

Holt lay on the roof of the five-story office building across the street from the Bestway Hotel in Sandy Lake and angled his rifle. Preparations for the weekend rally had already begun. Banners hung from windows, streets had been cordoned off, and the local shops were stuffed with rally souvenirs. In less than forty-eight hours, bikers would descend on the small town and the nearby campground, turning the place into one big party.

Without his cut to identify him as a biker, and falling back on the charm he'd once used to inveigle women into his bed, it hadn't taken Holt long to find out where Viper was going to be staying during the rally. Although the hotel desk clerk, a former house mama in a Sinner support club, had been willing to give him more than information, he'd felt guilty even kissing her cheek. There was only one girl he wanted. And he couldn't have her.

"Fuck." His loud curse echoed over the rooftop, fading into the evening sky. He flattened himself on the warm asphalt, and peered across the street, as he tried not to choke on the thick scent of tar.

From this position, he had a clear line of sight into both Viper's room and the front door to the hotel. He had two sniper rifles set up beside him—an M24 weapons system chambered for a NATO short-action cartridge, and an SR-25 with a rotating bolt and direct impingement gas system—thanks to the raid on the Devil's Brethren cache.

His groin tightened when he remembered holding Naiya that afternoon, how badly he wanted her—so much that fear had driven him away. He'd almost lost her then, but the feeling of despair was nothing compared to what he felt now.

How did they reconcile two different lives? Holt had always been part of a brotherhood—first with the street gang and then with the Sinners—and the time he'd spent between, alone with his thoughts day after day, had been nothing less than hell. He liked being around people. He liked being part of a tribe. The Sinner's Tribe.

"At least, I did," he muttered.

Now, he wasn't so sure. He'd felt uneasy around his brothers, uncomfortable in his skin. From the moment he stepped into the clubhouse, he wanted to be alone. No, not alone. With Naiya. She was the only person who knew the new Holt, the man who had survived, transformed into a harder, stronger, ruthless, more determined version of himself. A man who needed a strong woman by his side. A man worthy of a beautiful, intelligent, confident woman who had suffered and survived, too.

Because of Viper.

He leaned up, practiced tracking a man on the street with the rifle. Back on track. Focus on the goal. The one thing that had kept him alive in the dungeon—his reason for being now that he'd left Naiya behind. What the fuck had he been thinking?

His breath caught when he heard the scrape of a door. Rolling to his back, he pulled his Smith & Wesson Model

500 revolver from its holster. The large caliber handgun packed a punch, although it was damn loud and would draw the wrong kind of attention. No time to dissemble the weapons. Whoever had intruded on his surveillance was about to get an unpleasant surprise.

But the surprise was on him when Shaggy stepped out onto the roof.

"Christ. I almost shot you." Holt lowered his weapon, took a deep breath to slow his racing heart. "How did you find me?"

"Wasn't hard." Shaggy closed the door behind him, leaned against wall. "Lookin' the way you look, wasn't hard to find a coupla girls who noticed you wandering around. Viper's an arrogant ass. He's not gonna be slumming it, so we put our people in the big hotels. We got the intel last week that he's staying across the way. Figured it wouldn't take you long to figure that out."

Holt huffed and flipped over, checking out the hotel through his binoculars. "You here to convince me to give up going after him on my own? Come back to the club? Be part of the team?"

"No."

Frowning, Holt looked back over his shoulder. "So did Jagger send you to teach me a lesson? Do I get a beat down or a bullet to the head?"

"I came to give you shit 'cause you left your girl unprotected."

"She's not my girl."

Shaggy snorted a laugh. "Anyone that spent more than five minutes in a room with you two would disagree. She pulled a fucking gun on Jagger for you, and you did the same for her. The two of you are like goddamned Bonnie and Clyde."

Holt abandoned his surveillance and pushed himself to his feet. With the moon hidden behind the clouds, Shaggy was a dark shadow in front of him. And an irritating one at that. "What the fuck it is to you? You've barely said two words to me since I joined the club except to give me orders or ream me out for doing something wrong."

"Someone had to come and line you up," Shaggy said. "Tank's still trying to get a grip on the fact his best bud might not come back to the MC, and the rest of the senior patch are getting ready for the rally. You got a girl who cares about you, she's in danger, and you fucking ran away."

"She's safe in Conundrum, and she'll be safe wherever she goes after I'm done what I gotta do here."

Shaggy stroked his beard, gave Holt a considered look. "Arianne said she was a Black Jack. That true?"

"Her mother was a Black Jack sweet butt, Viper's favorite. Naiya said he turned her mother into an addict to keep her tied to the club. Her mom never told Naiya who her dad was, but she said he was a Jack. She lived with her grandmother for a time then had to live with her mom. She left the club when she was fifteen. Never looked back until she returned home to go to her mother's funeral and Viper caught her. So, no. She's not a Jack. Never was a Jack. Never wanted to be a Jack."

A pained expression crossed Shaggy's face, but it was so fleeting Holt wasn't sure if he'd seen it at all. "Rough life."

"It's worse than I told you," Holt said, gritting his teeth. "And it means Viper's got more to answer for than just what he did to me." He gestured to the rifles. "He's going down the minute he comes in range, and if he goes in the back, I'll get him through the window."

"How are you gonna get off the roof?" Shaggy swallowed, cleared his throat. "There will be over one hundred Jacks in town this weekend, not to mention their support clubs. You know Viper will have guards all over the block."

"I'm gonna jump to the next building from the fire

escape." Holt pointed to the brick building beside them. "Then I'll go down the stairs to the basement. I rented a mini van, filled it with sports equipment. Gonna put on a ball cap and pretend like I'm a civilian dad and drive myself outta town."

"You'll never make it."

"Maybe I will. Maybe I won't." Holt shrugged, feigning a nonchalance he didn't feel in the least. "All I care is that Viper is dead. That's what I lived for all those months in the dungeon. That's what Naiya deserves."

Shaggy walked across the roof and stared down at the road, fiddling with his ring, the gesture so like Naiya's that Holt's heart squeezed in his chest.

"You didn't live in the dungeon," Shaggy said. "You survived. I know someone who went through what you did. He came out of it a changed man. He lost his heart and soul. You don't want to wind up like him, but if you leave Naiya, you will. A woman like that can save you. Maybe she already has."

Holt joined him at the edge of the roof. By Friday, the main street would be a sea of headlights, everyone showing off their bikes before heading out to the campground for the real party. The rally organizers had booked a kick-ass headline band, and there would be all the booze, girls, and drugs a biker could ask for.

"You got something else to live for now." Shaggy shoved his hands in his worn, frayed pockets. "You got a girl who loves you. You got a president who was so overjoyed to have you back that he forgot to give you a chance to breathe. You got a club full of brothers who sacrificed themselves to rescue you. You got the kind of friend a man only gets once in a lifetime—the most loyal man I've ever known— who doesn't understand why you walked away from the club, and who's gonna spend the rest of his days waiting for you to come back."

Stunned, Holt just stared, trying to take it all in. Shaggy, the recalcitrant loner, the grouchy old timer with more miles under his belt than all of the MC combined, of all people, lecturing him, telling him Naiya loved him. That Jagger, the man he admired most in the world, had made a mistake. That Holt had meant something to the club. That Tank would never give up.

"She doesn't want to be part of the club, Shag. And I totally get it. She had a shit time growing up. She had no one to protect her, no one to have her back, no one to care when Viper . . . well I can't say what he did to her."

Shaggy made a choked, strangled sound, and thudded his hand on the concrete ledge, like he'd just done a shot of Gunner's moonshine. "We've let him live too long. First Evie. Now Naiya. Even the civilians aren't safe from him anymore."

"He didn't break her," Holt continued. "She's strong. Strongest woman I know except for Arianne, but then she's Viper's daughter so you gotta be made of steel to survive that. Naiya turned away from all that shit, went to college and made something of herself. She's a scientist now—she does forensic stuff like on the crime shows. She's gonna get a job at a crime lab out of the state. She's not part of our world, and I would never drag her back into it. It's better that I leave her. For both of us. And for the club." Except, coward that he was, he hadn't been able to say goodbye. For all he knew, Naiya thought he was coming back.

"Yeah?" Shaggy's eyes burned into his soul. "You think Viper's gonna just leave her alone? Did he leave her alone after she escaped? What if you miss? What if they catch you? What if they shoot you in the fucking heart? Who's gonna look after her then? Who's gonna protect your girl from the fucking ATF agent who was sniffing around her hotel?"

"What the fuck? How did he find her? Where is she?" Fear and regret stabbed Holt in the gut. This was Lucy all over again. He'd left her unprotected and she'd died for his mistake.

"She's safe at Rider's."

Holt drew in a relieved breath. "Tank will look after her."

Shaggy walked across the roof, pausing to kick at some small shards of asphalt. "Yeah, he will. But is that what you want? And I'm asking this 'cause long time ago, I fucked up. I had a girl, the other half of my soul, and I left her for something I thought was more important—my club. I broke her fucking heart. Abandoned her. She had no one, no protection, and it ended so fucking bad I can hardly breathe for thinkin' about it."

"Club first. That's the life."

"After all my years of livin' the life, I can say that's bullshit." Shaggy thumped his chest. "Without heart you got nothing to give to the club. And I'll tell you now, unless you want to wind up bitter and alone with a fucking beard you wear to pay for your sins, you gotta follow your heart." His phone buzzed and he reached into his cut and pulled it out. "Don't let Jagger know I said that. I'd never live it down."

"So why did you tell me?" Holt kneeled and folded down the M24.

A pained expression crossed Shaggy's face. "So you don't make the same fucking mistake. So that another innocent girl doesn't suffer."

Naiya sipped her second vodka and tonic and checked the clock above the bar. If Tank wasn't back in ten minutes, she was going out to look for Holt herself. Banks had let her use his phone to text Ally and Maurice her new location, but she couldn't wait. The thought of Holt in a prison cell or a dungeon did strange things to her stomach, and she couldn't just sit and let it happen.

"You want another?" Banks held up the bottle, and Naiya shook her head.

"I'm still working on this one. I've always liked to keep a clear head. Bad things happen when people drink too much."

"Sensible." Banks put away the bottle. "I rarely touch the stuff."

"But you run a bar."

Banks gave her a wink. "That's just the day job."

She wanted to ask about his night job, but his face shuttered quickly, and she took the hint. "Seems crazy for me to be applying for jobs in crime labs while I'm hanging out in an outlaw-biker bar."

Banks took a bottle of vodka off the shelf. "Just as crazy as me saying the Sinners are good guys for a buncha outlaws. But you fuck with one of their own, and nothing will get in the way of their revenge. They got each other's backs. A brother gets hurt, the club makes sure he gets the best medical care there is. A brother dies, and his family is taken care of for life. A brother falls on hard times, and the club is there to help him out. Civilians don't look out for each other that way. So who's good and who's bad? Hard to draw that line in the sand."

"There's good and bad in everyone." She toyed with her glass. So far the Sinners had been pretty decent for outlaws. They seemed to understand Holt's emotional turmoil, and as far as she knew, there had been no fallout after the incident at the clubhouse. Sure some of them were rough and crude, and she had no doubt they were involved in illegal activities, but they were different from the Jacks. The Sinners were all about honor, loyalty and brotherhood.

Banks glanced over his shoulder and his eyes hardened.

"You're all kinds of good. And now you're gonna have to be all kinds of brave 'cause there's a suit in the doorway, who looks like law enforcement, and I'm guessing he's here to cause trouble."

Naiya looked back over her shoulder and her heart skipped a beat. "It's the ATF agent from Trenton. I have to get out." She stared straight ahead, gripped the bar. "Do you have a back exit?"

"You run and you might as well slap a sign on your forehead that says 'Guilty.' Banks cracked his neck from side to side. "You're gonna have to play this one out, but I promise nothing's gonna happen to you in this bar. He's made the mistake of walking into Sinner territory and messing with a Sinner's girl. Now he's gonna pay the price."

"Skyler." He gestured to a young, blonde waitress at the end of the bar. "Your job is to make sure the fed's glass is never empty. To do that, you're gonna stand near him the entire time he's here. He'll be sitting at the bar, next to our girl, Naiya. If he gets up, you get in his way. If he moves to go anywhere except the door, you spill his drink. You clear on that?"

Skyler paled. "He's a fed? What if he—?"

"He won't," Banks assured her. "Not unless you've been in contact with anyone back home."

"No." She shook her head violently. "The Sinners have been real good to me. I wouldn't rat them out, and there's no one at home I want to talk to."

"Good girl." His face softened, and for a moment Naiya wondered if there was something between them. But Skyler looked to be two or three years younger than her, and Banks was . . . Well it was hard to figure out how old he was. Thirty? Maybe a year or two less?

Naiya braced herself when she heard footsteps, the scrape of a stool beside her, the rustle of a suit, and the heavy stench of cologne.

"Fancy meeting you here."

"Yes." Naiya fought back a wave of nausea when Michael sat on the stool beside her, impeccably dressed in his "I'm-a-federal-agent-attire"—dark suit, white shirt, and tight smile. "What a coincidence."

Michael lifted a dark eyebrow. "I thought you and your man were heading to Idaho Springs."

"We're taking the scenic route." She unclenched her hands and placed them on the counter. No point giving away her anxiety that easily, although there was nothing she could do about the sweat beading on her brow.

"What can I get you?" Banks asked Michael with a scowl. "We got a cop special on today. Water. Wet."

"Perrier. Ice and a slice of lemon." Seemingly unfazed by Banks' calling him out, Michael smiled. "I'm on duty."

"I'll bet you are," Banks muttered.

Naiya stared at the counter while Banks prepared the drink, wondering if Michael would indeed chase her if she ran.

"Where is . . . ?" Michael hesitated. Frowned. "Was it your husband? Boyfriend? I don't remember his name. Just that you had five kids." He stared pointedly at Naiya's stomach, and she pooched it out like she'd just had a big meal.

"Four," she said, quickly. What an idiot trying to pull the same trick on her. "He went . . . out . . . to get me . . . anti-nausea medicine." Since she was about to throw up and was no doubt pale and clammy, the lie would no doubt carry a ring of truth.

"Alcohol, medicine, and babies don't mix." Michael tapped her vodka glass and Naiya swallowed past the lump in her throat. God, she really needed that drink now.

"It's water."

"In a highball glass?" He reached for her drink. "Mind if I have a sip. I'm parched."

"I'll freshen it up for you." Skyler reached between them and grabbed the glass. "Actually, I'll just get you a new glass." She smiled at Michael. "And you, too."

Michael's lips quirked amused. "My apologies. I didn't think it would be untoward since we're friends."

"We're not friends," Naiya snapped.

"Hmmm." Michael stroked his chin. "Well, I hope we're not enemies. We had such a nice chat the other night in Trenton. You were wearing that cute Bolton Beaver sweatshirt. You know, I liked it so much that I drove down to Bolton so I could buy one for my nephew. It's his twenty-second birthday next week."

Naiya drew in a deep breath, gritted her teeth. He was still fishing for information, but there was no damn way he was getting anything from her. "That's very thoughtful of you."

"Well, it would have been." Michael sighed. "But I couldn't get one the right size. It seems the only place you can buy them is at the Yates Motel, and they sold the last of their supply to a woman with dark hair and hazel eyes who was the exact same size as my nephew."

"That's a shame." Her hand trembled. Banks poured a glass of water and pushed it across the counter, his fingers brushing over hers in a fleeting gesture that did much to calm her nerves.

You are not alone.

★ TWENTY-FOUR ★

"Holt! Holt!"

Holt parked his bike outside Rider's Bar and gestured to Shaggy to wait as Ally ran across the street with a pasty-faced dude in tow. Where the fuck was Doug and why was he letting his woman run around in a biker town un-protected?

"Who the fuck?" Shaggy muttered.

"Naiya's best friend. Don't know the guy she's with. Her husband is a cop, but he's a good guy. Not someone who'll rat us out."

"Have you seen Naiya?" Ally's face creased with worry. "We were supposed to meet her at the hotel and then she sent me a text telling me to meet her at this bar, but the bouncer at the door says it's a private club and he wouldn't let us in. He said he'd never heard of you or Naiya."

"Who's on the door?" Holt asked Shaggy under his breath.

"One of Banks's new hires. Civilian. Doesn't know all the brothers yet."

The dude tugged on Ally's arm, and pulled her to the side. "I don't think you should be talking to them," he said, making a poor effort at keeping his voice low. "They're bikers. Real bikers. They are the last people Naiya would ever hang out with."

"I know Holt." Ally pulled her hand away. "And so does Naiya. He's a good guy, Maurice. He helped her escape."

Maurice. Holt hissed under his breath as he took in the pathetic excuse for a man in front of him. Christ, the dude looked like that geek from *The Big Bang Theory,* except his forehead was even bigger, his head even rounder, and his hair so pale he almost looked bald. Although he couldn't be more than thirty, his shoulders slumped forward, he had arms like sticks, and he had the beginnings of a paunch. And those fucking thick glasses . . . Where had she dug this loser up? Geeks R Us? And what the fuck was on his legs. Were those . . . cords?

"Thank you for looking after Naiya. She means a lot to me." Maurice stuck out his hand, but Holt made no move to shake it. Like fuck she meant anything to him. If she did, he would never have let Naiya go alone to the cemetery. He would have been the first one out to rescue her. He would never have had an affair or sent his friends to tell her and break it off. And, although Holt couldn't even bear to think of Naiya with another man, this cord-wearing freak would never have satisfied her the way a real man could.

Shaggy glanced over at Holt. "Is this her boyfriend?"

"Was."

"Is." Maurice corrected him, proving just how stupid he was. "That's why I'm here. Naiya called and begged me to come. She's alone and afraid and she needs someone to protect her."

Ally frowned. "That's not really what happened."

Shaggy snorted a laugh, speaking as if Maurice wasn't standing right in front of them. "*He's* gonna protect her? From Viper?"

"Seems so." Holt pinned Maurice with his gaze. "She

must have real faith in your ability if she called and begged you to come. Let's see what you got."

Maurice glanced over at Ally for help and received a smirk. "I'm not sure I understand."

"What are you packing?" Holt pulled out his Smith and Wesson Model 500. "I carry this, along with a Glock 17 and a SIG P226. I also got a Ruger P Series across my chest, a .22 on my left leg and an assortment of blades.

"I don't carry a gun." Maurice took a step back. "I'm actually anti-gun."

"He's anti-gun," Shaggy said, amused. "That might be a problem, son, 'cause Viper is pro-gun. In a very big way."

"Don't give him a hard time." Holt tucked away his weapon. "Maybe he's got some fight training, or maybe he knows marital arts." He held up his fists, turned to the side. "C'mon. Gimme your best shot. Show me what you're gonna do to Viper when he comes at you."

Maurice held up his hands, palms forward. "No fighting. I'm a pacifist."

"Jesus Christ. He's a pacifist." Shaggy laughed. "He's gonna make love to Viper, not war."

Ally stepped in front of Maurice, and glared at Holt. "Stop this right now. It's like watching a cat toy with a mouse. You just want an excuse to hit him because of what he did to Naiya."

Shaggy's brow furrowed. "What did he do to Naiya?"

Holt rocked his head from side to side and his neck made a satisfying crack. "Well, let's see. He led her on. Told her they were gonna get married, have a life together. All the time he was fucking someone else. He was so busy with his little honey that he couldn't be bothered to go with her when she went to her momma's funeral or help her when she escaped from Viper. Instead he sent her friend to tell her about the affair and break it off."

"Son of a fucking bitch." Without warning, Shaggy

plowed his fist into Maurice's stomach, sending him sprawling on the sidewalk.

"That was my hit," Holt protested. "She's my girl."

Shaggy shook his hand, spat on the sidewalk beside a whimpering Maurice. "Sorry about that. Got carried away. I'm anti-cheating on nice girls who belong to my brothers."

Holt felt a prickle at the back of his neck. Christ. Had all the Sinners changed as much as Shaggy in the short time he'd been away? The dude had gone from barely tolerating Holt's presence to becoming his new BFF.

"You want me to hold him so you can have a go?" Shaggy moved toward Maurice, and Holt shook his head.

"We're wasting time. We gotta get her some place safe before that fucking ATF agent finds her."

"The ATF?" Maurice scrambled backward, cupping his jaw as he stood. "What have you dragged her into?" He turned to Ally and scowled. "Why didn't you tell me she was in serious trouble? I don't want to get involved with the ATF. I have a reputation to protect. I'm up for tenure in a few years. I don't want my name smeared all over the news, or associated with bikers or drugs." His face twisted in disgust. "That's it, isn't it? She's back with the bikers. Two years she held out on me but really she's just like her mother."

Holt lunged forward, grabbed Maurice by the collar and slammed him up against the brick wall. "You ever talk shit about Naiya again, I'm gonna break your skinny arms and legs and wrap them around your neck." He flicked Maurice's glasses off and Shaggy ground them into the sidewalk with his heel.

"Leave a piece of him for me."

"No way." Holt drove his knee into Maurice's stomach. "This dipshit is all mine."

* * *

Think. Think. Naiya twisted her ring around her finger wishing she'd never bought those damn Bolton Beaver shirts. But how could she have known where that night would lead? Certainly not to her and Holt going on the run all over Montana racking up the crimes and attracting the attention of the ATF.

Michael smirked as he lifted the glass, the same kind of smirk that had been on Viper's lips when he pretended to be solicitous seven years ago at the party when she said she wasn't feeling well after the drink he gave her. Michael was toying with her, just as Viper had toyed with her. Except this time she wasn't fifteen, alone, and innocent. She'd been through hell and back. And there was no damn way anyone was taking anything from her again. She wasn't a victim, and she hadn't done anything wrong.

Well . . . maybe she'd done a few things wrong, but nothing bad enough to warrant the kind of attention Michael was throwing her way.

And he had no evidence to tie her to Leo's death, or they would be having this conversation in an entirely different location.

She finished her water, and nodded at Banks for a re-fill. "So, Michael. What brings you to a one-percenter biker bar in the middle of a one-percenter biker town? Isn't this a dangerous place for an ATF agent to be?"

His head jerked toward her, and his eyes hardened. Well, too damn bad. She wasn't playing his game anymore. No more pretend. The very fact she was in the bar proclaimed her biker connections. After this was over she was heading out of the state for her interviews, and she would be done with bikers forever, so why not use her connections to her advantage while she could?

"My personal safety is never an issue when I'm looking for a cold-blooded killer." He puffed out his chest. "I'll do what it takes to keep the public safe and ensure justice is done."

"How noble," she said dryly. "And you think you're going to find him in this bar?"

Michael pulled a piece of paper from inside his jacket and laid it on the counter. "I think I'll find Holt Savage wherever you are."

Naiya stared at the mug shot of a young Holt and read through the text that set out his juvenile record in Laredo for assault, battery, theft, and violation of parole. His fingerprints appeared at the bottom of the page along with a note detailing his current known associates: the Sinner's Tribe MC.

"You printed him from the glass in Trenton," she said without thinking.

"Clever." Michael tipped his chin.

But not clever enough. How could she have missed the glass? She'd been hyperaware about evidence around Michael. But then Holt had made that comment about pizzas . . .

"Do you have evidence that he's done something wrong, except maybe indecent exposure with his girl outside the bar?"

"You think you're so smart, but I'm on to you." Michael gripped her arm so hard her eyes watered. "And as for evidence, in less than twelve hours I'm going to have a copy of the CCTV tape from the gas station that shows the faces of the two people in Bolton Beaver shirts who were riding the deceased biker's Harley. And I'm pretty damn sure I know who I'm going to see when I look at that tape. So why don't you stop playing games and start cooperating, and maybe I'll go easy on—"

His last word was cut off when a massive hand landed on his shoulder.

"This the guy you texted me about, Banks? The one causing trouble in our bar?"

Naiya looked up at the tall, giant of a man behind Michael. It took her a second, but she remembered him from the front door—Gunner. And behind him were Zane and Cade, and a dark haired, blue-eyed biker she'd only briefly met, Sparky.

"I think he's lost," Banks said. "Must be in the wrong bar. See the way he's holding Naiya? Anyone who comes to Rider's would know our policy about manhandling the ladies. In the civilian world, I believe unwanted touching is called . . . assault." Banks cocked his head and gave Michael a cold smile. "Isn't that right?"

Michael's lips thinned and he released Naiya's arm. "I didn't assault her. I was holding her so she didn't get away."

Catching on, Naiya twisted her face in a frown. "Look at the bruises on my arm. I believe a person convicted of assault under the Montana code faces a fine and imprisonment in county jail for up to six months. In fact it might even be aggravated assault, since I had a reasonable apprehension of serious bodily injury, and you do have a weapon, don't you?"

"I definitely think he was trying to intimidate you," Banks said. "I felt intimidated listening to your conversation. I think I might have even pissed my pants."

"He did make me afraid he might inflict physical harm or subject me to physical confinement or restraint." Naiya slid off her seat, paraphrasing the code as best she could remember from her criminal-law course. "That's an even worse offence. He could go to state prison for up to ten years or have to pay a $50,000 fine."

"Seems a shame such an efficient ATF agent would have to spend ten years in jail," Gunner said. "Maybe we could offer not to report him if he accepts Sinner justice instead."

Zane cracked his knuckles. "You're too kind-hearted, Gun."

"Gunner really is a softie." Sparky said. "That's why he gets all the girls."

"It's against the law to assault a federal agent." Michael pulled his ID from his pocket and Cade snatched it from his hand and tossed it over the bar to Banks.

"Is there a federal agent somewhere?" Cade pretended to look around, then stared at Michael. "Are you a federal agent? You got some ID?"

"Maybe he's not a federal agent," Naiya said. "Maybe he's just some drunk guy who sat beside me and tried to pick me up even though I told him I'm . . ."

"A Sinner." Banks smiled. "And the Sinners protect their own."

Holt spotted Naiya at a table with Ally as soon as he entered the bar.

Ever watchful, Tank stood beside Naiya, his hand in his cut, his eyes darting from side to side as he searched for danger.

"Darlin'." Holt leaned over to kiss her and she pulled away. He supposed he deserved that, but right now he wasn't in a mood to play games. His brothers had taken Michael out back to await Holt's justice and after Holt had let loose his anger, he wanted nothing more than to hold his woman in his arms. Preferably, naked and in his bed. But first he'd have to gain her forgiveness.

Naiya glared, her eyes dropping to his blood-smeared hand. "Is that Maurice's blood? Ally said you beat him up."

He pushed her hair back behind her ear, trailing his fingers down her neck. God, she was beautiful. Sexy. Fiery. And his. What the hell had he been thinking walking away and leaving her unprotected? "Nah. That's Michael's blood. I had to teach him a lesson. He made the mistake of messing with a Sinner's woman in a Sinner bar in the Sinners' town."

Naiya stared at him aghast. "You beat him up, too?"

"Anyone who hurts you. Anyone who touches you. Anyone who makes you scared. Anyone who makes you cry. I'll rip out their hearts, break their bones, and drown in their fucking blood to keep you safe."

"That's kind of romantic in a terrifying, morbid, ruthless, outlaw-biker kinda way," Ally said. "Doug just says 'love ya, babe' or 'keep safe.'"

"It's only romantic if the guy is actually around to do it," Naiya said, slapping Holt's hand away. "But if he drops you off at a hotel in a strange town and leaves you to fend for yourself while he drives off to get himself killed, it loses its effect."

"You looked after yourself pretty good." Holt pulled his chair closer, rested his hand on her knee. "Smart move coming here when you saw Michael sniffing around."

Naiya pushed at his hand, but he held her fast, stroking his thumb along the inside of her thigh.

"What was I supposed to do?" Her voice rose in pitch. "Go to the police? I may have been living a civilian life, but I spent six years with the Black Jacks. I know the kind of power the clubs have. I know how things work. And I know I'll be happy when I leave town and get away from all things MC."

"You also know you gotta listen to your man. And your man wants you to stay with the Sinners until I've dealt with Viper." Holt tilted her head back with one finger under her chin, then leaned in and kissed her, his free hand ready to grab her wrist if she tried to slap him.

Which she did, because his Naiya had a spine of steel.

"Who says you're my man?"

"I do." He met her gaze, watched her eyes darken to brown.

"It sure didn't feel like you were my man when you left." She pulled away, and Holt gritted his teeth. Didn't she understand that he had come back for her? That for now he had put aside his quest for revenge to keep her safe?

"When I put you in the position of having to pull that weapon, I realized I'd brought you back into a world you don't want to be in. I didn't want to waste any time getting you out." He traced the bow of her mouth, pleased when her lips parted at his touch. She couldn't be that angry. After all, she was still here, and she had come to the brothers to ask them to warn him.

"I can take myself out." She drew his hand away. "I've got interviews set up in different states . . ." Her voice trailed off when Holt frowned. How could he protect her if she left? Viper would send men to chase her wherever he went. Sweat trickled down his back. This reunion wasn't going exactly as expected.

"You don't leave," he blurted out. "You don't go."

She studied him for a long moment, and then she stroked a light finger over his jaw, her voice soft, as if they were alone and not in the bar with the Sinners watching them and Tank and Ally sitting at their table. Like she'd forgiven him for leaving her. "You're lucky I understand your bossy, evil biker ways."

Yes! Forgiven. Holt heaved a sigh of relief. "I'm gonna take you back to the clubhouse and show you just how evil I can be." He covered her hand with his, and pressed his lips to her fingertips. Her sharp intake of breath made him instantly hard. And suddenly it all didn't matter. Viper.

Michael. His status in the club. All he wanted was this woman who took away the pain and the darkness; who made him feel whole again.

"I'm not going anywhere until I get a proper apology."

Holt hooked his boot around Naiya's chair leg and dragged her toward him, feeling a power and confidence he hadn't felt before. He liked how the brothers had deferred to him when he walked into the stock room, and how they stood aside as he dealt with the fed. He liked that they'd looked after Naiya and that Tank had been standing guard. He liked that they didn't treat him like a junior patch but as a man to be respected. And he liked that he would have this woman by his side—strong and determined, fiercely intelligent, highly capable, and yet willing to accept his need to take control.

"Holt!" Naiya's eyes widened when he yanked her chair forward, but a smile played across her lips. "What's got into you?"

"Want my woman close so I can protect her." He slid an arm around her waist, stroked the curve of her hip.

"More like you want to feel her up in public." She gave him a sideways glance that made him laugh out loud.

"That, too." He leaned forward, pressed his lips to her ear. "What happened with that agent will never happen again."

"Apology accepted." She cupped his face between her hands and kissed him long and hard.

Ally fanned herself with her hand. "I thought I was coming here for a pity talk. Now I'm thinking I shoulda brought Doug along for a little hotel loving 'cause I don't know how I'm gonna drive home with Maurice in the condition I'm in after watching you two. Hopefully he drinks too much at that bar down the street where you left him to drown his sorrows, and sleeps all the way home."

Tank gave Holt a quizzical look. "So, you being here . . . Does that mean you're back with the club and you're gonna come with us to the rally?"

"I came back for Naiya," Holt said. "Nothing has changed my plan to go after Viper."

Tank stared at him aghast. "You're gonna take her with you?"

Fuck no. He wasn't letting Naiya anywhere near Viper. But to keep her safe he either had to rely on the Sinners or let her go, and the latter was no longer an option. "I gotta think things through. Then I'll make a decision."

"A decision that involves me." Naiya nuzzled his neck, distracting him. "If you're going after Viper, I'm coming, too. Actually, Ally and I were going to the rally anyway. Doug will be there giving support to the Sandy Lake sheriff's office. We're going to keep a lookout for a biker wearing a Skull Mark ring."

"We are?" A frown creased Ally's brow, smoothing away when Naiya gave her a nudge. "I mean, yes we are. We talked about it . . . over the phone. Earlier today. I love bike rallies. Lots of . . . dangerous bikers and bikes and rings." She gave an apologetic shrug. "I think."

"It might be dangerous," Naiya continued. "You should probably teach me how to use a gun."

Was she fucking crazy? Give her a gun and let her go with him? "No."

"No?" She lifted an eyebrow. "How are you going to stop me?"

"I said no and I mean no." Holt looked over at Tank for a little support. Maybe his brother would look after Naiya while he did what had to do. There was nobody he trusted more. "Tank?"

But Tank stared at his phone, his face pale and drawn.

Holt picked up on the tension in Tank's shoulders and leaned across the table. "What's wrong, brother?"

"It's nothing. Just . . ." His gaze flicked to Naiya and then back to Holt. "Nothing."

With a discrete nod of understanding, Naiya stood and gestured to Ally. "Next round is on me. I'll need some help at the bar, and I can introduce you to Banks. You'll like him. He's got the whole taciturn mysterious bartender vibe thing going on. I dare you to make him laugh."

After the girls left, Holt pulled his chair closer to Tank. "Talk to me."

Tank's head jerked up and hope flared in his eyes. "You're still not putting on the cut?"

"Doesn't feel right," Holt said. "I don't know if it ever will."

"So you're not a Sinner?"

Holt didn't know where Tank was going with this, but perversely he seemed to take comfort in the fact Holt wasn't presently a member of the club, so he ran with it. "I haven't handed in my cut to Jagger, and he hasn't taken it from me. But I'm not wearing it, so I'm not bound by the rules."

Tank let out a ragged breath. "Then I got a problem, brother. And if Jagger finds out . . ."

"He won't." Holt clapped Tank's shoulder. "Tell me what I can do. I'm here for you. Whatever you need, I've got your back. No matter what happens, that will never change."

★ TWENTY-FIVE ★

TANK

Tank wiped his sweaty palms on his jeans, but it didn't do any good. Ever since he received Ella's text, his body had been in stress overdrive. Heart-pounding, shirt-soaking, pulse-racing stress. If T-Rex hadn't been there to keep him calm and take charge of the situation, he didn't know what he would have done. Even now, in Hacker's office—a small computer room at the back of the clubhouse, set up for the club's IT whiz to deal with tech operations—he couldn't stop his teeth from chattering.

"I've got bad news and I've got good news," Hacker said, turning from the massive computer screen in front of him.

Tank glanced over at T-Rex and Naiya standing behind Hacker's chair. They'd had no choice but to confide in the MC's computer geek on his word as a Sinner not to share the results of his scan of Tank's phone with Jagger or the rest of the club. Tank didn't like putting Hacker in this position, but Hacker owed Tank a favor for the night he'd gotten drunk and knocked over Jagger's bike. Tank had spent the whole night fixing the damage and now he was calling in his mark for keeping his mouth shut about the whole ordeal.

"Gimme the good news." Although how much worse could it be? When he'd seen Ella's email with the gas station video attachment, he'd almost handed in his cut right there. No way would Jagger let him stay in the club after he'd broken the rule about fraternizing with reporters. Add to that, taking the video in the first place without authorization, getting so pissed he forgot basic safety protocols and left his phone unattended and unsecured, and now putting T-Rex, Naiya, and the club at risk, he'd be lucky to be kicked out without some broken bones, maybe even his life.

Hacker, tall and lean with unnaturally bright green eyes, and the kind of face that sent the sweet butts into a swoon, ran a hand through his long hair. "She emailed the video to herself. I can hack into her email account and delete it. I can also find out if she's sent it to anyone else."

"And the bad news?"

"If she's downloaded it, or if she sent it to someone else and they downloaded it, then it's going to be more difficult, if not impossible, to get rid of it. And if she's uploaded it to the Internet, then we're shit out of luck."

"I say we grab her. Bring her to the clubhouse and let Dax scare her a bit," T-Rex said. "We'll find out pretty damn fast who got it."

"And you'll find your way to a jail cell pretty damn fast once she goes to the authorities, as if you're not headed there already." Naiya snorted her derision. "She could have just put it on the news or sent it to the police, but she didn't. So why not meet her at the rally like she's asked. Find out why she took it and what she's going to do with it. Then make a decision. It might be she's planning to air it while she's reporting on the bike rally unless you give her what she wants."

"I don't know what she wants." Tank folded his arms. "And if I see her alone, feeling the way I feel right now, I might lose control. And she's got this way of twisting words around . . ."

"You won't be alone," T-Rex assured him. "I'll be with you."

Emotion welled up in Tank's chest. "Thought you had your own shit to do at the rally. You can't be in two places at once."

"The only place I need to be is at your back, brother. And it might be that the Sinners have a good plan I can go along with. While they're setting it up, and taking care of my girl, I can be with you."

It took a moment for T-Rex's words to sink in, and when they did Tank's heart seized in his chest. Was T-Rex really going to return to the club for him? Join with the Sinners instead of going after Viper alone?

"You and Naiya." T-Rex answered his unspoken question. "I trust you more than anyone, but I trust the brothers, too. I want Viper so bad it burns inside me, and for the longest time it was all I lived for. But now I got Naiya and you, and if I lost either of you, it would fucking kill me. I'll hear Jagger's plan. And if it's solid, then I'll work with them to take Viper down." A grin spread across his face, a flash of the old T-Rex. "But I'm still gonna be the one who pulls the trigger."

Tank's hands clenched and unclenched by his sides, and his throat tightened so hard he could barely breathe. He couldn't hug T-Rex here. And he couldn't fucking cry. Christ. Ever since T-Rex had returned, he'd been an emotional mess, and Tank didn't do emotion. Bikers didn't do emotion. Men didn't do emotion. But he was so goddamned grateful to have his best friend back, and even more relieved that T-Rex was going to talk to Jagger. Not just because it meant he had a chance of getting out of this mess without losing everything that mattered—his life, his cut, his club, and his friend—but also because T-Rex stood a better chance of surviving a confrontation with Viper with the Sinners at his back. And he wouldn't be able to take T-Rex dying all over again.

He forced his words past the lump in his throat. "Appreciated, brother."

"I got your back, Tank, like you always had mine."

Tank shot a look at Naiya to see what she thought of the new plan. Clearly, not much, given how tightly her lips were pressed together and how she was shooting daggers at T-Rex with her eyes. He figured that might have something to do with the fact T-Rex still wasn't backing down about her going with him when he went after Viper. Tank gave an inward chuckle, wondering if T-Rex had planned it out this way. Once the Sinners were involved, it didn't matter how much Naiya protested; she would be staying behind. Women were not allowed to participate in club business. Not even Arianne. And it wasn't that way with just the Sinners, but with all outlaw MCs.

"Holt," she said. "Could I speak to you outside?"

Tank shuddered on his friend's behalf at Naiya's icy tone. But he had T-Rex's back, whether it was in a gunfight, a revenge quest, or an angry girlfriend. "Actually, the board meeting is in fifteen minutes, so we gotta split if you want to talk to Jagger before it starts. He won't let you sit in without a cut, but I'm sure he'll talk to you in his office."

Hacker squinted at his screen. "I thought it started in—"

"Fifteen minutes." Tank cut him off, biting back a smile when T-Rex gave him a grateful nod. "Hacker, can you take Naiya out back when we're done? Shaggy's meeting her at the shooting range to show her the basics."

"You're learning how to shoot?" Hacker asked Naiya.

"Gotta defend my man." Naiya lifted an eyebrow. "Or maybe I'll shoot him. I'm not sure which."

If Tank hadn't been so damned stressed out, he would have laughed. He never would have picked Naiya as a match for T-Rex, but the man who stood beside him now was not the same man he had known. The new T-Rex was confident, determined, and decisive. He didn't joke around or try to smooth things over. He took control. Made things happen. Didn't second guess himself or try to find a middle road. He led rather than followed, and Naiya, with her quiet confidence and inner strength was a good match for him. One day maybe he would meet a woman like her.

Or, at least, he would have liked her not to run away.

"C'mon, T-Rex." He gestured to the door. "We'd better get going."

"Call me Holt, brother. T-Rex is dead." Holt brushed a kiss over Naiya's cheek, and Tank followed him out into the hallway.

T-Rex is dead.

Tank's lungs seized up and he struggled for breath, even as he acknowledged the truth of the words that hung between them, even as his heart broke all over again. That night. In the alley. When they had cried in each other's arms. If he'd known that was the last time he would be with T-Rex, the man who had been closer to him than anyone on the earth, he would have said the words that he had always wanted to say.

But the man who walked away from the alley that night was not the man who had walked in. Tank had seen it in the way Holt stood a little straighter, talked a little louder, laughed a whole lot less. He had seen it in his buddy's confidence and determination, his ability to take charge, and his fierce protectiveness over a woman who burned with the kind of inner strength and fire that once would have scared Holt away.

"T-Rex" needed Tank. In the alley, he needed Tank's arms around him, Tank's strength to hold him, Tank's friendship to endure. Before the dungeon T-Rex needed Tank and Tank needed T-Rex.

Did Holt need Tank, too?

Tank knocked on Jagger's office door, and Jagger called out for them to enter. Over the years, Jagger had transformed the once lavish office—decorated in old-world style with floral wallpaper, a massive cherry desk, matching built-in bookshelves, thick carpets, and a crystal chandelier—into something more fitting of a biker president. He'd kept the desk and bookshelves, but he'd had the prospects rip off the paper and paint the walls white. Now framed prints of motorcycles and scenic bike routes decorated the walls, and the patio doors leading out to the shooting range had been stripped of their heavy brocade curtains, allowing the light to flood in.

"I'll hear you out," Holt said to Jagger, without preamble or hesitation.

Jagger lifted an admonishing eyebrow, glanced over at Zane who lounged in the chair in front of his desk, and then back to Holt.

"You and I have some things to discuss, T-Rex. I'll speak to you alone."

"I'm staying." Zane folded his arms, leaned back in his chair. He always had Jagger's back, even when Jagger didn't want him. There was nothing Zane wouldn't do for Jagger. He was Jagger's rock, his shield, and his support. Where Jagger went, Zane followed, protecting him so he could focus on the important business of running the show.

Holt had it in him to be a leader. Tank had seen it in the clubhouse and in the bar and in Hacker's office. A leader needed a man at his back. A man he could trust. Holt might not realize it now, but he needed Tank, just as Jagger needed Zane.

"I'm staying, too." Tank folded his arms and leaned against the wall, just like Zane. If that's what Holt needed, that's what he would be.

Jagger and Holt shared a look—not the look a biker president would give to an upstart junior patch who had stormed into his office demanding details of his plan, but the look of an equal. Jagger nodded, and Tank pulled the door closed.

"You coming back to the club?" Jagger nodded at Holt's cut folded neatly on a table beside his desk.

"No." Holt took a seat beside Zane, although Jagger hadn't asked him to sit. Tank tried to hide his discomfort. It was going to take a while to get used to the new Holt who no longer shared the awe and reverence Tank held for Jagger and the senior patch members of the club.

"But we may be able to work together to bring Viper down. I have other things needing my attention at the rally, and I can't be everywhere at once."

Jagger studied Holt for a long time, assessing, considering while Tank sweated it out at the back of the room. What would happen if Jagger pulled on Holt? Or decided to beat him up and toss him out of the room? Where would his loyalties lie?

"This is my club," Jagger said. "I'll share our plan, but I will not be second guessed. I will not be challenged. I will not be questioned. You are in or you're out. If you're out, you stay out of the way."

Holt shook his head. "I'm not after your club. Hell, I don't even know if I want to wear a cut anymore."

"I'm beginning to think you shouldn't wear it," Jagger drummed his fingers on his desk. "There can only be one leader."

In that moment, Tank knew what would happen if Jagger pulled his gun.

There was only one man he could follow.

And it wasn't the man who had given him his cut all those years ago.

★ TWENTY-SIX ★

Naiya squeezed the trigger on the Colt Defender Series 90 semi-automatic pistol. Her first shot missed the target. But the next two shots hit not too far from the center. She turned to Shaggy, standing a few feet behind her, and grinned.

"You were right. It does have a smoother trigger pull, and it's easy to shoot multiple rounds quickly. When you first offered me a gun, I went for a .22 because it's small, but this is slim and lightweight and it packs more of a punch."

Although it was afternoon, the air was still cool and damp, fragrant with the scent of pine. Naiya fired another shot, and groaned when it went wide. She'd been practicing with Shaggy for almost two hours at the paper target handgun and small-caliber rifle range behind the Sinners' clubhouse, but she couldn't get any consistency with her shots. And it wasn't for lack of trying or even need for a better teacher. Shaggy had been nothing but patient and helpful, although the intensity with which he watched her put her on edge.

Shaggy leaned against the metal railing running the full

length of the field. "You got lots of practicing to do before you can approach a target without thinking through everything from your stance to your grip to the position of your arms and your sight. You got too cocky. Maybe it's in the genes."

"What genes?" She lowered the gun and sighed. "I never saw my mother fire a gun. My dad was a Black Jack, but I have no idea who he is. Maybe he was their top shooter or maybe he was a strung-out druggie like my mom. I'll never know."

Shaggy opened his mouth and closed it again. "Yeah, that's tough."

"I used to think he was watching over me when I lived with my mom," she said. "But I gave up that dream when Viper . . ." She cut herself off, reluctant to share that very personal information with someone she barely knew.

"When Viper what?" His face tightened and his hand closed in a fist. "What did he do? If that bastard . . ."

"Nothing. Just forget I said anything." Just what she needed. Yet another overprotective male in her life. Well, she was here learning how to shoot because she was tired of running and hiding, tired of looking for a man to protect her when she should have been looking for ways to protect herself.

"Christ." Shaggy turned and fired four bullets in rapid succession into the center of the already decimated paper target. He fired another round, lay the weapon on the table, picked up another and did it again. Was he angry she hadn't told him about Viper? Or was he tired of teaching her? Were they done for the day? He was the most enigmatic man she'd ever met and even after two hours she couldn't figure him out.

"Well, it's not like you gotta run out tomorrow and start shooting people." He raised his weapon, his body quivering like he wanted to punch someone. "You got lots of time to practice."

Naiya studied him as he fired at the shards of paper floating in the breeze. Despite the gray beard, he was younger than she'd originally thought—probably in his mid to late forties at the most—and no slower or any less capable than the junior patch from what she'd seen. As far as she could tell, he was an "old timer" through experience only, and maybe because of something in his past that had left him bitter and alone.

"I don't, actually. I'm going to the rally. I want to be there when Holt takes Viper out."

Shaggy laughed. "I thought you'd spent some time with the Jacks. If you did, you'd know there is no chance in hell you'll be going with Holt if he goes with the club. Women are not involved in club business. Women don't go on the road with the club. Women stay home. We don't put our women in danger." He cleared his throat, looked away. "At least the brothers that got women don't put them in danger. And Jagger takes care of the sweet butts and house mama, makes sure they stay behind."

"Club women," Naiya corrected him. "I'm not part of the club, and I'll do what I damn well please." She walked down the shooting lane to change the paper target, and Shaggy called after her.

"It's too dangerous. Holt's not gonna let you go. Jagger's not gonna let you go. And I'm not gonna let you go."

"Who are you to tell me what to do?" she threw back over her shoulder. "I hardly even know you." This is what she'd hated most about the Jacks, and all bikers, really. Misogyny at its finest.

"Not even Arianne is allowed to go," he countered, his tone dropping to something close to a plea. "And she probably has more reason than anyone else to want revenge. Viper killed her mother and her brother."

Naiya shuddered as she changed the target. She'd heard rumors that Viper had killed Arianne's mother, and that he'd had a hand in Jeff's death. She felt a pang of sadness at Jeff's loss. For all that he'd abandoned her that night of the party, he'd been a good friend to her after she'd gone to live with her mother. So how did Arianne reconcile her role as a woman in the club with the fact she could probably outshoot and outride most of the men here? How did she sit in the clubhouse and watch Jagger ride off to take out Viper on her behalf?

"I'm not Arianne," she said walking toward him. "And I'm not going to pull the trigger. But I want to be there. I want to see his face. I want him to know what it feels like to have your life and innocence brutally ripped away, to be totally and utterly helpless, to scream for help knowing that no one will come for you because your mother is high on crack and your father abandoned you." Her voice rose to a shout, the words coming thick and fast, words that she had never dared to say, emotions that she had been afraid to truly feel or express, a desire that had burned inside her for seven long years.

Shaggy stared at her, stricken. Like somehow he was responsible for what Viper had done to her. Like he was responsible for her life. She shouldn't dump on him like this. He was a stranger. And yet, she couldn't stop. The words kept coming, so she let them go.

"I want him to know what it feels like to be betrayed, beaten, violated, used, marked, and discarded like a piece of property." She tugged down her sleeve and bared the Black Jack tattoo for him to see. "He didn't just do this. He carved his initials into me, too." She yanked down her waistband just enough so he could see the top edges of her scar: "V" for Viper. "He scarred me inside and out and I am going to take back my life. No more running and hiding. No more looking for jobs in faraway states. Whether

Holt wants it or not. Whether the Sinners want it or not. I am going to that rally. I will be there when they catch Viper. I will watch him die. And I will shoot anyone who gets in my way."

Shaggy drew in a ragged breath, his face dark with emotion. "You won't be going alone."

Curiously calm after his meeting with Jagger, Holt made his way through the clubhouse to the shooting range. Everything was familiar and yet something had changed. He hadn't felt awed to be sitting in Jagger's office beside Zane, instead of standing in the hall, guarding the door, as was usual for a junior patch member of the club. They were just men, their mystique now wiped away by the brutal reality of what living beyond the law really meant.

He'd listened to Jagger's plan. Made comments and suggestions based on his intimate knowledge of Viper and the Jacks. Helped them revise. Insisted he take point. And they'd listened. With respect, even deference. They'd treated him as an equal. It felt good. Right. And when he walked out of the office, he knew he would never answer to another man. Whether it was a result of his time with Viper, or perhaps because it had always been inside him, he knew he needed to lead, not follow. Even if it meant he would die putting Viper to ground.

He'd hadn't shared the last part of his plan with Jagger because he needed the Sinners to bring the plan to fruition. But in the end, there would only be two people on the roof where Viper would have to flee the fire they were planning to set in the hotel. And only one of them would leave alive.

Tank walked by his side, unusually quiet, as if he knew Holt needed time to process everything that had happened during that meeting. Did he realize Holt would never return to the Sinners? Holt felt a pang of regret at the thought of leaving Tank alone again, either through death or voluntary exile as a nomad biker. Until he met Naiya, he'd never been as close to anyone as he was to Tank, never had a bond as strong. He didn't share the same intimacy he did with Naiya, and yet he needed them both to feel complete. Tank who knew him before and Naiya who knew him now. Naiya who had his heart and Tank who had touched his soul.

"Dunno why Naiya wants to shoot a gun so bad." Tank pushed open the back door leading to the shooting range and preceded Holt through. "I told her there's no way she'll be going with you."

"Naiya's got her own mind." Holt chuckled. "She'll do what she wants regardless of what I say. Short of tying her up, I won't be able to stop her."

"You want me to stay behind with her?" Tank offered over his shoulder. "I can lock her in a room."

"I need you alive, preferably uninjured." Holt clasped Tank's shoulder. "But if you could watch over her . . ."

"I've been watching out for her since the moment I knew she was yours."

Holt choked back a wave of emotion. If he survived the confrontation with Viper, he would have to leave Conundrum. And yet, he couldn't imagine going anywhere without Tank.

"What the fuck? He's touching your girl." Tank muttered under his breath as they rounded the corner to the shooting range where Shaggy stood behind Naiya with his arms around her, helping her aim her weapon at the paper target in the distance.

Holt took in the scene and gave Tank a calming pat. "I'm not worried about Shaggy. He's too old."

"He's not that old." Tank gritted out. "He's mid-life crisis age, which means he goes after the young honeys when we go out to the bars, trying to relive his fucking youth with twenty-year-old pussies."

"Well, right now he's touching her like he's someone's dad," Holt pointed out. "He's keeping a lot of space between them. But you keep an eye on him for me. The minute he steps out of line . . ."

"Yeah." Tank slammed his fist into his palm. "I always wanted to lay one on old Shag."

Holt tapped Shaggy on the shoulder, and the old timer stepped out of the way. After collecting his weapons and ammo, Shaggy took his leave, muttering something about leaving lovebirds alone. Tank followed behind him, clearly just waiting for him to step out of line.

Holt wrapped his arms around Naiya and pulled her against him. She fit perfectly in his arms, her head coming to rest just below his chin, her sweet ass at his belt. "I'm thinking you're planning to do something I won't like," he murmured in her ear.

"Saving your ass, you mean?" She turned and brushed her lips over his cheek.

"Like you did in the clubhouse when you threatened Arianne with the safety on? Made her almost piss herself laughing?"

She pressed her lips together and glared over her shoulder. "We don't need to rehash all the humiliating details. But it just made me realize I need to learn how to use a gun. I've wasted enough of my life hiding and pretending I'm not part of the biker world when no matter what I do it finds me. In the crime lab, we analyze bullets, trajectories, bullet wounds, and casings, but I've never known what it feels like to hold a gun, how the recoil impacts the body, and how it burns your skin, and having a biker skill doesn't mean I'm suddenly going to become a club—."

Holt growled softly behind her. "Don't say it. Even the thought of one of the brothers touching you . . ."

"Won't happen," Naiya said, teasing. "You see . . . I met this guy . . ."

"What guy?" Holt stiffened behind her.

"He's a biker." Naiya turned, nuzzled his neck. "Kinda cute. Longish blond hair. Perpetual scruffy beard. Rides a kick-ass bike. Has a serious overprotective streak. Not bad in bed."

"Not bad?" He grabbed her ass and ground his erection against her. "You didn't scream for 'not bad.' "

"Maybe I need a reminder."

"I'll remind you that you're mine." He nipped her earlobe, and then licked the hurt away. "And you don't need to use a gun 'cause you have me to protect you."

Naiya arched her back, pressed her breasts against his chest. "Are you sure? It feels like you've got a new weapon for me to try."

Heady with a newfound sense of power after his meeting with Jagger, torn between the need to protect Naiya and Tank and the need to avenge the grievous wrong done to him, and overwhelmed with the feelings he had for the beautiful woman in front of him, Holt wanted nothing more than to lose himself in her body, knowing it might be the last time they were together. "My room. Now. And I'll show you some heavy artillery."

"I have one more round to fire." She walked through the trees to the box in front of the low target and bent down to take aim.

Fuck. Didn't she understand? He needed her now. Crashing through the cover of the trees, Holt grabbed her by the hips and pulled her against him.

Naiya startled and the gun shook in her hand. She looked back over her shoulder and laughed. "Where did you come from?"

"Your dreams."

"I wasn't dreaming about a big sexy biker pressing his

package against my ass when I'm trying to shoot a gun." She gave a little wiggle and fuck she almost set him off.

"Too many men looking at this sweet ass." He smoothed his hand over her cheek. "Thinking things they shouldn't be thinking about something that belongs to me." He kicked her legs apart and held her against the box with a firm hand against her lower back.

"Holt! What are you doing? What if someone comes out here?"

"I'll shoot at them till they go away," he growled. "I want you like this. After what just happened at the clubhouse, I'm in a mood for rough, and I don't give a damn 'bout who sees us."

Her voice caught. "What happened?"

"Got things settled in my mind about who I am, where I need to be, and what I got to do."

She stilled, drew in a shuddering breath. "I don't like the sound of that."

But when she tried to get up, he pushed her back down. He would have her here. Hard and fast. And then he'd take her up to his room and give her slow and gentle, telling her with his body what he couldn't say in words, saying good-bye. He reached around her, unbuttoned her jeans and shoved them down.

"Holt!"

"We're in the trees. No one's gonna see us. And even if they were minded to come out here, Tank will keep everyone away."

Naiya dropped her head to the box and groaned. "He knows?"

"He knows me." Holt ripped open his fly, freeing his throbbing shaft from its restraint. He leaned over Naiya, pressed his lips against her ear. "I need you, darlin'. You ready for me?" He slipped a hand between her legs, found her wet and slick.

"Such a good girl. Always wet for me," he whispered as he positioned himself at her entrance.

"You have a way of turning a girl on."

"Only one girl I want to turn on." Holt rubbed the head of his cock along Naiya's slit, and she moaned.

"Pushing her down on a box at a shooting range beside a clubhouse full of bikers, telling her that you need her, and then ripping off her pants is a good start."

"You like that?" He pushed inside her with one hard thrust.

"I like anything to do with you." She arched her back, angling herself to take him deeper. Fuck. She was made for him. Holt grabbed her ponytail and yanked her head back, holding her still as he hammered into her.

"Yes." She bucked against him. "God, you feel so good, Holt. So big and thick. So hard."

Christ. He wondered if women knew what it did to a man to hear them talk dirty about his cock. He was so fucking jacked, Jagger could come around the corner and he wouldn't fucking stop. He pulled back and thrust inside her, faster, harder, gauging her reaction. He was right on the edge, but he wasn't going to come until she climaxed. After what she'd been through, the last thing he wanted was for her to feel used.

"Give it to me, Naiya." His balls slapped against her smooth round cheeks, his cock going so deep he could feel her cervix. "Give it up to me." He slid one hand around her hip and stroked on either side of her clit, feeling the little bundle of nerves swell under his touch. Naiya moaned, and her pussy quivered around him.

"I'm so close." She gripped the edge of the box, her knuckles white.

"Come for me, darlin'. I want to hear my name on your lips." He rubbed his thumb over her clit, and she stiffened, choking back a scream as she came.

"Holt. Oh God. Holt."

He pounded into her, his own release coming as hers ebbed.

Holt. Not T-Rex. A new man with a new life and a woman who had stolen his heart.

★ TWENTY-SEVEN ★

Naiya fell on the bed in the well-appointed hotel room in Sandy Lake as soon as the door closed behind Holt. They had been on the road all day, riding from town to town after they left Conundrum for Holt to pick up the equipment he needed for his secret plan that she hoped wouldn't remain secret much longer. Along the way, he bought pillion pegs for Naiya's feet and a back rest she didn't want, but was glad to have when what should have been a short trip turned out to be a day-long event.

"You okay? Riding's hard if you aren't used to it." Holt sat beside her and stroked his hand over her arm, frowned at the goose bumps dotting her skin. "You're cold."

"I'll be okay. The leather jacket you bought me at Big Bill's kept out most of the chill." She shivered and Holt pushed himself off the bed.

"I'll run a bath for you."

"I'm not really a bath girl. I usually take showers."

He headed for the washroom, ignoring her just like he'd ignored her when she insisted she didn't need the backrest he bought for his bike because after the rally they would be going their separate ways. It had been a hint, an opening for him to share his plans, or to reassure her that it would all turn out okay, but he'd ignored that, too. In fact, he had talked less over the course of the trip than he ever had before, and it tripped all the warning bells in her mind.

Naiya stripped down to her underwear and joined Holt in the bathroom. After filling the tub, he added some bath salts from a basket on the tub surround, and piled white fluffy towels on the cream marble counter. When everything was to his satisfaction, he tugged off his clothes and Naiya winced when she saw his scars under the bright bathroom lights. Damn Viper. There wasn't an inch of his torso that hadn't been marked.

He choked back a grunt. She looked up and saw him studying himself in the mirror, his eyes unfocused as if he was lost in memories she couldn't even begin to imagine.

"Holt?" Naiya wrapped her arms around him, pressed her cheek against the soft hair on his chest. "You okay?"

He stiffened, pulled away. "Yeah. Good. Bath is ready."

"I know what it's like," she said softly. "One minute you're here. The next minute you're back there—"

"I said I'm good." He turned off the tap, checked the water, and then stepped into the tub. "Come."

Anxiety curled in her belly, and she stripped off her underwear and stepped into the tub, settling between his legs as the warm water lapped over her aching muscles.

"Do you want to talk about it?" She looked back over her shoulder. "Sometimes talking helps."

"No."

Naiya drew in a deep breath, steeled her spine. No hiding. No running away. Even though this wasn't a physical problem, she needed to confront it head on. "What's going on? You haven't been yourself since the meeting with Jagger. Why are you being so distant?"

He kneaded her shoulders gently, working out the knots until she relaxed against him completely, shifting to accommodate his growing arousal. Well, at least one thing hadn't changed.

"Got a lot on my mind, darlin', but I'll tell you the plan. Viper and his bodyguards have the penthouse suite at the Royal Hotel. The Sinners have spent the last few months paying off the staff, security, fire department, and police. A couple of brothers are gonna go in as trades, set fires in strategic locations that will result in a lockdown of the elevators but won't put civilians at risk. Fire doors from the penthouse will be locked down. Telephone wires cut, and Wi-Fi cut. Cell signals blocked. Viper and his men will be forced up to the roof. Fire department and police will be delayed getting to the scene. If they come early, people will tell them the building has been completely evacuated. Meanwhile, Jagger and the senior patch will be on the roof of the building across the street with a few sniper rifles. They'll pick Viper's men off, go down the fire escape and head out of town in a van waiting for them in the street."

The Sinners. Jagger. The senior patch. Not once had he said "we" or mentioned his role in the mission. Maybe she was overthinking, reading too much into his words. "I want to be there. I want to watch."

"You will." He slid one hand around to cup her breast, soft and slick in the water. His cock stiffened, and he shifted behind her. "You and Tank will be on the roof of the adjacent building. Tank will be wearing a jacket over his cut, and after it's over, you'll go down the stairwell to the sixth floor pretending to be a civilian couple. Once the Jacks figure out where the shots are coming from, they'll be swarming the other hotel, looking for men in cuts. Tank will look after you."

She drew his other hand around, and he smoothed his thumb over the curve of her breast. "Where will you be?"

"I'll be there."

Another vague statement. Did he mean "there" as in on

the roof of the building across the street with Jagger and the Sinners, or "there" with her and Tank, or . . . "there" on the roof with Viper and his guards? Before she could ask, he nuzzled her neck.

"Spread your legs for me."

He'd never spoken to her in such a rough, commanding voice, and the incongruity of the warm, rose-scented bath and his harsh tone aroused her. She parted her thighs, and Holt stroked his fingers over her soft curls.

Naiya moaned, leaned back, her breasts lifting, her thighs parting wider, inviting.

"Good girl." He hooked her legs over his shins and spread her wider, his fingers working their way through her folds to her entrance, and then up and around her clit. Naiya melted against him, her muscles relaxed now in the warm water, a contrast to the tension in her core.

"I love your body," he murmured. "Your softness, your curves, the way the pink of your pussy matches your rosy nipples. I love how you respond to my touch, how wet you are when we're together, how you open for me and let me enjoy your beauty." He kissed his way down her neck, nipping the sensitive spot between her neck and her shoulder. "I love that you're mine, that you know the worst of me and still want my touch, that you know me as I am now, that I wake from my nightmares and find myself in your arms. I'm gonna make sure you're safe and happy and able to live that normal life you dreamed about."

"With you?" She looked back over her shoulder, the niggle at the back of her mind now a full-blown roar of worry.

"Turn around. I want to see you." He lifted her, helped her turn, and then positioned her over his shaft, her knees on either side of his hips.

"With you?" she asked again.

"I can't give you a normal life, darlin'. I'm leaving the Sinners. And even when Viper's gone, he'll still be a part of me."

"Maybe I don't want a normal life anymore," she said. "Maybe I want a chance to live free for a while, make sure the career I've chosen is what I really want to do, and not a reaction to my mom or Viper or what I went through. Maybe I want to go on the road with you. Maybe I love you, Holt. Just the way you are. Maybe I don't want to lose you."

Pain flickered across his face, and he cupped her face in his hands and kissed her softly on the mouth. "Maybe you don't have a choice."

Naiya jerked back as if he had slapped her. He was planning to do something stupid. She could hear it in his voice, and see it in his eyes. Well she wasn't going to let it happen. He'd already sacrificed too much. Clearly, he wasn't going to tell her what he had planned, so she would just have to outthink him, and she'd need Tank's help. She knew Holt now. He knew Holt then. Together they would be able to figure out what the hell was going on and stop him. She had a choice. And she was choosing him.

Holt eased into her slowly until he was seated to the hilt. So hard. So hot. He filled her completely, perfectly, like they were one person and not two. Naiya wrapped her arms around his neck and pulled him toward her until their lips met. Their breaths mingled, tongues tangled. She tried to commit him to memory, the warmth of his lips, the deep rumble when he looped an arm around her waist and pulled her against him. She wanted him. Needed him. She'd made it through hell, and he was her piece of heaven.

He leaned down, licked the perfect, pale swell of her breast, glistening with water, groaned as he closed his lips over the taut, pink peak, rubbing his thumb back and forth over the other.

"Oh God." Naiya bucked against him, rocking over his cock. He pulled out, gave her a teasing thrust, and then returned to her nipples, switching his mouth and his hand, rubbing with his thumb, flicking with his tongue.

She thrashed, churning up the water, shaking with need. "Please."

"Not yet." His slid his fingers between them to flick over her clit and then away. She moaned with delight, arched her back, and ground her clit against his hand.

"Holt." She threaded her fingers though his hair, and pulled him down as she writhed over his cock. He claimed her nipple with his tongue, and bit it gently. Unable to hold back, she lifted herself up and slammed herself down over his cock.

Just like that, he lost it. His cock surged inside her, and he yanked her up and brought her down again, driving deep into her channel.

"Oh, yes!" Her trembling thighs clamped his hips, water splashed, the scent of roses fading beneath the scents of sex and arousal. "I'm so close."

He lifted her up and yanked her down. Naiya let go of her anxiety and lost herself in the erotic sensation of Holt moving inside her, his long, hard strokes hitting her in just the right place to have her writhing on his lap, desperate for more.

Holt closed his eyes, quickened his thrusts, sending water splashing out of the tub. She could feel his need, his desperation flowing through her, his desire to lose himself in her body. She pressed her knees against his hips and worked her body against his, lost in passion, frantic to give him what he needed.

"Look at me," she breathed. "Open your eyes, Holt. See me."

His eyes snapped open, and she saw her need reflected in his eyes. Heat coiled in her belly. She rocked against him, riding his cock as he ground his pelvis against her clit, bringing her closer and closer to release.

"For me, darlin'. Come for me." He slid one hand between them and slicked her juices over her clit.

Naiya cried out as pleasure crashed through her, a burst of lightening that electrified her body. She sagged against Holt, and his grip tightened. He thrust into her, ratcheting up his pace, his deep thrusts drawing out her orgasm. He came with a raw, guttural groan, his cock pumping hot and hard inside her, the pain of his grip overshadowed by the pleasure of their mutual release.

She melted against him, warm in the fragrant water. She had never felt as complete as she did at this moment; never felt she really belonged until she'd stepped into the circle of his arms.

"I love you, Naiya." He stroked his hand down her back. "Never thought I had it in me to love someone after my sister died. But you were made for me. We fit together. I don't regret a single moment I spent with you."

He loved her, and yet he wanted to throw that love away. He had survived, and yet it was clear he planned to throw his life away. Well, she wouldn't let him do it.

He might think it was good-bye forever. But it was just good-bye for now.

★ TWENTY-EIGHT ★

TANK

When Tank turned the corner onto Sandy Lake's Main Street, he was engulfed in motorcycles. He slowed his stride, drinking in the shops decorated with the rally colors of black and gold, the welcome banner flapping overhead in the breeze. Hundreds of bikers lined the street to watch the parade of bikes that was a custom for everyone joining the rally. Hands in the pockets of his cut, he wove his way through the crowds and along the rows of vendor stalls, selling rally T-shirts and hats, bike gear, and souvenirs, searching for Holt. He'd received a text from Ella late last night asking him to meet her this morning, and, of course, Holt said he would come.

He pushed thoughts of Ella aside when he spotted Holt waiting for him inside the Sandy Lake Café. A wave of nostalgia hit him hard when he saw the waitress lean down and whisper in Holt's ear. They'd partied with that pretty waitress last year at the campground outside of town where the real party would start tonight. Although they'd both put on their best moves, she'd spent the night with Sparky, and he and Holt had made a bet about who would get her into bed this year.

Had it really only been a year since he and Holt had nothing more important to worry about than their next lay and their next job for the club? He felt a hundred years old now, aged by the loss of his best friend, and the realization that although Holt had returned, he was nothing like the man he had been before.

Holt looked up and waved a greeting when Tank walked into the café.

Tank joined him at the white Formica counter. "Hey, bro—"

"I got your text," Holt said abruptly. "Where does Ella want to meet?"

"She's in the Majestic Plaza Hotel." Tank looked over Holt's shoulder and frowned. "Where's Naiya?"

"Back at our hotel. Shaggy's keeping watch. I don't want her wandering the streets. I left her a note telling her to wait for you. After we deal with Ella, you can take her up to the roof. I figure by then everything should be in motion."

Tank shifted uneasily in his seat. "You don't have to come with me. I mean . . . you've got more important things to do. I'll understand."

"There is nothing more important to me than you and Naiya," Holt assured him. "I've got your back like always. We'll deal with this bitch together."

Emotion welled up in Tank's chest. "She's a fucking shark. Or maybe a snake. I can't keep up with her. She always seems to be two steps ahead of me, and when I start asking questions, she whips off her clothes, and I can't think about anything but fucking her. She's fucking hot, man. Beautiful, but dangerous."

"So the fuck am I." Holt threw a few bills on the counter. Tank laughed, letting some of his tension go as they walked out of the café.

"Not pretty enough, brother. If I recall she dumped a

beer on your head when you tried to get her into bed." Tank skirted around a group of Skull Crackers who had recently pledged allegiance to the Sinners.

"I pissed her off on purpose," Holt said. "She made my fucking skin crawl. At some point I decided the challenge wasn't worth the risk."

If Tank were as perceptive as Holt, he wouldn't be in this mess, but he'd been a long time without a woman and with Holt gone, he'd suffered again from the lack of self-esteem that had plagued him since he was a kid. "She's stacked, man. Tits out to here. Curves all over the place. Her skin is so fucking soft and smooth. Her hair is always perfect. She's like a doll. I never had a woman like her. Never thought I was worth—"

"Don't say it." Holt cut him off with a bark. "You're worth fifty fucking Ellas. No. One hundred. One thousand." Holt turned down a side street, and they made their way down the back alleys to the Majestic, a ten-story hotel overlooking Sandy Lake. "She's not even worth the time it would take to fuck her."

"That's not gonna be an issue," Tank mumbled as he took in the lavish gold-and-red reception area, the huge crystal chandelier and the slick marble floors. "I'm more worried about keeping my dick around her than using it."

They took the elevator to the tenth floor and walked down the hallway to door 1147. Holt made a quick check of the corridor and the exit then nodded for Tank to knock. Ella opened the door right away and gestured him inside. She looked perfect as usual, her blonde hair sleek and shiny, her voluptuous body encased in a form-fitting white dress, and her vivid blue eyes cold and clear. The only imperfection Tank could see was a fresh smudge of red lipstick at the corner of her mouth, as if she'd been kissed only moments ago.

"James. How nice to see you again."

Holt came up behind him and slammed the door open. "You get two for the price of one this morning, sweetheart."

Ella barely flinched. "And you brought a little friend. Your missing friend, if I remember correctly. The one who murdered that Black Jack back in Still Water. Are you really so scared of me, James, that you needed to bring him with you? You were very much in control when we were in bed together. Or don't you remember?"

"Shut the fuck up." Tank gritted his teeth and walked into the room. Decorated in dark, heavy wood, rich blue carpets, and gold brocade furniture, with a separate bedroom off to the side, the suite was at least five times the size of his room at the clubhouse.

Ella closed the door behind them and leaned against the wall, arms folded. "Don't be rude," she admonished. "I could have just handed this tape over to the police or aired it on the six o'clock news. I'm doing you a favor by offering to give it to you."

"How the fuck did you get into my phone?" Tank snapped. "I don't sleep that heavy, and the phone was in my pocket all night. I woulda felt you taking it out."

"Not if you were drugged." She lifted a creamy shoulder and shrugged. "Hard to tell the difference between a man who's had too much to drink and a man who's been given a little something to help him sleep, so I can use his thumb to unlock his phone."

"You fucking bitch." Tank started toward her, and Holt held out his hand.

"Hear her out, brother. You're on the back foot here."

Ella fiddled with the shiny gold doorknob beside her. "Listen to him, James. He's the smart one. He knew enough to stay away from me the first time we met. But then he went and got himself caught by Viper and left you all alone. Poor James. So trusting. So lonely. Such easy prey without his savvy friend by his side to warn him away."

Holt growled. "What the fuck do you want? Spit it out or quit wasting our time."

"We want you." Ella gestured behind them. And fuck, if it wasn't the ATF dude who had been after Naiya standing in the doorway to the bedroom, his weapon aimed at Holt. Tank reached into his cut for his gun, but Ella quickly pulled a weapon from the table beside her and pointed it in his direction.

"Hands where I can see them."

A howl of anguish ripped out of Tank's throat. Holt was here because of him. He was going to die because he had come to help Tank. How fucking stupid could he be? Why hadn't he realized the whole thing with Ella was a trap?

"Ah. The loyal hound." Michael chuckled, his bruised and battered face contorting into something like a smile. "I think he'd probably take a run at us if he thought he'd be able to dodge my bullet." His gaze flicked to Holt and his eyes hardened. "But then, Viper said you would do the same for him, which is why it was so easy to separate you from Naiya after Ella caught him in her web."

"What the fuck?" Tank growled.

"Still trying to catch up?" Michael glanced over at Ella and shrugged. "You didn't tell him?"

Her face tightened. "Tell him what? Viper didn't confide in me. We had a deal. He gave me a story and I gave him T-Rex . . . among other things." She swallowed hard. "My job is done. I got my story and paid for it with my damn soul and all my living-room furniture."

"Why?" Tank muttered. "Why does he want Holt so bad? Wasn't three months in the dungeon enough to punish him for saving Evie?"

"Viper doesn't want him." Michael smoothed his black suit jacket, and Tank wondered what had happened to the torn, bloodstained suit he'd been wearing when the Sinners tossed him in the alley behind Rider's Bar after teaching him a lesson about touching their women. Too bad they hadn't just offed him when they had the chance.

"He wants Naiya," Michael continued. "But Holt rarely left her side. And every time she was alone, Holt showed up to save her. He said you were the one person Holt called for in the dungeon; the person he thought would be coming to save him. Viper figured you were the only reason he'd leave her alone."

"You work for Viper?" Holt's lips curled in disgust. "He's got the fucking ATF in his pocket?"

Michael shrugged. "He's got everyone in his pocket. He owns most of the state police, a handful of ATF agents, judges, senators . . . Soon his reach will extend beyond the state. He'll lead the Jacks not just in Montana, but nationwide. But that kind of power requires money. A lot of money. The kind of money Naiya will have in a few short months."

Tank automatically turned his gaze to Holt. He looked calm, composed. And yet, a vein in his neck throbbed and his jaw was clenched tight.

"Naiya doesn't have any money," Holt said.

"Not yet. But, she will. And as soon as it's hers, she'll be transferring it all to her new husband." Michael cocked his head to the side, and for a moment he looked almost sympathetic. "Viper is on his way to meet his bride-to-be as we speak, and then they're heading down to Sandy Lake's city hall."

Tank glanced over at Ella. Her expression had changed from bitterness to disgust.

"That's why he wants her?" she spat out. "He's going to force her into marriage to get her money? I thought misogyny was dead, but now I see it's alive and well in the biker world."

"Don't be such a hypocrite," Tank snapped, seeing an opening. Ella may have been prepared to cross lines for her story, but she was a professional, educated, modern woman, and it was clear she was appalled by Viper's plan. "We're here because of you," he continued. "He's going to get her because of you. Was the story worth it? I know he was at your place the other night when I showed up. You sold your body and your soul. You're as much a part of this as he is."

His barb hit home, and she winced but recovered quickly. "I didn't want him there. It was just supposed to be about getting something to blackmail you with to keep you in line in exchange for a story. But Viper wanted more and more, and he had something on me."

"Shut the fuck up, Ella." Michael swung his gun to point at Tank. "And you shut the fuck up, too. Enough talking."

But the damage had been done. Tank had clearly rattled Ella, and she was no longer fully on board with Michael's plan, whatever that might be. Tank glanced over at Holt, flicked his gaze to Ella and back again. Holt gave an almost imperceptible nod. They might have an ally, but with Michael to contend with, the odds still weren't in their favor. And time was ticking. Naiya was in danger.

And now, she was alone.

★ TWENTY-NINE ★

Thump. Thump. Thump.

Naiya startled, yanking the curtains closed and casting her hotel room into semi-darkness.

"Look through the peep hole," she whispered to Ally. "Tell me who it is."

After waking alone with Holt's note on her pillow, Naiya had called Ally to come and help her track him down. But after making her way across town from the hotel she shared with Doug, Ally had convinced her not to go. Sandy Lake was swarming with Jacks, and there was no way Naiya would be safe once she left the hotel.

"It's an old guy with a long, dirty beard. He looks like a vagrant except he's wearing a Sinner cut." Ally turned and pulled her phone from her pocket. "I'll call Doug. He's on patrol, but he said he'd come if we needed him."

"No. It's okay. Let him in." Naiya let out a relieved breath. "It's Shaggy."

"Shaggy is right," Ally muttered as she undid the lock. "He looks like some kind of sheep dog." She pulled open the door and stepped back. "Smells like one, too."

"Viper's in the hotel." Shaggy waved his gun in Naiya's

direction, his voice frantic. "Holt asked Benson and Shooter to keep watch downstairs. They just texted me. We gotta get you out of here, and take you someplace safe. He's coming for you."

"Why?" Ally stared at Shaggy aghast. "Is he that desperate for a woman? Is he that obsessed with fulfilling a debt?"

"I don't think it's about the debt." Shaggy's voice thickened. "Or about getting a sweet piece of tail. But he wants her bad." He pulled open the door as Naiya stuffed her few belongings into her bag.

"Leave the bag," Shaggy barked. "We gotta go. Now." His gaze flicked to Ally. "They don't know who you are, and you'd better keep it that way. You need to be somewhere Naiya is not."

"I'm not leaving her." Ally pulled the door closed behind them as they exited the room.

"You'll be a liability." Shaggy gestured to the stairwell. "Viper won't give a damn that you're a civilian. He'll use you to get to her. And it's harder to hide two people."

"You go, Ally." Naiya followed Shaggy down the hallway. "I'll be okay."

Ally hesitated before turning toward the elevators. "I'll get Doug. Tell him something's going down. The police will protect you."

"C'mon," Shaggy urged. "No time to waste."

Naiya clasped his offered hand and they ran down the hallway. Shaggy pushed open the fire door and they raced down the concrete stairs.

"Where's Holt? Does he know about Viper?"

"No one can get in touch with him. Or Tank for that matter." He bounded down the stairs with the energy of a man half his age. "We've left messages for them. Holt knows I would never leave you alone. I've been in the hotel since he left."

"Why?" She'd been wondering about Shaggy since they'd first met in the bar. He had volunteered to help with everything from beating up Michael to looking for Holt, and from teaching her to shoot to being her bodyguard. He had no connection to her, and from what Holt had said, no real connection to Holt. He was the club enigma, a wild card. Not even Jagger knew his story, and the Sinners who did were all dead.

"I gave my word." He jerked to a stop, put out an arm to hold her back, and a finger on his lips to quiet her.

Naiya held her breath. Above, on the stairwell, she heard the thud of boots on concrete, the clang of metal, heavy breathing.

"This way." Shaggy pulled on the fire exit door leading to the fifth floor. The metal lock thunked, but the door didn't budge. "Fuck. It's locked."

They ran down the stairs, trying the doors for each floor without success. When they hit the ground floor, Shaggy gestured her toward the back exit and she ran full tilt into the alley and smack into a broad, hard chest.

"That was almost too easy." Viper grabbed Naiya's ponytail, pulling her to a stop, while his bodyguards slammed Shaggy against the brick wall. "Walk around the lobby so any Sinners watching will send a message up to warn you. Lock all the exit doors. Chase you down the stairs. Like flushing rats out of the sewer."

"Let him go." Naiya gestured at Shaggy. "He has nothing to do with this."

"He's a Sinner. Can't have him running off to bring in the cavalry." One of the bodyguards backhanded Shaggy, snapping his head to the side.

"Stop it." Naiya drew in a breath to scream, and Viper clamped a gloved hand over her mouth. She gagged on the taste of leather, the scent of sweat and diesel burning her nostrils.

"Tsk. Tsk. Don't you know better than to involve civilians in biker business? You don't want civilians to get hurt. You're already responsible for two deaths today. Three after we deal with the old man."

Naiya's eyes widened, and she bit his finger, her teeth finding flesh through his leather glove.

"Fucking bitch." Viper tore his hand away and cuffed the side of her head, knocking her to the ground. "You want to know who died today because of you? Your new boyfriend and his pal."

"No." She stared at him aghast. "They aren't dead. I don't believe you."

"Believe me, love. If they aren't gone already, they will be before we leave his alley. I was done with T-Rex. Had my fun with him. But for some fucking reason, he wouldn't leave your side. So I sent my reporter friend to find Tank, just in case I needed an insurance policy. And after my ATF mole tried and failed to bring you to me twice, I cashed it in. He's with Tank and T-Rex now, along with four of my senior patch with orders not to leave until they've both been put to ground."

Did she hear some hesitation in his voice? A hint of uncertainty. Would Michael really execute two men in cold blood? He might be a dirty cop, maybe blackmailed by Viper, but she'd sensed a streak of decency in him the few times they'd met. He wasn't a hardened criminal like Viper, soulless and beyond redemption. Even after the Sinners had beaten him for touching her in the bar, she couldn't imagine him pulling the trigger.

But maybe he had no choice. She'd known Viper owned the police, a few judges, and maybe a senator or two. But if he owned the reporters and the ATF, he was playing at a much higher level. Not even Jagger would be able to stop him now.

"Let her go," Shaggy said. "She can't help you. She's

nobody. And you can get yourself a finer piece of tail over at Peeler's Strip Club."

"She *can* help me." Viper pulled Naiya to her feet. "In fact, I can't do it without her. When Naiya turns twenty-three, she'll have access to a trust fund containing twenty million dollars. Imagine that. Imagine how many people I could buy with twenty million dollars. I wouldn't even have to run in the nationwide Black Jack election. I'd just off the National Black Jack president and take his place and no one would be able to do anything about it."

"Bullshit," Naiya spat out. "You know my mother was nothing but a drug addict, and my father was one of your Jacks. We had nothing when I was growing up. And my grandmother had nothing either. When I lived with her, we barely had enough money to eat and pay the mortgage."

"Your mother was definitely a drug addict because I made her that way." Viper's lips turned down in mock regret. "I had to keep her around in case your father showed up. The trust could be broken with both their signatures, and if he was a Jack, then that wouldn't be a problem. And I had to keep you fucking safe, because if you died before you turned twenty-three, the money went to charity. Your grandmother thought of everything when she replaced your mother's name on the trust with yours."

Naiya tried to take it all in, but there was only one thing she really cared about. "You know who my father is?"

"Don't be fucking stupid." Viper shook her hard. "If I did, I would have hunted him down and made him sign on the dotted line when your mother was alive. I got all the information out of her I could, but it wasn't enough. His name was Joe Johnson. He hid his identity from her, but she didn't know why. They had some pathetic love affair and he took off after you were born. Your grandmother was a smart woman. She musta known the deadbeat would never come back so the trust was secure until you turned twenty-three. I had to listen to the fucking sob story so many times I had to gag your damn mother every time she brought it up. She loved him. He left her. He broke her heart. He gave you his fucking ring and left her with nothing. Blah. Blah. Blah. I had a good look at that ring the night I made you mine" He leered and Naiya's stomach roiled. "Didn't mean anything to me. But that was a fucking good night. I want to hear you scream like that again."

Shaggy fisted his hands by his sides and shouted curses, throwing himself forward. Viper frowned and one of his bodyguards slammed the butt of the gun into Shaggy's head. Shaggy stumbled and went down on one knee.

"No. Stop." Naiya took a step toward him, and Viper pulled her back.

"He's nothing. He's gonna be yet another body for me to bury tonight after our wedding."

Naiya stared at him aghast. "Our what?"

Viper laughed. "We're getting married today, love. Then I'm keeping my bride chained to my bed for the next three months until she turns twenty-three, her trust vests, and she transfers all her assets to me as a wedding gift. After all, you've been mine since you were fifteen, and I claimed you to protect you and keep all the vultures at bay."

"You fucking bastard," Naiya screamed, her body heating with anger. "I'll never marry you. I'll never say yes. Never give my consent."

"Lucky for you I know the mayor of Sandy Lake, and he owes me a favor. He doesn't need to hear the word yes to solemnize a marriage. He's the one who helped me trace the source of the money. Did you know your great, great granddaddy invested in the railroads? The stock was handed down through the generations, but your grandmother wanted nothing to do with it. She put it in a trust for your mother, but when she found out your mom had got herself a taste for bikers, she changed the terms of the trust and all the money went to you."

"I would rather die than give you that money," Naiya spat out.

"You will die as soon as I have all the funds." Viper stroked her cheek with a thick finger. "But in the meantime, we'll have three months to enjoy married life together. Although I suspect, I'll be the one enjoying it, and you'll be the one suffering. Just like T-Rex."

"So what's the plan?" Holt asked Michael. "You gonna shoot us in cold blood?" He looked over at Tank who had his gaze fixed on Ella. She was definitely a weak link as Tank had silently hinted, but Holt had also picked up on Michael's hesitation. Michael was a lawman at heart and threatening to kill two innocent men clearly didn't sit well with him. Maybe he truly was a dirty cop, with only a big payout in mind, but Holt had a feeling there had to be something else that would turn a man of Michael's character into Viper's puppet.

"Yup. That's the plan." Michael shot a quick glance over his shoulder at Ella. Her eyes widened, and she took a step back.

"Are you serious?" Her voice rose in pitch. "You're going to kill them? I thought we were supposed to hold them until Viper got here."

"Change of plans," Michael said, his voice tight. "Viper's not coming. He's got the girl. He texted to say he wants them dead by the time he's done the wedding ceremony."

He's got the girl. Viper had Naiya. Red sheeted Holt's vision, and only the risk to Tank kept him from rushing Michael and grabbing the gun.

"You got all those forensic details accounted for?" Holt

struggled to remember all the things Naiya had made him do to clean the crime scene at the lake, all the things she'd told him she would be doing in her job. "Like the blood splatter on the floor? You got a silencer for your gun? How are you gonna get our bodies out during the day? And if you don't, how are you gonna keep the maids out until you do? Don't bodies decay? If you leave us too long, are we gonna smell? Is Ella gonna clean up the blood on her hands and knees in that pretty white dress. She'll have some explaining to do if this room is registered in her name. But then, you know all this 'cause it's your job. You catch the bad guys, protect citizens, and enforce the law."

Michael's gun wavered. "Shut the fuck up."

"I don't want to be a part of this," Ella snapped. "Viper didn't say anything about killing them or being an accessory to murder. I was supposed to bring James and his friend here. End of story. I'm not going to watch you shoot them. And I'm certainly not going to clean up when you're done. This is crazy. You're crazy. You're a federal agent, Michael. Yes, we both got in a bad situation with Viper, but we're not killers."

With their attention focused on each other, neither Michael nor Ella noticed Holt take a small step forward. But Tank did, and he goaded them on.

"He is a killer," Tank said, bitterly. "Naiya's gonna die because of him. Once Viper gets what he wants, he'll have no use for her. What does he want anyway?"

"He wants the twenty million dollar trust that's in her name," Michael said. "He's going to use it to take over the Jacks nationwide. His ambition knows no end."

Holt dropped one hand behind his back and wrapped his hand around the handle of the knife tucked into the sheath at his belt.

"Now that's a story," Tank said, keeping their attention.

"Maybe if Ella had been offered a story like that she wouldn't have made a deal with Viper. What story did he give you?"

"I got an insider look at the club. I got to see inside the clubhouse, interview some of the bikers about their day-to-day activities. No names. No identifying the club. His men talked behind a screen. But he let me in deep and he gave me the scoop on something so big it's going to rock the White House. It's Pulitzer Prize–winning stuff."

"He'll never let you show it." Michael gave a derisive snort. "Viper doesn't give out his secrets. I'll bet your tapes will disappear or you'll meet with a gruesome end before it's ever broadcast."

Holt pulled the knife along his back, calculating aim and trajectory. Someone was about to meet a gruesome end, and it wasn't Ella.

"What does he have on you?" Tank asked Michael. "What turns a good cop bad?"

Holt tensed, lifted his forearm.

"He has my boy."

At the last second, Holt flicked his wrist, causing the knife to veer a few inches above its intended target, embedding itself in Michael's shoulder instead of his heart. Michael stumbled back, dropped the gun, his face a mask of pain.

Ella stared at him for only a moment and then lowered her weapon. "Go."

"C'mon, brother." Holt pulled open the door. "We have a wedding to crash."

"We are gathered together here in the presence of these witnesses . . ."

The Sandy Lake mayor lifted an admonishing eyebrow

when Viper's Black Jack bodyguards, assembled in his large office at city hall, snickered. Naiya pressed her lips together and tried to hear his words above the pounding of blood in her ears. This was not happening. She was not being forced into marriage to Viper like they were living in the Dark Ages. Once she got these damned ropes off her wrists, she would grab his gun and shoot him between the fucking eyes.

"To join this man and woman in matrimony, which is an honorable estate, and is not to be entered into unadvisedly or lightly, but recently and discreetly."

More snickers. A belly laugh. At least the Black Jacks were enjoying themselves. She couldn't say the same for Shaggy whom Viper had brought along as an afterthought to be an independent witness at the ceremony, unconnected to the Jacks. He wanted to cover all his bases just in case there was an investigation into the legitimacy of the wedding after the trust monies were transferred, and with Shaggy in the wedding video, and his signature on the documents, no one would be able to say it was entirely a Black Jack affair. And, of course, Viper planned to end his life after the ceremony was over. Dead men told no tales.

Naiya looked around the ostentatious office for some route of escape. But aside from the two giant windows flanking an enormous oak desk, and the door they had come through, there was no other way out. She ground her toe into the thick red carpet and threw a beseeching glance at the heavyset mayor who had been happy to accept an envelope stuffed with money in exchange for performing the ceremony on short notice—and without the consent of the bride-to-be.

"If anyone can show just cause why this man and this woman may not lawfully be joined together, let them speak now or hereafter remain silent."

Viper dropped a warning hand to Naiya's shoulder.

How ironic that the last time she'd attended a ceremony it had been at her mother's grave and Viper had stood behind her, his heavy hand a precursor to the horror that lay ahead. Back to the beginning, except this beginning was an end unless she could escape from this nightmare before the mayor pronounced them husband and wife.

Naiya glanced around the room. This was the part in movies where the hero burst through the door and saved the woman from her impending marriage to a psychopathic biker who wanted her twenty million dollar trust fund. She still couldn't wrap her head around the fact that her grandparents had lived such a simple life when they'd had that much money available to them, but it made sense. They were good, honest people who didn't need more than the basics to be happy. Too bad Viper hadn't learned that lesson.

"I'm being forced into this marriage against my will. How's that for a reason?" She couldn't stop the words that dropped from her lips. She'd gone timidly with Viper that day in the cemetery, afraid to rock the boat, hopeful he would let her go, accepting of her fate. But no more. She'd protest this marriage until he gagged her or knocked her unconscious.

"Shut it, girl, or I'll off the old man right now," Viper growled, nodding at Shaggy who had been tied to a chair in front of the desk.

"Naiya Kelly and uh . . . ?" The mayor looked to Viper for help.

"Marcus Wilder," Viper offered. "But hurry it along. I don't have all day. Fractured Skyway is headlining at the rally and I hear they've got a damn good warm-up band this year."

"I'm recording this at your request in case there are questions about the ceremony." The mayor whispered his words. "It would be best to do the complete ceremony, with the small alterations you requested, and of course I'll edit out the extraneous conversation."

At a nod from Viper, the mayor continued. "Naiya Kelly and Marcus Wilder, I require and charge you both that if either of you know any reason why you may not lawfully be joined together in matrimony, you do now confess. If any persons are joined together otherwise than as prescribed by law, their marriage is not lawful."

"How inconvenient," Naiya spat out. "We're going to go through all this for nothing since forcing a person into marriage isn't lawful."

"I fucking warned you." Viper drew his weapon and aimed it at Shaggy. With a gasp, the mayor raised his hands.

"Please. Not in my office. This has been hard enough to orchestrate and it is very likely the marriage will be nullified and there will be an investigation if I have to explain a dead body in my office. No doubt the police will take the tapes."

"Do it." Shaggy glared at Viper. "I fucking dare you. Fucking pussy has to steal a young girl's money so he can play with the big boys. You got no balls, Marcus Wilder. You think you can buy power? Think again. You think you can lead a national organization 'cause you paid people off to get your throne? Jax Abrahams rules the Jacks on a national level because he fought his way to the top. Battle after battle. Scar after scar. He has respect because he earned it. Not because he bought it. I knew him when he was junior patch. I watched his rise to power. You don't have what he has. Even if you manage to get through his security and take him out, you won't last a week as national Black Jack president. They'll see your weakness. Tear you down."

"Shut him up before I put a bullet down his throat," Viper roared.

Two Jacks grabbed Shaggy and a third stuffed a bandanna in his mouth while the mayor looked on in horror.

Viper huffed his annoyance. "Keep going. I want the shortened version."

"Do you, Naiya Kelly, take this man, Marcus Wilder, to be your lawful wedded husband?"

Naiya turned to face Viper and put the full force of her anger in her words. "I, Naiya Kelly, do *not* take Marcus Wilder also know as Viper for my lawful husband and if you force me to marry him, I will bite, kick, scratch, and punch him. I will claw out his eyes, rip out his tongue, and twist off his balls. I will do everything in my power to cause him pain and make his life a living hell. I will try to kill him at every opportunity with whatever weapon is at my disposal. I will shoot, stab, burn, or maim him in health and in sickness, in prosperity and adversity, forsaking all others until he is dead. And then I will spit on his fucking grave."

"That's a yes," Viper said, his eyes cold and hard. "She said yes."

Naiya opened her mouth to protest once more, but before she could speak, the office door slammed open, and Holt stalked into the room. He had an automatic weapon in each hand, weapons and ammo belted across his chest, and weapons strapped to his legs and arms. Tank walked by his side, heavily armed and ready for battle.

Naiya had barely processed their entrance before Viper had his gun to her head.

"That's far enough," Viper warned Holt.

Holt and Tank froze, and Holt's gaze fell on Naiya. "You okay, darlin'?"

"I've been better." Her heart pounded in her chest, and she tried to remain calm and focused. She needed to be part of the solution here. Not the problem.

"Drop your weapons," Viper directed.

"Or what?" Holt cocked an eyebrow. "If you kill her, you don't get your money."

"It's not her I'm going to kill."

A gunshot cracked the silence. Tank cried out in pain, his weapons falling as he crumpled to the floor. Naiya glanced down and saw Viper's gun aimed where Tank had been standing.

"Tank!" Holt stared at his friend in horror.

"I know everything about you, Holt Savage," Viper said. "I know you inside and out. I know what scares you, what gives you nightmares, what keeps you up at night. I know how many times I can whip you before you pass out, how much pain you can take. I know how to make you scream and how to make you cry."

"You bastard," Naiya choked out. "He never did anything to you."

Viper looked down at Tank writhing on the ground and sneered. "Did you know he cried for you in my dungeon?" he said to Tank. "It was your name he called over and over and over again. It was you he imagined coming to rescue him. It was you he missed more than seeing the sun or feeling the rain or breathing the fresh air. At the very end, he gave up because he thought you had abandoned him." He shot a second bullet at Tank, missing only because Tank rolled to the side. "If you die, I'll destroy T-Rex in a way the dungeon never could. And it has been too long in coming."

"No." Shaggy leaped from the chair, the ropes that had held him secure falling to the floor with the wet bandanna. Taking advantage of Viper's surprise, Naiya spun around and jammed her knee into his crotch. Viper grunted, and Naiya slammed a well-placed fist into his solar plexus, knocking the wind out of him as she mentally congratulated herself on her thorough knowledge of anatomy.

Before Viper could recover, Shaggy tackled the Black Jack president from behind. Naiya jumped to the side and Viper fell the ground, battling a ferocious Shaggy. Naiya grabbed Viper's gun from the floor and aimed at the two men rolling on the ground as Viper's bodyguards closed in.

Naiya heard the door slam. And then the sound of boots. She looked up to see Sinners pour into the room, Jagger in the lead. Within minutes, the Black Jack bodyguards were disarmed and on the floor, while the fist fight between Shaggy and Viper raged on.

"Never seen him fight like that before," Jagger mused. "It's like he's possessed. If I'd known he had it in him I woulda sent him out on some of the more dangerous missions."

"He'd better not fucking kill him." Holt, still fully armed, stood on Naiya's other side.

Shaggy rose up over Viper and smashed his fist into Viper's blood-streaked face. Viper slumped back on the ground, eyes closed, his body struggling for breath.

"Everyone out of my way," Shaggy gritted out as he drew his weapon.

"He's mine." Holt stepped forward. "He owes me a debt."

"He owes me a bigger debt." Shaggy's body shook, whether from adrenaline or emotion, Naiya didn't know, nor could she tell whether his cheeks were wet with sweat or tears. "He destroyed the woman I loved. He raped my daughter. I won't rest until I pull that fucking trigger. My family needs to be avenged."

"As do I," Holt said.

Naiya caught movement out of the corner of her eye, and barely had time to shout a warning before Viper surged to his knees. "He's got a gun."

Two shots rang out through the mayor's office. Two bullets pierced Viper's heart. His mouth opened and closed again, and he dropped his weapon before his massive body sank to the floor.

Naiya looked over at the mayor, huddled in the corner. "You can take that as a no," she said. "And you can officially declare Viper dead."

★ THIRTY ★

Holt parked his bike outside the Sinner's Tribe clubhouse for the very last time. After the dust had settled, and the Black Jacks retreated to deal with the loss of their president, he had a long talk with Jagger, and they agreed it was time for him to leave.

Naiya slid off the bike behind him, her new riding leathers creaking as she followed him to the crowd of Sinners waiting by the clubhouse to say good-bye.

"They're giving you quite the send-off," she said. "After two days of partying I thought most of them would be comatose this morning."

"The party was the send-off. This is the good-bye." Holt threw an arm around her shoulders. He had no plans about what he wanted to do or where he wanted to go. Only that he wanted to be with Naiya, and since she had interviews at forensic labs all over the country, he would take the opportunity to explore his country before making a decision about where to put down roots—if he was putting down roots at all.

With her trust fund vesting in a few short months, Naiya was in no hurry to get back to work. She wanted a chance to be free, to live life without fear of Viper or the Jacks, to travel, see the sights, and think about whether she wanted to pursue a career in forensic science. She'd given up her apartment, sold her stuff, and paid a last visit to Maurice to say good-bye. Holt hadn't been happy to let her go to that bastard's apartment alone. He'd sat on his bike outside Maurice's building, counting off the minutes as he imagined all the things that could go wrong. But, of course, nothing happened. Naiya returned in one piece with a look of satisfaction on her face that was as close to a smirk as he'd ever seen. She seemed at peace with herself about that situation, which was all good with Holt, at least until she told him later that she'd punched Maurice in the face for being a two-timing bastard, and then it was even better.

"I was surprised you kept up with us."

Naiya snorted a laugh. "I didn't have a choice. You have some very pretty women at the club. I didn't want to leave you drunk and alone with them."

"After watching you beat on Viper, I'd be afraid to even look at another woman, darlin'."

"Good thing I still don't have a gun." She looked up at him and grinned. "Shaggy's a good teacher. After two weeks of shooting with him, I could really give you something to worry about."

Holt had his suspicions about Shaggy, but he hadn't shared them with Naiya. And if Shaggy had chosen to reveal his secrets to her, she hadn't confided in Holt. Except for the fact Shaggy had shaved his beard after the Sandy Lake shootout, nothing had changed. He was as ornery and grouchy as usual, except around Naiya, and everyone kept a safe distance from him.

"Holt." Jagger stepped forward and shook Holt's hand, and in that moment all his years with the Sinner's Tribe MC hit him in a rush. From the day he first saw the Sinners in a bar and knew he'd found a new home, to the night Jagger accepted him as a prospect, and from meeting Tank to the thrill of receiving his cut that marked him as a brother in the club. He had laughed and partied with these men. They had ridden together and fought together so they could live life on their own terms. Freedom. Loyalty. Honor. Brotherhood. Those were the principles that had governed his life.

Now he had love. And a burning need to find his own place in the world.

Holt handed Jagger his cut, neatly folded, as a symbol of his departure. His heart seized in his chest as he released it into Jagger's hands. The night Jagger had given him that cut had been the greatest night of his life. He had never been more proud, never happier, and he'd shared every minute of that glorious night with Tank.

"I'm keeping this for you," Jagger said. "The board has agreed to release you from the club on good terms. If you ever want to come back to us, you will be welcome, and your cut will be waiting for you."

"Appreciated, brother." He fought back a wave of emotion as his brothers surrounded him, clapping his back, and wishing him well. He shook hands with Sparky, Cade, Dax, and Gunner. Hugged Dawn, Arianne, Sandy, and Evie. He smiled at the sweet butts but, wary of Naiya's watchful gaze, he kept a respectful distance. He gave a few tips to Shooter, Benson, and the junior patch members of the club and said good-bye to Dax's five boys, Cade's three kids, and Zane's son, Ty. Zane insisted that he still owed Holt a debt before giving him a painful whack on the back, which Holt returned with twice the force.

Banks joined them with Skyler in tow. Holt almost didn't recognize the girl he'd saved in Missoula, now that she'd gained a bit of weight and stripped the color from her hair. She'd turned down Jagger's offer to join the club as a sweet butt. Instead she'd accepted a job working for Banks at Rider's Bar.

"I never really got to say thank you." She leaned up and kissed his cheek. "Thank you for turning me down that night and for giving me hope. What you did changed my life."

"Just happy things worked out for you." His held out his hand to a scowling Banks who had been in a rare good humor until Skyler had given Holt that kiss. "And don't worry about Banks. He's all bark and no bite. But you can be damn sure he'll look out for you."

"Damn right." Banks shook his hand. "Good luck going it on your own. If you rescue any more damsels in distress, just send them my way. I always need the help."

After he'd finished his good-byes, Shaggy took him aside.

"You take care of Naiya or I'll hunt you down and rip off your balls."

Holt met Shaggy's gaze, watching his eyes shift from hazel to green. "You gonna share with me why you think you got a right to do that?"

"No."

"Can I guess?"

Shaggy shook his head. "Nope. Some wrongs can't be made right. Some secrets are never meant to be shared."

Holt glanced down at Shaggy's left hand, noted the pale white skin on his finger where he used to wear a ring. Although he was tempted to force the issue, out of respect he let it go. Shaggy had to have a reason for keeping his own counsel, and maybe in time he'd change his mind.

Naiya joined them and they walked toward Holt's bike. "Where's Tank?"

"Dunno." Holt looked back over his shoulder at the crowd. Tank had been at the party last night, matching Holt drink for drink, and joking around like old times. It hadn't occurred to Holt that Tank wouldn't show up this morning. He had expected him to be here. Wanted him to be here. Needed him. How could he leave without saying good-bye to the man who was part of his soul?

"So what are you gonna do with your twenty million dollars?" Shaggy asked as they crossed the gravel.

"Nothing." Naiya looked over and shrugged. "I don't want the responsibility that comes with it. I don't want the risks. I don't want to fall into the trap Viper fell into. I'm going to take out enough to live on, and then I'm going to enjoy being free before I settle down and live a normal life."

"What about buying your old friend, Shag, a kick-ass bike as a going-away present to thank him for being so patient teaching you how to shoot?"

Naiya laughed. "How about I send you a picture of me riding my first kick-ass bike after Holt teaches me how to ride?"

"Not happening." Holt put an arm around her waist and pulled her close. "And I'm not saying that 'cause I'm an overprotective bastard. I'm saying it 'cause I love you and I don't want you to get hurt."

Naiya leaned up to kiss his cheek. "Because you're overprotective. But I tolerate it because I love you, too."

They reached Holt's bike and Holt shot a desperate look at Shaggy.

"I don't know where he is," Shaggy said. "You want to wait?"

"We can't. Naiya's got an interview scheduled first thing tomorrow morning. We're already late getting away." Holt swallowed past the lump in his throat. "Tell him I said good-bye."

"Holt." Naiya put her arms around him. "Let's wait. I can reschedule. Or we can ride at night. You can't just leave."

"If he wanted to be here, he'd be here." Holt swung his leg over his bike. "Tank is never late. He doesn't stand people up. He doesn't sleep in. He's not here for a reason. And I gotta respect that. Maybe it's better this way."

Naiya slid on the bike behind him and wrapped her arms around his waist. Holt took one last look at the club-house, remembering all the work he and Tank had done to help fix it up, and all the good times they'd had. Heart-sick, he started the engine. With one last look over his shoulder for Tank, he punched the throttle and accelerated down the lane, leaving the Sinner's Tribe behind.

★ THIRTY-ONE ★

TANK

He was dying.

Tank walked across the grass to join Shaggy on the clubhouse steps. His body followed directions, but he was empty inside.

"Where the fuck have you been?" Shaggy shifted to the side to make room, and Tank sat beside him.

"Riding."

"Riding? When your best friend is leaving the club and you'll probably never see him again?"

"Yeah." He rested his elbows on his knees, dropped his hands, stared at the gravel, wondered if the black hole in his chest would eventually suck him up and put him out of his misery. "I couldn't say good-bye."

He tensed, waiting for one of Shaggy's sarcastic or cutting remarks, but his brother gave a sympathetic murmur instead. "Maybe you shoulda gone with them."

"And leave the MC?" He patted his cut. "I made a commitment when I put on this cut. This is my home. These are my brothers. This is my life."

"So was he."

Tank bristled. "It's not like that. Not like what he has with Naiya. I don't love him. I like women."

"There's different kinds of love," Shaggy said. "I had a brother once. Loved him to death. He died a long time ago when he miscalculated a hairpin turn on the Going-To-The-Sun Road in Glacier National Park, and his motorcycle went over the cliff. Ever since then, I've felt like a part of me is missing."

Tank twisted his hands together. He'd felt like a part of him was missing until he met Holt. And after Viper took Holt, he'd felt lost. Now, Holt was back, but gone, and Tank felt nothing but pain.

"You want my advice?" Shaggy stroked his chin, as if he'd forgotten he cut off his beard. Tank still couldn't get used to seeing him without it.

"No."

"Too fucking bad, 'cause I'm gonna give it to you anyway. I didn't live through all those years of biker shit to keep all my learning to myself." Shaggy leaned in close, as if he was about to share a secret. "Follow your heart."

"Christ." Tank reared back, his hand clenching into a fist. "You making fun of me, Shag, 'cause I got energy to burn and your smooth baby face will make a nice target."

"I'm serious." Shaggy held up his hands, palms forward. "I made a fucking mistake twenty two years ago. I chose to follow the club instead of following my heart and now I'll stay with the club till I die. But I guarantee if you stay here when part of you belongs out there, you'll wind up a fucking bitter man like me."

"I've got no skills to make it in the real world," Tank protested.

"You're damn good with your hands. You understand engines and mechanics. If we didn't already have a road chief, you woulda been a natural to look after the bikes. You just never had the confidence to put yourself forward."

Tank felt a strange feeling in his stomach, a flutter of hope. "He doesn't need me. He's got Naiya."

"He needs you both. She's his heart, but you're part of his soul. He waited here as long as he could. Even when they drove away, he was looking over his shoulder for you."

"Jagger will never let me go." Tank threw the last of his fears on the table, held his breath.

"He already did."

Tank's head jerked up. "What do you mean?"

"The board met when you were trying to ride your sorrows away. I put a motion forward that we release you on good terms if you wanted to go. The motion passed. It was unanimous. Every man in that room wished he had the kind of friendship you and T-Rex share. No one wants to keep you apart."

Hope flared in Tank's chest. "Where's Jagger?"

"Waiting for you inside. He's got a place for your cut. Right beside T-Rex's where it's meant to be. But you'd better hurry. They've got a twenty minute head start, and I'm not sure which road they'll take when they reach the end of town."

"Thanks, man." He jumped to his feet, and Shaggy held out a small velvet bag.

"Take this. When Naiya and Holt get around to having a baby, you leave it in the cradle. Don't tell them it's from me."

Tank studied the bag but made no move to take it. He'd suspected Shaggy had some connection to Naiya when they first met—a feeling that had become stronger when Shaggy always seemed to be around when she was there. "Why don't you give it to them yourself?"

"Some mistakes can't be undone."

"But some can," Tank said, sliding his cut over his shoulders. "And I'm going to undo one now. Keep it, brother. Give it to them yourself. If I can give up my cut for friendship, you can unburden your heart for love."

★ THIRTY-TWO ★

Holt slowed his bike and stopped in the parking lot beside the charred remains of Big Bill's Custom Bikes and Paint Shop on the Conundrum border. This was where it all began, where he'd offered himself to Viper in exchange for Evie's life.

"Why are we stopping?" Naiya slid off the bike after he turned off the engine, her face creased with worry. "Is something wrong with the bike?"

"I can't." Holt choked on his words. "I can't go without Tank." He dismounted his bike and flipped the kickstand.

"Then we'll go back." Naiya wrapped her arms around him, hugged him tight.

"If we go back, you'll miss your interview."

"I'll reschedule." She looked up at him; her eyes warm with sympathy. "I'm not in any big hurry. I haven't even decided if it's really what I want to do with my life, and I've got six other interviews lined up. This is more important. I know how much Tank means to you. If you need to stay, then we'll stay. I can fly out to the other interviews."

Holt shook his head. "I can't stay in Conundrum and not be a Sinner. And I want to be with you. You're my heart, Naiya. I waited my whole life to find you, and I'm not gonna let you go. We'll find our path together. I just never thought we'd be doing it without Tank."

"Do you want to text him again?"

"I texted. I called. I left messages. He's not answering his phone." He kicked at the gravel, stared out over the highway. "Fuck."

In the distance he heard the unmistakable rumble of a Harley engine.

His skin prickled and his pulse kicked up a notch. If he'd been a praying man, he would have prayed for just one thing. But he wasn't. So he closed his eyes, held on to the woman he loved, and made a wish.

The rumble turned into a roar.

Holt opened his eyes and his wish came true.

★ EPILOGUE ★

Naiya parked her SUV in front of T & T's Auto Body Shop, carefully maneuvering around the row of motorcycles gleaming in the Montana summer sunshine. Every week that row got longer and longer. She would have been happy if the bikers had all been customers, although Tank and Holt had more than enough mechanic work to keep them busy, but many of them belonged to MC presidents who had come courting Holt to set up a new MC in Northern Montana, uniting them all under one patch—Holt's patch.

Tank came running out to help her unload her briefcase and boxes, his navy coveralls streaked with grease. Swamped with work, the Montana State Crime Lab had set up a new branch in Auburn, just north of Whitefish and after only one year working with them, Naiya received a promotion and the extra work to go with it. Sometimes she missed the time she, Tank, and Holt had spent on the road crisscrossing the country after leaving Conundrum, when they had nothing to worry about except where they were going to sleep the next night and how many women Tank would have to fight off at the bars.

"You should have called. I would've come to get you," Tank chastised. "Holt's gonna be pissed when he finds out you carried all these boxes to your car. You're supposed to be taking it easy."

"He'll only be pissed if he finds out, and you're not going to tell him." Her gaze flicked to the shop that Holt and Tank bought together after she'd accepted the job in Auburn. They'd fixed it all up themselves and within a matter of months had built up a reputation for quality work in the biker community. When Holt had started to seriously consider setting up his own MC, he and Tank built an office out back to keep their activities discrete and away from the prying eyes of local civilians.

Naiya glanced over at the shop. "Is Holt in the office?"

Tank nodded. "He's got four MC presidents in there with him. They sure want him bad. They see a leader in him, and once the biker is in your blood, it's not easy to let it go."

Naiya snorted a laugh. "I figured that when we were on the road, and you two would only go to biker bars, get your bikes fixed at biker shops, and let me wear biker gear when I wasn't in an interview."

"Those were good times." He dug his hand into his coveralls and pulled out two tickets. "Speaking of good times . . . you busy tonight? Fractured Skyway is playing down in Whitefish. I missed them at the big rally where we took down Viper. A customer gave me these comps and told me not to miss the warm-up band. He said they were just as good as the headlining act. I was curious so I looked them up . . ." His voice trailed off, and Naiya frowned. Was Tank . . . blushing?

"And?" she prompted.

"The band is called Snark Bite, and Connie is the front woman. Fractured Skyway is her parents' band. Looks like she started something up on her own. You never met her, but she's the one . . ." He cleared his throat—". . . who got away."

"And you need a wingman or woman?"

Tank toed the dirt. "Yeah. I don't know if she'll want to see me. She kinda started seeing Sparky, and then up and left one day without saying good-bye."

"Sure, I'll go." Naiya brightened at the thought of hitting the road and getting out of town. Holt hadn't had much time for her over the last few weeks. He was either working in the shop, visiting other clubs, or meeting with his soon-to-be-appointed board. Although she had been leery at first about him getting involved again in the biker world, Holt had assured her nothing he did would touch her or her work. His new club would operate in the gray—not quite criminal but not legitimate either. She couldn't take it away from him. Like Tank said, he had biker in the blood.

"Are you fucking kidding me?" Shaggy stalked over to them, his Sinner cut swinging around his narrow hips. She hadn't seen him when she drove up but she knew he would be around. After they had settled in Auburn, Shaggy came to see her. That first meeting had been gut-wrenchingly awful. She hadn't dealt well with finding out Shaggy was her dad, especially after what she'd gone through with Viper and her mom, and she'd turned her back on him and asked him to leave. He had left her with his ring—the Skull Ring—and a promise to try and make up for all the missed years if she ever forgave him. It had taken six long months of soul searching and Holt's full support before she made that first call. Even then the first few visits had been awkward as hell. But Shaggy—she couldn't bring herself to call him dad—didn't give up. They'd discovered shared interests in music, science fiction, and comic books and he'd slowly integrated himself into her life, limiting his visits to a few days every month.

At least until she told him that she was pregnant. Now she couldn't get rid of him. And with Doug and

Ally coming to see her and Holt every other weekend, their small ranch house was never empty.

"My little girl's five months pregnant," he spit out. "Are you seriously thinkin' of taking her down to Whitefish on your bike? Are you insane?" He scrubbed his clean-shaven jaw and scowled at a horrified Tank.

"No man." Tank held up his hands, palms forward. "I was gonna take her in my truck. Wrap her in coats and bubble wrap in case—"

"Your truck?" Shaggy rounded on Tank, cutting him off. "Your bike is safer than that piece of shit. And she shouldn't be goin' to a concert. There's gonna be drunks there and drugs, people smokin' weed and shit, and the music's gonna be loud and upset the baby. They can hear stuff and it should be good stuff. Not frickin' Indie Rock."

Tank bristled. "What's wrong with Indie Rock?"

"Calm down." Naiya put a hand on Shaggy's arm. "It's bad enough I have two overprotective men to deal with every day, but now that you're in the mix it's almost suffocating. I'll be fine. Pregnant women go to concerts all the time. Maybe if the baby hears enough music, we'll have another Robert Plant or Stevie Nicks on our hands."

"Jesus Christ," Shaggy muttered. "Not fucking likely if you're going to see Fractured Skyway. You stay here tonight. I'll play good stuff for the baby: Steppenwolf, Hendrix, Meatloaf, a little ACDC, Judas Priest . . ."

"Seriously?" Tank snorted. "You want him to have no musical taste?"

While Shaggy and Tank argued over what music would be best for her baby, Naiya headed over to the office and knocked on the door. Holt insisted that she come to him when she got home from work every day, no matter what he was doing. He stepped outside moments later and swept her into his arms.

"How's my baby today?"

"Which one?" She leaned up to kiss his cheek, bristly with the now-usual four days' growth.

"Both." His hand slipped between them, and he stroked her rounded stomach.

"We're both better now that we're home." She leaned her cheek against his chest and Holt hummed his pleasure. He had filled out so much since she'd first met him in Viper's dungeon that she sometimes didn't recognize his broad, muscular frame from a distance. He had a calm confidence now that commanded attention, and a way of getting people to do what he wanted without resorting to violence. Tank said he was a bit of the old Holt and a bit of the new.

"I could hear Tank and Shaggy arguing from inside." He pulled her close, brushed his lips over her hair. "No way am I letting you go to Whitefish."

Naiya stiffened and tried to pull away, but Holt held her tight. "Don't try to boss me around. You're not my president, Holt. If I want to go—"

His hand dipped down into her skirt, skimming over her mound, and his fingers brushed over her clit. "I had something else in mind for tonight." His voice was low, raw with sensual promise. "I've been neglecting you, darlin' and I want to make it right."

Naiya laughed. "We had sex yesterday, twice the day before, and three times on Sunday. I hardly feel neglected."

"But I do." He leaned down, brushed his lips over hers. "Shaggy can go with Tank, and I can take you home and do all the things I've imagined doing to you all day." He placed her hand over the bulge in his jeans, and she rubbed her palm over the ridge of his erection.

"Someone's been a naughty boy," she murmured. "How could you work when you were thinking about sex all day?"

"I'm a man."

"Yes, you are," she murmured. "All man and all mine."

"And you're mine. My sweet, beautiful geeky girl."

Also by

SARAH CASTILLE

Rough Justice
Beyond the Cut
Sinner's Steel

Available from St. Martin's Paperbacks

Read on for an excerpt from the next book by

SARAH CASTILLE

★ NICO ★

A Mafia Romance (Ruin & Revenge #1)

Coming soon from St. Martin's Paperbacks

"You think I won't hurt you because you're a woman?" Nico tugged his weapon from its holster and held it under Mia's chin, tilting her head back, forcing her to meet his gaze. "I don't give a damn about tradition, *bella*. All I care about is making sure justice is done."

"Holy shit. Oh god. Mia!" Jules sucked in a deep breath and Mia cut her off before she screamed.

"I'll be fine, Jules. He's not going to shoot me in a public place with family all around. But you go. Let Dante know we're here." She didn't drop her gaze from Nico's, didn't want him to have the satisfaction of seeing her scared because, dammit, she hadn't done anything wrong. And she wasn't going to be intimidated by anyone ever again.

"You underestimate me," he said softly as Jules' footsteps faded away.

"And you misjudge me." She palmed her knife and slowly moved her hand to his groin. "I suggest you lower that gun or you won't be passing on the tradition of shoving your gun in the face of a woman to any Toscani sons."

She jerked her hand upward, just enough so he could feel the blade.

For the briefest of seconds, surprise flickered across his face, but it was so fast she wondered if she'd seen it. His jaw tightened, and he growled. "Drop the knife."

"Drop the gun."

He held her gaze for another heartbeat and lowered the weapon. "You are your father's daughter."

"If I didn't hate him so much, I'd take that as a compliment." Mia hiked up her skirt to tuck the knife away and Nico hissed in a breath.

She looked up, her body heating at the raw desire in his eyes. "You like women with knives?" She slid the knife into its sheath and looked down as she straightened her dress to hide the flush in her cheeks.

"There's nothing as sexy as a woman with a weapon." He gave her a slow, sensual smile.

Mia snorted a laugh. "I think sex was the last thing on your mind when I had my knife between your legs."

The deep rumble of Nico's voice vibrated through her body. "Sex was all I was thinking about."

Electricity crackled between them, sparking the connection she'd felt the first time they met. "Are you trying to hit on me at a funeral after pulling a gun on me?"

Nico slid a hand around her waist and pulled her against him, his body hot and hard against hers. "I don't try. I do. And when there's something I want, I take it."

For some curious reason, the intensity of his desire scared her more than his gun. Nico Toscani had clawed his way to the top, eliminating every obstacle in his way through a combination of brute force, fierce intelligence and ruthless determination. He missed nothing, and from the way the corners of his mouth lifted in a half smile, it was clear he hadn't missed the way her body heated at his touch.

"Too bad for you I'm not available," she said.

With his free hand he fisted her hair, tugging her head back, holding her firm as he studied her face. He had beautiful eyes, dark and deep with a hint of gold. His heated scrutiny made her blood simmer and pool low in her stomach.

"You got a man?"

"A man" in mafia speak meant a made man, someone who had jumped through the hoops to be inducted into a crime family. If she were attached to a made man—either as a wife, mistress or girlfriend—then he couldn't touch her without causing the equivalent of a civil war between crime families. It would be considered the ultimate in disrespect.

Mia suspected Nico wasn't the kind of man who would care if he started a war to get something he wanted. And right now, with the evidence of his desire pressed tight against her belly, she was pretty damn sure he wanted her.

"I don't have a man. I'm my own boss, and unless you want me to pull out my knife again, you'll let go of my hair."

"Hmmm." He nuzzled her neck, his erection thickening between them. "I'd like to fuck you, *bella*, with that dress off and only your little knife strapped to your thigh."

Goddamn it. If he'd been any other devastatingly gorgeous man coming on to her so strong, she would have invited him home for a few hours of hot sex. Hell, she would have considered dragging him into the nearest alley and getting down and dirty with him before the reception. But Nico was the enemy, a powerful and dangerous man, and she couldn't risk starting a war between their families.

Falling back on the self-defense techniques she'd learned from Bennett, she smashed her hand down on his, trapping it against her head. In one quick move she stepped back and bent over, tucking her chin down and forcing his trapped wrist backward. With a grunt, Nico released her and Mia backed away.

Far from being angry, or showing even a hint of pain, he seemed amused by her escape, and no small bit aroused. He licked his lips, his gaze locking on hers, his body tense as if he were about to pounce.

"You shouldn't have done that, *bella*." His smooth, sensual voice was dark with warning. "Now, I will never let you go."